In One Life and in the Other

Tarik K. Montoro

In One Life and in the Other

First Edition: 2022

ISBN: 9781524318406
ISBN eBook: 9781524328412

© of the text:
   Tarik K. Montoro

© Layout, design and production of this edition: 2022 EBL

Dedicated to all the first responders, guardian angels in the flesh and blood. To your unending vocation and your enlightened souls.

Table of Contents

Chapter 1. This Is Not a Puzzle Piece 10

Chapter 2. The Reunion 19

Chapter 3. Change Is Coming 31

Chapter 4. Lost Directions 39

Chapter 5. Disclosure 52

Chapter 6. Back 66

Chapter 7. The Visitor 74

Chapter 8. The Conversation 86

Chapter 9. Voluntary Denial 96

Chapter 10. Sailors Without Direction 103

Chapter 11. A Matter of Attitude 117

Chapter 12. Demons in the Forge 125

Chapter 13. More Than a Fly 135

Chapter 14. Siblings 144

Chapter 15. Premonition 154

Chapter 16. Far Reflex 164

Chapter 17. Projection 178

Chapter 18. Scientific Method 190

Chapter 19. Mixing 202

Chapter 20. Liaison 214

Chapter 21. Days of Light 234

Chapter 22. One of Our Own 249

Chapter 23. To Run.. 265

Chapter 24. I Am Not Alone 283

Chapter 25. Superhuman 295

Chapter 26. Dustin? 312

Chapter 27. Nearby Universes... 322

Chapter 28. The Enigma 336

Chapter 29. Hitting Bottom 348

Chapter 30. Controversy 361

Chapter 31. Other Forms of Life.. 373

Chapter 32. Findings 388

Chapter 33. Grays 401

Chapter 34. Irreversible 415

Chapter 35. Betrayal and Pain 428

Chapter 36. Alliance 443

Chapter 37. Atlantic Blue.. 454

Chapter 38. Internal Debate... 469

Chapter 39. The Art of Disguise 481

Chapter 40. The Message 497

Chapter 41. Chambres... 507

Chapter 42. Mockery... 524

Chapter 43. Uncertain Destiny 532

Chapter 44. Responses 543

Chapter 45. The Purpose 556

Chapter 46. Love Is Salvation.. 567

Acknowledgments 579

If you are reading these lines, it is because you have followed the signs of 'The Order'. Recover your identity. Recover your memories, but, above all, do not remain indifferent. Do not disregard your purpose... your love, your destiny.

This book is a work of fiction. The events narrated, characters, names and nicknames are inventions and, therefore, any resemblance to persons living or dead is entirely coincidental. That said, I welcome you and encourage you to seek the truth that lies within these pages.

Go ahead.

Chapter 1
This Is Not a Puzzle Piece

I had just turned four years old. I was just a child, although I was already speaking fluently enough to start worrying my poor mother. One of my first clear memories is of holding her hand as we walked to an appointment with the village priest. My mother had already tried to talk with him about me but until this moment there had been no opportunity.

Let me give you some background: my family and I live in a small town in the north of Spain, called Andrín. I am an only child, my mother is a housewife, and my father spends long periods of time away; he is a fisherman, and at that time he would often leave for more than three months at a time. In the village, and very close to home, live my uncles; I'll tell you about them later.

Apparently, my mother became concerned that I was not understood correctly when I spoke. Yes, I was able by imitation to reproduce some words, but others I made up. It was this failure that had my mother a little distressed. A few months earlier she had taken me to the ear, nose and throat specialist, worried that something was wrong with my vocal cords. The doctor's diagnosis: all normal.

What really got her worried was when, a few weeks later, some backpackers, pilgrims on the Camino de Santiago from who knows what country, asked my mother for a hostel, or someone in town who could rent them a bed for the night. They struggled to make themselves understood and used all sorts of gestures to describe a bed, a shower, something to eat. It was comical. It was a couple of blond guys, almost albino, light-eyed, languid, and with faces so pale that next to them we looked really dark.

Laughing, the albinos already considered it impossible. I don't remember any this, not the slightest thing; I only know what my mother told me much later. Apparently, I started talking to them, with the classic clumsiness of a four-year-old. What puzzled my mother was that I did not do it in Spanish, but in perfect English. According to what she told me, she had never had such a fluent conversation with me as this. Naturally, my mother froze in shock, and after a while of conversation, the albinos stroked my head and said goodbye to us with a comical "mochaaas grasiasss". This was the reason my mother had made an appointment to speak to Father Damián now.

The day finally arrived. My mother dressed me for the occasion as if I were a miniature sailor: blue suit with white trimmings, shiny shoes and my cheeks rosy; I gave the impression that I had never broken a dish in my life. As we walked to the priest's house in silence, my worry grew. I knew I was responsible for our short journey.

I was not used to seeing my mother so quiet. We stopped in front of the old oak gate, whose purpose was to separate the earthly world from this small sacred plot, and my mother crouched down to my level and said to me,

"David, my son, speak only if I tell you to; otherwise, remain silent."

She then asked me again what I should do. I repeated her words and then we knocked on the door of the priest's house.

"Good morning, Father Damián. May I?"

"Of course, come in, the house of the Lord is always open. How are you?"

"Very well, father. I came to talk to you about something"

"No problem, my child, we'll talk now. Let me offer you a cup of coffee and a snack."

My mother had never been to the priest's house, she was curious to see it, but at that moment the desire to alleviate her fear was stronger. Although she did not feel like any coffee, politeness and formality pushed her to answer,

"Thank you, I'll have a coffee with milk and, of course, I'll take one of those great cakes."

"That's better, Leticia. If a worry prevents us eating, it becomes a disease," commented the priest, laughing.

Father Damian, in the village, was more than just a spiritual advisor. I would dare to say that at that time he was one of the most respected men not only in the neighborhood, but in the whole region. He was effective, affectionate with everyone, and equally intense in his firmness, especially when it came to mediating disputes between neighbors. Altruistic and dedicated, he never left anything half done. Generous and discreet, he helped many families in their most difficult moments. Spokesman for all the neighbors when it came to land disputes, he was also a respected marriage counselor, Father Damián was a chameleon with a single purpose: to help others.

"Well, tell me, Leticia, what is this important thing you wanted to talk to me about?"

"Don Damián, I almost don't know where to start. Since you were a missionary and have traveled halfway around the world, surely you can give an explanation to a humble country girl who has never gone beyond these borders."

"Yes, Leticia. It is true, I have traveled a lot and met many people and have many opinions. Latin America, Africa, the

United States, Canada, Asia. And, in the end, despite all that travel, and without knowing very well how, I find myself back in the land where I grew up. It must be true what they say, that a leopard never changes his spots!"

"And what are those conclusions, if it's not too much to ask?" My mother was afraid to broach the subject too directly, and Father Damián loved to talk.

The tone of his voice, his body language, the gestures on his face, everything blended in harmony with his words. Even the most boring topic became interesting if he was the one talking about it.

"Well, Leticia, I have seen so much. The world is changing very fast, and people are gathering in bigger and bigger cities. Here, despite proximity and different points of view that generate misunderstandings, fraternity and the goodwill of the just will always end up surfacing, because every individual, no matter how serious or rude he pretends to be, always wants to love and be loved, and generally nothing makes people happier than this simple principle. But nowadays, oy, oy, oy, we are ruining everything, we are blinded by greed, selfishness and indifference. The human being is becoming a scavenger animal without values."

"Yes, father, every time I watch the news on the Channel One, I switch to the Channel Two to watch a documentary and I wonder if all those horrible things I see on that box can really be true."

"But my faith, in God and in humans, makes me convinced that before long people will stand up to the selfish interests of their leaders and proclaim loudly, "No! I will not harm my brother, I will not steal from him, and I will not be unjust."

There was a short silence,

"Sometimes I get carried away and no one tells me when to stop but thank goodness, Leticia, that your face is more transparent than the April rain." And he began to laugh out loud at himself for the sermon he had just given my mother.

Suddenly, the expression on his face changed, like someone distracted by something pending and forgotten, and who upon remembering it is filled with worry.

"Anyway, Leticia, you didn't come to see me to listen to the battles and ravings of a chatterbox. Tell me what's wrong, and I hope I can help you, or at least put you in touch with someone who can."

"I'll get to the point, Father. You know that David is my only child and, despite having no previous experience with children, there are small details in his behavior that are, at the very least, striking or special, let's put it that way."

"And what's so special about that, Leticia? Because all I see here is a very attentive and formal boy. He hasn't moved from his seat; he hasn't even twitched this whole time."

"Well, look, Don Damián, at home he is a boy who, yes, runs around, can be mischievous, but at the same time behaves in a strange way. Look, this is one of his last drawings."

Father Damián was skeptical and, before seeing the sketch, his eyes reflected the memory of the experience, as if he was about to see something very bad.

Without further ado, she pulled the drawing out of a folder and Father Damián breathed a sigh of relief, smiling a huge smile. It was an architectural drawing. It showed a large building, bordered by several streets, a river, trees, a recreational area, and so on. My mother explained to father Damián that to make it I had used a Betamax tape as a ruler and a Carioca marker inserted in the cap of a Bic pen, so that only the edge of the tip was showing, creating a very fine line, which gave the drawing the appearance of having been drawn by a dot matrix printer.

The priest kept looking at the drawing with a certain skepticism, while intermittently watching my mother and me.

"So, Leticia, you say that you yourself saw how this little guy made this diagram?"

"Yes, father, just as I described."

"And tell me, Leticia, has he shown other skills?"

"Yes, father, and this is what really frightens me. He speaks a language that we have never taught him at home."

"And what language is that?"

"I think it's English, but I'm not sure."

And it was then that she told him the story of the albinos. While she spoke, the priest held my gaze, like one who tries to discover the identity of the soul in the depths of the eye. That is why this is one of my first clear memories. Father Damián, in front of my mother, began to ask me some questions in English, but I did not answer. He asked me several, but I still did not articulate any word, I just looked at my mother, obedient, waiting for her to give me permission to speak. After a few moments during which the priest almost felt ridiculous asking questions to the air, my mother realized and said to me,

"Speak, son, speak without fear."

So, without my mother understanding a word, we began to talk.

"Do you understand me?"

"Yes, sir, perfectly."

"I saw that you have made a very nice drawing. Aren't you going to color it?"

I still remember his soft voice. I replied,

"Something tells me that would spoil it."

"Where did you learn to speak English?"

"What is that?" I asked, ignorant of myself.

"It doesn't matter, my son. Don't worry. Do you think you could teach me to draw like this?"

"I could, Father, but it would be easier if we could get a technical drafting table with integrated Parallax."

With my answer he fell silent, because for a moment he stopped paying attention to me, staring at the floor for a long time with his eyes directed to infinity and, after meditating those moments, he turned to my mother with the expression of one who has run out of words. And then something restored his composure, he turned to me again and answered me,

"I can get the table, but you have to explain to me what the Parallax is."

My mother was biting her lower lip, a reflection of her anxiety, reliving the particular scene that days before had stolen her sleep. Finally, I answered,

"The Parallax is a ruler supported by wires, usually metal, which is used to draw straight and parallel lines; it is so that in the same amount of time we can print more sketches."

And from his mouth came the timid whisper of a vowel,

"Aaahhh."

And here came the million-dollar question.

"Who are you really? Uncover yourself!"

Now I was the one who was silenced for a moment; in my little head I was thinking, "But if this gentleman knows me perfectly well, what is he talking about?"

"I'm David Fonseca, I'm four years old and I live on San Roque Road," I said.

My mother, who could only hear us talking like babbling drunks, was waiting for the illustration that Father Damián could offer her with his knowledge and experience. My innocent reply filled the priest's face with a huge smile, which turned into a fit of laughter.

Over time, I deduced that in his mind he saw himself as the protagonist of the movie *The Exorcist shouting aloud,* "The power of Christ compels you! The power of Christ compels you!"

I was ordered out of the parlor of the priest's house and marched to the backyard of the house. The priest assured me that if I dug a little in the earth, I would find living treasures; I think he was referring to earthworms. Meanwhile, my mother remained talking alone with Father Damián.

"And, well, Father, what explanation do you give me for what has just happened?"

"Look, Leticia, there are many enigmas that, even with all human effort, we are unable to understand, but I will tell you something, your son's ability is a gift."

"A gift? But if that's a gift, where does it come from?"

"I have already told you, Leticia, that the virtues that the Boss, the Big Guy in the sky, gives us are mysterious, but everything has a purpose in this life."

"But how is it possible that my son speaks another language? Where did that come from?"

"Nowadays, the vast majority of songs, television reports, and even, as you yourself have said, the pilgrims who pass through the village are English speakers. And children at this age are real sponges that absorb all the information that surrounds them. Your son must absorb more than most."

"What do I do now?"

"Well, Leticia, the same as you have done so far: take care of him, pamper him and live a normal life. I am sure that your son will become very successful if he continues to develop these abilities. He will be able to be anything he wants: a renowned scientist, engineer, magistrate, notary. He has the talent, and he will have the support of his family and, of course, of the village priest."

"Thank you very much, Father, I feel much calmer. What you have told me makes a lot of sense."

"It was my pleasure; go with God and bring your son to me as often as you can to monitor his progress."

"Thank you, Father, I will."

And that's how she took a big weight off her shoulders. She tried to go on with her normal life, excited that her son was going to be someone very important.

Now I feel very ashamed of everything that happened afterwards.

But all in good time.

Chapter 2
The Reunion

Andrin, autumn 1983

She seemed delighted with the idea of her son being an outstanding little man of achievement, special among the rest. Hers was a child of power, as if the vast mass of humanity were a night sky and I were the brightest star, and the less fortunate were part of that innocuous, dark void that functioned as a contrast.

I remember perfectly the return home; it was a particularly sunny day even for this part of Spain. Just as we had gone, we were returning the same way. Now everything was different, my mother was back to her old self. She talked on and on, describing the plants to me.

"Look, son, do you see that tall tree with those pale leaves? It's a white willow. We use its bark to make a medicine we call aspirin. Breathe deep, smell the forest; the smell comes from the ferns, roots and mosses that cover our Asturian land."

On the way home we met Matilde, my mother's sister, and as soon as she saw me, she dropped to one knee, and stretched out her arms and smiled. Naturally I ran up to her and we melted into a tight embrace.

"How are you, *little one*? How's my champion? You're getting bigger every day!"

"Hello, auntie! I'm well. We were at the priest's house, it's a fantastic place, and now my pockets full of treasures."

I pulled out a handful of six or seven worms. My aunt stared at them for several seconds, obviously trying to hide her disgust, but failing when I brought them close to her face.

"David, are you *crazy*? Those are not treasures, they are the Lord's creatures and they're trying to escape from you! Can't you see they are scared to death?"

I stared at them and realized that my aunt was right.

"Oh! I don't want them to be afraid of me, I want to be their friend and take care of them."

"Well, if you want to be their friend, leave them next to a tree with soft, moist soil, so they can hide underground, which is where they like to be."

"And so I did. After that, we went home, and my mother and my aunt made themselves some coffee and went out to the little table outside to drink it. Even though I was very small, my mother always kept me active.

"David, get some cookies from the lower kitchen cupboard, the one with the curtain."

I ran to get the cookies.

"Leave them here on the table and sit with us."

My aunt didn't hesitate to sit me on her knee so that I could see and reach almost the whole table. Then I saw the box of cookies, and for the first time I read aloud:

"Maria Cookies. The authentic flaky, soft and tasty, delicious for children and adults."

My mother almost choked on her coffee, and my aunt stared at me as if she didn't recognize the boy on her lap. My Aunt Matilde and my Uncle José had been together for many years. They'd always wanted their own children and had tried everything, but science then was not so advanced as it is now, and religion also played its part in how we understood conception. So, my uncle and aunt never had children but never knew why and never doubted divine will, either. In those days we didn't talk much about the pain of childlessness. My aunt and uncle were happily married, enjoyed their life and treated me as the son they never had.

My mother again had to explain the sudden changes in her son's behavior. She told her that we had just come from the priest's house precisely because of this question, and my aunt seemed delighted with the idea of having a little brainiac with a good future in the family.

Uncle José was the classic big country man: round face, pale complexion and rosy cheeks. His expression was, as a rule, the living reflection of honesty, kindness and full confidence, but at the same time, when the circumstances demanded it, his face became the greatest image of seriousness, discipline and forcefulness. He had a dairy farm that gave work to several neighbors in town.

That trade requires constant attention to livestock, their conditions and quality. As I said earlier, technology didn't make things that much easier. It was still common to see animal-drawn carts, to milk and then distribute by hand, and to act, on many occasions, as a veterinarian. Not to mention that the workday began at four o'clock in the morning and ended, well, that work never ended. My uncle wanted to delegate a little to his employees and not worry about his business, but it was impossible, so he rarely took a break.

At that time, chores were divided into men's and women's roles. As a rule, it was the wife who took care of the household chores, which involved proportionally more effort for her than for him; although it must be said that, in general, the respect for these tasks was so great that we would sit down at the table, fill our mouths and proclaim praise for the cook. She was always the beloved mistress of the household.

Going back to the subject, my aunt began to talk about the need to invest in my education in order not to waste such an extraordinary talent. It was the first time I heard the name of the city of Gijón.

My mother, true to herself, began to organize all the details with incredible precision and planning. At that time, my father was at sea. He had left on September 3, and it was October 11. There were still at least two more months before he would arrive in Santander with his full fishing boat and then he'd have to travel home to us. I could not, therefore, count on him to support me now.

If my mother, in agreement with her sister, wanted to take me to a respectable school in Gijón, the first thing she had to do was to find a means of transportation. My uncle could help as often as his chores allowed, but my mother, used to being an independent and determined woman, started by buying a bicycle. Her goal was to be able to take us to the nearest town, Llanes, in order that she could start taking driving lessons.

I remember clearly the first trip we took to the driving school. In fact, my butt still hurts to this day! Fortunately, my mother noticed that little detail and the next day she put a cushion in the luggage rack, which became my VIP seat.

The relentless and unforgiving rain would also regularly be a faithful traveling companion. My mother, though, was determined to get her driver's license before father arrived, so some days we drove twice. I was happy, because in the garage I had father's latest whim waiting for me: my uncle was under instructions to move it from time to time to ensure the battery didn't die and the tires didn't get flat.

We had a brand-new French car, a Renault 11; the whole town would ask my father to show it to them. It was the latest model, which was unusual because generally, the villagers would take advantage of the cars coming from big cities like Madrid, where the rich had the strange habit of changing cars as often as others change shoes.

My father preferred to buy new, because he hated to see license plates from all the provinces of Spain, except Asturias, and he knew that he would not fill it with tools, chickens or goods.

I was given the model cars and trucks that the driving school had to teach mechanics, and it didn't take me long to impress the teacher, Tomás. He left me the model on the condition that I would take care of it, but I don't know if it was a professional defect or what, he gave me a short lesson on the basic components of the vehicle.

"Look, David, this big metal box in the center of the cabin is the engine, this next is the gearbox, in front is the steering, which is what allows the wheels to turn where we want to go, and this back here is...."

"It is the drive shaft, made up of cardan joints, reinforced leaf springs, boilers, chassis..."

"I see you like mechanics, kiddo. Does Dad work in a garage?"

"No, sir, my dad is a fisherman, but I really like cars."

"How can you not like cars if you're a big boy? When you want to be my assistant, just let me know. I'm going to trust you to take care of the truck, it's the only one we have."

The driving schoolteacher became engrossed, seeing that I was not playing with the truck, but rather turning it three hundred and sixty degrees in all directions and carefully placing it back on the desk. Soon, he resumed the course of the class, and I could see my mother taking endless notes in her notebook.

It didn't take her long to pass her driving test. The country was immersed in a wave of progress that encouraged society to change its patterns. Few women were seen behind the wheel. Perhaps that is why, after passing the theory test on her own merits, the examiner was more benevolent with some mistakes that, as is natural in an inexperienced driver, must inevitably come to the surface. She passed without any minor faults.

When the expected return date was approaching, the women from the neighboring towns would gather at the Tina Mayor lighthouse. The lighthouse keeper already knew the women well, and the fishermen's wives would gather there and talk to him all at once. This old psychological trick quickly bent the will of this little man accustomed to the solitude of his work, and the women all but took over his job. They lost all the disciplines inherent in marine communications and began to call the boats of their husbands, who usually fished in groups and then returned from their campaign on the coasts of Africa.

The sailors loved to listen to the sweet and sensual voices of the women on the radio. For the fishing group and the rest of the merchant and recreational vessels, it was their particular modern version of the sea sirens. The ship my father worked on was called The Beluga. Its captain had bought this boat from an unnamed German shipyard and adapted it for fishing. Its design was conceived to perform well in areas of thin ice, hence the shape of its bow was more rounded than other boats, and although he wanted to call it The Arctic, it was finally christened The Beluga by his colleagues in the port of Santander because of its resemblance to the cetacean. The life of a sailor is full of dark humor and ominous portents so the captain didn't think twice about the name and, actually, thought it was pretty great.

That feature gave her an advantage when she sailed on her North Atlantic campaigns, but on this occasion her cruising speed was noticeably slower, and the radio failed to make contact with The Beluga although the San Vicente confirmed that they were behind and had not suffered any incident. They were about seventy nautical miles away, so with any luck my father would be home in three days.

My mother proudly installed the L on the rear window and set out to familiarize herself with the car. Normally, it was Uncle José who was in charge of taking us to the port, and although on this occasion my aunt and uncle were not going to miss it either, it was my mother who was at the controls of that beautiful silver Renault 11.

I remember it being so comfortable that, except for some train seats from that same era, I have not since been able to feel that same level of comfort. I remember that the car had such a distinctive and undefinable that even today when I smell something similar, I am immediately transported back in time to sitting in this car as a small child.

The ride was short, but God knows it was intense. The three of them didn't seem to stop arguing the whole way. My mother and aunt in the front, and us in the back.

"Leticia, put it in fourth."

"Don't listen to him, you do it very well. José-José, you'll kill her."

"I'm just saying that the engine is very strained, that's all. Beware of the guardrail, the guardrail, the guardrail. The guardrail!"

"I see that you're afraid of the guardrail, aren't you?"

"I think I'm going to close my eyes, and if the Lord decrees that my time has come, so be it."

"Relax, brother-in-law, I passed on the first try and everything is under control."

As my mother, who was looking at my uncle through the rear-view mirror, said this, she gently began to invade the oncoming lane, with a bus coming right for us. Lights, horns, screams and pale faces of passengers on that first trip to Santander. Against all odds, we arrived in one piece and without incident. My mother put on the handbrake, turned off the lights, pretended that the big guy, my uncle, wasn't there, and neither was I. She locked the car and we walked to the dock, laughing and chatting, as if we had just ridden on a placid cloud. My uncle fixed his gaze on me and, wide-eyed and nodding his head several times and very serious, he said,

"Get used to it, they're all like that."

And then he started laughing non-stop. It was such an attack of laughter that I, without knowing very well what he meant, cried with laughter too.

'The girls', as my uncle called them, however, turned around without understanding what was happening, but with the undeniable intuition that it was them we were laughing about. The two in unison raised their chins in disdain, turned their faces and continued. My uncle continued laughing for a long time, well aware of the marital consequences that would take place that very night if he did not fix it.

So, as the wait was going to be indeterminate, my uncle came up with the idea of asking for forgiveness by buying chocolate and churros for everyone. In this way, that little roughness was eliminated while we waited, along with the rest of the relatives, for our longed-for sea-wolf.

We positioned ourselves on the most solitary harbor breakwater. Slowly, in the distance, the lights of the ships could be seen, and incredibly, although they seemed like a dot on the horizon, they sounded their horns and could be heard with perfect clarity. Those sounds coming from the sea were the spitting image of joy. Seeing the approach of a loved one from whom one has been separated for so long, and knowing the inherent dangers of the profession, makes every reunion a cause for celebration.

It is strange. The more you are separated by distance and obligation, the greater the nostalgia and the desire to have that person close to you. That fear and uncertainty while that person is away produced a soothing effect on the whole family upon his return. Of course, no one denied my father anything when he was at home, and no attempt was made to bother or contradict him; and he, who was aware of this, interpreted it as a nice gesture of love and respect. My mother instilled this behavior in me because she knew that at sea the hardships, the abstinence and the hard work required huge efforts of body and mind.

My father was a man of medium height, strong, yet lanky. His hands looked like sandpaper, full of badly healed wounds and deep cracks. He faithfully fulfilled the stereotype of a northern sailor: a fortnight's beard, a woolen cap, a stiff face and a penetrating gaze that conveyed the experience and echo of countless adversities overcome. A true soldier of the sea with scars on his body and soul, and, of course, his black briar pipe, his inseparable travel companion, whose punishment by corrosion gave, as it did my father, that old and mysterious touch on something young and healthy.

We had to wait much longer than the rest of the families to see, greet and smile at my father as he stood on deck. In the hierarchy of the ship my father had a position of special relevance; he was the first officer, only the captain was above him, and that saying "the captain is the last to leave the ship" is as true as you might assume.

When The Beluga docked and moored, my father stayed with the captain until ordered to leave for home, with the promise that they would soon get in touch. The advantage of a port like Santander, among others, was that the loading and unloading operations were carried out by stevedores; but the captain had to stay to sign the logbooks and check that the weights were correct.

My father's name is Jeremiah, but everyone calls him Jemy. When we were finally able to greet him, my mother burst into tears. I guess feeling his absence for several months meant the build-up of sadness that eventually erupted like a volcano when she eventually saw him.

My mother's exaggerated reaction was not surprising. A few months prior, another Galician fishing boat had disappeared without a trace, leaving the families of all its crew members with no idea what kind of tragedy occurred. Later, my father told us that they changed their fishing routes on an unsuccessful search and rescue mission. Inexplicably, the radio beacon was not fired, and the trawler ended up lost in the ocean. Nothing was heard of it, not the slightest clue, not a single trace of the vessel's components. All kinds of violent, accidental, smuggling hypotheses were speculated upon.

The honesty of the captain, the ship and its crew was sullied by stupidity. If all that enthusiasm had been focused on the search, maybe and just maybe the families would have gotten some answers. That's why my mother felt luckier than ever to see her husband return. And although she would always have liked to urge my father to pursue something else, she knew him well and was aware that his profession was more than just a trade: it was his life, it was his identity. My parents embraced, my mother cried on my father's chest, and my father stroked her hair and kissed her cheeks. I could hear them speaking to each other, but it was so low and subtle that it was not discernible. They looked into each other's eyes, both resting on their foreheads, and did not stop kissing until my father saw my mother calmer.

"How is my little boy?", my father exclaimed as he picked me up and swung me around.

Next, he gave me a very tight hug and a kiss with that bushy beard, and even though it prickled like a hedgehog I could feel his lips on my aching face.

He then gave my aunt two energetic kisses and followed up with a hard hug full of back slaps to my Uncle José.

As we walked to the car, with me on his shoulders, my uncle was updating my father on the news. The real reason my mother got her driver's license, though, was something she and my aunt had kept even from Uncle Jose. My mother to be the one to tell him about their boy.

The night caught up with us on that cold and wet December afternoon, and my father insisted that the protagonist of the last nightmarish trip drive. My brave mother started the car under his watchful eye from the back seat and we finally headed home between accelerations, braking and counter-steering. Little by little we approached the warmth of home on that dark two-way road, towards Oviedo, only interrupted by the yellow headlights of the few vehicles that crossed our path.

We arrived at the town of San Vicente de la Barquera. At the entrance of the town, we were greeted by the imposing bridge of La Maza, and until that moment nobody had noticed the Christmas decorations that illuminated all the little streets with bright colors. The adults decided to stop with the excuse of enjoying a carnivorous supper. San Vicente is a town with a strong seafaring character, but at the same time you can eat a great grilled steak, and that was precisely what the uncle knew my father needed, although he also had other plans. While we were all at the restaurant table, my father got up and told us that he had something to do, that he had to leave for a moment.

He walked along the edge of the fishing port. At the end of the port, a small green path of bushes and hedges led to a landscaped passageway adorned with saplings of poinsettias, foretelling the entrance to a special place. Next, a majestic portico with semicircular arches safeguarded the entrance to the sanctuary of La Barquera.

When we were waiting in the port of Santander and heard the sirens of the ships, I thought they were a greeting to our friends and relatives who were patiently waiting; however, it was part of a ritual of gratitude, greeting and offering respect for the protection given by the Virgin of Barquera, whose image was now just a few meters away from my father.

The chapel was always open and my father, in strict solitude, said a few prayers at her feet, looked up, thanked her and said goodbye, blowing kisses into the air with the palms of his battered hands.

He returned just seconds before dinner was served, happier, more content and calm. Resolved by the duty accomplished, we enjoyed an unforgettable family reunion, full of complicit glances between my parents, displays of affection, laughter, anecdotes, wine, meat and Christmas atmosphere.

Chapter 3
Change Is Coming

Principality of Asturias (Gijón), 1989.

She kept her promise and took me to school in Gijón every day. It was a fee-paying school, but at that time my mother had obtained a scholarship for rural children from the autonomous community. We were not a financially buoyant family.

Naturally, my unexpected talent attracted a lot of attention during the first years of school. It was commonplace for the subject to come up in faculty meetings and informal faculty gatherings. Some felt that the school was not up to my abilities, others downplayed the fact, and the less professional ones, well, the less professional ones were simply indifferent.

Soon, however, I was no longer the topic of conversation. Gradually I stopped paying attention in class and, even worse, I sat at the back of the class, that small area furthest from the teacher's gaze. This change meant my refuge. Others like me, but with different motivations, sat at the back with me. They tried to talk to me, threw pieces of the eraser at me, but I remained impassive. It wasn't that I was a disruptive student. I simply preferred to use the time to let my imagination run wild and create a parallel universe that would make me forget all the boredom of classes.

I turned ten years old. At that time, about a hundred of us passed the grade. We were on fire, proud of having passed. Enthusiastic. That vanity was explained because the difference lay in a change of building. We were moving from the little ones to the older ones, and, of course, the playground was also a new universe to explore. What we had not calculated was that before we had been the oldest of the group of little ones and now, we were the opposite. That slight detail would become crucial in the happiness of recess.

We could already feel that winter was coming on strong. It was November, and the cold weather gave us all the false illusion that we were smoking. Some kids would even do the whole finger movement for minutes at a time. I don't mean that they simply put their fingers in a V shape to their mouths; they even pretended to tap the ash out with their thumbs, while they talked about something else, while keeping their eyes on their fantasy cigarette.

It's funny: when you are little you long to be an adult and, the older you get, the more you want to return to your youth. I imagine that this premise responds to the natural nonconformity of human beings. Anyway, that frigid morning, while we were in class, the recess bell rang. I was not a big sports lover, but I knew the rules of the playground well.

My classmates would leave their anoraks on the backs of the chairs and a minute before the bell they would start to put them on slyly. The eagerness was to get to the playground and grab the soccer fields before the other classes. The golden rule of the playground was that the first one to arrive on the field would get to pick who played with them.

If you think about it, schools have many similarities to prisons. There is a wall that separates you from the outside world and there are guards who watch over your stay, your behavior, only in this case they are called teachers. As in every prison there are gangs, and those gangs are usually led by a bully, and, in our case, that cretin had a name: Jonathan.

Jonathan was in seventh grade, but in reality, he should have been in eighth grade. He had surrounded himself with other students who, along with him and like me, were also hiding at the back of the classroom. It seems incredible, but at that age, a year makes a lot of difference between boys. This cretin had managed to seduce some sheep with the false promise of turning them into wolves, and that little group of five walked around the courtyard in a triangular formation.

Our class had already been on the block for months, and little by little we all observed the evolution and negative progress of the little mafia. Generally, the ringleader liked to sit on the disused stairs of the sports center, from where he had a global perspective of the playground. But sometimes he would approach the wall of the soccer field and kick out whoever was there, with the sole purpose of establishing his dominance and reinforcing his authority.

During all those months, his schoolmates actively and passively avoided any direct confrontation with him. Jonathan was a stout young man, he had matured physically very young, at the age of thirteen he was already smoking, and he really smoked. When he wanted something, he simply took it. If he was hungry, he would take snacks from the first person who passed by. If he wanted to play soccer or basketball, he would simply kick out the players. He dared everyone, even the eighth graders, and not even the teachers said anything to him when he jumped over the fence behind the sports center and went to buy cigarettes or a chocolate bar.

I'll never understand the way the girls reacted to him. They fought each other for his attention, and he kissed and touched them all at will. It gave the impression that they were hypnotized by this evildoer, and to receive a spank on the butt or a kiss from this creep represented success among them.

This boy was known for his violence and, although at that time my class had little experience with him, the legend, perhaps exaggerated, preceded him.

We had already heard about this little punk even before he changed blocks. It is said that the previous year he hit a teacher because he refused to go out in the hallway, as punishment. He was almost expelled and, although he was moved to a different class and required to repeat a grade, none of that solved the problem.

I always spent recess with my friend Javier Alvarez. We had been the best of friends since I arrived at school in 1985 in the middle of the school year. My good friend and I always got "A's", although in that grade I was already drifting away because I was bored with everything. Javier, so enthusiastic, always tried to encourage me by reminding me that we were the best in the class, that we had won all the science, language and social studies contests, and that we had to keep it that way.

The truth is that he felt a healthy envy for me, because, while he never stopped studying, I helped my uncle on the farm, did all the errands that my mother sent me, read adventure books, and when my father was at home we went hiking in the woods and, when the time came, I collaborated in the outfitting of The Beluga.

To me, everything I heard in class was strangely familiar, and just attending was enough to get me top marks. By the way, my English teacher could not speak English, she tried to avoid me whenever she could because she felt ashamed of not being able to maintain a conversation with me, although the secret of her ignorance always remained between her and me. She was a very good teacher; she was very interested in helping any student who had doubts. On her own, she organized games to learn the language, and in this way all the boys kept their attention in a subject that would otherwise become very insipid.

Gradually, I found myself more and more distracted in all subjects. Instead of listening, I began to draw in class, and the truth is that it seemed that I was not bad at it; the bad thing was that I had caught the attention of the teachers, especially the Natural Sciences teacher, who was the same one who taught us Mathematics, Mr. Antonio Jarras. So, before leaving for recess, he told me to stay after class, that he wanted to talk to me. I stayed at my desk while everyone ran out to the playground, and alone with my teacher, he came to my side and sat down on one of those little chairs. He looked ridiculous sitting there, but, on the other hand, I thought it was a very humble gesture on his part. So, with half his body out and the backrest at the edge of his kidneys, he began by saying:

"Well, David, tell me, where are we going wrong with you?"

"I find your question very curious."

"Why?"

"You are deflecting blame for my behavior and redirecting it to the faculty; I get the impression that you are trying to avoid victimizing me."

"David, I'm used to treating you all the same, and I forget that you are different."

"I'm sorry for my lack of attention in class. If that is your concern, I will try not to raise any further concerns that could be communicated to my parents."

"Look, David, I didn't want to address your case in Thursday's tutoring hour because I preferred that we talk privately. Do you know where the word "stake" comes from? It is a word that comes from gardening and consists of a straight stake inserted vertically next to the plant that is in the growing phase. That stake has the job of making that new little plant grow strong, healthy and straight. So, if I am the tutor, you can guess who you are?"

"I am the little plant that is growing."

"That's right. So, David, I don't want to beat around the bush with you and I'd like to ask you something, and I'd like you to answer me honestly. Do you think this school is falling short of your abilities?"

"No, sir, I am very happy here."

"Well, I get the impression that everything we teach in class is too easy for you, and that's why you're not interested anymore. What do you think?"

"You are right about that. I can't tell you what's wrong with me, although I understand that sitting in the back and drawing pictures might be disrespectful, I can also assure you that I will not fail the exams."

"I don't doubt it, my boy. That's precisely why I wanted to talk it over with you. Your father works on a ship, right?"

"That's right, Don Antonio."

"It's diesel-powered, isn't it?"

"Right, it has a four-stroke inboard diesel engine."

"And how long does it run?"

"It is not a vessel designed for speed; it can reach twelve knots, which is about twenty-two kilometers per hour."

"I understand that when entering the port all vessels must idle, right?"

"Yes, sir."

"Well, I think that's the speed at which you work here, your brain is a very powerful engine running at idle speed in the sea, am I wrong?"

"I wouldn't know, Sir."

"Well, David, I firmly believe that you are underutilized here, but I don't know where to turn either."

"Don Antonio, I am very grateful for your interest, but I don't need anything."

"Relax, David, let me think about it and we'll see what I can do with you. For now, go out into the yard and have fun with your classmates and we'll talk about it."

"Thank you very much, Don Antonio."

"Give me five."

I slapped the teacher's hand hard and ran out of the classroom throwing on the heavy coat my uncle had given me a few weeks earlier. I loved that dark green coat; my uncle told me that the furry lining of the hood was from an Alaskan bear.

I still had about twenty minutes of recess left, and as I opened the vestibule gate leading to the courtyard, I felt the force of the cold combined with the damp and struggled for a moment to keep my eyes open.

I looked for Javier scanning the horizon, slowly from right to left. I couldn't see him. This seemed strange to me, because he and I in these situations always waited for each other at the exit. What I could see was a crowd of boys, shouting upwards, forming a perfect circumference that hid what was going on inside, as if we were talking about a Roman circus. The girls stopped playing rubber bands and skipping rope. The basketball and soccer games came to a complete halt. Even the Strange Ones - the school's little group of "peculiar" students - stopped playing baseball to see what was going on.

Next, a teacher, whose nickname was Smirky, ran over. I remember the sight of her running conveyed a very unsettling look; it was like watching a stick insect move. She pushed the boys away and squeezed into the circle as best she could. I moved in as well. My heart skipped a beat. I felt every beat so hard it felt like it was going to burst out of my chest. There was fucking Jonathan, stepping on my best friend's head, raising both arms with his fists clenched in victory, while Javier lay on the ground unconscious, his face full of dirt and his saliva, thick, sliding down the piece of tongue coming out of his mouth.

The teacher ran to push him to stop him from stepping on Javier. All the boys were silent, as mute witnesses, and at the same time accomplices of the morbidity and taste for violence. As she approached, Jonathan removed his foot from my friend's head, and directed his foot to the stomach of the teacher in a kick with all his strength. She dropped to the ground. Barely able to breathe, she held her hands to her belly cowering on the floor in a fetal position, now also surrounded by all the students. Between gasps, we heard,

"Someone tell the teachers' lounge."

No one paid any attention.

Chapter 4
Lost Directions

Principality of Asturias (Gijón), 1989.

Jonathan's foot returned to Javier's head, in the same position it had been in previously. I was paralyzed. I had never witnessed anything like this. I began to feel a brutal energy inside me, my breathing was got faster, and fury took over my whole body. I looked around me, I was slightly outside the circle, and I could see the tennis ball and the wooden stake that the Strange Ones used to play baseball. I hurried to pick up the stick, when I heard that sick kid screaming:

—This is what happens when people piss me off! I'm going to smash his head in!

I understood that I had to hurry as fast as I could.

I grabbed the stick firmly with both hands and ran towards the inside of the circle; I was determined to hit him as many times as necessary and with all the strength that nature had endowed me with. Everything seemed to be going in slow motion and at the same time very fast. As I got closer to the circle, and ran towards it, I felt my breaths deepen and become more frequent. It was the first time in my entire life that I felt the irrepressible desire to hurt another fellow human being.

I was only a few meters away from arriving as a gladiator when something happened that I did not expect and that left me astonished. A very big boy, an eighth grader, came out of the circle and walking calmly grabbed me by the arm, with just enough strength to stop me, but not enough to try to hurt me. I knew him by sight, but nothing more. He was a young man who must have been about six feet tall, very corpulent, almost fat. He stared into my eyes with a calm and peaceful expression, completely out of context for the circumstances. I had the impression that we knew each other very well, but there was no room for distractions. My best friend was lying on the floor like a rag, and the teacher was trying unsuccessfully to get up between sobs and winces. Then this boy spoke, and, more than what, it was how he said it.

"David, take it easy. I'm here to help you. Relax and let me take care of this. Javier has nothing serious. Trust me, everything is going to be fine, my friend."

How did that eighth grader know who we were? We continued to look into each other's eyes; he kept that smiling expression. His temperance frightened me and at the same time transmitted something very familiar to me. I relaxed my muscles, and he immediately released my arm. With both hands, like a samurai master, I offered him the wooden stake. He smiled at me and said,

"I don't need it."

I said, "Please hurry!"

His smile grew bigger, and he nodded.

Then the almost fat guy began to separate the boys from the circle with the same movement as one who dives into a pool. He walked very calmly towards Jonathan; the latter looked at him and exclaimed,

"Would you like to be next? You greasy pile of dung with eyes!"

He continued walking. Jonathan got off Javier's head, readied his fists and directed them toward our unexpected friend. He walked with his arms relaxed, his fingertips pointed to the ground, like someone walking bored down a shopping street. Even today

I can remember perfectly the sound of Jonathan's fist crashing into his face; it sounded the same as when you slap your fist hard. I was surprised because in the movies it sounds more spectacular. To everyone's surprise, he didn't even flinch, he didn't even seem to feel it; he continued walking with his half smile.

For the first time I saw the fear in the cretin's eyes.

In a very serious voice Jonathan threatened,

"If you resist, it will be worse for you."

With his mitten he turned his face to one side, not hitting him exactly, but with force and speed. His body seemed to want to accompany the head, at the same time refusing to leave his guarded position.

Finally, the body obeyed the impossible position of the spine and turned, his back against his chest. His right forearm tightly squeezed the base of his throat and with his left hand he pushed his head forward, as if his chin had to touch his collarbone. He struggled to get rid of the oppression, while the almost fat one whispered in his ear,

"Shhhhhhhhhh, shhhhhh!"

He lost consciousness and was placed carefully on the ground. We were all dumbfounded. He knelt down beside him and began to move his now inert body. He laid him on his side, brought his right leg and arm forward, placing the back of his hand under his face.

He seemed to be sleeping peacefully.

The loud clang of the gate on its hinges sounded like a small bomb announcing the arrival of the cavalry. The teachers, among them Don Antonio, assessed the scene, looking at each other as if they didn't quite know what to do. The social studies teacher, Don Alberto, rushed to put Javier's head on his thighs, shouting,

"Bring water!" He slapped Javier's cheeks.

Don Antonio helped 'Smirky' to stand up as best he could, but she was still not strong enough. He ran to the head teacher's office, returned two minutes later and informed the other teachers that ambulances were on their way.

The janitor, Don Emilio, ran with his bunch of keys to the school's exit. We always went in and out through that access, but when I saw the two sides of that metal door open, I understood that it was actually designed for vehicles.

Soon the acoustics of the ambulances sounded, louder and louder, warning of their approach. They arrived and several operators with huge blue square backpacks got out and hurriedly attended to the injured from the small chaos generated at our school that day.

Fortunately, it was no big deal, but even so, an unfamiliar car also arrived at high speed. We all thought it looked strange. It was a dark blue Peugeot 405; inside was a couple, a man and a woman, looking very serious. They approached to talk to the teachers. The gentleman with the mustache was chewing on the stick of a lollipop, he was as tall as a castle and as thick as an oak tree, and his expression was very observant. She, slim, younger, wore bell-bottom jeans and a dark green shirt, the contrast with her straight blonde hair was very striking. Both were interested in what had happened, and soon we all found out who they were when Don Antonio addressed them.

"Good morning, officers. We apologize for having called you here, but for some time now we have been unable to keep this young man under control."

"Don't worry, we are here to help you."

"This boy seems incorrigible; his behavior is increasingly violent and unpredictable. He subdues the boys through threatening intimidation and in cases like today, through physical aggression he violates all the rules of the school."

"I need to meet with the health officer, first to assess the facts, and then I need to talk to all the adult witnesses, if possible, in the presence of the school principal."

The police had taken matters into their own hands and were talking about something about an examination of a minor. My friend Javier had regained consciousness by now. He was still a bit dazed but was obviously relieved that it was all over. He told me he had been waiting for me by the wooden gate, rubbing his hands together to warm up. Then Jonathan and his henchmen approached him. One of them was from a nearby class, and in a defiant tone they asked him,

"Cousin, was this the one who hit you and stole your lollipop?" he said, snapping his fingers.

"I'm sorry, but I didn't do anything like that," Javier said, frightened.

"What's the matter? Are you calling us liars?"

"Was it this little wretch?" asked Jonathan, shouting at the boy who was in his class.

The young man stared into his eyes, as if apologizing for what was about to happen, while Javier, shocked, made subtle signs of denial. The boy lowered his gaze, embarrassed, and exclaimed,

"Yes, cousin, it was this one."

"I'm going to bury you, you bastard!"

Poor Javier, like me, unaccustomed to these things, ran towards 'Smirky', who at that moment was smoking a cigarette as languid and stretched out as she was, looking outside the school, as if dreaming of freedom. And the rest, well, that you know.

Jonathan never went back to school; he was taken to a reform school very close to Oviedo, Sogrande, or something like that was called. Eventually, we learned that his parents, both hooked on drugs, did not feed or clothe him. He had to fend for himself. At home he was forced to steal from the department store, 'El

Corte Inglés', to pay for their drug use, and if he didn't get the required amount he suffered constant beatings from his father, who thrashed him at will with a sock full of stones or with a belt strap. I suppose that violence only generates more violence, that sometimes monsters are manufactured, and that not everyone was as fortunate in life as Javier and me. With the passing of time, one can't help but remember him with some pity. He was a victim of himself and his context. Javier never held a grudge, but selfishly we were all glad not to have him around.

Don Antonio was an exceptional teacher. He had a very particular way of teaching his classes: he was extremely demanding with the studies, but then suddenly he would teach us how to play with a spinning top in class, or he would tell Andalusian jokes. But, above all, he made us feel grown up, because on occasions like this he was transparent, fair and upright. He explained to us all the misfortune surrounding Jonathan, how hard he had tried to help him in vain and his feeling of failure over the matter.

But I guess, as always, life goes on. What kept Javi and me on tenterhooks was the eighth-grade classmate who helped us, how did he know us, why did he help us, and why did he look so familiar?

The *dude* ignored us. We would stare at him, but in the playground, he would go his own way, with the boys and girls in his class. He looked studious, because he took his books with him to recess and also seemed to help his classmates with their schoolwork. We couldn't hear him, but we could see him gesturing with his hands, giving explanations, sitting on his knees, writing things down for others. Recently, he had acquired a lot of prominence because of what had happened, and although he did not look like the typical hot boy, for a while quite a few girls greeted him and smiled at him with flirtatious glances.

I was very curious, and I couldn't help it. I had to talk to this guy, so Javier and I approached him.

"Hi. Sorry to bother you. We just wanted to thank you for what you did and tell you that we are indebted to you."

"Don't worry, it was nothing. My name is Carlos, and yours?"

Here I was really taken aback. Javier and I looked at each other. I doubted myself, my memory and my recollection. Pale and embarrassed, I took a few seconds to respond.

"My name is David, and this is my best friend, Javi."

"Good to meet you, guys."

"The truth is that I was surprised by your calmness with Jonathan. No one had ever stood up to him before, let alone like you did."

"I did judo until third grade. Maybe that's why."

"I guess that's why you didn't want the bat."

"What bat?"

"The baseball bat I offered you, from the Strange Ones."

"Oh, yes; it's just that I was a little far away."

Well, I would be going crazy by now if it weren't for the fact that some of my classmates saw me take the stick and offer it to him. Anyway, I don't know.

"Well... In any case, you were great, and we wanted to tell you that you have two good friends here for whatever you need."

We both shook his hand. I noticed that he looked very different. He seemed to be lacking that self-assurance that had impressed me so much. He shook my hand, but it was as if he left it dead and weak, I had to regulate the intensity of my grip because unconsciously it seemed to me that I could hurt him.

I couldn't stop thinking about why Carlos, this large guy, didn't remember any details, why at the time of the fight he called us by name and now we had to introduce ourselves. Why did his face have no mark from the punch he took, and why he didn't remember anything about the bat I offered him. Definitely, nothing made sense, but maybe the adrenaline of the moment and the stressful situation caused us all to have a false memory. I didn't want to give it any more thought; in all seriousness, everything went well and that was that.

Autumn passed and winter came in very cold that year. It seemed incredible to see the frozen puddles in the courtyard. Some completely bare trees seemed to resist the cold with a latent spark of life. As every year, Christmas passed again, this time with the sad absence of my father, who was at sea.

Andrín, years 1991-1995

His periods at sea were getting longer and longer; he and the captain often discussed the difficulties of the business. The fishing industry was going through very bad times; working at sea was becoming practically uneconomical and unsustainable.

My father tried to convince the captain of other options for the ship and the crew, but stubborn, and barely a year away from retirement, he did not want new changes, new risks, new challenges. Tired, but aware of the situation, his captain proposed to transfer the business to him. It was strange to imagine Captain Jemy and his ship, The Beluga. Being in the second line of battle is a lot of work, but in the end one can always rely on a superior. But if he accepted, he would have no one to protect him, no one to lean on when a sailor asked for explanations about the orders. It used to be easy to say, "because that's the captain's orders," but now he would be the boss, the one responsible for all the important decisions at sea.

Being a captain is not just a command position, it is not just any job. The life of each of your men is in your hands. On many occasions, you have to choose between staying moored in a port waiting for a storm to pass, losing huge amounts of money, or risking and fighting in the storm to earn a living, trusting in the protection of God and the Virgin of La Barquera.

The responsibility and risks are scary, and as soon as my father arrived home at the end of January, he spoke with his wife. He explained the pros and cons, and my mother, true to my father and herself, eagerly accepted the opportunity as a blessing from heaven.

Soon after, my father found himself as captain of a fishing boat, during one of the biggest crises in the sector. One afternoon, when we were all gathered at home with my uncles and aunts, my father explained the situation to us.

"Right now, the fishing world is going down the drain. It is no longer worthwhile to fish because profits are almost non-existent. Once you take out the tax, social security, repairs, fuel, gear, etc., there's hardly anything left, and I'm not willing to lay off any of my men or overload them with work, which is already hard enough."

"So, then what is your idea, Jemy? Because something very similar is happening to me with cows, the middlemen earn more than I do, and without doing anything."

"Change, risk and taking a gamble are the key."

My mother and aunt listened attentively to the men's conversation, ready to intervene at any moment should the need arise.

"I don't want to be negative, but what if that change goes wrong?"

"Give me a moment, I am going to explain a very recent situation. Detroit, one of the largest cities in the United States, was specialized in the manufacture of American vehicles, gigantic asphalt titans, gasoline cars with huge engines and excessive fuel consumption. These were huge cars, more than five meters long, difficult to park and expensive to maintain. Manufacturers such as Ford and General Motors have not been able to react in order to maintain their production, their rhythm of work. And, despite the patriotic sentiment of Americans, ordinary citizens have opted for Japanese models, that are better designed, with more interior space, have more efficient engines, lower fuel consumption, are easy to park, more reliable and affordable.

"American manufacturers, despite seeing what was coming at them, have not known how to react, have not understood the evolution of the market, have not taken risks and have been content to continue doing the same thing. Now, Detroit is labeled as the most dangerous city in the whole country, infested with crime and arson. Thousands of working-class families fled because of the lack of jobs. Hollywood studios shoot catastrophe and zombie movies in the hundreds of abandoned houses and streets, without lights or services, where nature reclaims its space, taking over the city and casting an apocalyptic image."

"Okay. And what do you plan to do?"

"Well, I've thought about taking The Beluga to the shipyard and first of all overhauling the entire hull, and secondly and more importantly, to make a drastic transformation to become a transport vessel. If we are already on credit, asking for a little more won't make much difference."

"Continue."

"Over the years, I have met the right people to dedicate myself to this, and taking advantage of The Beluga's icebreaker status, I will be able to supply the populations of the North Atlantic with oranges, wine, oil, espadrilles, everything that any Spanish producer wants to export."

"Well, Jemy, that's your world, you're the one who is in charge of it. If you're so sure about it, go ahead, we're here to help you with anything you need."

And the two shook hands, as if it were a business deal. That handshake meant: "I am with you, you will not be alone, your family supports you and our optimism will accompany you on those journeys".

To celebrate, my father and uncle went to get a good suckling pig, brought it home, prepared the barbecue on the patio; and although God knows it was freezing cold, the two of them with a beer in hand were laughing and stirring the meat as if they were at a summer *campground*.

I remember clearly that night, in the outdoor gazebo, surrounded by trees, the smell of plants and the occasional sea breeze. The bugs and owls going about their business; the women and me near the embers so as not to catch cold; and the men, a little impaired by the beers, goofing around, recalling old anecdotes and telling jokes non-stop. I ate so much dinner, and I was still so small, that I fell asleep on my mother's lap, and, as if by magic, I woke up the next day perfectly tucked up in my bed with my pajamas on.

My father was fully focused on his idea. He tried to be discreet, but the excitement was evident on his face. Every three days he would go to the shipyard and check all the changes. He always talked about the engineer who carried out the theoretical part of the modifications. I remember arguing with him, coming home and boasting that the engineer didn't know what some of the modifications were for, and when he explained them to him, he was amazed at the sea dog's creativity. His idea was to take advantage of every cubic centimeter for cargo, but the layout was to allow, if necessary, that same space to be occupied by sea containers, making loading and unloading processes quicker. At the same time, and together with the engineer, they had designed a system of pneumatic doors that, when opened, would change from the aforementioned cubic stowage to bulk cargo, taking advantage of the entire concave surface of the ship and installing automatic devices for anchoring the *containers.*

He also added cranes for autonomous loading and unloading, increased the fuel tank, enlarged the crew's common area a little and renovated the cabins, reinforced the hull, overhauled all the mechanics and adapted the engine to the harsh northern conditions with more powerful antifreeze, auxiliary batteries, thicker hoses and pipes, more lighting and an enclosed watertight rescue skiff with heating, flares and provisions. The skiff alone cost him fourteen million pesetas, but my father would pay more money to never have to use it.

Finally, by the beginning of July, everything was finished and by the middle of the month he had his first load scheduled. He was to transport four all-terrain vehicles, a container with household appliances, another with furniture, a cargo of red wine bottles and a tank container with chemicals; and with all that loaded, the ship was barely half full. So on the coast of France, he was to pick up more goods, flour and grain, all destined for a supplier in the Faroe Islands. My father was very happy with his new venture, and everything was going smoothly.

On the other hand, I was already enjoying my vacation and, as I promised Professor Don Antonio, I passed everything with straight A's. I did not study, this was without studying and without focus or effort. Time went by and my boredom only grew from year to year. It didn't get any better when I moved to high school. Javier was no longer with me, he had to go with his parents to Seville; work stuff, he told me. I had to go to that classroom full of unknown kids who, for no reason, looked at me like I was a reserved nerd. I admit that the classes were long and heavy, and the only classmates who approached me did it out of self-interest, so that I could explain trigonometry, physics or technical drawing to them.

It was no longer like in elementary school. The teachers hardly knew us, nor did they pretend to. Big classrooms full of young students, taking notes and sitting for exams. Tests and results, nothing more. If you missed class, no one took roll call; and if you snuck into another class, no one noticed. And Christmas passed again, then Easter, then summer; and another course faded away, lonely and nondescript. My mother worried about me. My loneliness had her on tenterhooks, and a part of her needed to change things, so that summer she forcibly signed me up for a summer camp with boys my age.

My parents were still recovering from the investment in The Beluga, but with the help of my aunt and uncle they made the decision to force me to go on vacation. They were given a two-page list of all the things I had to take with me: sleeping bag, sleeping mat, flashlight, ten-meter rope, whistle, compass, swimsuit, raincoat, etc. I didn't know if I was going on vacation or being sent to war, but the truth is that the fact of being surrounded by unknown boys in the interior of the Peninsula aroused in me a strange desire, but also panic.

Chapter 5
Disclosure

In class we studied the geography of the entire national territory, physical and political maps, but traveling by road and going through all those places is something very different.

The camp was located in the province of Avila, specifically in a small town called Arenas de San Pedro. My mother, aware of my lack of enthusiasm, forced my trip with the insistence of my uncle.

Someone told him that I was gifted. That in these cases it was common to have an attention deficit in class because everything was so simple and the interest was lost, and this was extrapolated to the rest of the facets of my personality. Others told him that I probably suffered from a strange disease called Asperger's syndrome. The affected person usually shows extraordinary virtues in the use of language, mathematics and abstract concepts. That-that's all well and good, except that I was being called autistic. It's not like I was Rain Man, counting chopsticks and cards.

I am not supposed to be offended by this diagnosis, given without any guarantee, speculated and unconfirmed by a psychologist, since historical and prominent figures, such as Isaac Newton and Albert Einstein, suffered from this syndrome.

Certainly, yes, I admit it, he was a bit reserved, but he didn't show a strictly hermetic personality either. He wasn't the funniest guy in the world, but he began to whet my appetite for some sports.

My uncle and aunt always talked about taking a route through the southern half of the country, and my trip to Ávila was the perfect excuse to get away. They had insisted that my mother accompany them, but she said she couldn't be any further away from my father.

The camp bus left early on August 5, 1995, from the central Plaza de Atocha in Madrid. The trip was a blast, and almost at nightfall we were greeted by the urban immensity of the capital. We spent the night in a small and comfortable hotel near the Retiro Park, and the next day, after breakfast surrounded by businessmen in suits, we walked downhill towards Atocha, following the directions of the hotel receptionist.

It was nine o'clock in the morning, and the sidewalk was packed with kids with giant backpacks and family members everywhere. The bus was guarded by Smurfs, a monitor told us. I thought he was joking, as if I were even more of a kid. After a while I understood that this was how they nicknamed the Local Police of Madrid, since they wore light blue shirts. Of course, the local jargon could be a barrier to communication.

They were all carrying giant professional backpacks, they looked like they were marching to the Himalayas. I, on the other hand, was carrying a backpack that my father was given when he did his military service. In reality, it was a green bag with rings at the top and a pin inserted through them to close it and fastened with a carabiner. Everything was inside, unlike the others, whose canteens and utensils had their place perfectly measured and designed for their correct transport. Next to the others, I looked like the little bogeyman.

My parents had invested every peseta they had in the boat project, and I wasn't going to be squeamish about it. They were about to sell the car and so it seemed strange to me that they could send me camping. My uncles and aunts and uncles helped out so that I would not suffer the tremendous family effort.

I was walking down the aisle of the bus. Out of embarrassment, I was one of the last ones to get on the bus and I was looking everywhere to see where I could sit. I got to the end of the bus and had to go back to sit in the only free seat. Stuck to the window, there was a boy so skinny and squinty that his eyes looked twice as big as normal.

"Excuse me, is this seat taken?"

"No, you can sit here."

"Hi, how are you? I'm David."

"Hi, I'm Mario, but everyone calls me Picueto. Where are you from?"

"I am from Asturias, and you?"

"I am from Albacete. Do you know if it takes a long time to arrive?"

"My uncle told me about two hours."

"I can't wait to get there to start my vacation."

"And me!"

I immediately liked the guy. I admit that, at first, I passed him by on the bus, but I was very lucky to meet him.

You have to see what two hours of driving can do to the landscape. Suddenly it felt like I was back home, only it wasn't as green, and the sun was shining brightly for most of the day. The monitors were hilarious, not serious at all, but no matter how much they told me I didn't get used to calling them by name, and a "teacher" always slipped out. The camp was beautiful; it reminded me of the Playmobil fort that Javier had and that had given us so many hours of happiness a few years ago. There was a wall made of logs without branches, all placed vertically and sunk in the ground almost a third of its length. Inside there were some brick constructions, but mostly it was wooden huts, also made of logs arranged in a conical shape; they were called tepees, because of their resemblance to the tents used by the Native American.

The first day was all about settling in, arranging our hygiene items and leaving the clothes in the backpack. There were no lockers. We were told to spread out the mats on the ground in a circular shape. In each teepee *we were* a total of six boys. The girls slept with girls, and the boys, well, with boys and spiders.

We were told that the place was a military installation, sometimes used as a staging area for soldiers. All I know is that, although there were bugs in the hut, our camp was very nice. Soon they gave us a sandwich and told us to get into our bathing suits, we were going to the natural pools.

"Oh, no! Not the pool, please, it's the worst thing for me."

"But what's wrong with you?"

"Well, haven't you seen me? I look like the little bones in science class!"

"No, you don't! You look great! Come on, hurry up, I don't want to be last."

"Well, okay, but you'll see how the girls laugh at me, and I don't go for any of them."

"I don't care about that; I don't care about girls."

"Ha! That's because you haven't kissed one yet, nor have they made eyes at you, or even written you a love letter. Oh, my friend, what can I say to you, you little baby, you don't understand anything about the feminine world."

"Well, yes, I'm more innocent than a little nun, but, *damn it,* hurry up and put on your bathing suit."

"Which one would you wear: the red floral Hawaiian style, for the carefree and rebellious young man, or the psychedelic striped one, whose straight parallel lines hypnotize girls from side to side?"

"Man, you're ridiculous. And they say I'm the weird one."

"I need your opinion! There's only one occasion for a first impression! If we're going to be friends…"

"The psychedelic ones! Happy now?"

"Mmmmmm, good. I'll take your advice and wear the flower one."

"Fuck you."

Of course, this boy had one a small defect. For him, girls were his only thought. And me, I hadn't even noticed them. That's why on the bus he kept pointing them out to me with his eyes, making those weird eyes even more bulging.

Every fool with his own theme.

I thought, "Well, I'll just do my own thing".

The camp was turning into the best vacation of my life. We had a routine of activities. We tried everything and every day we did new things: craft workshops, hiking, fishing, learning about flora and fauna, dance and singing lessons, and the best part, the stories at night.

It was great to listen to Germán, the counselor. Every night, around the fire, he told us all kinds of stories. He left us all spellbound. Not even the best movie in the world could compare with his stories. Some were intriguing, some funny, some scary. Nieves, the cool camp counselor, would accompany his stories on the guitar. To tell the truth, I had no time at camp to be bored, abut eventually, like all good things, the end drew near.

It was already the penultimate day, and all the Picueto's attempts to seduce the girls had failed. He said, however, that some of them had been looking at me, but the truth was that I wasn't interested at all, and that seemed to make my new friend even more angry.

I had to learn what love is in the strangest way in the world, so as not to lose the habit. It was noon and we were playing non-stop in the natural pools of the Arenal River. The diving boards, the bridge and even the concrete ramp were all so much fun. I, unaccustomed to the sun's rays, had slightly burned my shoulders and had to start applying sunscreen. We queued up to jump from the diving board, but Picueto took advantage of his thinness to get in between the others and advance along the edge of the board, sneaking in again and again. He was ahead of me. There were four other boys in front of me when he jumped into the water and emerged again like a spring. He never respected the order of the line, and sure enough, what was bound to happen happened.

My face was practically in the butt of the boy in front of me as we climbed the stairs, all of us standing there in a tight line. I could hear Picueto from behind muttering,

"That's my friend, step, step, he's saving my place, move aside, I'm coming, move, move, I'm coming with my friend."

He was full of cheek and his face was a poem, he even had the gesture of speed with his lips pressed together and those bulging eyes like eggs. He looked like he was going to get something.

As is so often the case, the one who is least to blame pays the price. The two of us were juggling to fit on the long board. Someone pushed him just when he was almost next to me and, as it could not be otherwise, Picueto pushed me, in turn, to regain his stability on the platform. So I was the one who got the big kick in the ass.

My feet slipped to the side, and my entire ribcage hit the diving board. My body was slippery thanks to the sunscreen I had just applied, which prevented me from catching myself. At least I was far enough forward not to fall on the rocks and concrete. When I emerged from the crystal-clear water and tried to catch a breath of air, my body wouldn't obey, and the more scared I got, the worse it got. I seemed to be breathing through a straw. My face went through all the chromatic phases of the rainbow; I could hear, above all, the girls screaming with their high-pitched nervous voices calling the counselors.

The first to come to the rescue was Nieves. Her warm, soft hands sat me on the floor. She grabbed my face and pulled my head back a little.

"Focus on your breathing, try to relax it and little by little your lungs will open up."

It was like a magic trick. In a matter of seconds, the feeling of being overwhelmed dissipated and I could take those much-needed deep breaths. I wanted to get up, but she told me that it was not yet the moment, that I should rest like this for a while. Germán came running along the edge of the pool. The sound of his flip-flops slapping on the surface reflected his haste.

I didn't like being the center of attention, and so, even though I was in a lot of pain, I kept saying I was fine. Nieves told me we should go to the infirmary. It was a square hut perched on the lawn. She knocked on the door, and while I looked at the ground out of both embarrassment and shyness. A female voice greeted us, calling only me to go in, Nieves staying outside the cubicle.

I was in the middle of the room, standing, while she had her back to me dressed in the classic blue uniform. She picked up a small pen-shaped flashlight and placed a stethoscope around her neck. The walls of the booth were decorated with posters of the human body, ophthalmological signs, freehand drawings, glitter hearts and photographs of her hugging summer groups.

I call this moment in my life the revelation.

I stared at one of the pictures where the nurse was with a group of girls, all of them looking like geese; my attention was only focused on the nurse, the rest I didn't even notice. It was like flicking a switch in the kitchen. The light wants to turn on, but it starts with something dim, to give way to intense flickers of memory, and after a few seconds everything lights up clearly.

Suddenly I remembered, in part, who I was. It was as if my whole life as David Fonseca overlapped with other memories, other remote experiences. Another person, being myself. Something very disturbing and difficult to assimilate. I looked at my hands, recognizing myself, asking myself, "What am I doing like this?" but remaining aware of my true identity. The effect was very disconcerting. I looked at the photograph again. Displaced, I removed the thumbtack from the cork to take a closer look at the image, when his voice brought me back to reality,

"Come on, champ, sit down here on the stretcher."

Nervous and frightened, I turned around and when I saw her in person, my strength left me. My legs bent in two, I fell to my knees, and my hands rested by inertia on my thighs. I could not lift my head; tears flooded my face and fell on my bathing suit like an open faucet. It was followed by a kind of retching that came from my chest, not my stomach. I can't describe it any better. It was so much homesickness.

She rushed to my side and hugged me, asking me,

"What's the matter, young man? Come on, honey, take it easy, whatever it is, you're going to be fine, honey."

I looked up, saw her big green eyes, her small, upturned nose, her straight brown hair in a ponytail and her beautiful lips. For me, time stopped in the reunion, in our complicit gaze, in the whirlwind of confusion, and, without further ado, I kissed her. I kissed her with all the love in the world, and I melted with her, returning her embrace, while caressing her cheek.

"I have missed you so much, Angie," I told her in English, and she looked at me again.

There was a few seconds of silence and, quietly, she said to me,

"I don't understand you; I don't speak English and we can't do this, kid. It's not right," she replied with a blush.

Suddenly, two loud bangs sounded on the door of the tin hut, like someone was hitting it with the edge of their fist. She stood up like a flash, afraid that someone had seen what had just happened, but I couldn't stop staring at her, dazzled. What a beautiful woman. I let go of her forearm, letting my tiny hand slip, caressing the back of hers. Nervously, she repeated for me to sit on the trolley. She was in her thirties, still youthful looking. Her little teeth stuck out like those of a small mouse, making her look even younger.

Although it wasn't necessary, she quickly checked that all her clothes were properly laid out and fastened. I heard her take a breath, and she opened the door. It was Nieves, the instructor, waiting outside. She was asking for me. The nurse answered,

"He looks good, but I still have some checks to complete." Is it a trade-in?"

"Let's say he's... a special boy. Could you ask him to step outside for a minute? I'll just be a minute."

"Yes, of course," she said almost stammering.

I was trying to digest everything that was happening to me. Nothing was adding up. Hopelessness was taking over me, giving way to anger, impotence, almost madness.

Nieves waved me out, looking at me questioningly, without actually entering the stall. I don't know what she wanted. At that moment, she struck me as the most unwelcome person on earth. I gave a little jump, leaning with my hands on the stretcher. I felt I looked ridiculous, out of context. My glassy eyes and shuffling gait gave away my mood. Nieves smiled at the nurse and thanked her, promising to return me at once, closing the door quietly.

Suddenly, Nieves grabbed me forcefully by the back, by my shirt, and led me towards the huge trees that shaded the lawn.

Almost aggressively, she pushed me, and I could barely keep up with her walking pace. I began to worry.

"Nieves, Nieves, let me go, what are you doing?"

"Look at me, David! Look me in the eyes! Look me in the eyes and answer my question! Do you want to die? Answer me! Do you want to die?"

My heart was beating a thousand beats per minute; my dry mouth was throbbing, and the rush of blood was pounding in my temples. My vision became somewhat blurred.

"No! I don't want to!"

"Say it, say it! What is it that you don't want?"

"I don't want to die!"

Then she let go of my neck and Nieves began to walk around me, as if in thought, catching her breath. Her walk was very different from her usual one; the feminine subtlety had disappeared in her.

"Look, David, or Dustin, or whatever you want me to call you. Right now your life and mine are in grave danger."

"I don't understand anything, Nieves."

"You still think I'm Nieves? Don't you recognize me?"

"I'm sorry, but no. I don't know who you are and I'm scared."

"Don't you remember me? Jonathan and your schoolyard, do they mean anything to you?"

"As soon as she said those words, my eyes started to spin. It was as if all my reality had escaped like a liquid down a drain. How did the counselors know who Jonathan was? Why did that nurse remind me so much of Angie?"

"I remember the fight," I began to vocalize with broken words.

"Well, I'm the same one who helped you that day."

"I remember, it always seemed so strange to me. Who are you?" I sounded fearful.

"This is not the time to ask questions, but you can assume that if I am here, right now, it is because your situation is compromised."

"I don't know what's wrong with me. What's the danger?"

"Your little number with Alicia, the nurse. Listen to me, I will give you precise instructions and you will obey. Do we agree?"

She repeated, louder this time, "Do we agree?"

"I agree. Whoever you are, and wherever you come from."

What was happening to me was inexplicable, but there was also a familiar ring to the encounter.

"My existence is also in grave danger. Every time, as now, I occupy a body, I become mortal. I know this is a lot of information all at once, but there will be time for you to understand, for you to remember. I am your protector, your custodian, and my duty is to resolve the dangerous situation that you yourself have created; you fool! Get this through your little head! That woman is not Angie. She just reminded you of her, but she's not. You're confused."

"What should I do? And why am I in danger?" I felt short of breath.

"I will tell you. And, as I have told you, I will explain later, when my very existence is not in grave danger."

"Okay," I said, startled.

"Before Alicia sleeps, you must make her memory of the day less intense and strange."

"Right. And how do I do that?"

"That, my friend, is your business; figure it out."

"Help me!" I begged.

"Believe me. I already do way more than I should. I have to go now. I'll see you soon."

"When?" I was very aware of my breathing at this point.

"Soon. In the meantime, be cautious with your secret. No one must ever, ever, ever know what is happening to you. If you make a mistake just once, it may be the end of you. If you are not dead when the nurse wakes up, you will have done well. If you fail, I'll be waiting for you."

As soon as she finished speaking, Nieves' gaze faded. She stood there, rigid as the trunks of that small forest. From her back an elongated humanoid-looking shadow began to emerge, as tall as a basketball player with long arms and legs. I could basically see the forest through its almost transparent head. It would have been utterly terrifying had I not I had just met this creature, and, paradoxically, I felt a strong link.

He stepped out of Nieves' body like someone taking off overalls. He raised his hand in salute and vanished like cigar smoke into thin air.

I held Nieves' hand, watching to see if she would come to her senses, while I pondered the meaning of it all. I doubted my own sanity, and at the same time I panicked, because deep inside I knew that I had always been different. For the first time in my life, and even though it seemed crazy, I was being offered a reason, an explanation for my strange circumstances. And, of course, I wanted to understand. As I told my newly acquainted and elongated friend, I didn't want to die.

Nieves came round. She stood with her gaze unfocused for a while, reflective, looking a little worried, as if she had suffered an absence. Then she looked at me, trying to focus. She smiled at me with her usual tenderness. And she said to me,

"I've been lost in thought for a long time, sometimes I think I'm losing my mind. Let's go to the infirmary."

I chewed over what the silhouette in the forest had just told me and realized that, although I didn't understand, I had to put the whole thing right before Alicia went to sleep. And then I began to think. Soon it would be lunchtime and maybe she was going to take a nap. I understood that I had to solve it quickly. And I bet everything on one card.

Nieves approached me again to take me to the infirmary. Confused, she told me,

"David, it's funny, but I think I dreamt this."

She didn't remember that just fifteen minutes before she had taken me to the same place. She knocked on the door and, as I heard Alicia's footsteps approaching, I asked Nieves if she could please bend down for a moment, as I had something important to whisper in her ear. A secret. She did not hesitate to oblige, blinded by my innocent and youthful appearance; moved by curiosity, she bent down beside me, and I whispered in her ear,

"Thank you."

The door opened, and then I kissed Nieves with such passion and intensity that she herself also seemed to forget that she was making out with a fifteen-year-old boy. When I parted my small, thin lips from hers, she stared at me in such a way that she seemed to sense that I was using her. Somehow, she had found me out and knew she was part of my plan. Still, I went ahead, and told her how beautiful and pretty she was, and how much I loved the sound of her guitar playing on those magical summer evenings. I thanked her and apologized for making her an unwilling participant in this misfortune. She understood almost nothing, because I told her everything in English. Almost enraged, Alicia jumped up.

"You damned midget Casanova! So you're doing this with all the older girls, do you think it's funny?"

Nieves sat up and stroked my head.

"You're a rascal, David. David the heartbreaker, ha! Well, life is short, and you have to enjoy it."

In my heart, I agreed with her, because if my strategy went wrong, my life would be short. Very, very short. But at least no one suspected anything, and my plan had gone perfectly.

Now all we could do was wait, pray and cross our fingers.

Chapter 6
Back

Evidently, the nurse did not want to see me again. She told Nieves that if he was able to shower her with love and affection in that way, that was a sign that I was fine. The group walked along the trail, as we did every day to get back to camp. As always, Picueto was by my side the whole way. He ran back and forth fooling around, he knocked caps off people's heads, drank water from other people's canteens, stopped to pick flowers. He was a restless guy.

I was just walking around pondering everything I had just remembered. Nothing fit me properly. I couldn't erase from my mind the dark, elongated silhouette leaving Nieves' body. If I told anyone about this, they would lock me up for life and throw the key into the sea. In my mind I had Alicia's picture; now that image was a faithful witness of my sudden memory and her amazing resemblance with that love called Angie.

Picueto, in one of his comings and goings, saw me crestfallen. Like a flash of lightning, he approached me. I didn't stop him. Somehow, he needed to talk to someone, even if it was a little boy.

"Jesus Christ, man! *You are* very sad, aren't you? If you want, I can take you to the love of your life."

"I wish, Picueto, I wish."

"You see? I told you, no one escapes the clutches of love. Ha ha!"

"You were right, Picu, absolutely right." I sighed, feeling sad and misunderstood.

"Of course! Girls are the best thing in the world. The best thing in the world!"

He liked them all, all of them. Short, chubby, tall, skinny, brunettes, blondes, redheads. Sometimes he even scared me because he always repeated himself to me,

"My friend, I like them all, all and then more!"

Now he was laughing like a madman, staring at me and licking his lips. I was in no mood for jokes. But I still caught his unbridled laughter.

I began to live with a maturity that worked at two rhythms.

As we approached the camp, we tried to guess the menu by distance-smelling. The cook had an incredible way with food. Every dish she cooked was delicious, even if it was vegetables. But that day I had a pit in my stomach. I was very worried about what the shadow told me; and now all kinds of memories were jumbling in my head, past and present. I was having a real internal debate.

I ate what I could and went to the tepee to lie down for a while. I kept thinking about the nurse. There, lying and meditating on it, I realized that indeed it was not her; she looked very much like her, but it was not. However, she had provoked in me a rush of memories. Memories that, thinking about it logically, could not be of this time. They were so precise that they could not be my imagination, but at the same time I was a mess. It's going to sound impossible, I know, but I'm going to do it anyway. I introduce myself again, partially, with what I managed to remember.

My name is, or was, rather, Dustin Sanders. I was born in Philadelphia, USA, on September 18, 1943. Yes, you heard, in the year 1943. I know how that sounds. I grew up in the city of brotherly love, but I think my family was traveling all over the country following my father, a sergeant in the AA, which stands for All American, 82nd Airborne Division. Fortunately, I managed to get away from the military world despite my father's hopes for me, and, encouraged by my mother, I studied at Harvard University, Massachusetts, so fashionable today. I have no clear images of my parents, no matter how hard I try. I specialized in neoclassical architecture. I was enthusiastic about it, and I am still enthusiastic about it, after all that has happened.

I can't remember how or when I met Angie. What I am sure of is that our house was beautiful. We lived in New Yor, in an old factory that had been closed and redesigned as a home. Our open plan space blended Victorian style décor and the natural industrial feel of the building seamlessly.

We loved it and at the weekend we would have a leisurely breakfast. We would both dress according to the day's plan and head outside. I vividly remember my love of motorcycles and motoring. We had a beautiful Harley Davidson parked on the landing of our floor. We could leave it there because the forklift, the only elevator on the property, had retained all its originality and usefulness. I remember as if it were right now when I closed its fan gate to lift it up.

I could go on telling hundreds of vivid details, but the reality is that I am now someone very different. I am a fifteen-year-old boy from Asturias, son of a sailor, worried about whether the next day I will die and appear somewhere else, as a different person again, or not remembering anything at all. Actually, maybe that would be for the best.

Lying there, alone, on my mat, I tried to use my analytical capacity to the full, trying to glimpse a plausible hypothesis for these experiences of mine. Obviously, the only thing that could explain all this would be reincarnation; but, even so, I could not find any explanation for the appearance of the visiting shadow. Nor did I have any recollection of my death or any time in an afterlife. I could not ratify any objective data about my past existence, and nothing could confirm or disprove whether everything I thought I knew was real or the product of some hallucinogenic suggestion.

It was supposed to be my last night at camp, and maybe on the face of the earth as well. That afternoon I was more distracted than a *voyeur* on a nudist beach, I couldn't focus or pay attention to anything. The uncertainty, and the new feeling of being trapped in that little town in Avila, and having to be interested in youth activities, was leaving me in a daze. But, without a doubt, my main concern was to get through the night, and if the outcome was satisfactory, to meet the shadow again. I had a lot to ask.

That night I didn't sleep a wink; I stayed up all night trying to remember another time, another life, I was obsessed with bringing back the distant memories of Angie. I liked her so much. I needed her so much and I was so in love with her that I kept wondering if she was alive and how I could visit her.

But, of course, the visitor told me that nobody, nobody, nobody could know what was happening to me. It was all very complex. I remember the dark morning blue of dawn coming in through the tepee's timbers. Everyone was snoring; some of the boys were even talking in their sleep. The new day arrived with the cheerful birdsong, and I finally fell fast asleep as a result of exhaustion and nighttime wakefulness. I think I slept less than three hours. It was nine o'clock in the morning and everyone was hurrying with unusual impatience to breakfast in the shed. The boys were talking about enjoying the last day to the fullest, because at eight o'clock in the evening the bus was leaving to return us to Madrid.

I let myself go with the adolescent flow, but strangely, although almost adult inside me, I also felt the contradictory need to have fun and do childish things. I analyzed that feeling, that duality between childishness and maturity, and my limited imagination wanted to conclude that it could be some hormonal absence, or some physiological process typical of my current physical age.

I woke up from my short rest happy not to have died. I had passed the test, and everything was going well. For the last time we went to the pool. And from a distance I looked at the hut where Alicia was, without having made any decisions. Any false step could be a blunder, and I still didn't know what I could and couldn't do. Much to my regret, I decided not to approach the hut and contemplate it from afar, like the mute vestige of a cruel resemblance.

Sadness took over my mood as I sat on the edge of the pool, staring at the infirmary. As it could not be otherwise, Picu was in charge of pulling me out of my lethargy by throwing a one peseta water balloon at me. The icy liquid against my warm, sun-bathed skin almost gave a heart attack.

I jumped up and ran after him, he ran like a frightened lizard. I could not catch up with him, and little by little I got over my annoyance, so from a distance I told him that I forgave him, and when I had him close, I grabbed him by the neck with my left hand and gave him a full nuggie although then we called 'doing a Coke'.

Peaceful and somewhat distracted, we bathed and enjoyed our last day together, almost completely forgetting our worries; and, for that short time I was, again able to just be David Fonseca, a fifteen-year-old boy at camp. When we all begged the counselors to let us stay a little longer, I looked at the hut for the last time, waiting for Alicia to come out to stretch her legs, to smoke if she smoked, or to get a little sun on her face. But nothing, that fragile door never opened. Something inside me was pushing me to that tin door, to face my fears and to disregard the danger signs, but I did not give in to the temptation.

It was time to go, so I joined the group. I said goodbye to the pool trying to keep its image in my memory, looking back over my shoulder as we walked to the camp for the last time.

That last meal tasted like glory. It was clear that it was a very special day because the menu was also very special. We had a country salad for first course, steak and fries for second course, and for dessert there was ice cream and chocolate yogurt. The table was full of soft drinks of all flavors. This time the counselors did not order us to sit on the benches or prevent us from going from table to table, chatting as we wished.

After lunch, we had to prepare and collect all our things to put them in the bus. We had a couple of hours to spare, so the counselors took us to some nearby ruins to see the atavistic lifestyle of the ancient inhabitants, and, this time, unaccompanied by the night fire, told us a story of love between two young villagers. It was a forbidden love between a beautiful young woman and a young peasant, whose feuding families rejected their relationship, forcing them to escape from the community in search of their destiny, in search of freedom, far from hatred to fight for their love. I don't know if he made up these stories or what, but Germán had a special talent of making you feel, he always had the right words; he was an exceptional orator. Finally, it was time to go back to the camp.

As a final touch, the cook, always so dedicated, had made five giant cakes of various flavors, which were waiting for us in the shed as the icing on the cake of this wonderful, eye-opening summer trip.

Almost all the boys hugged Carmen, the cook, to thank her for all the good things she made for us. That woman had earned our eternal love by putting so much effort and love into what she did.

We boarded the bus that would take us back to Madrid and sang our way home while Nieves accompanied us with her guitar.

Even the driver joined in with the chorus of Kumbaya. Little by little, and like the first time I approached Madrid, the sky was illuminated in the distance with that fluorescent orange color.

Picu and I exchanged telephone numbers, which at that time were only domestic numbers with long prefixes, in the hope of seeing each other again someday. In the Plaza de Atocha, the sidewalk was once again full of relatives awaiting our arrival.

We gave Germán and Nieves a big hug. The kids were crying with sadness, knowing this was the end of our adventure. Soon school and unsavory obligations would take up most of the time.

I was delighted to find my aunt and uncle, who were returning from their Andalusian road-trip. Josito had left the car parked near the Scalextric that went down to Legazpi, which is where the Smurfs told him he could park more easily. As soon as she saw me, my aunt sensed that I was not well at all; although without slacking off, I insisted that I was perfectly fine, that I was sad to end that wonderful vacation. My uncle was fully convinced, my aunt, a little less so.

I put that green duffel bag in the trunk of the car again, now even more filthy and dirty, except that this time it was loaded with unthinkable memories.

We spent the night for the second time in this small but comfortable hotel. It was nice to be able to take a shower in a bathroom with so many comforts, to get into a well-made and clean bed and let oneself be carried away by tiredness to the world of dreams.

The next day, the smell of toast and coffee pervaded the corridors and rooms of the hotel. I brushed my teeth, took off my pajamas, and together with my uncle and aunt, went down to the restaurant for breakfast, attracted by the sweetness of the pastries. It was self-service, so you sat where you liked and got up to take whatever the counter had to offer, as you pleased.

My aunt asked me what I wanted, and I insisted on making my own breakfast. I arrived back at our table with a small tray laden with a plate of toast, butter and honey, a glass of orange juice, a saucer of eggs and bacon, and a well-filled cup of black coffee.

My uncle was surprised, and skeptically thought I had the wrong drink, making secret gestures with my aunt to see how I reacted when I tasted the coffee. Of course, I didn't even think about that detail, for me it was as natural as drinking water when you are thirsty. My aunt and uncle were surprised to see me finish the cup, and of course, they asked about it. I evaded their confusion as best I could with pretexts, that I wanted to feel older and so on, to hide it, but they told me that I was not going to drink coffee again without my parents' consent... not even if I was a junkie!

I wanted to forget about my meeting with the shadow and stop wondering when and where it would show up again. and I wondered why it was taking so long to come. I was impatient for the promised explanations.

I would look for it in the eyes of any stranger, to see if it was him.

Chapter 7
The Visitor

Madrid-Asturias, 1995

We returned to Asturias by the northern road. The north, how nice that sounded. Leaning against the window, I enjoyed the changing landscape with my absent gaze.

At dusk we entered the village of Andrín, our home. For quite some time, the mixture of the smell of vegetation, land and sea had been giving us its particular welcome. I couldn't wait to get home and hug my mother. My uncle phoned her from Aguilar de Campoo, where, seduced by the aroma of cookies, he could not resist buying a few boxes. By the time we arrived home, dinner was almost ready, so that, gathered together, we could tell her everything we had done during those two weeks.

It was rather rude to brag about vacations while the poor thing must have been left alone with nothing to do. For that reason, my uncle and aunt did not put much emphasis on describing their route through the southern cities, their dreamy beaches, and the hard working and easy-going style of the locals, always generous with smiles and jokes.

Exhausted from the car ride, after showering and eating dinner, I found that my bed and I had missed each other too. I made a titanic effort to pull the covers back and not just throw myself on it. I remember letting myself go, like someone who falls into a cushioned depth, losing all his strength, trapped by Morpheus.

My aunt and uncle and my mother stayed in the living room, talking non-stop, and Josito's deep voice stood out from the women's', despite their failed efforts to lower the tone. The orange light of the lamp passing through the doorjamb was an added soothing balm, like a nightlight.

I was in the confines of the deepest part of sleep, when a sound, sharp and intermittent, began to tug at me, forcing me to awaken. It was a resonating sound like an ungreased door, yet sharper and more strident. I could hear it, but I could not define where it came from.

Finally, it woke me up completely. I looked at the alarm clock on the bedside table, and saw it was three-thirty in the morning. I looked across the room, where just before I fell asleep, I had seen that orange glow. Now there was only darkness. A faint white light, from the street lighting, was streaming through my window, printing the outline of its lattice between the foot of my bed and the floor. Out of the corner of my eye I thought I saw something move, near the door. I focused my attention on the black darkness without ceasing to hear that annoying noise, which little by little seemed more like the rubbing of a fork on a blackboard. I leaned on my hands to sit up, resting sleepily on the headboard of the bed. And at that moment I distinguished its outline clearly, motionless at the foot of the bed, almost as high as the ceiling; erect and elongated, it seemed to stare at me, although its silhouette could barely be glimpsed in the blackness of the night.

I blinked repeatedly to try to adjust my vision. As much as I wanted to calm down, the fear was in my body, and that sharp sound like the thinnest note of a violin kept ringing in my ears.

Camouflaged in the shadows, I saw him move slowly towards the light of the window, revealing, at last, the shape of his elongated and shadowy body. There he was, illuminated by that subtle, whitish light coming through the window of my room. The same gesture, standing there, raising his outstretched right hand to the height of his shoulder, just as I last remembered him. Waving, as if he were a Comanche chief.

He walked slowly and smoothly and stood right in front of the window. His back seemed to be towards me, but the direction of his body was not clear. The sound was changing through different tones, and now I was sure that its origin came from my special visitor. I remained motionless, waiting, not wanting to do or say anything. I watched attentively, terrified, but also curios and fascinated. Suddenly, he sat on the edge of the bed. Neither the mattress nor the comforter moved under him, and I realized that his presence must not have been tangible.

That annoying sound began to define itself as a distant voice intermingled with stridency. Suddenly, I clearly differentiated a sentence with a low, slow tone,

"If you hear me, speak to me."

I immediately reacted, trembling, stuttering and mumbling,

"I hear you; I hear you."

"I have a serious problem and I'll be honest with you; I came here because you are my last resort."

"What do you mean?"

"I need you. I need your help."

"My help? Me?" I said, puzzled.

"On occasions like this, my capacity is very limited. We have no time to waste."

"I know I am indebted to you; I know you are good. I trust you, shadow."

"Shadow? I suppose that will do."

"What can I do for you?"

"One of my protégés is badly wounded, suffering and trapped. I have tried everything and to no avail. I need you to go and help him as soon as possible."

We both sat up straighter; and, without wasting a second, I went to the closet, grabbed the first clothes I saw and began to get dressed in a hurry. I tried not to make any noise, so as not to wake my mother. Finally, I put on my sneakers, got back on my feet, and, in a firm tone and in a low voice, I said,

"Where is he and what happened to him?"

"It is behind the church of San Juan, in Oceño. You will find it on the outer western edge of the village."

"Shadow, that's far from here!"

"Have you forgotten to drive?"

At this my face broke into a half-smile.

"Understood, I'll take my parents' car."

"Even if you don't see me, your intuition will tell you which way it is. Trust it."

And he disappeared, his image fading into the darkness. Stealthy and excited, I grabbed my backpack. The first thing I threw in was the flashlight I took with me to camp. In total silence, I walked past my mother's room. I saw her resting, sleeping, placidly and soundly. I stopped for a few seconds and then continued. I knew that time was short, but on the other hand, I was aware that it was bad to leave this way. I continued down the hallway, took the car keys from the coat rack, and stopped at the bathroom at the entrance of the house. I slowly closed the door, but the damn hinges couldn't keep quiet. I close the in a hurry, before snapping it shut.

I opened the closet and checked for the essentials. I put the whole first aid kit in the backpack. Closing the zipper was quite an effort, between my nerves, the pressure and the rush. I opened the window wide and threw the backpack on the grass. I carefully climbed up leaning on the toilet and jumped out. I grabbed the backpack again, and squatting and hunched over, ran to the car. It was parked on the street, just by the lamppost. I left two stones by the driver's wheel, next to the curb, to mark just where my mother had parked it. The central locking sounded like lightning on a silent night. It made me angry, and I couldn't help but look around, worried that someone was watching me.

I climbed into the car with a weight on my stomach, shaky from following my impulses. I slid the seat back and placed my backpack on the seat next to me, controlling my breathing. I left my door ajar so as not to make noise and turned the key in the ignition. The steering wheel unlocked and the dashboard glowed red. I felt my heart in my throat. It wasn't wise to start close to home. I released the handbrake, turned the wheel slightly to the right, separating the car from the curb. The car began to move s under the effect of gravity. Once I felt I was far enough away, I shifted into second gear, released the clutch by pressing the accelerator and the car woke up with a tenacious roar. I closed the door, put on my seat belt and, with no time to lose, I began to drive, rushing through the gears, heated with nerves, excitement and haste.

It was four in the morning when I crossed the village of Caldueño at full speed. Like a *flash,* my attention was focused on an SUV pulled up and stopped behind the last farmhouse. It caught my attention for several reasons. It was at the foot of the road with its lights on and, well, so far, so good. The problem was that on the roof of the SUV two blue, permanent lights decorated it picturesquely contrasting with its two-tone green and white bodywork.

I shouted in frustration as I hit the steering wheel and cursed my luck.

As expected, the police did not take a second to activate their sirens and their lights. In the middle of the night, in the most resounding silence and without warning, a mobile fair began to follow me.

For a moment, and as a reflex, I lifted the accelerator pedal. I looked in the rearview mirror and realized that, between the time they started and now they were picking up speed, but I was still well ahead of them. It was all wrong. I would never normally have done anything like that. But on this occasion, I had to do everything I could to escape. Someone was hurt and trapped. My mind was racing, and I concluded that evading justice was a necessary evil in honor of the greater good.

I downshifted to third gear and pushed the Renault's accelerator pedal to the floor. Showing off its power, the car's engine surprised me with a push in the back. I don't know how, but those damned guards were following me in the distance; I passed a curve and lost sight of them, but when I reached a straight section of road they appeared again with their blue flashes, like indefatigable pursuers.

That Nissan Patrol seemed to be running faster than it should; and the guards, relentless, did not give up. I turned off the lights of the car to camouflage it in the dark, taking advantage of the gray of its paint, so that the red rear position lights would not reveal my position. It was useless, I couldn't see a damn thing, and when braking before each curve, the powerful brake lights shone like a lighthouse in the night. I was trapped by the law. I doubted myself, what I was doing, my deepest values. And, for the first time in a long time, I felt alone, a failure, and realized I would probably soon to be captured.

"Don't slow down, there's no time to lose! Keep going, I'll take care of it!"

Those words of encouragement and cheer echoed in my ears, and I immediately recognized the voice of the shadow. It was coming up the winding mountainside, our gazes met. Then out of the strangely clear sky, a very bright light the size of a fat marble appeared. Suddenly, that light grew larger and larger, approaching the two cars, all the while increasing in size. It was an oval light, bright white in color. Around it seemed to rotate blue, green, violet and red glowing lights. The light came between us, and the two of us, impressed by the sight, slowed to a stop. The lights of the police car began to flicker and finally went out.

The SUV stopped, and so did I, absorbed by the sight. I could see the agents as they got out of the car with their flashlights in hand, the driver was also wielding his pistol, and the co-pilot was walking perplexed looking at the colored light that did not seem solid. They were trying to turn on those long, crude flashlights, but only a few timid intermittent beams of light emerged from them.

The luminaire levitated next to them, almost in contact with the ground. It must have measured about eight meters in diameter. My height-advanced vision gave me a clear perspective. Still amazed, I could see thousands of colors inside that bubble. Suddenly, I heard his voice again, very loud,

"Come on! What are you waiting for? Run away, run away!"

I put the car back in first gear and revved the engine to the maximum, obeying, heading towards the church of San Juan. No one was chasing me this time.

After a few minutes and after crossing through several detours at full speed, behind me I saw the light rise from the surface, rising in a perfect vertical, very slowly and then fading like a firework. I deduced that it was a distraction maneuver, very effective, by the way, of my ally.

Finally, I arrived at my destination. As I climbed down with my backpack over my shoulder, a faint smell of burning, coming from the car, warned me that I had abused it. I caressed its hood and, when I reached the headlights, I patted it twice. I realized that it was a gesture from my previous life. It was my way of thanking the car for how well it had behaved.

In a hurry, I took out my flashlight. I didn't want to leave the lights on in order to not to attract the attention of the guards. Who knows, how many could be looking for me. I started to walk around the old church. There was no one there. I was already in the back and still could not find any wounded. I walked through the meadow, illuminating the field with my sad lantern, which offered a humble amber color full of stripes. A four-legged animal, perhaps a dog, stood vigilantly on top of the small hill. He had noticed me long before I noticed him, that much was certain. I kept moving forward and thought it was a good idea to shine the flashlight on myself, as a gesture of trust, so that he wouldn't take me for a threat.

A few meters away, I could distinguish that it was not a dog, but a wolf. The brown color of its frizzy fur, the elongated gait of its paws and its indomitable gaze made it clear. It walked towards the trees and the vegetation. I lost sight of it, but followed in its footsteps, entering its terrain.

A metallic clang caused me to direct my light toward the source of the sound. A wolf came out of nowhere, heading towards me at speed. Stopped by the tension of a chain attached to its hind leg, it failed to catch up with me. Frightened, I tried to retreat, falling and then crawling backwards on my hands and heels. A shuddering shriek accompanied the tension of the chain. Another wolf, the one that had led me to this one, patrolled restlessly and alertly. Hearing the whimper, it came closer, as if to calm the other down, while I could not stop looking at the aggressive fangs, the violent, inclement face, without blinking for a second, warning me that if it could escape from that chain, I would be minced meat.

I shone a light on its hind legs, and one of them was literally soaked in blood. The right thigh was caught in a trap that was biting in relentlessly. The other wolf was licking the wound helplessly. Its sad look and the bloody muzzle of the other's wound was the living image of fraternity.

I had to sit and wait patiently for quite some time while the trapped animal calmed down. Suddenly, the other wolf, who until then had remained at a distance, approached me.

Having this wild animal so close with its rapid breathing, strength and, why not say it, a wolf's bad reputation was quite an exercise in impulse self-control. My body was screaming for me to run.

The wolf lay down next to me and rested its head on my legs. This wolf knew that I had come to help them.

Little by little and influenced by its companion, the wounded animal began to relax, loosening the chain and laying down on its side. Cautiously, I approached. Its expression was totally different. As a predator, it must have understood that if it were my prey, I would have already ended its life, or at least tried to. Nevertheless, its ears, the opening of its eyes, its muscular tension, everything about it made it clear that this was an animal always alert and on guard.

I approached the trap that held it prisoner. I felt a shiver as I put myself in the wolf's place, empathizing with its pain. Then I could admire the courage, wild strength and bravery. Stroking its back, its snorting became less and less frequent. I told it in the sweetest voice I could muster,

"This may hurt you, partner."

I looked closely at the design of that trap, and nowhere did it feature any opening device, handle or latch. It was clear that it was a resistance trap. Only by prying it open or levering it open, counteracting its tension, could I free the poor wolf.

I stuck my fingers as best I could between the teeth of that metallic jaw and with all my strength tried to force it open, without success. The wolf seemed to give up, but not me. I began to think about what I could do with the meager resources I had at my disposal. I thought about my clothes, the car, stones, everything. And, out of nowhere, like a click, my mind got an answer. I stroked the wolf's head again, looked into its eyes and said,

"I'll be right back, don't give up."

I ran to the car as fast as I could, opened the trunk and under the wheel cover grabbed the jack.

I returned breathlessly to the place and at full speed took off my sneakers. Almost forcibly and in a matter of seconds, I extracted the laces. I tied each of them to both ends of the well-reinforced jack with several turns and did the same with each prong of the trap.

It was the moment of truth. I began to turn the crank of the jack and the gag accompanied its opening with astonishing ease. There, barefoot, almost in the dark and among shadows and wolves, I felt happier than I had ever felt in my entire life. The wolf stuck out a paw in a reflex movement, trying to stand up on it. I calmed it down again and said,

"Wait, let me cure you a little."

I opened the backpack and took out the first aid kit. I parted the thick fur to see the extent of the wound. It was a good bite. I poured out some hydrogen peroxide, which bubbled up like an effervescent pill. With all the gentleness in the world, I cleaned the wound with gauze and I soaked a good piece of absorbent cotton with iodine and with a compressive bandage I attached it to the flesh, secured it with plenty of adhesive tape, and said,

"That's it." And I gave the wolf a loving slap, celebrating the end of the agony.

The wolf stood up and turned in on itself. It barely limped. I found the tough, strong, resilient temperament unbelievable. It brought its eyes close to mine, sniffing me relentlessly, and nuzzled me with its head rubbing against my neck. I could see tears welling up in the wild animal's eyes, though not a sob was heard. He was sad and grateful at the same time. That is how I understood it. I told him again,

"It was nothing, don't worry." And although I knew it might not understand me, I added, "Thank our protector, he brought me to you."

A few meters away, the other wolf seemed to be waiting, impatient to leave that place of danger. They marched off into the darkness of the forest, but not without turning around one last time to look at me.

As quickly as I could I untied the laces and put them back in my sneakers. I picked up the first aid kit, put it in the backpack and looked at the snare, which was totally closed. Chained to the tree, I tried to pull it off, but there was no way. I gave up, but I threw it into the branches where it remained hanging on one of them.. I ran to the car, opened the trunk, and the light from it illuminated my bloody hands and shirt. I took off the shirt, wiped my hands with it, put the jack back in place and got back behind the wheel. I looked at the time; it was half past five in the morning. I had another hour to get home, and I had to drive slowly so as not to attract attention. I rolled down the car window slightly and in the distance I heard the free howling of the wolf.

I admit that I felt proud and it seemed to me that all the difficulties had been worth it.

I went back through Unquera, which is the opposite circular road to the one I came on, thus avoiding the places where the police had chased me. Relieved to get home, I placed the car on the marker, under the lamppost, threw the stones into the bushes carefully, and like a *ninja* I entered the house through the bathroom. I closed the window, took off my shoes and walked barefoot down the hallway. I closed the door to my room and turned on the lamp on the headboard. All my clothes were stained. I took them off and hid them between the mattress and the box spring. I put on my pajamas and, still on a high from everything I had experienced, I tried to digest, to understand. I watched the day dawn without being able to sleep a wink again. The effect of the adrenaline and the stress of danger still lasted.

I fell asleep, as if I had never left home.

Chapter 8
The Conversation

Andrin, 1995

My mother should work for Interpol or the CIA. Gee, she almost caught me. I was anxiously awaiting the shadow's return. I had a lot of doubts and questions about my past, but most of all, I would have loved to celebrate how well I had done rescuing the wolf. My mother noticed that someone had touched the driver's seat and also commented to me that she could have sworn the car had half a tank of fuel but now the needle was almost showing empty. I tried to disregard everything she was telling me by playing it down, but just in case, I decided to throw the clothes in a dumpster far, far away from home. I couldn't leave any more clues. All this served as a lesson for me to realize the mistakes I had made, although I also gave myself a pat on the back for the things I did right.

Days went by, and every time I saw a police car I would think about my tenacious pursuers, about whether they would have caught the license plate and whether they would be looking for me.

My doubts were dispelled a little more than a week later, when they announced on an entertainment program the story of a police officer who claimed to have witnessed a supernatural sighting. Only one of the two was on the program. He maintained that his partner did not want to back up what they saw because he was afraid of the psychological board of the military corps and also of what people would say. Still, he told his story. I was sorry to see how the presenter mocked him, skeptical, about the details of the sighting.

"So, agent, do you think that huge flash of light could be a worldwide threat?" And he laughed sardonically.

"I only know what I have told you, what my partner and I saw. We were chasing a gray Renault 11 that was driving at full speed, invading opposite lanes, and tracing the curves and crossings as if it was running away from something. Maybe it was being chased by the luminaire, maybe it was just a madman behind the wheel, I don't know."

I felt my pulse quicken; my face was pale again. My mother, who was watching it, was very interested because it was a local story and picked up the phone to call my aunt. I could see how the agent was almost making a fool of himself for telling his story, when suddenly the program received a call from a witness who, awakened by the sirens and in the distance, had seen the light rise into the sky and vanish.

The police officer seemed to breathe a sigh of relief and regained his lost composure; his testimony was supported by another witness, although his partner did not want to share his version. This agent had to write the report of what happened alone, his partner refused to give an account of the facts. It all made more sense to me than it did to them, although I could not blame the presenter for his natural, sarcastic and unserious reaction.

Going to a program to be taken for a madman, not being paid any attention and suffering comic skepticism makes me, today, still take my hat off to that officer. The police officer only wanted to warn that this light could represent a danger or an opportunity, but no one from the institutions paid any attention to him and television was his last alternative.

I was just worried that my mother would connect what she was hearing with the lack of fuel and the date of the narrative. On the other hand, I would have loved to call and tell the whole truth, and stick up for him, but that was out of the question.

Days went by, and I did not receive a visit from my good friend, the shadow. I tried to justify this, but sometimes bad thoughts would come out of me. We were already in that repetitive process of returning to class. My mother, already drowning under expenses, couldn't afford to buy me new books, and the second-hand ones she got must have belonged to someone with an obsessive fixation on phallic illustrations. Anyway, I wasn't going to look at them much, so I didn't care.

Every night I waited for his visit and finally he deigned to come and talk to me. Like the previous time, he woke me up in the middle of the night. This time, I was not the least bit startled, and even allowed myself the luxury of reproaching him for his absence. He immediately motioned with his hand for me to be quiet, moved to the side of my bed and looked at the wall in front of us. He clasped both hands together and a beam of light emerged from them.

In front of me I had the clear image of a forest, like a projector illuminating the wall, filling it with light and color. It was not exactly like going to the movies, there was depth and you could breathe the air of the foliage. Attentive and surprised, I kept looking at the wall, now turned into a window to another place. The vision was moving up, as if rolled by a giant. Then I saw several wolves walking, and the image focused on the one we had helped, apparently his protégé. He was not wearing the bandage and was walking normally. The animal was looking towards us, as if it saw nothing, but sensing that someone was watching it. The wolf pack started to run and the vision began to shrink on the wall until it closed the frame. The shadow walked a few steps forward and turned and stared at me.

"You have done a good job. Without your help, the wolf would have died for sure."

"We did it together, shadow."

"Well. Before you start with your questions, I must tell you that I don't have answers for everything. I am but a step above limited human knowledge, but we are both about equal in order. I will lay the groundwork for you to understand, and then you can ask questions. I am part of a countless number of fellows. All of us have assigned protégés. As you may have guessed by now, you are one of mine. We are beings of light and you are beings of water. Our existence is relatively immortal, unless we borrow the body of a water being. Doing so is a last resort, because when you occupy it, you are not protected by your light being; it is as if you are disconnected.

"Apart from us, other beings, invisible to me and those like me, occupy this reality. They are called beings of fire, although you will know them by the pseudonym of evil genies or demons. You must understand that the concept of good and evil is relative, nothing is black or white, but simply lighter or darker. You have mistakenly thought that spiritual evolution has to do with these two antagonistic concepts, which undoubtedly influence, but are not determinant. The key is in the effort, the overcoming and the constant struggle from birth; that makes you worthy of spiritual evolution. For example, you have carried out an animal rescue mission, haven't you?" he asked in his booming voice.

"Correct."

"And how do you feel?"

"I feel good about it, but..."

"I know what you are going to tell me. You feel bad for running away from the police, for breaking the rules. For betraying your mother's trust and doing something as serious as driving a car."

"That's right," I sighed.

"But at the same time, you have saved a life, a free life, of incalculable spiritual value. Those are the grays, my friend. Nothing is so simple. Everything is blurred in a strange reality between life and death, between the right and the forbidden, where the small details are important, but the result is the key."

"So, anything goes?"

"You're missing the point. Not everything goes. Basically, the evil produced should never outweigh the evil one is trying to avoid. If the scales tip the other way, we have lost, and if that tendency becomes constant and predominant, your destiny will be to evolve into a being of fire."

"I'm getting it, but what about me?"

"You are an anomaly in this evolutionary process."

"Please explain that to me, how am I an anomaly?"

"One must overcome different difficulties in life. These tests cannot be offered in a single existence; each vital context makes you suffer and strive spiritually in different ways. Sometimes, when passing from one life to another, the "basic erasure" does not do its job properly. If the erasure has not worked, it is because something in that lifetime has marked your spiritual personality. Every living being brings with them "remnant" experiences."

"Explain it to me, I want to know." I was perplexed.

"The most imperative is the survival instinct. Other behavioral tendencies obey slight imprints, such as being left-handed or right-handed. And sometimes the remnant manifests itself in talents imported from previous lives, indelible and already permanent. Let me give you an example. Talent in painting, music, craftsmanship, combat, social skills..., I could go on and on and on. But what has happened to you is unusual. Not uncommon, but special."

"So, there are more like me."

"Of course. The universe was already invented before you and I existed. The order establishes several types of existence: the currents and the inverses."

"I'm listening."

"I would have to start with diffuse and abstract concepts, misunderstood by your civilization. Time does not exist as such. It is an invention to measure the rotational cycles of your world on its own axis, on the celestial orbit of light that you have baptized as the Sun. It is so pitiful that you have had to apply intermingled decimal and sexagesimal measurements, and, even so, every four years you must correct the excess. Well, I will tell you that time is somewhat elastic, it can go forwards and backwards, although the most normal thing is to go forwards. There are existences whose reincarnations go back in time and that, like you, remember perfectly not only a previous life, but many; it is the example of Jules Verne or Nostradamus. They also had to hide their anomaly or singularity by means of fantastic literature or encryption.

"This quality of yours is more frequent in retrocedent existences. In the currents, the anomaly usually corrects itself automatically in childhood, so yours is something very special. Remnants can manifest in many ways. There are individuals whose spirit remains anchored to a sexual identity. Often, there are other cases of cognitive inheritance, phobias and fears of experiences from another life, vertigo, panic of blood or needles, unfounded obsessions, innate abilities, unexplained knowledge and even blurred, unconnected memories. But I have never known of a case as complete as yours. Because, in addition, you have retained the gift of connecting with other realities. So we must tread very carefully, because this is all new to both of us."

"I want to know more," I insisted.

"Regarding time, I will tell you that all beings of light can travel to the recent future and contemplate coming events. It is our way of trying to avoid them. When they are small dangers to oneself or others, the being of light tells his or her protégé, without revealing themself, discreetly. It is like a telepathic communication, or the voice of the conscience. This communication generates a bad feeling, a warning, an alarm is turned on. Some turn a deaf ear and finally tragedy strikes; others hear the warning and dodge it, and others have never noticed the signs. Intuitions, premonitory dreams, *déjà vu,* chills, slight tugging at clothing or feelings of alertness in normal situations. All these impressions foretell an almost imminent risk, you have to know how to listen, to identify the signs; this is the help we can give you."

"Tell me about the beings of fire."

"They share the reality with you and me, but they are far removed from my perception. They sweeten their guests with false promises, gifts and presents; facilities, after all. Nevertheless, I can perceive the altered and dark aura of their guests, but I cannot see them."

"How so?"

"You will understand it very easily. You call it luck; others, more refined, call it magic. The beings of fire always get their work done by directing the spiritual orientation towards their own nature. They need their host to become one of them. It is their reproduction system. Your world, like many others, is a game board where everyone freely chooses their path. You are a blank canvas that allows itself to be seduced by facilities or, otherwise, struggles relentlessly at every instant to achieve the same result by doing the right thing.

"Now you will understand why there are people to whom everything seems to work out wonderfully, with an unusual ease;

and others, on the other hand, to have less, they fight three times as hard. That has nothing to do with the social context, make no mistake. It's about proportion, I don't know if you follow me. You could be a king of the Middle Ages and yet your life will be more sacrificed than that of a peasant. The key is in the will and in not succumbing to the charms of those aids that lead us to the wrong side of the scale, the path of eternal servitude, the wrong path."

"Tell me about what you have called The Order."

"Light and darkness. Matter and antimatter. Yin and yang. Everything intermingles and competes for a piece of space. You just worry about the next step. Don't want to run before you know how to crawl."

"Why were we in danger at the camp, when I thought I recognized Angie?"

"I'll start with me. I have already told you that if I occupy the body of a water being I become vulnerable. The bond between that person and his protector is broken. If at any given moment a danger were to cause my death, I would return again reincarnated to the lower step, having to coexist with that soul united to it in the same body. Now you call it multiple personality disorder, before it was called Gemini. Finally, when The Order corrects the disturbance after harmonious cohabitation, it divides and separates them with the birth of twins. That is why when I entered the body of that boy in your school, or that of the teacher, I was in great danger."

"Can you get into any body?"

"No. Or, rather, yes, but if I do it in the body of a person who enjoys the favors of the beings of fire, they would try to kill me at all costs. That is why I must choose very well. And the situation must be truly require me to do so. We are the ones who fill with courage an ordinary person who throws himself on the tracks of a train to help a stranger. We are the courage of the soldier who in a war carries a wounded stranger amidst the whistling of bullets to save him, even if he is on the opposite side."

"And... me?"

"Severe disturbances such as yours tend to be corrected. When any living being sleeps, it transmits in the rem phase all daily memories to the Order; if another individual notices the anomaly, it can be corrected, and you know what would happen: start over."

"It's clear to me. And where is Angie?"

"You can't ask me that. It would be breaking all the rules."

"What if I travel to the United States and do some research?"

"If you are a good chameleon and no one discovers you, you can do it. But it would be risky."

"I think I remember where we used to live, I'll start there."

"Don't forget that you are fifteen years old. You're already attracting a lot of attention with your skills. I would wait."

"Where is she? I helped you, you help me!"

"Lower your voice. You woke your mother. I have to go. Remember everything I said. Maybe we won't see each other again. Maybe this relationship doesn't suit us."

"It's only good for you when you want it! I didn't hesitate to help you! Help me find Angie!"

The appearance of the shadow began to blur, fading away, diluting next to the window.

"No hurry, my friend, all in good time. Start where I told you and be very careful."

"Don't go! Wait!" I shouted in desperation.

The light in the room came on. My mother looked at me in fright as I screamed at the window, at nothing, full of rage. With clenched fists I pounded the bed incessantly as I screamed,

"Come back! Come back here, you wretch!"

My mother ran to the bed and began hugging me and trying to calm me down. She repeated over and over again,

"Calm down, it's over, it's over."

I couldn't wait to tell her everything. About the camp, about the escape with the car, about the shadow, about my past, about Angie. But I held back and pretended; just as she thought, I pretended it had been a bad nightmare. And, in part, it was. A bad dream.

My life without Angie was exactly that.

Chapter 9
Voluntary Denial

Andrin, 1996

Days went by and I felt as if I was caught in a loop. There was nothing I could do. I was too young to leave home and too poor to dig into my past.

For a few months, I couldn't stop thinking about everything that had happened to me. I tried to tell myself that Angie was far away from me. Far away in time and distance. That she would have rebuilt her life. That what was between us was impossible. I told myself so many times that I finally accepted it.

I wanted to focus on my new life, keep my secret on a shelf in the storage room of my heart and focus on my future. Because looking back I felt only nostalgia, sorrow and doubt. And in this future, everything was new and unpredictable. I had a chance to build my happiness.

I also wanted to forget about the shadow and the strange things I did. I focused on being happy with my beloved family, my friends and my future. I decided to enjoy the future by renouncing the past. Anyway, I could never tell Angie who I was. If I found her, the only thing that would happen is that I would be left with the desire to return to my past existence. Still, I was just trying to convince myself like a pushy salesman. I used my usual logical syllogism to do so, but, in reality, something inside me was struggling to emerge and look for her. I only set out to tame that beast so that it would leave me alone, so that it would let me live.

I no longer wanted to know anything about the hidden mysteries of life, of fate, of yin or yang, of beings of fire or light. All that started to get too big for me and I tried to ignore it completely. Or so I thought.

Easter vacation was just a few days away. I had hit a growth spurt and had been focusing more on exercise for some time. I found that it helped me to stop thinking. The suffering and pain of exertion made me live a more balanced life. It's funny that my conversation with the shadow was very brief, but he certainly seemed to be right about a lot of things.

I happened to be the young man with the best grades in all of Gijón. That's what I found out later. I was focused on getting the best results to make my parents proud and not to increase in the least their concern for me. I often thought about my projects: what I was going to study at university and what I would do for a living. I thought I was in control. Nothing was to alter my new goals. I wanted to be just another person.

I remember it was a Friday and my mother had prepared several sponge cakes. She carefully removed one lemon cake from the cake tin. While it was still warm, she placed it on a paper plate, protected it with crisscrossed strips of hard cardboard, wrapped it with brown paper and decorated it all with a navy-blue ribbon. My mother called me. It was five o'clock in the afternoon, and I had planned to go for at least an hour's run. But my mother is my mother. Her errands come first.

"Take this sponge cake to Father Damián, I hear he is feeling under the weather."

Since I that first encounter years ago, I never met him again. Yes, I passed him in town many times, we went to mass, etc., but since then I had always tried to avoid his conversation. I was driven away by the way he looked at me. He would stare at me as if he knew something about me. That's why I tried to refuse to take him the cake, offering weak excuses. My mother took my bicycle out of the garage, attached the cake to the rack and exclaimed,

"It will take you ten minutes!"

What to do? We might have been short of many things at home, but stubbornness? There was plenty of that. I arrived at the door of the priest's house, I stood there for a few seconds, as if looking for the courage to knock, and just as I raised my hand to knock, the door opened. As it rotated on its hinges, the priest's back could be seen walking with difficulty towards one of those wooden armchairs. Aided by a cane, he sat on that bench straight and firm, fixing his eyes on me. He said nothing. He just waited in silence, still resting his hands on the knob of that staff. I, half nervously, felt in a hurry, I don't know why. I untied the cake, took it in my hand, and asked,

"May I?"

"You may, you may. Come in, boy," he answered.

"My mother made you a lemon cake."

"I can smell it already. Mmmmmm, my favorite. Leave it in the kitchen."

"Well, that's it, Father. Is there anything else I can do for you?"

"Sure, of course you can. Cut two good slices of that great cake, get me a drink from the fridge and have another one for yourself."

I hesitated for a few seconds and reacted.

"Okay. Hold on."

I walked around unwrapping the cake, looked in the kitchen and everything was in full view on horizontal shelves. I grabbed two plates and some silverware, the glasses and drinks, and headed for the living room with a corrugated wooden tray, thinking how much Father Damián had aged in such a short time.

"I wanted to talk to you, young man. Since you came here with your mother, we haven't talked again. And I think it's necessary."

"I remember, father. I didn't say much on that occasion," I said, to let him know that I kept the memory fresh.

"Are you still fluent in English?"

"Yes, more or less."

"Are your grades good?"

"Yes, sir."

"Have you had contact with beings from another reality?"

"I'm sorry?" I tried to hide my reaction but lying was not my thing.

"-I'll put it another way and don't act surprised. Here, neither of us has to look like we fit in. If you haven't already had a visit from a guardian angel, you're one of the bad guys, and I don't think you're bad. Or are you?"

"No, sir, I'm not bad. But I have done some bad things."

"Have you made them to do good?"

"I think so. But I have not received such a visit. I have nothing special."

The father took a gulp of his fizzy drink, blinked hard as if affected by an itchy throat and stood up with the help of his cane. I remained seated, not quite knowing what to do. This was precisely what I had feared most; but alas, I had calculated that this could not possibly happen. And now this old man had taken it upon himself to contradict me. I would have loved to grab him by the cassock and shout at him that I wanted nothing to do with all that, that he should leave me alone, he and all the angels of the heavenly kingdom. Don't ask me for anything and I won't ask for anything either. I want to be normal, just that.

"Well. Let's pretend you did. That you've had that visit, right?"

"It would be too much to imagine, Father, but okay."

"You must not resist destiny. You were born to do good and help others. I don't want to tell you that you are a chosen one, or anything like that, don't get confused. All I am telling you is that you have the faculties to see beyond earthly simplicity."

"Have you, Father, received any guardian angels?" I wanted to divert a little attention from myself.

"Not vividly, but I have always felt his presence by my side. I have counted on his help in the best and worst situations of life, and I am convinced that I have been blessed with his and our Lord's support."

"And how are you so clear about that?"

"Angels have always existed, with very different names and interpretations. The Virgin, guardian angels, protectors, guiding souls, valkyries, cherubs. Now they call it with the nickname of the third man; dozens of meanings to name the same phenomenon. Every human being has been able to feel their help at one time or another in life, but, of course, most are pragmatic and assume it's nothing more than a hallucinatory experience or the fruit of delirium and then bury the memory and continue their existence. Is that what is happening to you, young man?"

"No, I don't think so."

"I am glad, so much the better. Because to waste the gift is to sin against God. Don't forget that. Your destiny, David, is to help the angels; know that you serve a much greater purpose. Even if you give me that skeptical face and continue to carry the attitude of a comedian to the end of this conversation, we both know what we're talking about. I respect that, though. You'll have your reasons. As for me, you can leave whenever you want. Thank your mother for the delicious cake."

"A question. Are there bad guys? Bad angels, I mean."

"Of course, there are, and they are very powerful. Inclement and capable of the worst atrocities. They feed on hatred, envy, fear, pain. They are very dangerous and can change a good person. They seduce by finding human weakness, transforming it into something terrifying for others."

"I've heard that before," I said resignedly.

And Father Damián burst out laughing. As if happy to confirm his hunch and his belief in the gift.

It seemed to me that I had put my foot far into my mouth.

"Well, my son. Go do what you want to do, but wait a second," he said, raising his index finger.

He walked to his room, not without effort, and brought a small transparent bottle with water inside. He approached me and grabbed my head with his left hand, gently shaking it with his left hand, while he murmured in a very low, accelerated voice. He opened the little bottle with his thumb and began to pour holy water on my face. I closed my eyes in acceptance of the ritual, and when he was done, he slapped me quite hard. I opened my eyes right away, looked at him with a disbelieving look; to him it seemed that everything was correct. On top of that, I felt an obligation to thank him. It wasn't until I walked out the door and closed it that I put my hand to my cheek to try to ease some of the pain. Wow, what a slap he gave me.

I peeked out of his window to see if he was laughing his head off, but no. He went to his seat and sat quietly. In the end, I laughed all by myself.

I pedaled slowly home, with the heat throbbing in my face. Now, once again, everything I wanted to forget was more present than ever. Father Damián encouraged me to actively participate in the path of good, but that clashed drastically with my desire to remain unnoticed. In any case, it had been a long time since I had seen the shadow, or should I call him a guardian angel? For the moment, I preferred not to give the matter anymore thought and selfishly continue in my world, trying to remain oblivious.

The vacations were approaching, and my father called from Calais, France, informing me that he would dock in Santander to pick me up and continue with a transport to Civitavecchia, very close to Rome. I was excited to travel and get to know the capital of the Roman empire, to delight in its architecture and glorious monuments.

I packed my backpack carefully, so as not to miss anything: my camera, my flashlight, my knife, my winter clothes, my raincoat and, just in case, my swimsuit. My father arrived at midday, and we went to lunch. He rested a while at home with my mother, and after dinner he had to set off again to the port to continue the trip. The whole crew took a short break, albeit a very short one. But at least it was something.

My parents' business seemed to be doing quite well, but, of course, my father preferred to pay off and repay his loans in order to achieve what he called financial freedom. So our austere and humble lifestyle did not change at all.

We boarded The Beluga, and now I was on the opposite side of the ship from the usual one. Accompanied by my father, we were saying goodbye to my aunt and uncle and my mother. I have no explanation for this, but I suddenly felt so sorry to leave my mother there alone that I was tempted to return the ship to port.

The smell of diesel, the dull hum of the engine, the seagulls screaming in the night, the lights of the ship, everything gradually seemed to dissolve in the distance, watching the streetlamps and the houses lit on land from the gently rocking of the sea.

From ruminant restlessness.

Chapter 10
Sailors Without Direction

Cantabrian Sea, 1996

I settled into Alfredo's cabin, although everyone called him Fredy. My father boasted of having one of the best mechanics in the world in his crew. He was a man who was not very talkative but was extremely meticulous in all his chores. He would set his alarm clock at odd hours to keep up with maintenance. That was probably why he slept alone in the cabin. He was corpulent, but without being very big, the classic body of a strong and sturdy man. Bald as a billiard ball, he shaved his head every day and then covered it with a visored beret. His hands were the color of aged wood, and his nails were never clean, no matter how much he washed them.

Logically, I got the top bunk. To be honest, I liked it better. The skylight dipped in and out of the water with every sea sway, and I found that relaxing and soothing. Fredy had checked that the nightlight, the bed and the small closet were in perfect condition upon my arrival. The cabin had a strong smell of cedar. Going from the sea to the forest was a matter of crossing a couple of narrow corridors and a few doors.

Alejandro, the chubby chef on the boat, showed me around his kitchen. It was so small that watching him move around in that tiny space was quite a feat. He was making coffee for me and for my father, who had to stay awake on the bridge until a little after four in the morning. I decided to accompany him on that first half-night of sailing.

We chatted about this and that, the places we would pass through, the difficulties of his work, his youth and how he ended up as a sailor. It gave me time to get to know some aspects of his personality better. And that first when I didn't go to bed until almost five in the morning helped me to respect the hard work of all seamen. Santiago, my father's right-hand man, the deck officer, relieved us so we could sleep. My father looked him in the eyes and said in a very disciplined tone,

"If there is anything new, do not hesitate to wake me up. He who does nothing shrinks."

I entered the cabin very carefully so as not to wake Fredy. I saw him open his eyes. It was clear that everyone on the ship was resting in a state of wakefulness. I, on the other hand, unaccustomed to danger or sudden awakenings, was lulled to sleep by the gentle tide.

I woke up at midday and the captain had already been awake for a long time. I don't know if it was me or what, but for me, resting for eight hours at a time was essential. We had already rounded Finisterre, and about nine miles offshore was the Portuguese city of Porto. Soon we would see Lisbon, albeit from a distance.

Again, late at night, Alejandro insisted on making us coffee. I made him promise to let me do it the next day. My father warned me that crossing the Strait was always a risky task. We sailed zigzagging because the easterly wind blew like a hurricane; according to the captain, it saved fuel. Nevertheless, we were always moving within the maritime half of the national territory. Finally, two days after passing the Strait of Gibraltar, we reached the islands of Sardinia and Corsica, crossing between the two. We were already close to our destination, the imposing Rome.

My father and Santiago had worked hard and moved things to ensure reaching Rome coincided my vacation time. He knew that I was a great lover of classical Roman architecture, that it was in my DNA.

We docked at the port; I was anxious to visit the city. Ricardo and his companion, the stevedores, took charge of loading and unloading, for the first time without the supervision of their captain, who delegated operations so he could accompany me to the heart of the city. We spent that night in a modest hotel in Rome, very close to the Colosseum, and I had a wonderful time in the company of Japanese, Russian, French and people of all nationalities. All were fascinated by the ingenious grandeur and artistry of the constructions. Occasionally, I saw my father yawning. He made a strong effort to seem interested in all the monuments we visited; it was the best gift he could have given me.

At noon we had to return to port: permits, tempos and frenetic deadlines were unforgiving. It was what my father called whirlwind tourism. So we set sail again with the ship loaded once more. The stevedores informed the captain of a special cargo from the Italian government bound for their embassy in Oslo, Norway. It was a very large wooden box with a phosphorescent sign that translated read: "Diplomatic Pouch"; along with the side padlocks it had security straps all with the same reference number, but in different colors.

My father did not give it much importance, he seemed to be more concerned about the shipment of Murano glass and porcelain from Florence. He was interested in their packing and positioning on the ship, confirming that everything was in the right place. The right place for the captain was the center of gravity of The Beluga, as this point is the one that suffers the least heeling during rough seas. The cargo had to be mathematically positioned taking into account many variables, primarily dynamic stability and secondly, the nature of the cargo.

It was evening, and I seemed to be used to the sea routines by now. I prepared coffee for both of us. My father looked at infinity, the dark horizon of the night only altered by the play of the waves and the reflection of the moon in its foam. The weather forecast was good. The sea was not a raft of oil, but it was safe to sail. We were at the midpoint of the Alboran Sea; it was approximately two o'clock in the morning.

We talked, we imagined what life must have been like at the height of the Roman Empire; we both pretended to be soldiers in battle and I thought it was a great moment to immortalize the moment. I got out the camera and we took a picture of us embracing. The *flash* left us seeing sparks for a few seconds. Just one more of many. It was right there that the look on my father's face changed completely and he dropped his pipe on the floor. He picked up the binoculars and went out on the port side deck. I, between picking up the pipe and still having my vision affected by the *flash*, didn't understand what was going on.

A red flare, very faint, was slowly falling from the sky. I watched but was not able to see anything. My father pressed a button with a transparent cover that sounded an intermittent alarm on the ship. In a matter of less than a minute, the entire crew was assembled on the bridge. Immediately, my father cut the sound of the alarm and steered the vessel toward the distant flare light. The captain ordered Santiago to turn off all the lights on the ship so that he could make out this something in the night, while he watched steadily through the binoculars. He ordered the reduction of speed so as not to collide with any possible vessel. He positioned the transmitter on the emergency channel and began to modulate:

"Attention, attention, attention. Attention, attention, attention. Emergency call to all stations. This is The Beluga, this is The Beluga, this is The Beluga. Position thirty-six degrees, twenty minutes, forty-one seconds north latitude, three degrees, twenty-five minutes, fifty-six seconds west. We have a marine emergency flare from another vessel. We are on scene. We are requesting precautionary assistance from Maritime Rescue. We will provide further information on the emergency when available. This is the general cargo vessel The Beluga. Over."

There was a brief silence when the PTT was released and for a few seconds only the fog of the radio could be heard.

"Received vessel Salvamar Spica, we are heading to the point. I am inquiring if your vessel and crew are well."

"Roger."

"Be careful, provide information and don't take risks. We are going full speed ahead."

"Received."

My father ordered the lights to remain off. It was logical, because if we turned all the lights on, our visibility would only be a few meters. Out of the darkness, about a hundred meters away, a small wooden boat emerged, white with a green horizontal stripe. Before us, a group perched on the boat: between ten and fifteen sub-Saharans, men, children and women. My father had all the lighting on The Beluga turned on. He had kept all the lights from his previous fishing activity, so the light penetrated deep into the sea and could reach a distance of about thirty meters.

As we approached, you could see the terror on their faces. They were all shivering from the cold and, despite their dark skin color, their lips so blue from hypothermia, it was clear that the situation was critical for them. I stared at a young man about my age. We held each other's gaze for many seconds. A worry began to form in my stomach. It was an unfamiliar situation for me, but I still felt that something was not right.

If there was one thing I learned at that point, it was to listen for the signs. Some danger was lurking for all of us, but I was unable to identify it. My father immediately began directing the operation, ordering the small dinghy loaded with blankets and slings to be lowered. My father's plan was for the stevedores to make a good lashing to the boat and pull them all up at once with the crane arm. The stevedores were rushing around the deck, they were so heavily laden that you could barely see their heads. They knew the ship so well that they could go from side to side blindfolded. Despite their confidence, I couldn't stop worrying. A bad feeling was sticking in my soul like a splinter between flesh and nail.

I was looking again at that small boat trying to identify the origin of the omen, and the sad eyes of that young man were looking for me again. We stared at each other and, this time, he very, very slightly shook his head. Everything about him conveyed horror, panic and fear. It was as if the salvation of such a large ship did not make them happy at all and as if the danger wasn't in the wandering aimlessly on the wide sea. I ran to my father, who was ordering Santiago to give news over the radio and I had to tap him on the shoulder to make him pay attention to me. I was a kind of tourist on the ship, an inert piece with eyes, a maritime hitchhiker.

"What's the matter, son? Help carry blankets to the zodiac, don't just stand there!"

"Dad, wait. Hold on a second. Something's not right about this."

"But-but what are you saying? Those people need help, there are children on that boat! Cut the crap and help! Otherwise, get out of the way and stay out of the way!"

"Dad, something bad is about to happen, listen to me! I know!"

My father ignored my warnings and focused on recovering all the battered passengers. I watched the port side intently, gazed at their faces, and despite the absence of joy at their salvation each and every one of them radiated kindness. I took the shadow's advice and looked around for it. Maybe I wasn't right. Maybe it was all my paranoia. Maybe I should just actively help and be glad that my father saved all those people's lives. Then I felt something move behind me in a hurry. I couldn't explain it in words. It was like when you see something moving out of the corner of your eye. I could feel the evil on the deck of the ship.

I started skirting the bridge gangway and reached the starboard side. A long, black, seat-filled powerboat with four engines at its stern was waving empty, tied to our ship's rail.

"No, no, no!" That was all I had time to think before I heard the roar of about fifteen shots in the air emitted by an assault rifle.

I knew well the feeling of adrenaline rushing through my body. We all looked up at the roof of the wheelhouse. It was the only unlit part of the ship. A man standing there was holding a very long machine gun with the barrel pointing skyward.

"Stop whatever you're doing, good Samaritans. Or, next time, I swear I won't waste a cartridge. Do you hear me?"

My father stood completely still. His expression was one of genuine concern. He was reluctant to pay attention to the man. He didn't understand what was happening, he seemed incredulous.

"Who is the captain?" asked the man, who was now squatting down and holding on to a ledge of the roof with his left hand.

"I am the captain!" my father replied in a firm and hard tone, offended.

"And you will continue to be, my friend. You will be a hero who has saved the lives of poor little black people full of dreams and hopes. But if you make it even the smallest bit difficult for me, you will all die and be thrown to the bottom of the sea. We'll set the rudder and leave this beauty on the sea, sailing unmanned like a ghost ship, ungoverned. What do you decide, do you want to be a hero or a brave man?"

Eternal seconds of silence lingered in the tense atmosphere.

"I want to be a hero, not a brave man."

"We're going to get along then. Order everyone to stand at the bow."

There was no need for my father to order it. The six of us gathered there. More men came out. They were dressed in black with balaclavas. They were all armed. In all, there were four of them, including the one who looked like the leader.

"We've come for a few things. As soon as we have what we need, we'll leave here peacefully, and we'll all go on with our merry lives."

At that moment, one of the men said something in his ear. And the two went to the bridge. After a few seconds, they returned. And Santiago began to pray the Lord's Prayer in a low voice, while a tear ran down his cheek.

"Who was the smart one?" He repeated, "Who was the smart one?"

No one knew what he was talking about. What did he mean? Suddenly, Santiago spoke up.

"It was me. It's my fault. I didn't understand anything."

"Well, that's all right. We caught you and that's it. We'll talk about it later. Don't worry."

I could not believe my eyes, but, between the light and the darkness, and apart from the four men, I saw two small beings scurrying back and forth. Their presence was intermittent. They were the size of large children; their appearance was not very defined, they seemed muscular or perhaps naked. I could only see them if I really looked hard. Once I saw them and tried to focus my vision on them, they became invisible to me. It was obvious that they were accompanying these men. It was clear that no one else saw them. Only me. Not even the bad guys.

Those reddish, distorted beings were the ones who discovered that something was happening on the bridge. They were gesturing from there, pointing to the control panel. And, as if by magic, one of the men entered and focused his attention on something. It was curious to watch because at no time did they interact with them; it was as if those bugs aroused the suspicious intuition of the bad guys.

Thanks to these little creatures, the other three invaders seemed to move around the ship as if they had known it forever. They led them, unbeknownst to them and without any detour, into the cargo hold, into the bulk compartment. Meanwhile, the leader stood watching us at the bow, with the barrel of his rifle pointed at the ground. His index finger remained resting on the frame of the gun. He was strangely calm. He looked like a military special ops guy, like in the movies. In addition to the long gun, a pistol was sticking out of a leg holster. He also had a knife holstered in his belt, several magazines, a small flashlight, and a lighted *radio* connected to an earpiece in his left ear.

These people were prepared. I couldn't think what they could want from us. What was clear was that they were well armed. One of them was carrying several empty bags and a backpack with tools that were placed in compartments for that purpose. Among them I could see a shear and a crowbar, pliers and so on.

The leader was chewing a piece of gum. He was looking at all of us, or rather, watching us. I had the impression of being in front of a soulless man. I looked at the small skiff to see where he was, and then I understood the message from the dark-haired boy. He couldn't tell me anything, but he still tried to warn me.

It was of no use.

"You're too young to be part of this crew, aren't you?" the leader asked me.

"I'm on vacation. That's why I'm here. Please don't hurt us."

"Are you afraid, boy?"

"Yes, I am afraid. I will not deny the obvious."

He pulled a piece of gum out of the side pocket of his tactical pants and tossed it. I caught it on the fly in a reflex action.

"Human beings are animals by nature. While chewing gum, unconsciously, you tell your brain that you are eating, and then fear, nervousness and stress disappear, because your body would never associate eating with danger. Chew, kid, and you'll see what I mean."

I didn't accept it, and threw it back at him again.

"Thank you, but I don't like tricks."

"You've got guts. You almost caught us getting on the boat. I gotta hand it to you, kid. You've got instincts. You'd make a good mercenary."

"Is that what you are, you? A mercenary? I'd say you're a pirate!" I stepped forward.

"Shut up already!" my father burst out with a shout.

"Hold on, Captain. Take it easy, man. Your son and I are having a friendly chat. He is your son, isn't he?"

"Yes, he is my son. Please forgive him, because he is at a very difficult age."

"No, man, no, each thing by its own name. It's all right, partner. I like talking to your son. It's been a long time since anyone has disagreed with me."

Then, looking him straight in the eye, holding his gaze, I inform him tersely,

"You are doomed. You are a servant of evil. Your fate is already written."

"Boy, you talk funny. I'm being nice. Why are you saying such ugly things to me?"

He continued to chew his gum exaggerating it a bit, and then exclaimed,

"Well, if I'm already condemned, I might as well kill you all!" he shouted.

He pointed the gun towards the skiff and fired off several rounds. My father knelt down and with joined palms began to beg him to stop, not to do it. But he continued with another burst. I was looking at the little green and white boat and, fortunately, none of the projectiles hit it. It was no coincidence. That man knew what he was doing.

Then, with a bang, the door of the hold opened and out came his henchmen with full packs. They seemed to be carrying a lot of weight, and, as they reached the deck, one of them approached the leader and said,

"That's it, we have it all."

"Don't be rude. I was talking to my hosts. We were having a momentous talk about good and evil. Now, Captain, do you want to know what we're here for?"

"No. I don't care about that, I'm not curious. I'll settle for you not harming us."

"Captain, captain, captain. Shhhhh! Too bad. You have to inform yourself better about the goods you are transporting. Beginner's mistake."

"Well, you tell me," said my father, resigned, playing his game so as not to anger them.

"Look what we have."

He opened the backpacks a little, and hundreds of blank, new, unused passports and identity cards could be seen inside. Another backpack full of Beretta semi-automatic pistols and ammunition, and the last bag full of money in Norwegian bills.

I understood that all that was in the drawer of the diplomatic pouch and, somehow, those people had planned it all; they had precise data of its contents and our route.

"This little talk about good and evil reminds me of something. What could it be, what could it be? I forget something and I don't know what it is. Ah, yes! Our friend the brave one."

I could hardly remember what he was referring to. Immediately, Santiago's repentance and confession came to mind, and of something he did on the bridge. He raised his chin knowing that he was referring to him. Then he handed the assault rifle to guy next to him, he approached Santiago, and, in a flash, pulled his knife from its sheath and stabbed him twice in the left leg. Santiago fell to the ground, and the pirate crouched down to his full height and wiped the knife on his sweater before putting it away again. He stood up again and repeated loudly that he didn't want any braves. Strangely, I could feel the stinging pain in his leg, a kind of empathetic cringe. These people were deadly serious.

"I am a fair man. The first thing I said was that I didn't want any bullshit. And this moron couldn't help but leave the radio button locked with a rubber band so that everything that happened here could be heard! Clever but reckless. These are the things that fill me with rage and make me angry. Bad behavior needs to be corrected," he said in a convincing tone, opening his arms in explanation.

My face was filled with rage. They already had what they wanted. He really seemed to be enjoying himself now. I was furious and felt powerless. We were at the mercy of this criminal.

"Come on, boy! You seem to be the only worthy one here. Pick one thing out of the backpacks. Take your pick." I looked at the guns without blinking. "Do you see yourself capable of wielding a gun? Would you have the balls to use it?"

I didn't make any gesture, but I didn't stop looking at the bag full of weapons. He took one of the pistols from the backpack, removed the magazine and opened one of those cardboard boxes full of golden cartridges. Slowly, he began to feed it and finally inserted it into the grip. He pulled the slide back, and the gun stood ready to open fire. He grabbed it by the barrel and held it out to me by the grip.

"Come on, take it. Take it and kill me." Even his sidekick looked at him uneasily. "One single action, just stroke the trigger and you'll be rid of me. Come on. Come on. Come on. Come on!" he shouted at me.

"I could do it, but I'm not like you. You think I was born yesterday and you underestimate me. You're offering me the loaded gun, but with the safety cap on. You trust too much in your luck, in your arrogance and in the ignorance of others." It was clear that he was shocked. "Please leave at once and take your demons with you."

"I like you, boy. You're special. We'll leave you alone. You've earned my respect. I wish I could more with you. He clicked his palate. "This is nothing personal, it's just work. Your father's partner will be fine, it's just two minor cuts. If I'd wanted to kill him, I'd have severed his iliac." He lifted his chin with a curious skepticism, without taking his eyes off me, "Cover the wound until Maritime Rescue arrives, and raise his leg."

At that moment, I could see his side of kindness, his gentle and human side. He shouted to his guys,

"Let's go! Let's go!"

And as I was about to disappear down the deck of the ship, he called me and told me to go. And, reservedly, he said to me,

"Maybe you're right about me being doomed, maybe not. Either way, accept what you wished for. Hide it or throw it into the sea, that's up to you."

And he gave me the pistol, another magazine and a small box full of ammunition. And, seeing that I accepted it, he went down the ladder smiling and victorious. I looked at the gun lying on the deck and thought about throwing it into the sea, but something inside me refused to do so. I kept it all in my clothes, well concealed, while the motorboat sped off into the blackness of the night. Soon after, the engines stopped and peace came to The Beluga. I was in charge of assisting Santiago, while my father continued with the small skiff, to take the crew onto the boat.

Now they seemed happy to be saved. Now they could breathe a sigh of relief.

I learned a valuable lesson. Evil takes advantage of goodness as a weak point. That makes you feel stupid, deceived and betrayed by yourself, by your values and convictions. That's why, now, my father didn't seem happy to help those people. It was the strategy of evil. It is his way of punishing the fraternity. I understood that these chastisements can transform any good person into a bad one. Or, at least, into an indifferent one. Indifferent to any state of need of others.

Watching those two reddish creatures for the first time left me with more questions than answers. Now I could see how evil worked. My senses were sharpening and I needed to know more. I needed to be more prepared. I could not remain indifferent to injustice and abuse. Using those poor innocent strangers to distract us, lure us into their trap and leave us completely exposed was petty and mean. Miserable.

I guess honor is a word from other times. Something extinct and forgotten.

Something dead.

Chapter 11
A Matter of Attitude

Strait of Gibraltar-Andrin, spring 1996

After helping those poor people and taking them up to The Beluga, my father communicated the number of castaways to Maritime Rescue over the radio. They arrived about twenty minutes later. They came from Melilla and were the closest to us. A doctor confirmed that Santiago's injuries were not serious. Fredy, my good cabin mate, watched the whole scene with his beret in his hands, asking all the time how he could help.

Of course, my father was well protected by loyal men, full of courage and heart, fundamental to the principles of the sea. However, they all felt deeply cheated by obeying that maritime law, inherited from human frailty in the face of the immensity of the water, and which had now been turned against them.

I understood many things I did not know. The assailants knew that no armed Civil Guard vessel would ever show up at that point. Their margin of action is ten miles from the coast, maximum twelve. That is why they were in no hurry. They worked with alarming impunity. In addition, the entire crew had to keep the robbery secret, so as not to provoke what they called the "call effect". What a disgrace.

Once ashore, the captain gave a statement and promised not to make the details public. The Italian embassy seemed to be resigned to the loss of the stolen goods, without asking for too many explanations. In any case, much of what happened had been recorded, thanks to Santiago. Although the poor guy had to pay the consequences. Someone was supposed to take charge of the investigation, but the truth is that nobody asked us again about what happened that night at sea; never. What stayed with me, and forever, was the image of my father, sailing in the wee hours of the morning in absolute solitude, containing his emotions like a house in disrepair.

It was the only time in my life that I saw my father like that. And I swore by the most sacred thing that I would never again remain impassive in the face of evil.

I went down to the galley. Without haste, giving him time to pull himself together, I prepared two piping hot coffees and the ding of the microwave bell served as a warning of my arrival.

"Forgive me, Dad, for my reaction to those men." I broke the ice in a quiet voice.

"Don't apologize, my son. This is not the first boarding I have suffered. But it is the first time I have feared for what I love most in this world: my family. You are not to blame for anything. You reacted very well. I am proud of you."

No one had ever transmitted so much tenderness, sincerity and affection with so few words.

My father was an exceptional man.

"I love you very much, Dad."

And we gave each other a very strong and long hug full of relief.

It was all over the news that our boat had picked up the lost people. Everyone was praising the crew's feat, their coordination and humanity. A Red Cross spokesman said we were angels of the sea, the warm and gentle hand of God picking up the homeless. Those who have lost everything, those who cling with serene and long-suffering struggle to fragile hope almost lost. Nothing was as they said, but I imagined that people want simple stories with happy endings.

I had the opportunity to meet Kingsley, the young Nigerian who tried to warn me of the danger. Only I understood him and the rest of the group. They all spoke correct but old-fashioned English. Kingsley confessed to me that he had been running from the clutches of death for more than half his life. He had seen his parents, siblings and friends murdered all because of his country's political and military instability, for control of power and resources. Now, alone, starving and stripped of all possessions, his fighting spirit gave off in him the joy of success, the success of not giving up at any time and staying true to himself in the face of so much violence and injustice suffered.

He told me many things about his culture. I was interested in the matter of the intermediate deities. According to them, they could satisfy the wishes of the sorcerers in exchange for sacrifices and deeds, depending on what was requested. I understood that a good dominator of that religion could cause pain, discomfort, illness and tragedy to another person by means of those divine creatures. Immediately, I associated it with the demons that accompanied those mercenaries.

Kingsley certainly did not speak on the subject by speculating hypotheses or expressing conjecture. He spoke with complete conviction on the subject. With absolute certainty and true knowledge. With absolute faith.

My father and the rest of the crew offered everything they could spare from their belongings, what they could replace in Santander: money, clothes, a *Walkman,* a Rubik's cube, towels, backpacks. Everything could be of some use to them. They refused to accept the help. We had to convince them conscientiously not to refuse. They were not used to receiving something for nothing.

For them, all this altruistic charity was a clash of mentalities. For the sub-Saharans, being towed by those awful people and used as human bait cost each of them everything they possessed in life. Ignorant of the men's intentions, they accepted the deal without knowing the conditions, and now felt ashamed of their involuntary participation.

With father's permission, I gave our home phone number and address to Kingsley. I explained that this boy had warned us from the skiff, with discreet gestures, of the danger that was looming over us. Besides, we immediately became good friends. He had a wild and funny touch. Every time he smiled his face seemed to double in size. He reminded me a little of my long-missed camp-friend, Picueto.

We said goodbye to them, leaving them at the port of Algeciras, where, guarded by the National Police, they were taken to a reception center. The government promised to regularize their stay in our country if they so wished. Some opportunistic politicians did not miss the appointment for the usual photo.

My father insisted on not telling anything about the ambush. Everyone on the ship seemed to be in agreement and strangely accustomed to keeping such information to themselves. I wondered how many stories were hidden from the world and how big was that sailor captain's trunk of lost secrets.

After the relay on the bridge, parallel to the Portuguese coast, I went to bed watching that skylight plunging into the night sea. I kept thinking why I did not see the shadow anywhere at that dangerous moment. Honestly, something inside me told me that my life was not in danger, but any help would have been welcome. I came to the conclusion that I needed to prepare myself much better to deal with any future situation. Physical exercise alone was not enough. Gaining endurance in running is good to control my breathing at a given moment, but I had to learn to fight, to swim with technique, to know my body as that mercenary would.

I was determined to get involved in being a real foil for evil. It was clear to me that I was not going to change the universe, but I would at least try to improve my immediate environment. I refused to stand idly by.

You could say that those bastards completely ruined my vacation. They invaded our privacy, violated our peace of mind, and now my father and I were returning home with a latent resentment.

Before arriving in port, my father gathered the crew in the mess hall. He left me at the helm. He pointed out the direction to steer and I was left alone in the captain's chair. It was clear that they were talking about priorities, from then on. He told them that from then on, they should be wary of any unforeseen event, and the first rule should be personal self-protection of the crew and the boat. Expect the unexpected. Take nothing for granted.

I was left at the port of Santander as if I were a stowaway. My parents were reunited for a few minutes, but the unbridled rhythms wait for no one. Everyone said goodbye to me. Santiago had to get some stitches for those cuts, but he was fine. Fredy and the others, and, of course, my father, bid me an affectionate farewell and I watched them march north committed to make their deliveries. Fredy gave me one of his berets. It was dark gray, with a white and green checkered interior. It was almost new. I accepted it without complaint because I knew that refusing it might offend him. And much to my chagrin, I was back to my hamster-wheel life. But this time it was different. Now I had my ideas in order.

It was clear to me from that unpleasant event that I had to prepare myself physically and mentally for any possible situation.

I needed to be able to join a gym or several gyms to develop my abilities.

A Thai master was teaching an unknown martial art. It was a small, spartan, gymnasium in a garage near my high school. The floor was covered with small mats. They seemed to have been donated, because they did not cover the entire surface. There were several punching bags. The practitioners wore forearm, head and shin guards. They trained barefoot and half-naked. I was cold in there, even though I was well wrapped up.

I couldn't imagine myself there, but something told me it was the right place.

I wanted to talk to the teacher, and he received me with haste while keeping his focus on his few students. He spoke Spanish poorly, but he was well understood.

"You too young *train* here. *Everyone* here is adult."

"It doesn't *matter to* me. I *train* hard."

No wonder this guy doesn't speak Spanish well. Everyone seemed to speak it just as badly as he did. I, at least, never did again.

He turned me around to look at my legs and back. He seemed happy and said I could start the following week, after class. One hour a day, three times a week.

Now I had to talk to my mother to convince her. The gym was not cheap. Five thousand pesetas a month. I had already thought of everything to be able to cover that extra expense: I was going to teach other students a few hours a week, and everything was solved. It was obvious that so much was going to take up a lot of my time, but my mind was made up.

I looked for a place to hide the Beretta pistol. I hesitated between several, because it was not exactly small. Finally, I found the right place with some old wood in the garage. In my other life, as a good American, I had military training and, after that, I always kept my gun license. The last pistol I owned was a Smith

& Wesson 59. I find it amazing that I can remember such precise details, and yet others remain buried in lost memory.

I'm not sure why I accepted the Beretta. Maybe it was the fact that I always had a pistol, maybe it seemed like a good idea, or maybe one day I might need it, you never know. Anyway, I bought the right oil at a hardware store. I disassembled it, properly oiled it and put all the parts in airtight bags. I didn't plan to handle it or carry it for a single second.

The academic year ended and the whole class was going on an end-of-year trip to the Canary Islands. My mother kept encouraging me to go. She said that she would get the money wherever she had to, but that she didn't want me to miss out. Naturally, and given the way things were going at home, I turned her down flat.

That early summer of '96 I spent it giving classes to boys from my old school. I charged three hundred pesetas an hour, although sometimes I was generous and stayed a little longer without asking for anything in return. It felt good to be able to help those kids. I could feel their fear of repeating a grade. Repeating a grade at that age makes you separate from your core group of friends and classmates. You are stigmatized forever, watching how you get off the train, wait at the station and catch the next one full of strangers. I could not allow it.

I was very sorry to see that the kids had high abilities, that they were very intelligent. What happened was that nobody taught them how to learn. They were required to study, but they were not told how. So the first thing I did was to teach them study techniques, mnemonic rules, outlining, work environment, sleep and rest discipline, and then perseverance and self-confidence. Once this was explained, we started with imagination. Learning the list of the Gothic kings is a real pain in the ass if you don't put a face to them and contextualize it a bit in their time.

I trained non-stop for as long as I could. With no friends and no plans, I would go alone into the woods and train on my own. My body was completely sore, and my mother started to worry about the bruises and blisters on my feet. It was my way of escaping from reality and releasing energy. I admit that I would have loved to go on that end-of-year trip, but I couldn't be so selfish. My uncle Jose's business was getting more and more squeezed, and he was overwhelmed with vet bills, permits, and more.

My mother had begun to trust me with a lot of freedom, and by that summer I was already traveling alone by train from Gijón to San Roque del Acebal. It was the town with the closest station to home. If I left late, I would tell her by phone so she wouldn't worry. I understood that freedom and responsibility go hand in hand.

My father, increasingly committed to his clients, could not cope with so much work. He phoned from Helsinki, Stockholm, Reykjavik, and in the timbre of his voice there was always a common denominator: disguised sadness.

My experiences with the supernatural were already distant in time. Not a single day did I stop thinking about Angie, but I could not find the solution to confirm my strange memories. At least, I didn't worry about it much anymore. I needed to keep my attention distracted and I managed to do so with my daily obligations.

I vented my unbearable frustration by training in the woods, until that summer night.

Chapter 12
Demons in the Forge

Andrín, summer 1996

As usual, I waited on the platform for my noisy train that always took me home. It was quite a busy afternoon between training and the math classes I gave to Nicolas' little boy. The sky was orange, and the weather that evening was warm. In summer it was always usual for the region to multiply by four its population, between family and tourists coming from all over.

I waited patiently on that yellow metal bench, with the chattering purr of the other passengers in the background. The train in the opposite direction arrived before mine. I liked to amuse myself by looking at the diversity of people of all styles who scampered freely across our land. Many of them appeared to have a false sense of belonging. They looked at everyone else as if they were outsiders. It was a curious behavior.

One tall, very thin man immediately caught my powerful attention. One of those reddish beings did not take off from him. Rather, this being seemed to be leading him on his way, going ahead. In the distance I could see the light of the convoy that would take me home and, for a few seconds, I hesitated. I looked at the train and saw the tranquility of another day having dinner with my mother and watching TV for a while. I looked back at the man and knew that things could get complicated. One way or another, I had promised myself not to remain impassive, oblivious to the success of evil. I was committed to stopping it.

I crossed the footbridge and left the station following him. That man was walking briskly, and chasing him without taking long strides was costing me. Suddenly, he stopped at a gift store. He was looking all around, watchful. He seemed to do it mechanically. I thought he might have noticed that I was on his heels, but it was clear that I didn't get his attention at all.

His lean, elongated face, stubble, shaggy hair and dark circles under his eyes made it easy for any mortal to guess that we were looking at a singular man, to say the least. He picked up a couple of tourist key rings and tucked them into his long three-quarter length jacket. To my mind, that petty theft was not the worst thing that individual came there to do. He was a nervous man. He was fidgeting. I was surprised when he sat in a small square in the city, because he gave the impression that he couldn't sit still for a second. He was looking around anxiously, looking for something.

I watched him without being able to understand what he was up to. I tried to see the demon that accompanied him. But I could no longer see him. I didn't quite understand how the help of these beings worked. He had been sitting there for about ten minutes, biting at the dead skin on his fingers. I could see him sitting, leaning, standing in a corner of the square, at a safe distance. I started to feel a little cold. I decided to take my sweatshirt out of my backpack and put it on. At that precise moment, I could see again the reddish silhouette of that being. He seemed to be pulling hard on the guy's coat. Without knowing how, that man received the signal and got up, trying to find something. He knew it was time, but he was hesitant.

Suddenly, I saw the reddish man's silhouette move swiftly; he approached an older woman who was walking at a good pace for her age along the outer edge of the square. A long brown coat covered her almost completely. Over her shoulder, the leather strap of a black handbag clutched tightly against her side.

The reddish being seemed to point at her as a target without leaving the lady's side. The thin, nervous man focused his vision on her and, suddenly, I understood that something bad was going to happen. He tightened the belt of his pants and started walking after her. It was obvious to me that the bastard was going to yank her purse or, worse, smash her head against the asphalt and rob her mercilessly. I didn't know how to act. I kept telling myself, "Think, think. Hurry, think."

I ran towards her, overtaking the man as we walked down a narrow and lonely street in the center of Gijón. I caught up with the lady and broke into her walk, exclaiming loudly,

"Grandma, it's so good to see you! Let's go home together," I said as I winked at her. Then in a low voice I whispered, "Listen to what I say. There's a man following you from the square. I think he wants to mug you."

A gave a small cry.

"Take my arm. And stay with me."

She trusted what I told her and obeyed without asking any more questions. I looked out of the corner of my eye and the man was still following us about ten meters away. He seemed full of fury. He was clenching his fists in a grimace of frustration and, out of nowhere, he kicked the air. I kept my cool, but the bastard wouldn't give up. He wasn't resigned to losing, and I guess a sixteen-year-old wasn't enough of an obstacle. He got closer and closer; the woman squeezed my forearm with all her strength; she sensed the danger. I was confident that he would pass me by, but he did not.

He pushed us both against a gate. We almost fell because there was a step and a small space between it and the wooden gate. He took out a switchblade and put it next to my face, pricking me a little with its tip.

"The backpack and the bag! Let's go!" he shouted to us in a low voice, with that broken drunken voice and rapid breathing.

"Please, please, please, please. Take everything, but don't hurt us. Here," I said between nervous cries and sobs, trembling as I took off my backpack and the lady offered her the bag unreservedly.

He pulled the razor away from my face, with a clear expression of disgust at my hysterical cowardice. He felt in control of the situation. He ordered me to open my backpack and stuff the lady's purse inside. And so I did. He left me some space while he hid the open knife inside a pocket of the coat, whose sharp relief was marked on the fabric. She urged me to do it quickly. I closed the zipper and looked at him with a terrified face, holding out the backpack by the small top handle. He grabbed it with his left hand pulling it, and then I thought, "Now or never!" I pulled the backpack hard towards me again, kicking him with all my might in the neck. This was followed by several elbows to the face. Grabbing his head from the back of his neck, I rammed it into my knee. He pulled out the knife waving it from side to side trying to reach me. I disarmed him by dislocating his wrist in an impossible position until a crack sounded and he seemed to writhe in pain.

The woman was screaming, distressed by the violence, and several people were observing the events without intervening in anything. Then I began to hear from those people words that would stay with me for a long time: "Criminal! Criminal! Savage!" They were saying it about me; about me, who almost had my eye gouged out with the razor. To me, who had just prevented that bastard from dragging that poor woman to the ground and robbing her without a second thought.

Without wasting a second, I took the bag out of the backpack again and handed it to the lady. She took it, looking at me as if she saw an alien. The bastard was lying on the ground clutching his hand and moaning in pain. I walked over to him, kicked the knife that was on the floor hard, and reached into his other jacket pocket and pulled out the key rings he took from the gift store. Visibly upset, I turned to the woman,

"Ma'am, I'm out of here," I said.

I closed my backpack, strapped it tightly to my back and ran away while those witnesses threatened me with the arrival of the police. Nervous, scared, but also happy, I noticed a wetness on my arm. I couldn't believe it. I was bleeding from a cut at shoulder level, and I hadn't even noticed.

Behind a hedge, I sat down and assessed the wound. It was an ugly but superficial cut; I remembered Santiago, aware of the similarity. I could not ask for help without attracting the attention of the authorities. I decided to return to Nicolas' house with the false excuse of an accident, a carelessness with the protruding glass of a construction container and full of debris.

Nicolas' parents wanted to see the wound, but I refused with evasions. I asked good old Nicolás for the contact glue I had seen on his shelf a few hours earlier. They left me the box from the first aid kit. There were only pills of all kinds, alcohol and band-aids. I did what I could with what was available.

I grabbed the roll of toilet paper that was about to run out and bit down hard as I poured the soap and water on my wound. Cold sweat ran all over my body. I pulled the flesh together with my fingers wrapped in toilet paper and outlined the cut, pressing the flesh together and sealing it with the adhesive. I grabbed the hair dryer next to the sink and used it to speed up the process. By the bathroom door I felt the presence of Nicolas' parents, worried, wondering whether to call an ambulance or take me to the hospital. Fortunately, my sweatshirt was dark so the blood was somewhat camouflaged. I wiped everything well with paper and flushed the toilet several times.

I came out of the bathroom and showed them the wound covered by three band-aids. I saw them breathing with relief, because it looked less serious than they'd imagined. I looked at my watch and thought that I would miss the next train if I didn't leave now. Nicolas' father insisted that I call home to say that I would be arriving later, offering to drive me to the station.

I thought it was a good idea. That way, if someone was looking for me, it would be harder for them to find me. I was becoming an expert at lying. I didn't like that, but I had no other choice. With my education and the experience of two lives, I knew everything I had to say at all times to win the appreciation and affection of adults.

Was I turning into a wolf in sheep's clothing?

I returned home reflecting on everything that had happened. As usual, being self-critical, I drew the conclusion that I was very happy with myself. That lady could be my mother or my aunt. I was glad to have given that bastard a good hiding. The few passengers, almost all of them tourists, who were in the carriage with me, looked at me as if I were crazy. I laughed, looking at my reflection in the glass of the train. I tried to imagine myself pretending to be cowed, whimpering in fear of that dude and how I made him let his guard down and took the opportunity to give him a "haircut".

It was clear that *muay thai* had served me well. That was a good thing. I looked at my hand and saw those two key chains from the *souvenir store* and couldn't stop laughing. I was glad I had been victorious. Bruised but victorious, I was congratulating myself and feeling proud.

This was only the beginning of my struggle. I clutched those key chains tightly. And I cursed that it had to be like this. To have to fight to protect the right. To be one of the righteous.

Then I noticed that a small group of four young men seemed to keep their eyes on me. To this day I don't forgive myself for what I did. They must have been in their twenties. They were quite a bit older than me. And, from their accents, I guessed they were not from the area. They looked like they were from the south, but I'm not sure. What I do know is that they threw me out of my thoughts. I got the impression that they were laughing at me. I stared at them, very serious, and they held my gaze. One of them made a gesture with his chin. I interpreted it as a questioning signal, as if he were asking me: "What's wrong with you? His gaze was defiant and haughty. In any other circumstance I would have avoided the conflict altogether.

Circumstances were key.

I got up from my seat like a wild boar and headed towards them. I slapped the one who held my gaze with all my might. As soon as he was able to pull himself together and I saw his face again, a red hand was drawn, almost in relief, on his face. And I returned the question,

"Now I'm asking you, you moron. What the fuck is wrong with the four of you?"

They looked at each other skeptically, not believing what was happening to them. And I shouted at them again, while the whole passage fell silent with my actions. I felt invincible as if I was capable of beating them all up and sitting back down to look at my notes.

"What? What the fuck is wrong with you? Little piece shit with eyes!"

I could see the fear in all of them and that fed my vanity. I pursued them with an inquisitive look and none of them answered. They just stared at each other endlessly, looking at the rest of the travelers, waiting for I don't know what. In the end, the one who got the slap spoke.

"No-nothing's wrong with us, man. We don't want any trouble."

"When you meet your match, then you can behave like that. Do you know me at all to look at me like that, you ass? I'm asking you!"

"No. We don't know you at all. Forgive us."

The train was slowing down, arriving at the next station.

"Get the hell out of here. This is your stop. You're getting off. I won't say it again. Either here or to the hospital. Choose, hurry!"

They all stood up and hurried to the door. They looked at the station as if the train would never open its doors, impatient to get away from me. Finally, they got off and didn't look up again, avoiding another glance at me. I had had a long afternoon, between gym, classes and then all this shit.

"Appearances can be deceiving. And with me, even more so. So they will learn their lesson," I said to myself, and I sat back down on the seat next to my backpack.

I did not remember the carriage being so quiet. It was clear that my behavior had provoked a sudden mutism in the passengers, which gradually began to dissolve back to normal.

My confrontation with the young people did not stir my conscience in the least. I was satisfied. And, at the time, it even seemed little reprimand for their foolish daring. I arrived home at last. My mother was sitting in the doorway, worried that I had caught the train and about the cut I had mentioned. Upon my arrival, my mother walked toward me. As soon as I was level with her, she gave me an affectionate squeeze, asking me, while pinching my cheek,

"How is my little man?"

"Fuck, get off, Mom!" I exclaimed in disgust.

I just didn't feel like that nonsense at all. She withdrew her hand and adopted a slightly disappointed gesture. She had to get used to the idea that I was growing up, that I wasn't a ten-year-old anymore. I wasn't going to be her baby forever.

I took off my ripped sweatshirt and threw it straight into the trash. I went into the bathroom to take a much-needed shower. I examined the wound and it looked good. I showered, being careful not to get the band-aids wet and felt as good as new. The stress of all the fuss had taken its toll on me and now I just wanted to get into bed and rest.

I was putting on my pajamas in the bathroom, when there was a power cut.

"Fuck, it's always the same!" I shouted.

My mother did not answer. My eyes tried to adjust to the dim light. In front of me, the mirror subtly reflected my outline. And suddenly I saw what I had never thought I would see before. The reddish being of that delinquent was beside me. He accompanied me from there. An emptiness pulled my soul inward.

I understood then that I would never normally have behaved like that with those boys. That I would never have done that ugly thing to my mother when she received me with her tenderness. That damned being, who now did not leave my side, altered my behavior, made me be mean and even foul-mouthed. It had the ability to bring out the worst in me, I don't know how.

I watched him next to me, but I could never see him in focus. I always had to look into the far distance to make out his blurred color and shape, preventing me from making eye contact with him. I believe he knew I saw him. But it never manifested itself. I just wanted to get rid of him. I wanted my guardian angel to come and help me with this dreadful thing. I was terrified that

I couldn't get rid of him. The light came back and now it was harder to see him in the brightness.

The first thing I did as soon as I came out of the tiny bathroom was to apologize to my mother, give her a very, very tight hug and a kiss with all my heart. I apologized so many times that she was already laughing with an understanding and tolerant expression. I told her how much I loved her and how grateful I was to have her for a mother. And, almost excited and as usual, she told me to accompany her to the kitchen so she could heat up my dinner. In the meantime, we chatted about insipid town gossip. Something inside me encouraged me to be rude to her. I wanted to tell her to go fuck herself for talking to me about such nonsense. But I was strong and aware that it was what I called the reddish effect.

I finally got into bed. And again, in the dark I felt his constant presence. I tried to think of a plan. And the only thing I could think of was to go the next day to talk to the priest. I had no choice, especially in the absence of my interested friend, the shadow. My good friend who had disappeared, and who called himself a guardian angel. That dark angel who suddenly seemed to have abandoned and forgotten me.

I don't remember anything about the time I went to bed, only that I was thinking of some logical strategy to get rid of that evil being. Unable to resist, I fell into a deep sleep, as if my weight had multiplied several times.

The weight of evil.

Chapter 13
More Than a Fly

Andrín, summer 1996

The night passed and a new day lay before me. I woke up as usual. I went to wash my face and, suddenly, I remembered about the evil being I had stuck to me. I was overcome with worry. I didn't need to see it to realize that it was close to me, attached to me. At that moment, I did not know why.

I would generally wake up around on vacation, but that day, between my late return and all the accumulated stress, it was already half past eleven.

I had a quick breakfast while my mother prepared the food and rushed off on my bike to talk to Father Damián. I longed to talk to someone. Everything that was happening to me was like a volcano about to explode. I needed to contain all that visceral force. Someone had to calm me down a bit, because my attitude was the spitting image of the calm before the storm, you can feel the air change, but nothing has started yet.

This time, his door was not open. Last time I thought he was some kind of fortune teller or something. I myself realized that I knocked anxiously by insistently banging on the knocker of the gate at the priest's house. He opened the door timidly, peeking through the gap with his nose and one of his eyes. He did not smile at me as usual when he saw me. I suppose my uneasy countenance did not invite him to do so.

"Come in, son. What's the matter, do you look out of sorts?" He was leaning on his cane.

"I have some questions."

"For a moment, I thought you were the police. What a way to call."

"Sorry Father. I'm a little nervous about a delicate matter."

"Does it concern you?"

"Hey, no, no..."

"Good. Come in and we'll talk quietly. Let's see, my boy, what is it about?"

"I want to talk about demons: who are they, how do they behave, how can one get rid of them?"

"No one knows exactly that. The devil is an antithesis of good. He usually seduces us with the fulfillment of the most mundane desires, in exchange for a compromise."

"That... is something very generalized, father. I need to know what causes a demon to attach itself to a human being. And, above all, how to get rid of one."

"Speak more calmly, there is no hurry. A demon can attach itself to any human being. Generally, they choose between two very defined profiles: either individuals with a high potential for evil, or the opposite."

"Why would they want to approach a good person, Father?"

"They gain twice as much. First, if they succeed in transforming him into a bad person, he achieves the same goal and, second, they also avoid all the good he could do."

"And how does one get rid of that?"

"The Church does this through exorcism and other cultures have developed other rituals. The most important thing is to be very strong. Do not bow down to them. The more ground they gain from us, the more difficult it will be to drive them out. It is an inner struggle against oneself, rather than with the demon itself.

Overcoming is a matter of denial, fortitude and perseverance. Denial towards evil, fortitude to continue self-sacrifice and perseverance in maintaining the two previous ones."

"Thank you very much, Father, that's very good advice. And how is it that other cultures practice other rituals? What do you mean?"

"Well, look, son. As you know, there are many beliefs about these beings. Each religion holds a concept, basically identical, although with subtle differences. Not, of course, though, those who worship the evil one, who are a world apart. Why don't we go for a walk, so I can get my old body moving a bit?"

We left and walked for more than an hour, although we covered very little distance. Father Damián was a trunk full of anecdotes and wisdom. That walk in his company calmed me down a lot. It made me forget about "that little problem" that followed me everywhere. Walking by his side, one could feel the affection and true respect of all the neighbors. Every villager who greeted him seemed to be indebted to him. And now, no doubt, I owed him a favor too.

He asked me to sit in a pew. He told me he wanted to pray for me. And so he did, silently, for more than half an hour. I felt that the weight with which I arrived had been almost completely relieved. Apart from his religious character, Father Damián was an extraordinary person, he transmitted inner peace and that, like any other virtue, is contagious.

I returned home and helped my mother as much as I could, mixing the Russian salad with a paddle, setting the table and putting everything out on the patio. My aunt and uncle were coming over for lunch, and would soon be there, so I made a run to the store and bought several sodas. I was now in control of my own finances, and I liked being able to have niceties like that.

Being busy during all that time mitigated the anguish that had gripped me the night before. But my peace of mind was short-lived. I went to my parents' room and, lowering the blind, I contemplated my reflection in the mirror of their closet, at the greatest possible distance. The reddish, humanoid-shaped being seemed to be standing next to me with his arms crossed behind his back. His image was distorted like the heat of the asphalt on a hot summer afternoon. I tried to see his face, but it was impossible.

"What do you want from me?" I shouted at him. Seeing him there was driving me out of my mind.

I didn't get any answer, although I had the feeling he was laughing. I tried to pull myself together as best I could, pulled up the blind again and listened to my aunt and uncle arrive for lunch. I remember that every time my uncle saw me, I got a slap in the face. He was already doing it as a system. As a greeting. And, of course, with such a big hand and so much strength, anyone doubted his peaceful intentions.

We finished setting the table. We took the roast chicken out of the oven, I brought out the soft drinks and we all sat down to eat. We talked about trivial matters: the weather, the state of the sea, tourism. My aunt and uncle found me very distracted from the conversation. And then I began to see the little being hovering among us. He stood next to my mother and suddenly her plate of meat broke in half. She gave the explanation of the temperature contrast when serving the roast chicken. She got up to change it and the tablecloth got caught on her watch strap, and several glasses full of soda were knocked over. The bread got soggy, and my pants were almost completely wet.

I knew that all this was no coincidence. Of course, although my mother camouflaged her anger at the alleged clumsiness, her effort at self-control was evident. It was clear to me that the damn reddish being was doing its thing. I would have loved to tell her, but I could see myself in a mental institution, enjoying the passage of the electric current through my fried brain.

We changed the tablecloth, my pants and the plate, took another loaf of bread and refilled the glasses again. The chicken was already lukewarm, almost cold. Then I saw the figure next to my aunt. Suddenly, she hiccupped. But what hiccups, some inverted screams that were not even half normal. To top it off, a fly kept landing on her face. It really seemed to have taken it out on her. From her nose to her eyes, it landed on the corner of her lips; such was her desperation between the hiccups and the damn fly that she tried to eat it, but the fly escaped to land again and scurry around her face.

Then it was my uncle's turn, who with all his good intentions told my aunt to stay still, very still, while he brought his hand close to her face. I could see disaster coming. Her distrust-laden eyes foretold exactly what happened. I guess handling that ten-pound hand would be no easy task, and my aunt got a major slap and, worst of all, the fly landed on her face again.

My uncle kept apologizing to my poor aunt, when suddenly he began to complain of an itchy foot. Out of the blue, he quickly removed his shoe and took off his sock, hanging it over her shoulder like a pirate's parrot. He could be seen enjoying the unexpected foot-scratching. It was an insane pleasure. He spent his whole hand rubbing the sole as best he could, because he had no nails. It itched so much that he picked up a fork to relieve it. That itching had revealed several things: that my uncle had a serious localized body odor problem in his lower extremities and that the holes in his socks did not solve the problem with ventilation.

What a picture: my mother angry about the tablecloth; my aunt with superhuman hiccups, fighting a persistent fly and recovering from her husband's well-meaning giant hand; and the latter stinking up the table scratching himself with a fork and showing off his leaky, smelly sock. I couldn't help but burst out laughing uncontrollably. The bad thing is that the fork got mixed up with the others and I lost sight of it. Otherwise, I would have thrown it away for good.

Of course, I knew it was all the work of the damned red bug, a small demonstration of power. It ruined the food my mother had been cooking all morning. At least we had our coffee more calmly. My uncle wasn't getting on my nerves anymore. I looked at my watch and hurried to the station on my bicycle to catch the train back to Gijón. I had to train and to give a couple of classes.

I sat by the window, my favorite spot. This time I was facing against the direction of travel, in one of those four seats facing each other. Next to me was a crumpled and wrinkled newspaper. Bored, I opened it to read it. A discreet headline caught my attention: "Young stranger avoids the robbery of one of our grandmothers and collaborates in the arrest of a dangerous criminal wanted by Justice". I couldn't believe it, there it was, in the news of the Asturian newspaper.

Apparently, the lady had been carrying five hundred thousand pesetas in her purse, and the man had participated in numerous robberies in Barcelona and was hiding in pilgrims' hostels that had little or no police control. It was obvious that the bug had given him a good indication of the victim to choose. He had a good nose for money.

I put the newspaper in my backpack when a man and his son sat down across from me.

"Good afternoon. May we sit?" he asked me with exquisite politeness.

"Of course. It's not taken. Please."

The boy accompanying him must have been about nineteen years old and, from the way he behaved, it seemed clear that something was wrong with him.

"Don't be afraid for my son, boy. He's harmless."

"I wasn't scared. You can tell he's a very good person."

"And so it is. We just have to take him to have his medication increased a little."

The boy would look around as if he heard something the rest of us did not. From time to time, he would raise the index finger of his hand and move it from side to side, commanding silence. Wanting to pay attention to something else.

"Excuse me, what's the matter, if it's not indiscreet to ask?"

"It's all right, my boy. He's been diagnosed with schizophrenia."

And then the boy told his father to shut up.

"Just a moment, Dad. Quiet, someone wants to talk to David. Uh-huh, uh-huh, uh-huh."

"Your name isn't David, is it, young man?"

Instinctively, I was going to tell him the truth, but I reacted well and lied to him. I was finding it less and less difficult to play the part.

"No, sir. My name is Alexis."

"You're lying, you bastard! Your friend told me. He said you screwed him over yesterday with the old lady, and now he's going to pay you back by giving you a hard time."

Instinctively, I folded the newspaper, hiding the humble headline.

"He says he knows who you are and that he knows your secret. He knows you have a gun, and if he finds a way, he'll kill you with it. But he also says that if you choose the right side, if you choose him, he will help you with anything you need, anything at all," he repeated in a whisper.

"Forgive him, young man. He doesn't mean it. He suffers from auditory hallucinations, it's part of his illness. We won't bother you anymore, we'll go to another seat."

The boy interrupted his father again.

"He is shouting in my ear: 'Only I can help you! Only I can help you!'".

"Don't apologize, sir. If you wish, I'll leave you here quietly, so you don't have to get up."

I got up like a bolt of lightning. I slung my backpack over my shoulder and shifted in my seat. All this stress, the bug's threats, what he knew about me was getting on top of me. I was trying to calm down, but no one could really reassure me. I needed to talk to the shadow, but it didn't deign to show up. I was in relative danger, but he wouldn't come. I figured he had a lot of people to protect, I didn't want to be selfish, but my situation was getting a little too dark, and although I would never make a deal with him, what he said about help made me think of Angie right away.

I needed to meet her again. To see her one more time. It was my greatest desire. That's what the nasty bug was playing with. Everyone wants something. I was aware of it, but even so, it raised doubts in my mind. I will find her by my own means, I kept repeating to myself so as not to fall into its trap.

I looked at that young man with his father and felt sorry for him. What he had been diagnosed as a disease was really, in my opinion, simply a sixth sense, an amplified perception of parallel realities. But his mind was not prepared for such a barrage of information, and it was incongruous to skeptical eyes and even to himself. He hoped that he would get better and that this medication would alleviate his finely tuned sensory perception.

I got off at my station and they continued on their way to Oviedo. I said goodbye to them from the platform with a friendly wave and the father waved back. The son kept looking at me, following me with his eyes as the train started again, he placed his fist against the glass, and with his other hand he extended his middle finger like a crank. The father saw this and tried to correct it. I returned his cold stare with sharp eyes and stuck out my tongue as much as I could, very seriously, without looking away as the train pulled away.

I had seen that technique in a documentary; in it, Hindu religious people claimed that it scared away evil spirits. I was not sure about the latter; however, from the outside, I looked like a deranged person, that's for sure.

I was running out of ideas.

Chapter 14
Siblings

Principality of Asturias-Cantabria,
summer 1996.

I headed straight to the gym, where I took out all my frustration on my partner's bag and protective gear. Almost two hours of physical beating helped me to reduce tensions. I took a shower in those austere locker rooms and got dressed in a hurry so as not to be late for my student, Julio. This kid had failed one of the most important subjects and was carrying it over to September, Natural Sciences.

I was trying to concentrate on the matter at hand: the cell. I made him understand the genetic importance of the mitochondrion, and its inheritance only through the maternal line. I explained all its parts, as if it were an egg where the nucleus is the yolk, the white is the cytoplasm, the shell is called the membrane, and so on. He seemed to understand it well with that simile, but at the same time I could barely concentrate.

At the dining room table were his older brother and his father, both discussing the structural stability of an asymmetrical construction. I asked Julio about his relatives. His father ran a successful architectural firm and taught at the University of Oviedo; the brother was to present a project as a paper, and the two were discussing how to effectively, economically improve the structure of a major sports stadium and auditorium with a retractable roof without losing the integrity of the building.

They both took a break for a drink and went to the kitchen. Curiosity pricked my insides. With a silly excuse, I peeked at the plans they had there. They were dirty because there were some erasures and corrections with question marks. I understood that the desire of their design was somewhat irregular, and with the shape of the sketch I drew up a plan of all the supporting pillars, the necessary proportions, diameters, location of vomitories, buttresses hidden inside the structure, etc. The interior layout of the stands and exits followed the pattern of my recent visit, the Roman Colosseum, a historical monument for the people and the spectacle, very difficult to improve in design and evacuation capacity.

I was engrossed in drawing the location of all the components, I would stop for a few seconds to mentally calculate the cadences, mathematical notations, rational distribution of the elevators. I even had time to draw places restricted to the public and accesses for buses. I began to think of a subway parking lot, to enlarge the sketch at the bottom. The father and brother had been behind me for a few seconds. They looked at each other perplexed. I left the room and apologized for sticking my nose where it wasn't wanted. I was about to leave the room when they called me again. It was Julio's father.

"Excuse me, can you come here for a moment?" he said softly.

"Of course."

He didn't start asking me the usual questions about how I knew how to do this or that.

"Why have you placed these two buttresses here?"

"The asymmetrical exterior design forces the loads to be distributed transversely to the foundation, and by using these two buttresses hidden within the aesthetic design, the vertical forces of the retractable vault can be compensated. This is the first thing that came to my mind."

"And it's brilliant! I'm impressed. Let us check your calculations and then we'll talk."

The father and son looked at the quick shot I had made and were asking each other why they hadn't thought of it. For me it was as simple as putting on a jacket. That jacket has to be stuffed with a solid body that can breathe and still have freedom of movement.

"Does my son have your home phone number?"

He does. You must excuse me, sir, but it's time for me to go. I've had a lot of fun and I don't want to miss my train."

"Of course, of course. You go ahead. We'll be in touch." And he kept looking at that half-dirty paper with his eldest son, asking himself questions in between nervous laughter.

To be honest, I had developed a strange habit. It had become almost a reflex. Whenever I saw a building, I imagined its entire internal skeleton, mentally tried to conceive my own vision of its structural organization, and then contrasted it if I had a choice, by accessing its interior.

For the moment, none of that worried me in the least. I kept thinking about that blurred reddish silhouette accompanying me. I looked at myself in the shop windows and there it remained, like a limpet. I needed to do something about it. I could hurt my loved ones or myself. In fact, it had threatened to kill me.

Death. What a concept. I had lost all respect and fear for that word. The only thing I feared was to be reborn again and remember nothing. To be one of many, with my mind closed and unknowing, and the memory of Angie faded.

I thought of all the options to get answers. I imagined stepping in front of a car so it would run me over, but then I would think, "What if it goes wrong and there's no way the shadow could help me? I'd be crippled for life." I also didn't know if my shadow would appear if the danger was voluntarily sought. It seemed like a bad idea to force its presence in this way. I was running out of options. And then I remembered Kingsley, his vast cultural knowledge of these matters. But, of course, we left him in Algeciras, and who knows where he was now. Maybe I could try calling him at the reception center, to see if he was there.

As soon as I got home, I called Information and they gave me the number of the center. I wrote it down and called.

"First reception center, good evening," someone replied, cheerfully.

"Good evening."

"How can we help?"

"I am one of the sailors who assisted in the rescue of a group of foreigners shipwrecked in the Alboran Sea. I would like to know if I could speak to Kingsley. He is a friend of mine."

"Let me see, because there are many of them here. Let's see, okay, here it is. Oops. Bad news. He has gone to Madrid. He is going to regularize his administrative situation and is in one of our centers in the capital."

"I understand. And could you give me the telephone number?"

"-Of course, of course. Do you have a notepad?"

I wrote down the phone and then called. I got a very sour woman who said she couldn't help me. I could tell from the tone of her voice that Kingsley must be there. She refused to give me that information because she said it was her duty to preserve his privacy. hung up and thought, "Well, I'll call tomorrow and find another, nicer worker."

I had dinner with my mother as usual, we watched TV for a while and I lay down on the couch. I got up to go to bed, I felt like I was dragging a thousand kilos, I was so tired.

The next day, I called again in the morning. The same disgusting voice picked up the phone. I hung up without saying a word. At noon, the same thing. At night, the same thing. I couldn't believe it, that damn lady was always there. The next day, same operation, same result.

I went to Father Damián again. It was unbelievable. A call from him to the shelter in Madrid changed everything. If I had known, I would have pretended to be a priest. It's clear that the Church and these help centers are closely related. He was immediately put through to Kingsley. I was very happy to hear his voice, to feel him happy and in good health. Father Damián left the house to let me speak freely.

After the greetings and some polite small talk, I got straight to the point. And I told him I thought I was possessed. He began to refute me. I, of course, had no doubt about it. Convincing him while feeling quite unable to confess my encounters with the unknown was quite an effort in the use of language, although it escaped me that at one point I had seen it.

Finally, he accepted my invitation to come and stay for a few days. I had no option to travel alone, and if I did it would have been against my mother's wishes. I immediately went to the bus station and got the ticket in his name, for him pick up at the station in Madrid. I was looking forward to his arrival and the hours seemed to take forever.

I continued with my daily duties. I was more careful than ever, since I was stuck with this malicious bug, everything kept going wrong. I guess it was what people commonly call bad luck. Everyone treated me badly, they were surly and impertinent: the social worker, the bus ticket saleswoman, etc. Everything was much more difficult for me than usual. I was a "stinker". While training, I sprained my wrist a little. Household appliances that I touched mysteriously stopped working. While in the bedroom, a window broke in the breeze. I almost slipped to my death in the bathtub. While in Gijón, a police car stopped me and looked at my backpack, asking me about drugs or if I had problems with the law. I asked them very politely why they had looked at me. They made up an excuse about the control, carrying and possession of weapons among the youth. I knew it was not that. The policemen stopped me because they sensed the evil that accompanied me. I am sure of it.

Before leaving the station, Kingsley phoned home to let me know his arrival time. I insisted my mother let me go alone to pick him up from Santander. She agreed. And there, at a quarter to five in the afternoon, I was, impatient for his arrival.

The huge bus was full of people, but I immediately found him among the passengers. For many it was the first time they had ever seen a black man in their lives. And, contrary to popular belief, many people looked at him and greeted him with sympathy, without knowing him at all. It was their way of compensating for their indiscreet glances at him. It was like a constant welcome. Kingsley always answered with his huge smile and that crazy gesture he made, shaking his head in circles. He seemed to be very used to it, and he seemed to be getting on well. He was not yet fluent in Spanish, so everyone knew he came from far away.

We gave each other a big hug when we saw each other, and I helped him pick up his backpack. He was delighted with the trip, surprised by so much vegetation and natural beauty. The first thing we did was to go for a drink at a nearby bakery. He was feeling the cold from the humidity, and we remedied it with a hot Cola Cao and some sugar donuts.

Right away, he brought up the conversation of why he had come. We spoke freely because in those days it was very difficult to find someone who spoke English. He was telling me that in his culture demons, or evil spirits, are fought with prayers and sacrifices. If I had one of them attached to me, it was only for three reasons. The first, being heartless. As the term says, who has given up his soul in exchange for favor. Second, being cursed or suffering from an evil eye or voodoo. And, third, that this demon works under the orders of a sorcerer and is at my side to convince me of something. According to his explanations, this is done on special occasions; for example, when a man or woman asks the wizard to make someone fall in love with them, when an important contract is to be obtained, or similar things.

For me all the options he gave me were unfeasible. None of them matched my case and I could not reveal my full circumstances to him. I was forbidden to do so, the shadow warned me. I had formed my own idea. That bug was attached to me because its previous host had already cashed in all its favor, and it realized that I could see it and, worst of all, fight it. I embodied a threat to the bug and so many others like it.

He told me about the good sangomas, witches who only use white magic to do good, rejecting any act of evil or manipulation. He told me that for many years it has been used to heal at a distance or to protect a loved one from danger including on the risky trips of the tribe in search of game and resources. On the other hand, black magic was used by other witches for very different purposes and objectives, malicious purposes, such as making a person sterile, making them seriously ill or causing an accident, among others.

Then what he told me next chilled me to the bone. He began to tell me about his family. They had an older sister, and when I say they, I mean Kingsley and his brother. The small village where they lived was occupied by an armed rebel group that claimed to be fighting against the oppression of the ruling government. They raided and looted all the food stocks. Anyone foolish enough to complain was killed unceremoniously. They killed the cattle to eat them, something unthinkable in their custom until that animal is very old and they have milked it thousands of times. They occupied their house, and they also refused to let them leave, forcing them to take up arms and fight for their cause.

With his eyes full of anger, he kept telling me about the terror his family suffered. Of course, for the opposing side, everyone in that village was already an enemy. That is how his whole family perished. His brother died in his arms, hit by a shell, he bled to death. Then he began to describe his words in his last seconds of life, almost suffocated and in his death throes. His wounded brother claimed to feel no pain. He could see an elongated tunnel with a huge, bright light that encouraged him to come without delay. He claimed to feel great and could see several family members waiting for him on the other side. He removed the pendant around his neck and handed it to Kingsley.

"Grandpa says you should keep it, and when the time comes, give it to a very special person who will cross your path. That man will be your new brother. You will know who he is because his incorruptible soul can see both good and bad spirits. It is your duty to help him. That is your destiny."

His eyes went out of life, wide open and with a sweet expression. Bullets and explosions rumbled all around, but time seemed to have stopped before him. He grabbed the pendant, squeezed her eyes shut with his hand. He screamed with rage and pain as loud as his lungs would carry him and fled relentlessly northward.

I listened to his story. I was speechless. All that suffering seemed to come back as I remembered it, and Kingsley's face appeared to me like that of a warrior who has defeated death. Without another word, he pulled a pendant from the jacket of his scruffy old corduroy coat and hung it around my neck.

"Now I am sure that you are the man my brother told me about. I give you this amulet in obedience to my grandfather's will. It will protect you from all evil."

Gently, he pulled out from under his shirt an identical amulet to show it to me. He pressed my hand against his joining our foreheads and said,

"Now we are brothers forever."

I closed my eyes and gave him an affectionate hug. I was sorry for his loss. I was sorry he had to go through all that.

The pendant was a very small square of dark brown leather, tightly stitched and closed. It seemed to have something solid inside. The strap was black and looked very sturdy.

Kingsley could not stop thinking about his entire family lying in the ground, mortally wounded, without a decent burial. He had to abandon their bodies to survive. His journey to The Beluga was a heroic feat. He was a fugitive on his own continent. Hunger and thirst accompanied him throughout the journey. He slept in the open, hidden, and every sound in the night was a shock. Images of violence accompanied him at all times. When he crossed a border to the north, he was still greeted with gunfire. Unable to explain it, he stayed alive, moving forward. When he reached North Africa, others like him paid the mafia for their journey with diamonds, gold and jewelry. Many of them hid them in the anus wrapped in a condom, or in a latex glove. Kingsley himself was mugged by bandits bent on searching for treasure with their fingers uncovered. I couldn't help but burst out laughing, and together we giggled at this for several minutes.

Apparently, it was a situation that was a regular occurrence near the coast. So every time he saw two or three guys following him around a bit, he himself would drop to the ground and pull down his pants, offering himself up for exploration. Fortunately, he had got over his mania for doing so, although he was sometimes tempted in Spain. And we laughed non-stop again, joking. Funny how humor can repaint the darkest scenes of the soul.

With nothing to bargain with to take a paying boat, he heard of an offer to get on a barge without paying. All his countrymen warned him of the danger. Even though it was free, they refused the trip because they knew there had to be a catch. Kingsley had no other options, and, like him, many others gambled everything for everything, riding on that little boat towed by a zodiac full of men armed with balaclavas.

Men with gray hearts.

Chapter 15
Premonition

Kingsley was impressed by everything. As soon as we left the bakery, I could see the reddish figure walking away from me. Without wasting a second, he stuck to a man carrying a briefcase, wearing a suit and tie. His hair was slicked back, and he was smoking a cigar with an air of arrogance. He seemed to be arguing with another skinny suit-wearing man with loaded folders in his hands, perhaps a clerk. I don't know. What I do know is that as soon as it hit him, I felt completely liberated. Nevertheless, the gentleman in the suit stared at me without blinking; for a moment, I stopped my walk. Then he stuck his tongue out at me without taking his eyes off me for a moment and brought his hand to his genitals, shaking them up and down. I had to restrain Kingsley because he was going straight for him. I simply let him pass.

I knew that the culprit of those mocking and provocative gestures was the bug. That bug that I had gotten rid of, thanks to Kingsley's amulet.

I couldn't tell Kingsley how immensely grateful I felt, nor could I tell him anything about what I was able to see. I did tell him that the amulet made me feel more protected. Some time ago I wondered why so many drivers wore a figure of St. Christopher in their cars, or the ribbon with the image of the Virgin of the Pilar as a bracelet. I don't know if the effect was auto-suggestion or placebo, the fact is that it worked wonders for me.

Many people came to mind who treasured small, usually worthless, belongings of deceased loved ones. They claimed to bring them luck and protection, as well as to be able to feel in those objects the slight imprint of their lost and missed friends or relatives.

Something I had always underestimated now appeared before me as a clear and undeniable truth: the amulet worked perfectly. With time, I understood that the mechanism and functioning of these talismans was based on love and faith, acting as latent shields against evil.

For Kingsley everything was new and spectacular. We were on the train and he looked like a child in a toy store, asking me about everything. He saw the beach in passing from the railroad and marveled at its beauty, those atypical contrasts of turquoise, blues, yellows and greens of our northern nature. He loved seeing the stone and wood houses, their mountainous appearance and the assortment of colors with which their owners decorated them. I enjoyed seeing him so enthusiastic and excited about his future.

After so much pain, he deserved to be happy.

At last, we arrived in town, we shared between us the weight of his luggage and when we arrived home Kingsley showed off his exquisite manners. My mother did not understand a word our guest said, although she interpreted his body language without words. I would translate what my mother could not understand and vice versa. She scolded him for barely knowing two words of Spanish, because since he was in Spain, but almost everyone spoke to him in English.

We left the duffel bag lying in a corner of my room. It was too late to go around unpacking. We had to shower and get ready for dinner. I lent him some pajamas, and soon after my aunt and uncle arrived. As soon as my uncle saw Kingsley, he gave him one of his classic Bud Spencer-style affectionate slaps. Dinner was especially fun, because our guest was so salty. He tasted the food and his eyes seemed to pop out of their sockets, approving and exaggerating the pleasure of the meal. He managed not to lick the plate clean but he did have several helpings. The whole family was delighted with him and his sense of humor. My aunt and uncle tried to get him to learn some Spanish, and they would point out the names of everything on the table. When he tried to repeat the words, they always came out with a very strong, African-style pronunciation. And we couldn't help but laugh with him.

Having him in our home was a breath of fresh air. When we were about to have dessert, my mother told me about a phone call she had received. She told me that Don Manuel, Julio's father, had called because he wanted to talk to me and her, but he didn't want to do it over the phone. She had arranged to meet him the next day. He would come to our home in the morning and, he said, it was about my future.

I told my mother that he was a professor at the University of Oviedo in the field of Architecture, and she seemed delighted. I did not take a second out of my thoughts and went on my own way with my dear African brother. My mother had been trying all her life to improve my teaching education and take advantage of my abilities. For her, Don Manuel was a positive step in that direction.

My aunt and uncle said goodbye to Kingsley and, strangely, my aunt gave him a long, loving hug. Then she stared at her José with a trembling gaze. It was obvious that somehow they had connected very well. We made up the bed and, after kissing Mom goodnight, we got into bed, and talked in whispers until well into the early hours of the morning.

The next thing I remember, it was about five o'clock in the morning when Kingsley startled me awake. I was drenched in sweat, my heart rate was through the roof and my body was shaking. My mother also woke up and was standing under the door frame.

Apparently, I had had a nightmare. Kingsley told me I was screaming a woman's name, Angie. I could have sworn I saw my dear friend, the shadow, in the opposite corner of the room for an instant. Maybe it was my imagination, I don't know. My mother was holding a wrapped, damp cloth in her hand. Thus I learned that for quite some time I had been suffering from some nightmares and my poor mother tried to relieve them many nights without waking me up. She had heard that it was very dangerous to wake someone while dreaming or sleepwalking. But on this occasion, Kingsley bypassed all her protocol.

I apologized for the inconvenience and we all tried to fall asleep again. I knew I had dreamt something important, something about my longed-for Angie, but I couldn't remember what. The dream images faded against my will. I pulled the blanket over me, tried to control the shivering in my limbs, and promptly fell asleep again.

The sun was shining brightly, bidding us good morning. It was Saturday and I had no obligations to fulfill, except for Don Manuel's visit, which I hoped I could dispatch quickly. I prepared breakfast for everyone. Although this time, and not knowing Kingsley's tastes, I brought the Cola Cao can, a full pot of coffee and a pitcher of milk, flooding the table with local delicacies I wanted him to try, toast, butter and jam, olive oil, juice and fruit. When my mother got up, she was delighted, because it reminded her of a hotel buffet.

We were about to start serving breakfast when a shiny black Mercedes Benz pulled up next to our house. I peeked through the little window at the entrance and immediately recognized Julio's father. He was dressed in a shirt and pants, shiny shoes, and was carrying a leather folder in his hand. I didn't wait for him to knock on the door and quickly went out to greet him.

"Good morning, Don Manuel. You are just in time. Please come in."

"Good morning, David. How are you, young man?"

"Good, good. And Julio, is he you?"

"No, no. He has gone shopping with his cousins and his mother."

"Come in, come in, we were just about to start breakfast. Coffee?"

"Oh, yes, of course, with milk and a teaspoon of sugar."

I formally introduced my mother and Kingsley, and we had breakfast in relative haste because we wanted to go to the beach and enjoy our morning. We tidied up the kitchen like well-oiled machinery while my mother and Don Manuel chatted in the living room. I started to help Kingsley unpack his luggage, and I could see that in that faded bundle he was carrying only old and torn clothes. I felt embarrassed, and very assertively encouraged him again to put on one of my T-shirts and a bathing suit.

When we were about to leave, my mother called me and told me that Don Manuel also wanted to talk to me. He then explained that he wanted to give me a little test. He took out several stapled papers from his briefcase and told me to choose one at random. I suggested that my mother do it. They were all tests, each one had one question with four choices and a box next to it. Once I picked one, she asked me to go to the kitchen and do it; I had sixty minutes.

I sat in the kitchen and started to do it. It was an architecture exam. In fifteen minutes I handed it in while Kingsley finished putting his stuff in the room, and we hurried off to the beach to have fun. We took the paddles and the tennis ball and soon I could see some boys from town. We all sat together on the sand while the village boys kept an eye on Kingsley. He was trying to make himself understood with gestures and loose words. Many were unaware of my command of English and, fortunately, attributed it to my studies in Gijón.

The day went off without a hitch, although Kingsley didn't get in beyond the waist because he couldn't swim and the sea had unintentionally ripped his soul out. He didn't tell me, but I sensed his conflict. When we arrived home from the beach, my uncle José was preparing the coals for a barbecue; dinner looked great. We missed my father's presence very much, from whom we had had no news for several days. His absence was a taboo that we did not talk about, it was embarrassing for us to enjoy ourselves while he was risking his life mile by mile.

On the patio counter, my uncle had displayed a magnificent assortment of wild asparagus, meat and potatoes wrapped in silver foil. Kingsley had a great variety to choose from. We were all surprised at how much he enjoyed the food. He explained to me that they are great hunters of wild animals, but the domesticated ones they keep only for dairy products. Although they often went for long stretches without eating, or rationing their provisions very cautiously. That is why he was so grateful for such abundance.

"Seize the moment," he repeated to me, "because tomorrow is not assured for anyone."

How right he was.

While we were having dinner, my mother commented that, after taking that exam, Don Manuel had the correction template right there. He corrected it in front of her and there was not a single mistake in any of the answers. He explained to my mother that it was an Architecture final year exam. She couldn't get over her astonishment, and he insisted that it was clear that I had an innate gift for that subject, and that he would be delighted to take advantage of all that potential.

He started comparing me to Mozart. He also showed her the asymmetrical sketch of the stadium that I had made in his house and assured her that, once all the parameters had been entered into a computer software called AutoCAD, the design worked brilliantly, without overloads and really economical, leaving spatial freedom for the interior design, and, most importantly, with total security and stability. That was nothing new to me. Modesty aside, I used to make a living that way in the old days, and I was one of the best in the world, but of course, that was a thing of the past.

Don Manuel said that he had to talk to certain people and that soon my parents would hear from him. I didn't want to give him too much importance, mostly because, although I was passionate about architecture, my main goal in life was to meet Angie again before it was too late. Of course, that required money. I had to find a way to earn more and be able to travel to the United States.

The phone at home rang. At last, news of my father. He was docked in Belfast. You could hear the tiredness and sadness of being far away in his voice, although he tried to hide it. He seemed to curse himself for being absent in those summer days. He planned to leave port as soon as he hung up and get at the helm to return home in about three days. I was out entertaining my Uncle José and Kingsley, while my aunt seemed to be at my mother's side, giving her support.

I looked out the window and thought I saw my mother arguing on the phone. I walked down the hallway until I was almost to the living room, and I heard her ask my father to please stay that night in a hotel and leave tomorrow. She said she had a bad feeling that night. My father seemed to be arguing with her, justifying himself with deliveries, port costs and personnel.

"What's wrong, Mom?"

"Nothing, son, your father is a big-headed melon," she said without hanging up the phone.

"Pass her over to Aunt Matilde and don't let him hang up," I said softly in her ear. When she did, I asked her, "What did you see? I mean the feeling, mom, what did you see?"

"I don't want to tell you. No."

"Tell me! It's not nonsense. What did you see?" Then my mother burst into tears.

"This afternoon while I was taking a nap, I saw your father floating dead in the darkness of the sea, rocked by the waves, face down and drifting."

I was petrified. I knew for a fact how important these precognitions were. If my father hung up the phone, there would be no solution. And he wasn't about to believe in that kind of nonsense. My father has always been superstitious about seafaring canons, but this was too pithy. He would tell my mother that he would listen to her and then set sail as if nothing had happened. I had to think of something and fast. Then I hit upon the key. I grabbed my mother's face with both hands, trying to calm her down.

"It's not time to cry, Mom. It's time to think. I believe you. I need you to close your eyes and, even if it's hard, you must remember that image again with all kinds of details."

My mother, after several attempts, finally listened to me. Her tears were falling on her lips. She closed her eyes. I could feel her dread. Meanwhile, my aunt was talking to her on the phone about Kingsley, his gluttony and how little he understood Spanish.

"Mom, are you seeing it?"

"Yes, I'm looking at him, I see his body swollen and bluish."

"Don't look at that. What clothes is he wearing in your dream?"

"He's wearing his brown wool hat, the one his mother made him. A maroon scarf, and a navy-blue sweater with a red flag and a white star, there are some letters underneath, but I don't know what it says."

"Very good. Now give that description to dad, tell him how you saw him in your dream."

My mother picked up the phone again. She had to insist to my father, because when he gets stubborn no one beats him. He didn't want to hear my mother say those things again. He only started to pay attention when she told him the clothes he was wearing in the picture she dreamed. Apparently, my father was quite silent and astonished. I don't know if out of pride or why, he didn't tell her that he was dressed precisely that way. I guess the irrational is scary. I think it's something that happens to all of us. After a few moments of silence, my father assured my mother that he would not sail that night. He swore that he would listen to her and leave at dawn after breakfast.

And so he did. There was nothing to regret. That night, however, another shipwreck claimed its victims. A sudden storm with waves of more than nine meters took the lives of two sailors from a fishing boat. Precisely at night and more or less along the route where The Beluga would have sailed. In time, and although he always tried to hide it, we learned that while he was in the port of Belfast, he bought a blue sweater with the logo of the White Star Line company in honor of the now defunct passenger and cargo shipping company. That's the same one that commissioned the construction of the ill-fated ocean liner Titanic. Of course, the emblem of that company was none other than a red flag fluttering in the wind, firmly attached to a flagpole with a white star inside. Underneath it, on letterhead, was the name of the company.

Reflecting afterwards, I couldn't help but wonder if that beanie my late grandmother had made for him, had he put it on by chance or if there was something more to it. I was very curious to expand my knowledge in that regard, and I was ignorant of too many things. That night I was thankful that I didn't have to mourn any family misfortune and that made me feel indebted.

Indebted to life.

Chapter 16
Far Reflex

Principality of Asturias, summer 1996

My aunt and uncle slept over and, even though it was the middle of summer, Kingsley couldn't stand the coolness of the night. His body was slow to adapt to our climate. After that unbeatable dinner, we chatted, again, until well into the early hours of the morning. My uncle never ran out of stories to tell, and they were always very funny.

The next morning, I planned to take Kingsley to see the caves in Ribadesella. He told me a lot about caves near his village, where they made offerings and collected bat guano to mix with water to make fertilizer.

My mother, now calmer, prepared us some tortilla and tomato sandwiches and we set off. We took the train to Ribadesella, and there we started our hike. We headed towards the caves crossing the bridge over the river Sella and got ourselves the tickets by using my local contacts.

Kingsley seemed to enjoy every inch of the cave. The geological formations inside and the paleolithic paintings made him marvel, literally with his mouth open. I was translating to him in a low voice everything that the guide was telling us. Finally, we visited the Ardines cave, with a height of more than forty meters and its vaulted natural light passage, which made that natural structure a grandiose monument.

After lunch, we took the train again and got off in Llanes. I talked to him about the importance of fishing in the area, showed him the medieval fortifications and the cannons with which they defended themselves. We put ourselves in the shoes of those who had to live in those times, full of looting, and where the law of the strongest was the only law.

Finally, we headed to the city's lighthouse. Seeing it shining with its intermittent and powerful light was a spectacle to behold. It was already dusk and its light was beginning to win the battle against the orange sky that melted into the infinity of the sea.

We were arriving at the main road of the town, concluding a fabulous day of hiking and sightseeing. It was then that I began to feel strange. As we approached the bridge of the boats, I began to feel worse. Kingsley noticed, I slowed down and had to lean on the railing that ran along the river path through the town.

I remember it with millimetric accuracy. With no apparent explanation, all that tourist bustle was mitigated until it disappeared completely. I could see the whole street completely empty. It was still nighttime, but much later. In front of me a gift and souvenir store was presided over by a huge clock, like a train station, which read a quarter past twelve. My vision was somewhat dense but sharp. A lone young woman, about fifteen years old, was approaching the edge of the bridge. She was wearing a white dress with a brown leather Ibiza-style belt and matching pumps, carrying a brown cloth bag over her shoulder. I felt confused and exhausted.

With my hand tightly gripped on the railing, I sat on the ground without losing my vision. The young woman took a rope out of the bag, a folded piece of paper and a round stone. She discarded the bag by throwing it into the river. I could see the cloth floating towards the harbor carried by the current.

She firmly tied one of the ends to the metal railing of the bridge and dropped the other end of rope down into the abyss, like someone doing a preliminary test. I watched that scene as if from another time, between hot and sweaty chills. I didn't quite understand what was happening to me, I was just a spectator. Without thinking twice, in a hurry as if to avoid being discovered, the young woman placed the rope around her neck with a simple slip knot, nothing elaborate, although undoubtedly effective.

Determined, she pulled the rest of the rope, about three meters, through the gap in the bridge. She carefully took off her ballet flats, taking care to leave them perfectly aligned with the wall, and next to them the folded sheet of paper under the stone. Between balances, he climbed up to the edge of the cliff. I wanted to stop her, but I could not move a muscle, or even articulate a word, it was as if I were daydreaming, paralyzed.

Many thoughts were running through my head, I wondered what serious problem could make such a beautiful girl want to take her own life. The voice inside me replied, demanding respect for her circumstances and my lack of knowledge about her. Entertained by my inner debate, the girl, dark and slender like a ballerina, seemed to count to three, hesitating to take the step into the void, her last step in life.

Finally, like someone who decides to jump into the water of an icy pool, I saw her throw herself into the void.

I wanted to scream, to run to her, to beg her not to do it, that I would help her in any way I wanted! I kept repeating to myself, silently and dozens of times: "No! no! no! no!", I refused to see it, I wanted to spare myself the horrifying inclemency of death. Still, the whole sequence happened before my open eyes, unable to avoid looking. She leaned forward straight ahead, letting gravity do its work. Her arms attached to her waist accompanied her as if she were an inert body. As the rope tightened, her body flailed in the air like the end of a whip and the swing of the rope rattled against the stone with a coarse noise. Her mind was ready to die, but her body struggled relentlessly to try to free itself from the tight knot. She kicked her legs in a vain attempt to relieve the tension, and her delicate hands were ambitious to undo the knot.

Life was slowly leaving her body as her strength faded away. That beautiful girl, dead, swayed in the air like a pendulum. From then on, my vision blurred like a badly focused photo, and the blackness of the darkness gave me a visual respite, a peaceful rest.

In the distance, far away, I heard Kingsley's voice shouting my name. I still couldn't move, it was like being asleep and at the same time unable to wake up. I would later learn that they call that sleep paralysis. I was getting more and more scared because I could not regain control of my body, I wanted to scream or say something, but I could not. However, my hearing, touch and smell were at full capacity.

Through stimulation, basically pinches and blows to my face, I regained control over my muscles and gradually recovered my voice. Without being able to open my eyes wide, I could see the dark silhouette of many people around me. I thought I had experienced that vision before, but I couldn't remember how or when. I could only hear Kingsley asking me to please not scare him and kissing me on the cheek uncontrollably, perhaps reliving past experiences.

When I regained full consciousness, everyone around me was speculating about the cause of my fainting. Whether it was low blood sugar, low blood pressure or heat stroke. The fact is that a hand, coming from the crowd, forced a sugar cube from the cafeteria across the street into my mouth. I spat it out immediately. I looked at that clock, and it read half past nine.

I got up as best I could with the help of my friend and some other good Samaritan of the town. I kept looking at that bridge remembering the image of the girl throwing herself into the void. That girl must have committed suicide there and her imprint was engraved in the atmosphere.

Somehow I had been able to see it. After all, energy always lasts. I gave my own explanation and, after convincing Kingsley that it was okay, we continued on our way home zigzagging through the streets, always heading west. I was setting the pace and, truth be told, I wanted to get home for dinner, have a good shower and take off those boots that were giving my feet a hard time.

In my haste, I heard the rusty hinges of a gate opening. Presuming that someone was coming out of the estate, I increased my pace a little more to get in front of their exit, so that the person coming out with his back turned to lock the gate crashed into me, or me into him.

My first impression was one of disgust for the encounter, although both of us, slaves of good manners, apologized. The difference was that she did it in a sweet, subdued feminine voice. As I looked up at her, I almost fainted again - it was the girl from my vision! I just stood there, looking stupid, while Kingsley's piercing eyes asked me without speaking, "What are we waiting for?" Standing abstracted, I stared at her unblinkingly. She, also self-absorbed, was finishing locking the door. Without turning her gaze back to me, she began to walk down the sidewalk that seconds before we had walked. As a reflex action, I grabbed her hand, her fingers almost slipped out of my grasp and I held them with just the right amount of force. She stopped walking and turned around to look at what or who dared to disturb her, she wasn't dressed the same, but I'm sure it was her.

"Excuse me, do I know you?" she asked fiercely.

"No. I don't think so. But I would love to. If you give me the chance, of course."

"I don't think so. Give me my hand back, please."

"Of course. Forgive me."

She turned around again and started walking toward the center of town. Then I asked her,

"Are you going out tonight?"

She froze motionless for a few seconds and, without turning around, answered.

"Maybe so, but alone."

"You're not seeing anyone?"

She sighed, wanting to cut the conversation short and added quietly,

"I have a date with destiny." And she went on her way.

As she walked away from us, I just stood there, stunned and staring, while Kingsley had already advanced a few meters and turned around to ask me if I had fallen in love or what. The girl was surrounded by reddish creatures, at least three or four of them. I wanted to tell my good friend all the strange things that were happening to me. I really would have loved to.

The secrets were piling up, and so were the lies and half-truths. Their weight was felt in my soul, and the worst of all was not being able to tell anyone. It was finding myself so lonely. Kingsley asked me if these dizzy spells were frequent. I answered his questions but distractedly. I couldn't stop thinking about that girl. Those beings were not around her to help her do evil, what they wanted was to do evil to her, fulfilling someone else's dark desire.

Something strange was happening, it was my first vision and coincidentally the day before my mother dreamed of my father drowned and swollen in the sea. At this point I did not believe in coincidences; something was causing those premonitions, although at that moment that was the least of it. My main concern was to think about how to approach that same night without arousing suspicion and how to prevent the girl's suicide.

With that last sentence of hers, encrypted, I understood that I would do it that very night. Suddenly, my aching feet and my desire to rest took a back seat. When I got home, I had to talk to Kingsley; I had to lie again. Taking advantage of the fact that I didn't understand any Spanish, I made up the bullshit that I had a date with that girl and that he had to cover for me. He made a surprised face and did not stop praising me saying that I was a Casanova, a winner, that things were so easy here in Spain, that I should bring friends for him who spoke English, and so on and so on. Of course, he was more excited than I was. So I asked him just for the sake of asking,

"Kingsley, do you believe in visions of the future?"

"Why do you say that, brother? Have you seen a wedding with her?" he asked, looking sideways at me mischievously.

"No, seriously, visions of bad things."

Then he became very serious. And he grabbed me by the shoulders with both hands,

"What have you seen?"

He didn't know about my mother, and I told him about her vision to see where it would come out.

"These amulets are especially for that," he answered as he pulled it out from under his shirt. They are to avoid pain, to be able to react ahead of time. Someone very sensitive to the energies of the other side can transmit their visions to those around them without realizing it. I wouldn't be surprised if you had given that vision to your mother in your dreams. The amulet knows the smartest way to avoid tragedy. That's how the magic of my village works. Without a doubt, you are the man my grandfather pointed to."

"I hope I never lose it, Kingsley."

"In time, you won't need the amulet. That pendant is just a small window through which to look. You will soon leave these walls; you are predestined to be a shaman."

The truth is that it was literally going to be like that, because I had planned to escape as usual, through the window. This time, I would leave the car in its place and take off with the bicycle. After dinner, and with the invaluable help of Kingsley, we both claimed to be extremely tired and quickly went to the room. I looked at the clock, and it was already half past eleven; I had to get the hell out of there. I jumped out of the window and on the other side I said goodbye to Kingsley, who was looking proudly at me as if I were a champion of love. He kept repeating to me,

"Friends. Friends for Kingsley."

"Yes, my friend but lower your voice."

And we both had to laugh ourselves silly. I had to lift the bike by hand so that the sound of the sprocket and chain would not attract attention. I had to hurry as fast as I could. Fortunately, the last stretch was downhill, and that helped me a lot in my accelerated ride.

It was twelve o'clock according to my watch, three minutes past twelve according to the one in the gift store. I wiped the sweat from my brow and sat down to wait, to find out if this was really going to happen, if my premonition would come true in the real world. My mother's vision we could never know if it was real or not, fortunately, but on this occasion, if the girl appeared at the time envisioned, it would prove to be true.

I was looking at that clock embedded in a hard black metal frame, with that aged glass, and it was almost the announced time.

A few footsteps could be heard arriving at the Barquera bridge. My mouth was dry, and I was very nervous. The first thing I saw around the corner were several reddish beings, as always small, blurred and fiery looking. Behind them and at a slow pace came the girl, like the procession of the Santa Compaña. Her image was exactly the same as the one I saw a few hours before: her white dress with a brown belt, the matching espadrilles and an esparto grass bag with *hippy-style* decorations hanging from her shoulder.

This was the first time I felt a change in the rhythm of time. As if out of nowhere, a shadow-like being appeared. Time was slowed down in the outside world, the girl walked about a hundred times slower than she had been walking, which was already depressing in itself. I believe that, at a given moment, especially in the face of danger, we have all felt that slowed-down experience of time. What happens is that in this case I was much more conscious of that temporal alteration. That other shadow was approaching me. Its hand with its fingers spread wide was approaching my face. Suddenly, I felt him wanting to penetrate my body, wanting to take control of me. I refused completely. It was like a spiritual battle to take the steering wheel of my material dimension. I could feel him pushing me into myself, as if my soul was falling gently down a figurative well. I forced him to have to ask permission.

"Let me do it, don't make it difficult for me. You and I both know it's for her sake."

"I can do it alone. I can avoid the fatal outcome without you," I replied.

"It's non-negotiable. Whether you want it or not, I will take control over you. You must respect that I can't risk it. You don't know anything about her, you won't know what she must feel and hear."

"I won't resist, but I don't want to be absent. I need to know what you do with me."

"I will grant your request. You came because you want to help her. I showed you this afternoon what would happen if there were no one here. I saw the goodness in you, I felt your anomaly, your perceptiveness. Thank you for helping me; I will repay you."

Hardly had the girl taken another step in our short conversation. I stopped resisting and this being entered me. The sensation was incomparable. I felt light and placid. The experience was very similar to the most pleasant dream one has ever had, but while awake. I could see myself walking towards her, but I was not the one giving the orders. She seemed amazed to see me there, waiting for her.

She stopped walking and it was I, or rather, her protector who slowly but steadily approached her, who was looking at me with glassy eyes and a melancholic gaze. Without a word, I took her by the waist and the two of us melted into a passionate kiss. She began to stroke my hair and I pulled her tight against me, still kissing her.

"Who are you?" she asked as if a thought had escaped her lips.

The esparto bag slipped off her shoulder and fell to the ground. Holding back tears welled up in her big, beautiful black eyes. I kissed her soaked, salty cheeks. I hugged her very tightly and stroked her hair for a while as she calmed herself down. Now her protector let me feel her pain, sadness and her almost destroyed soul of loneliness.

I had to admit that his protector's way of acting was the most effective. Sometimes I give advice that I don't follow through on. A short conversation I had with Kingsley earlier that afternoon came to mind. I was complaining about the stubbornness of many people, their inflexible square mentality. I was making a destructive comparison, and I told him a curiosity of aeronautical design.

The Comet commercial airliner was the first jet-powered airliner, traveling much faster than airplanes of its time. It is said that an executive saw the original design and complained that the passenger windows were rounded like a ship's skylight. The designer understood that this rounded shape distributed the stress of the metal evenly, but the executive was unhappy with the circular design and insisted that they be square. After a few months of service the fuselages suffered micro-cracks, specifically in the windows. These micro-cracks developed into small cracks caused by metal fatigue under the pressurization cycles. The result: several of these aircraft exploded in mid-flight due to the "square" stubbornness of an ignorant person. Aviation windows never again had straight corners. The square mentality transferred to physical levels caused deaths. And I, without realizing it, had behaved that way with his protector, and now I had to agree with him and, if necessary, apologize.

My bicycle was where I left, and we took a ride hugging each other along the road to the beach of Toró. Impulsively, she threw away the esparto bag, I guess with the rope, the stone and her farewell letter. Soon she disappeared submerged in the surf. I was still not in control. I was a mere spectator to a couple's leisurely conversation. It was clear that every word that came out of my mouth was completely accurate. It seemed to be just what she needed to hear to change her mind, to make her feel better, and at times she even died laughing. I would scoop her up and throw her over my shoulder like a sack, and in the middle of the silent night she would scream,

"Potatoes! Potatoes! Potatoes! Potatoes! To the rich potato! Hey!"

With those things she smiled endlessly. In those moments, I would dare say she was happy.

"I want to spend the night together," she said in a firm, sensual voice.

I wanted to talk to his protector, and he sensed my call. Again, time slowed down and I could hear his voice, deep but pleasant sounding.

"You are in great danger by spending so much time adopting my form. I don't know if you know it, but Natalia -that was the girl's name- is surrounded by evil beings. If they find the form, they will kill you, and I will go with you without remedy. And, honestly, I don't feel like having multiple personalities."

"I see that you know more than you should. But that doesn't mean that I don't agree with you."

"You can trust me, from here on I think I can do it on my own," I insisted pleadingly.

"I will do as you say. I know you will protect her. You are a link."

This phrase would make a lot of sense later. At the time, it just seemed like a catch phrase. As on that occasion with Nieves, the camp instructor, the shadow came out of me like a surfer taking off his wetsuit with the promise to meet again.

Natalia was a girl from a well-to-do family. Specifically, her father was an important and successful businessman. Our walk along the seafront was no coincidence. Almost unnoticed, Natalia approached a huge single-family house with a plot of land. She removed one of the bottom bricks and took out some keys. She opened the outer perimeter door and with a suggestive "Let's go!" invited me in. It was a huge house. I had never seen anything like it. In the minimalist living room an attic window let you see the whole sea, not an inch of land was visible. It was like being on the main deck of a motionless ship. The clouds illuminated by the full moon were reflected in the undulating tide of the Bay of Biscay.

She explained to me that this house was one of many empty homes that her father owned. That was not what gripped me. I could not tell her that my body and soul were attached to a woman from another time, and that I felt a duty of fidelity, it was madness. Everything would have been ruined, or worse, even worse than at the beginning.

Despite her young age, she was quite a woman and refusing her would have meant breaking my word to her guardian.

I had made a promise to myself, to fight evil. And I had also just made promised to be her protector. However, I was wrong. She only wanted to feel my selfless presence, my company, to reverse the cold of her loneliness. This was no time to hesitate and hurt her feelings further.

We took a small mattress and dragged it into the living room, facing the sea. We put it on the floor next to the window and sat looking out at the vast sea. We talked, but we also kept long silences. The situation was embarrassing and pleasant at the same time. She never confessed to me what she was planning to do that night, nor did I want to inquire about it. We were together, breathing at the same time, living the furtive freedom of an unshared secret. I took her hand and we intertwined our fingers, she gasped. I took off Kingsley's amulet and put it on her, still looking into her eyes.

"I'll lend it to you tonight, it will do you good, you'll see." I kissed her softly on the cheek, with true and pure love, with no ulterior motives.

We lay on the bed, and I covered her tenderly, wrapping my arms around her. We kissed slowly, her thin lips and dark eyes lost in wonder, asking, "How did we get here?" She whispered something in my ear:

"I can't do it, David."

"-I know, Natalia." I caught my breath, "I'm a little scared, I confess. I just want to be with you and for this moment to never end."

She leaned on my shoulder and wrapped her dancer's leg around me, holding my hand. Her breath gently relaxed as I stroked her hair, her back, her bare shoulders and her soul. Meanwhile, with her body on mine, sleeping with the peace of babies, I was unable to sleep a wink. I forgot to blink. Too many mysteries in the same day, too many sensations and novelties in a very short time.

The memory of my true love grew stronger and more distant, if that was possible. I didn't want to think about her, but it was inevitable. My heart was pounding in my chest like a boxer's fist. Inside me a disloyal lingering hidden in some corner of my memories seemed to nag at me, although it also made me feel the distant reflection of being with her.

With Angie.

Chapter 17
Projection

The sun was beginning to touch the surface of the sea. I would have loved to go to sleep that night, but it was impossible. I had to get home before I was discovered after my nocturnal excursion. She was sleeping peacefully on my chest; I was afraid to move, but I had no choice. I began to kiss her as I whispered her name in her ear, trying to wake her as gently as I could. Her eyes opened and her lips accompanied them with a smile.

"I have to go. If my mother catches me, she'll kill me," I said very quietly.

"You're lucky someone cares about you. My father is always traveling and the house maid stays out of my business. Will we see each other again?"

"Tomorrow after training and teaching, I can be at the station around nine o'clock, and then I'll take you to dinner. Is that okay with you?"

We sealed our date with a kiss full of newfound love.

"Well, I'll see you tomorrow at nine o'clock. But don't forget your pendant."

I stood there for a moment wondering whether to leave it with her until the next day, but I knew Kingsley would be very upset and it would be disrespectful.

"Tomorrow, when we meet, I'll lend it to you again."

"Don't worry, it's a very ugly pendant."

And she laughed without malice, ignorant of the immense power of the amulet. I laughed too, because she was partly right. I explained that it belonged to Kingsley's deceased brother, without mentioning its protective capacity. She immediately understood its value to me and apologized for her accidental rudeness.

"Come on, let's go, I'll pick all this up."

I helped her put the mattress on the bed in the main room and rushed out of there hoping to find my bike where I left it. Fortunately, I did, because in summer, with so many tourists drinking so much of our cider, you never knew what would happen.

That uphill climb was steeper than usual. I arrived home and the bedroom window was ajar. I opened it very carefully so as not to make any noise. I had to enter as a stealthy burglar would. Still, when I noticed Kingsley's face, I got quite a shock, because I didn't expect to find him staring at me so intently. I started to take off my clothes and put on my pajamas.

"How did it go?" he asked in a mischievous tone.

"All right, but go back to sleep; I'll tell you tomorrow."

"But it's already daylight."

"Yeah. Well, I'm dead sleepy. I'm falling down."

It was the truth. Before I fell asleep, I held the pendant up to my face and it still smelled like her. To be honest with myself, I was afraid of falling in love with this girl. I was full of turmoil. Tiredness took care of it all by making me forget and transporting me to the world of dreams.

"Are you all right, son?" my mother said to me, sitting on the edge of the bed, while stroking my bangs.

I woke up feeling unbearably tired. My eyelids weighed a ton. I struggled to open my eyes.

"Don Manuel, Julio's father, called me. He says he'll be here in half an hour and wants to talk to both of us. Are you getting up? Come on, it's already ten."

"I'm coming, Mom."

I sat up in bed, struggling again not to fall asleep sitting up.

"Were you with a girl yesterday?" my mother questioned me as she sniffed my sweatshirt. That woke me up, alright.

"Yes, I met a girl yesterday," I confessed, rubbing my eyes sleepily. "I might meet her today. She lives in Llanes."

My mother seemed strangely pleased and looked at me with a proud expression. Although she never told me, she had always been concerned about my reserved and introverted behavior. For her, seeing me with friends and girls was a source of joy.

"Well, tell me all the details later. Now hurry up, Don Manuel is on his way."

The truth is that Julio's father was already seeming like a pain in the ass to me. I just wanted to give those classes to his son, so he wouldn't have to spend more of his summer working on such dull subjects. And now, seeing so much interest on his part made me think that I should have been more discreet. I wondered what he would want from me. Because I know that no one insists without having an interest, so when he came to my home I kept a cautious attitude.

As always, my mother prepared coffee and brought out an entire army of pastries. We sat at the outside table. Kingsley had been gone, helping out my Uncle José since eight o'clock in the morning.

"Well, Leticia and David, I must admit that I am amazed at this boy's capabilities. He has an innate talent, that's no secret to anyone. What we have to decide now is whether to exploit this gift or, on the contrary, to ignore it and squander this virtue, like a flower that withers without attention. I ask you, Leticia, but the decision must be made by your son."

"Yes, Don Manuel, my son has always had high aptitudes, but can it really benefit him? Because my main concern is his happiness."

I kept silent, trying to figure out why don Manuel was really there. They kept talking.

"That is why the decision is your son's, as I have already told you. As a university professor, I have some room for maneuver, but it is very limited; however, I know those who can give your son the opportunity to take advantage of his full potential."

"What do you mean?" my mother asked skeptically as I listened attentively.

At least there was one good sign, and that was that Julio's father didn't have those reddish creatures hovering around him.

"There is a multidisciplinary program for high-performing young people. Every six months, tests are held in Madrid. The tests are individualized, and the number of participants is not exclusive. What I mean is that it is not a competition, it is an evaluation."

"And are these tests conducted by Ministry of Education officials?"

"Not exactly, ma'am. From what I understand, it is a very well positioned international and private collective. The recruitment of promising young people is only a very small part of their activity."

"And what do they get out of attracting talent?"

"Good question. They are like sports scouts. They are not an NGO, or the Little Sisters of Charity. It's about mutual interests, an opportunity for both entities, in this case your son and the corporation. How many geniuses today are working in a supermarket, or a gas station, or a bar, or whatever, wasting their gift?"

"I understand. However, this must be discussed with the boy's father and, most importantly, my son must want to take part," said my mother while she kept looking at me.

"You see, we have been fighting for years with the educational system, precisely for these exceptional cases, but for the moment the most that has been achieved is to study two years in one. If it were up to me, I would have him take the selectivity test tomorrow, and I am sure that in just one or two years later he would already have a university degree. I don't want to reproach myself for not having done everything I could to give him his chance."

I kept listening, thinking that sometimes less is more. A quiet life as before, at my own pace, was really comfortable, without having to prove anything to anyone. On the other hand, it is true that I was stuck, and for me time was running very slowly.

"And then, how do you deal with the studies of those who pass the tests?" my mother asked, puzzled. And this is when my interest was piqued.

"Look, it is a collective with a very hermetic policy. Their procedures in the preparation of candidates are approached with great discretion, but I do know that they generally study in the United States, where there are no brakes for the development of these young geniuses. Then, it is not necessary to validate anything, because there are no better universities in the whole world. This is what I have been told by the rector of our university, who is the one who would give us an invitation to take the tests. In fact, the next ones are less than a month away. That is why I am here so soon, to give you some time to think about it."

He finished his coffee and took a bulging white envelope out of his briefcase. He put it on the table.

"What is that?" asked my mother.

"It's an unfair amount of money for your son's work. We presented the project to the board with David's design and won the competition. It's just a small gesture, a down payment on everything that's to come, a remuneration as an external consultant, call it what you will; in any case, it's small, because fiscally I can't draw attention to myself. Now I must go. As soon as you have made your decision, whether it is affirmative or not, let me know."

"Thank you very much for everything, Don Manuel."

He got up and shook our hands, leaving the envelope on the table. We walked him to his Mercedes and just as he came, he left.

When my mother opened the envelope, she almost fell on her ass. It was a huge wad of blue ten-thousand bills. In all, there were a million and a half pesetas. My mother was nervous and uneasy. Neither of us had ever seen so much money together. Accustomed to austerity and radical scarcity, our situation at times bordered on poverty and need. My mother looked at me and said,

"Son, this money is yours, you have earned it with your ingenuity."

I downplayed the importance of the matter, and told her that what mine is the family's, just as they had always instilled in me.

When your priorities are clear, decisions become easy. I would fight with all my might for a chance in those exams, so I could travel to the United States. Now I had to talk it over with the old man. I hoped that my father would not object too much, because I knew that he and distrust went hand in hand everywhere. In my mind and in my heart, I had only one goal: to see Angie again.

The day was pretty typical: a hard workout at the gym, classes with the kids and back home, but this time with a stop in Llanes. I felt a little embarrassed. Natalia was waiting for me sitting on a wooden bench. Our eyes met before the train stopped, and her beautiful smile welcomed me. She looked lovely in that blue lace dress. I could tell she was fidgeting, though she tried to conceal it by tightly clutching her matching handbag.

It looked like something out of a movie. I got off the train and she came toward me giving me an effusive hug. Without meaning to, I lifted her off the ground, and as one of her feet tried to reach the firm one, her other leg bent backwards in a very feminine pose. We kissed uncontrollably, oblivious to people watching, we were in our own world. Her indelible, sweet, fresh scent transported me back to the night before. I was afraid, so afraid of falling in love. My heart was filled with the memory of Angie, but for some reason something encouraged me to live this new life. To look forward and leave the past behind. It will be the strength of the present, I thought.

It was absurd. I put up a shield for myself. I told myself that my relationship with Natalia was all theater. I thought of it as a job, an obligatory task that had to be finished off. I would be lying if I said that. The truth is that Natalia had something very special. It was her contradictions that made her so interesting; she seemed fragile, but at the same time she was very determined. Smiling, funny, affectionate, attentive. Who was I kidding, I liked her a lot. We looked like the Lady and the Tramp. She was so pretty and well-groomed, and I was in my almost worn-out tracksuit and dirty sneakers. It seemed that none of that mattered to her. Any excuse was a good one to hug me, taking my hand and forearm to be even closer as we walked.

My mother had given me a five thousand pesetas bill. At that time, that amount was a lot of money for a kid. I insisted on inviting her to dinner. She, who was from the village, had to choose the place. We arrived at a nice restaurant downtown. Its rustic but modern decor gave it a very original touch. When we arrived, the *maître d'* recognized Natalia and asked about her father, she gave short and diplomatic answers. It was clear that this detail had influenced our treatment, because they went out of their way to serve us with surprising care, preparing a table with beautiful views of the harbor. It was a very elegant place to go in a tracksuit, but what could you do?

The evening was going great. Without realizing it, I had lost my sense of reality. I let my guard down, I thought I was in control of the situation, until her appearance in the restaurant left me frozen. Undoubtedly, she realized something was up. My face had always been, from a very young age, the mirror of my soul.

She asked me about the reason for my sudden seriousness. I would have liked nothing better than to be able to tell her the whole truth, to tell her about the reddish men who were stalking her. I wanted to tell her that they were there to hurt her. And that, if nothing prevented them, sooner or later they would achieve their goal. They appeared out of nowhere, four of them again. From the way they moved around us, it was clear that they were up to no good. My main objective was to keep them from knowing that I was able to see them, although I wasn't sure if that was working. Seconds later, they disappeared.

With little finesse and pushed by the strange lightning visit of the beings, I began to ask uncomfortable questions, out of context.

"And you, Natalia, do you have any acquaintance who wishes ill for you?"

"What kind of question is that?" she said in an irritated tone.

"Forgive me. It's just that you seem to be worried about something, and I wondered if you were worried about someone specific. But don't answer if you don't want to. I don't want to spoil your dinner."

"Well, there is something, but I don't feel like talking about it, maybe another day."

"Don't worry. I understand, it's hard to talk about pain, I know." I was trying to get her to give in with that little challenge, but without being too insistent.

"Well, it's nothing very serious, but it worries me a lot because it has to do with my father," I kept silent, to encourage her to continue. "For a little over a year now, my father has not been the same. He is less and less at home, and when he is, he is more and more unfair and tyrannical with me. Just yesterday, before he left on his trip, we had a shouting match like never before, and I ended up saying some horrible things to him abusing my late mother's memory. I have always been, as he used to call me, his little fairy girl, but for a while now, it's all conflicts and bad feelings, and yesterday I unintentionally blamed him for my mother's death just to hurt him. I feel very very bad, and the only thing I want is to be able to ask him for forgiveness and for everything to go back to the way it was before, but I see it impossible. I think it's going to get worse and worse, that it's beyond repair, and that I'm going to be left without the only family I have left."

I held her hand, caressing the back of her hand with my thumb while I offered her the napkin as a handkerchief to dry her tears. Things were going well, now I needed to know the cause.

"And what has changed in your father in the last year, to make him so different?"

Now I could feel that she was letting off steam by talking about it. The conversation no longer had to be strained.

"It's all Gallego's fault. That bastard and his filthy business are driving my father up the wall. Damn it."

"And what does this Gallego do, if I may ask?"

"It doesn't matter. He's a jerk, arrogant and arrogant. Sooner or later, he will pay for everything he is doing."

"I'm sorry, but I don't really understand."

"Well, it's very simple, my father has several businesses going, but the most important one, what he calls his *modus vivendi,* is a chain of mechanics' workshops spread all over Spain. All these workshops require a logistics network for the distribution of spare parts. Well, this guy, under the pretext of investing capital in the company, wants to use this national network. Firstly, for the transport of drugs and, secondly, for money laundering, injecting the proceeds of crime and issuing false invoices of companies, all of them invented.

"They are just a smokescreen to bring the dirty money into the legal system, making it justifiable, in turn, with other companies that, according to his plans, will be clients of the first ones. A whole tangled and orchestrated plan to launder the countless amount of money he amasses at the expense of the health of so many people. My father, who has always been a man with an impeccable and honest background, does not dare to contradict him, he is terrified. If nothing else helps, in a month he will become part of the mafia headed by El Gallego and his thugs. It's the end, damn the day that man appeared in my father's life!"

I could feel her rage, it was as if she felt like hitting the table to vent so much anger. I tried to calm her down by stroking her face, so tense and enraged.

"I know someone who can help you. He deals with this sort of thing." I couldn't tell her it was me.

"That would be ideal. Too perfect. But I haven't believed in miracles for a long time."

"He's a professional. You'll never know who he is, but what he does always works. Don't you trust me?"

"I've known you for two days, David. That's all I'm saying." And he laughed without malice.

"Yes, but answer me this simple question: Am I good or am I bad?"

"What a crazy question. You are good. One of the best."

"Then trust me and let me help you. This is the chance to do something and that Gallego will never know who it was. He'll just leave you alone forever. I'm sure of it."

"And how much do the services of this friend of yours cost? I want to meet him."

I had to improvise on the fly because none of it was planned in my head.

"He never deals directly with the client. He always uses an intermediary, in this case me. It's better for everyone. I'm not even sure if he works alone. He only charges when he's satisfied that his operation is successful. A colleague of my father's, for something similar, was charged three hundred thousand pesetas."

"Okay. Then let him deal with it. The dog is dead, the rabies is over. And, if necessary, I'll take the money out of my father's safe myself."

"Natalia, no. He doesn't work like that. No one will die. He will you get him to divert his plan and forget about your father. I'm sure you'll be a united family again."

"And how do you know him?

"He is an ex-military man from the Special Operations Group. I know him because on occasion he has had to "mediate" in matters of sailors and merchants, both to finalize and to adjust those relations."

She thought for a moment, looking at the dessert plate.

"It doesn't hurt to try," she said, wrinkling the line of her lips.

"I am very glad to hear that. You will need all the information you can get: residence, places he frequents, relatives, vehicles, spouses, photographs. Get what you can, he'll take care of the rest."

"Tonight I'll take care of it and make a good summary of everything. But please let it go well, because that man, unlike your friend, has killed quite a few people. My father calls them the disappeared, because they are never found again."

"It will be fine. You have my word. Natalia, we have to go. The last train leaves at eleven."

"Won't you stay with me tonight?"

"I can't, I shouldn't lie to my mother today, she's a very astute woman. Bring that to me tomorrow and we'll get going with the solution."

I could stay and somehow work it out with my mother, but the truth was that I felt, in a way, that I was betraying Angie. I remembered our vows, especially the "till death do you part" vow. I suppose Angie would have rebuilt her life with another man. The logical part of my thinking told me that must be so. My greatest wish in life is that after my death she would be happy. I could never reproach her for anything, because the one who was gone forever was me. However, I had no excuse, because I was alive, in another place, with another body, but the same heart full of her and her memory.

Everything changed when I regained my memory in that infirmary at the swimming pool.

All.

Chapter 18
Scientific Method

I was trying to be my own best friend, to somehow stay the course of sanity, to see my chaotic situation and give myself advice from another perspective. I couldn't talk to anyone about this. My own shadow had forgotten me. I know, I knew that seeing the shadow was almost forbidden, but with that conversation in my room I had felt really free and understood, almost everything started to fall into place. Now, I had many doubts, because the risks I was taking were very high, I almost ended up seriously wounded the last time, and with this new commitment the risk was even higher. This was a very dangerous drug trafficker, with an organization behind him. All I was worried about was dying and losing the chance to see Angie, even if it was just once.

Natalia walked me to the station and made me promise to stay overnight tomorrow. I could not allow myself to fall in love with her. I refused to acknowledge that strong attraction. Again, half-truths.

I felt overwhelmed by the deadlines. Now I understood my father perfectly. I had to solve Natalia's problem in less than a month. In any case, within that time limit, I would have the test in Madrid. In a little more than two weeks my father would return from the campaign, increasing the difficulty of my maneuvers, and, if for whatever reason I did not pass that strange test, the new school year would begin soon after. Not to mention my commitment to the students I was helping and my daily attendance at the *muay thai* gym. The thought of it all was a little overwhelming.

I can say that the next night with Natalia was better than the first; also somewhat shorter. I was happy. I didn't have a heart attack, nor did my eyelids forget to work. Nor did the air trip over my parched throat nor had the feel of my tongue turned to sandpaper.

Natalia and I tested each other, alone, with delicate calm; but neither of us dared to jump the limits of romanticism. I think she needed time to recognize the moment and I needed time to try to escape it. Rather, that was my intention. The reality was quite different, for I could feel that she was capable of stirring my convictions by unleashing the irresistible hurricane of desire.

I assume, it was in her hands. My emotional block was barely holding when I had her in front of me and I won't be so hypocritical as to deny it.

My faithful and rational personality told me that the important thing was that she had given me a folder with all the information, but if I only said that I would lie again. I loved being with her and it scared me too. It was turning into an uncontrollable weakness that I didn't want to part with. I don't know which of us was more of a rascal; well, yes, it was me. Because as much as I wanted to build a wall, as much as I wanted to reinforce myself, her femininity, her sweetness, her love and what she was capable of making me feel was like a battering ram.

I admit it, men find it hard to say this because we have been taught that it makes us fragile and vulnerable. Now I don't believe that anymore because I'm sure it's the opposite, so I'll say it straight out: I was falling in love with Natalia.

Back to the subject, to the folder. There were several pages written in her own handwriting. It was nice to see her handwriting, as wavy as she was, little circles over the I's, colors under the headings of the information, the I's and the E's looked like U's. But, without a doubt, the most important thing, to get to the point, was that she had done her part.

I quickly got a picture of his profile. He was a man in his late forties, had two daughters and an ex-wife who lived in Ferrol. Currently, he was not married and, from some information about lunches and dinners he had with her father, I could deduce that every week he boasted of a new woman. He lived in a secluded house, with a good plot of land and access to the sea, located in a small village not far away called Lastres.

I guess the small sea dock was to have more exits in case of escape. He had several cars, but he mainly drove a blue Range Rover SUV. Unobtrusive, no outlandish fenders or weird pipes, but that, no doubt, in my imagination, I assumed that vehicle also obeyed an escape or reaction strategy.

Basically, and although there was much more information, this was the most relevant, because the rest did not mark lines of behavior, habits or customs, so I would have to observe all that on my own. However, a photograph of both of them hunting allowed me to put a face to the man who made Natalia and her father's life impossible.

I was worried about time. I wanted to do things right. I could not rush without making the necessary inquiries. I had to study the security of the house, the staff, the mode of access, their tastes and hobbies; and all this without the means at my disposal, trapped by my own limited domestic freedom. Needless to say, I had to do everything on my own. I had to think of everything.

First, the plan to get him to leave Natalia's father alone, and second, how I was going to be able to carry it out. Fortunately,

Kingsley would not be a problem to hide my nights out, and he was spending more and more of his days with my aunt and uncle, helping them with the farm and spending a lot of time with them.

I couldn't ride my bike or take my parents' car either, with my mother's keen sense of smell that was too risky.

Then I noticed my neighbors, the Albertis. They had a son who was studying in Salamanca. They were a very old married couple to whom I had more than once lent a hand with some errands. Mr. Alberti was almost deaf and used a hearing aid. His wife suffered from Alzheimer's, and the poor man had to be constantly on the lookout for her because on more than one occasion she had run away from home.

What was important for the plan that I began to formulate was that his son had a motorcycle in the garden of his house, wrapped in a cover and with the keys always in the engine. It was a country motorcycle, but more than enough for my job. Doing these things made me very nervous, but I had to learn to control my excitement, to stick to a well-thought-out plan so as not to be discovered, neither by my mother, nor Kingsley, nor the Alberti family, nor Natalia, nor, of course, Gallego; all that in less than two weeks.

I started by making a copy of the keys to my uncle's farm. There he had a huge fuel tank for the generators. That way I could avoid getting gas and being seen with the motorcycle in public. I went to a hunting store in Gijón and, under the pretext of the birthday of a civil guard relative, they did not question me at all when I bought a quick release holster for the Beretta, a belt, a knife, a tactical flashlight and binoculars. I imagine that my young age, my education and my innocent face were a perfect visa to avoid arousing suspicion.

Although the hunting store had camouflage clothing, I thought it was too much, so I went to several sports stores and bought the rest: mountain clothing without reflective elements, Kevlar gloves with wrist adjustment, a balaclava and some sneakers, all black. In addition, I bought a large waterproof sports bag, eight meters of black climbing rope, kerosene and a shovel. That same morning, before going home for lunch, I put everything in the backpack, except for the flashlight. I dug a good hole in the ground of the pine forest at the exit of the village, not without first making a mark on the tree under which I hid it, burying also the folding shovel closer to the surface. Then, stressed and in a hurry, I headed home to my mother.

My uncle and Kingsley looked like they had just come from war, both with their clothes full of mud and grease from their daily chores; they were talking funny because they were laughing out loud. Soon my aunt arrived with a chickpea salad, and we sat down at the table to eat. It was funny to see that my aunt and uncle had saved a place in between them for Kingsley. My mother kept thinking about when my father would return. I was looking forward to it too, but at the same time I needed time to accomplish this risky "mission".

After lunch and the usual coffee, almost everyone took a nap, and I took the opportunity to approach the Alberti's house. I could see that the cover was covered in leaf litter, so I deduced that nobody had touched the bike for a long time. The gate at the entrance to the driveway was always open, held in place with a small stop on the top hinge. At first, I thought about taking the bike out and putting it in every night, but then I came to my senses and concluded that it was a better plan to assemble some branches together in the shape of a motorcycle and put them under that cover. And that's what I prepared that afternoon, a scarecrow in the shape of a motorcycle. Nothing sophisticated, just a similar stuffing, and I left it on the side of the farm.

Then back to my usual routine, to the gym and teaching classes. Without them, I couldn't have bought any of it. I postponed my meetings with Natalia for a while to carry out my task and, despite her subtle insistence, I kept making excuses to avoid her.

That same night, I stuffed my bed with clothes, like a fugitive escaping from prison. While Kingsley, who was slowly learning Spanish thanks to my aunt and uncle, asked me when he could meet Natalia's friends. I couldn't do everything, but I made a mental note to do this for him; I owed him a lot more than he imagined.

Once again, I felt that familiar sensation of doing the forbidden: the tingling, the agitated breathing and the racing pulse. I breathed and calmed myself inside the Alberti's lot, crouched in the dark. I could see the glow of a television set on in the nighttime blackness of the alcove. I dragged the branch frame up to the height of the holster and uncovered the motorcycle; the gun was heavy, but in the holster it would be more comfortable. The flashlight had several colored filters, so I shined it with a dark shade of green, and I could confirm that it still had the keys and next to it a full-face helmet. I put it in neutral and pushed it a couple of meters supporting it again on the kickstand. I placed the branches firmly with some rocks and covered everything with the cover. Then I threw some dead leaves on it and contemplated it without haste, confirming its stability and making sure that the lure would not fail me.

Before leaving, I put on the helmet, in case I needed to hide my identity, and pushed the bike to a secluded spot. I turned the key in the ignition, crossed my fingers and pulled the starter lever while accelerating with my fist. The magical rumbling noise of the engine flooded me with joy. Let's go! To the backpack and to Lastres.

I reached the place where I had hidden the bag. I cut a piece of the rope and tied it to the back seat. The paranoia that someone was watching me kept me on my toes the whole time. I covered the hole again with sand, twigs and leaves, hid the shovel again, and hooked a branch to the back of the motorcycle so that it would drag along the ground and erase the tire marks behind me.

I will not deny that at one point I was plagued by doubt. I asked myself why I took so much risk and if I wanted to get into trouble. The first thing that came to my mind was that I was doing it to fight evil, what I told myself last time, to improve my environment as much as possible. This time I dug a little deeper and realized that, despite behaving altruistically, deep inside me there was also an egoist, an addict to the curiosity of pushing limits, strong emotions and the taste of success. I had to be careful with the abundance of zeal or it would become another weakness.

I was beginning to like what I was doing.

It took me a little more than half an hour to get to Lastres, and another half an hour to find the Gallego mansion. The dark night was my involuntary accomplice. I passed through the gate without slowing down too much. Here I saw four white glimmers with an almost invisible red spotlight facing in all directions: they were closed-circuit television cameras.

About fifty meters from the entrance, I examined the terrain calmly to decide which would be the best strategic observation point where to set up my position. I rode the motorcycle up to a small path at idle speed, without lights, as in the old days, and from there I continued on foot, hiding the motorcycle among the trees, ready for my escape.

I once heard a police chief in a television series narrate how they had caught a small gang of professional thieves. According to this policeman, every thief who enters a place usually takes things, but also leaves other things behind. He was referring to evidence, traces, vestiges, instruments. This small gang, in its first robbery, was exaggeratedly cautious with details, but little by little, who knows if it was due to overconfidence, clumsiness or simple laziness, it began to make mistakes in planning and attention, to the point of being identified, located and arrested by the servants of good and order. Attention to detail, more attention, and then a little more attention. That's how I wanted to do my task.

Completely hidden among the vegetation, I applied the well-known scientific method of investigation, starting with observation. Armed with a pair of powerful binoculars, from the intermediate height of that hill I took out my notebook and pencil and began to make a sketch of the entire residence, so to speak, because it was a full-fledged security complex.

Lying there, vigilant, I realized that my behavior was part of a behavior internalized by the military training received in the United States. A *flashback came to my* mind of that sergeant shouting,

"Never go near the crest of a hill! Your silhouette would stand out! Tell me you understand, Private Sanders!"

I still had no definite plan. The fact of reassembling the Beretta was still against the most fundamental of my principles: to do no harm to anyone. I understood its use as a final solution and deterrent. It was a tool to bend the will of anyone who was willing to kill me. Something that, when the time came, would offer me an alternative for survival. That was the reality, but there was also another underlying reality, deeper if possible and also simpler. I was afraid that everything would go wrong.

At ten past one in the morning, someone came out of the farm. He was wearing a kind of work uniform; he looked like a household employee. In his right hand, a white garbage bag. I saw a thin man watch him walk slowly and sluggishly to the end of the street with to the bins. The one watching had an attentive gaze, was about six-foot-four, with a sharp face, serious countenance, long sideburns, pointed boots, tight-fitting clothes and long coat. The classic guy who isn't scary, but who you wouldn't think of disrespecting. The key to that look was in his eyes, full of pain and strength; later I understood that that inherited and transported energy was the key to his atavistic look. Undoubtedly, it had to be him, his security chief, the one everyone calls "Sideburn."

As the garage door opened, I noticed that the interior walkway was flanked on its edges by a thick wrought metal fence, the end of which was again presided over by another mechanical garage door. This time, the gate also opened into the corridor. I could understand that this design must have been intended to slow down and hold back as much as possible the entry of police vehicles or other unpleasant visitors, giving them time to make the evidence of their dishonorable business disappear and flee.

While staring at Sideburn from a distance, perfectly hidden in the brush and motionless, without any apparent cause he stopped looking at the employee and directed his gaze directly at me.

As if a sixth sense had told him: "Hey, buddy, there's a guy up there planning to screw you over". I almost made the grave mistake of moving in fear. I took a deep breath to calm myself as I held his defiant gaze. I knew the lenses of my binoculars were anti-reflective, so nothing physical could get his attention. Only his intuition alerted him to my presence. But like so many people, he still did not know how to interpret that intangible perception that had warned him of a threat.

He turned his attention back to the returning employee, if possible, even more slowly. From his body language, I knew that he gave him several instructions, and stood in the street waiting for the door to close. He took some keys out of his right pocket, unlocked a car of Swedish origin, rare in Spain, which was parked outside the compound, and placed his coat stretched over the back seat. As he was about to sit in the driver's seat, he looked up again right where I was, sharpening his eyes as if trying to see the invisible. I guess he felt that strange sensation of someone watching you, sometimes you look up suddenly and, without knowing why, you find someone staring at you, smiling or not, but it doesn't usually fail. At other times, that same feeling comes over you and when you look you find nothing, but that doesn't mean that there isn't someone watching, it just means that you can't see them.

Finally, Sideburn left, and I saw in that garbage bag an opportunity to discover something more about Gallego's habits. It was going to be gross, but this is not a glamorous movie. I made all the notes from that stakeout. As I could see, after two o'clock in the morning all the lights were turned off, all except for one small one where a watchman stood guard during the night. I was not entirely sure, but it seemed to me that he was armed. From time to time he would make a round, lazily, rather short. Then he would just sit there, with the only company of a small stove. I could put my hand in the fire, and I don't think I'd burn it, I mean he'd get a good night's sleep. Better for me.

From three o'clock onwards I devoted myself to burying the waterproof backpack, and although it took a lot of effort, I put the pistol and the magazine inside it. As I did near home, I left the shovel close to the surface and paid close attention to cover the marks of my passage there. With great stealth, I climbed back down on the bike, and before leaving I quietly opened that garbage can and hooked the bag onto the handlebars; a little further on I placed it firmly. On the way home I could see blue lights patrolling on the horizon in the distance. I stopped and waited for them to disappear before continuing my journey.

I was really tired, between all the ruckus of the day and the tension of my observation post, I was really fatigued and terrified by the humidity of the terrain. I hid the motorcycle and next to it I left the garbage bag to check out the next day. I didn't know where else, but in my village, I know well where hunters, hikers, rangers and any spontaneous strangers hang out. The place where I hid the motorcycle was the safest of all, despite this and true to my self-imposed discipline, I thoroughly cleaned any fingerprints I might have left on it and again with a branch I erased all my tracks to the roadway. Then I continued on foot home. With every car, with every strange sound I heard in the distance, I hid.

Prudence was my standard, and darkness my consort.

As usual, Kingsley had left the window ajar for me. This time no one was waiting for me awake; I guess routine normalizes habit. I tucked the little notebook under my mattress, put on my pajamas and went to sleep contentedly. The night had been very productive.

The next day, I opened the notebook to analyze the data I had written down. That handwriting, written in the dark, looked like that of a madman without eyes. With difficulty, I wrote down all the information. I had recorded the time it took for the doors to open and close, the time and frequency of the watchman's walks, approximate distances, structure and hypothesis of the interior of the house, the place where the alcove where the Gallego slept must be, access to the wharf, etc.

At noon I returned with all the care in the world to the place where I had left the motorcycle and the garbage bag. Crouching down and looking around, I began a thorough examination of the inside of the bag in chronological order. The first thing I pulled out was a small carton of orange juice; I figured he'd had it before bed. He had roast chicken with mashed potatoes for dinner. He must have showered before dinner: a disposable razor confirmed it. Shortly before the shower he had to open the mail; I only found one envelope, the return address was his two daughters. Perfect, now I had the exact address of her family in Ferrol. Another crumpled paper was nearby, several sheets of paper with quantities and places, printed with a dot matrix printer, indecipherable, but relevant.

It was obvious that this criminal did not take the proper measures of caution and erasure of traces. I wondered how such a good-for-nothing had amassed such a fortune by being so stupid. Suddenly, his mistakes made me more confident and also gave me a powerful lesson in caution. Little by little, my plan was taking shape and a clear idea was building in my head; a little more information over a few days would give me the final key.

The time stopped overwhelming me, it was going to be less difficult than I thought, but not easier.

Chapter 19
Mixing

Galicia-Principality of Asturias, summer of 1996

I met Javier, my dear friend from school. Coincidentally, his parents were coming home for a few days to visit family. I wondered if he would have a Sevillian accent now. We owed each other more than a quick visit. I had the strange impression that our lives would never again run parallel, but, at the same time, his timely presence was necessarily part of my goal.

I have never been materialistic, but in order to fulfill my plan, I needed certain objects that were difficult to acquire. I needed a small loan from Javier. I knew he would not object or ask annoying questions. He never had any doubts about the direction of my actions. It could be said that he was one of the people who knew me best, and not because I went on at length explaining my personality, quite the contrary. We practiced the language of silence.

He knew that all kinds of ideas could arise within me, but they all had to pass through certain filters to become reality: the filter of opportunity, the filter of reasonableness, the filter of feasibility, but undoubtedly the last and most important, the insurmountable one, the filter of goodness. Curious subjective concepts, clear and at the same time diffuse, so intermingled at times that they become impossible to distinguish, and, although much time had passed since we last saw each one another, our relationship was identical to the day he left.

I spent that whole morning with him. I brought him up to date, telling him about the trip on The Beluga, Kingsley, Natalia and my possible test in Madrid. I noticed his concern. He and I had been as thick as thieves. The possibility of studying abroad reflected the vivid image of loss on his face. Everything else was unimportant to him, he just wanted to know about that possibility, the possibility of an infinite ocean between us and, with it, the unlikely possibility of seeing each other more often. I understood his insistence as a show of affection for me and made him think it was unlikely I would even pass.

This time it didn't work, he took it for granted that I would be noticed, and, suddenly, an expression of sadness escaped him imagining our mutual absence. It seemed so far away at the time, so immersed in executing my plan. Now I know myself better and I know that my mind works in stretches, tasks accomplished, first A and then B, even though they are very close. I was infected by his emotion and, with my good friend Javier there, I already began to miss him before we parted again. Unfortunately, that is a feeling I know all too well.

In the end, I almost came back without what I was going to borrow from Javier: a Polaroid instant camera. My small savings were about to disappear almost completely; luckily Javi did me this big favor. Finally, he said he would give it to me, in exchange for one last snapshot together. I told him he was an exaggerator, like all Andalusians, but he didn't smile and with some reluctance looked at the picture before putting it away.

I had to ask my best friend to do something out of the ordinary: to lie for me. I needed to be away from home that night, and he had to be my alibi. I made up that Natalia and I wanted to spend it together. I knew him very well, he never wanted to get off the right track, but at the same time he was enthusiastic about my love affair and, in anticipation of my coming change of continent, he agreed to cover for me that night. I told him that in the afternoon I would return, and so call my mother from his house, with him in front so as not to arouse suspicion. He seemed surprised at the coldness of my terse orders.

That day I had to cancel my classes and gym attendance. I didn't care about the boys' classes, but missing *muay thai* made me feel a strong remorse. I had to travel to Ferrol as part of the plan. At five in the afternoon I arrived at Javi's house, again, and from there we called my mother to confirm that I had arrived and was staying with him at his parents' house. A metallic sound rang in my backpack, it was some tools that I was carrying along with the balaclava and some gloves. Javi didn't want to ask anything, but I could feel him doubting the veracity of my story. I guess he preferred not to inquire any further. My romance with a girl from Llanes, wanting to spend the night together, and now the sound of tools in my backpack, was far-fetched enough. But we went back to practicing the language of silence.

I didn't dawdle a moment longer, and hurried to the bus station. I got a round-trip ticket to Ferrol, and waited in the dock for a long time, among strange people and smells of diesel. Finally, the bus from Santander to La Coruña arrived, making numerous stops along the way, like the one in Llanes.

I tried to sleep a little, but nothing, the rattling and my nerves prevented me from doing so. I started to watch the movie they were showing, and the five-hour trip was quite short. Finally, I arrived at the village. It was completely dark, I oriented myself with a map that I had previously photocopied in the library and eating a chocolate bar I went straight to the house of the ex-wife of the Gallego. I watched quietly from outside, out of sight of the neighbors, but nothing as sophisticated as usual.

It was clear that the place did not have any security measures out of the ordinary in a normal house. I visually confirmed that there were indeed two girls inside. Around eleven thirty, a man came out of the house; they seemed to be arguing about why he couldn't stay the night. She explained that the house belonged to her ex-husband and that he had strictly forbidden another man to spend the night there. It was clear that the bastard didn't know anything about her ex-husband, because he said stupid things like: "Let him come here and say that to my face, I want to talk to him and explain a couple of things to that retard". She was worried that a neighbor might hear this outburst, and at the same time she begged him to shut up, and he replied again. He looked like he'd had a couple of drinks or was just trying to be macho. Whatever it was, he was foolish and ignorant, a man who didn't know who he was talking about.

Finally, and reluctantly, the man walked away with his jacket in his hand, grumbling until I lost sight of him. I noticed that, as he left, the door of the little house was not locked. I remained standing there, motionless and hidden by some reeds. I waited for a couple of hours until all the lights were off. I did some running on the spot for a few minutes to unwind my body and returned to the door of the house. I felt strangely calm, because besides the fact that it was only a woman and two girls, in case something went wrong, I had the whole forest to get out, escape and hide.

Before approaching, I pulled out the flexible plastic, which was nothing more than the classic fluorescent emergency exit signage found in every garage. I approached the door with my ski mask and gloves on. I slid the plastic into the doorjamb until it gently bumped against the slider, spun the plastic around on its wedge shape forcing it into the crevice and click, the door opened without making the slightest noise. I carefully closed the door, holding the latch, and then I began to feel it was for real. I turned on the flashlight with the navy-blue filter, with a very dim intensity, and climbed the stairs leaning on the railing and the extreme side of each step, thus avoiding the warping sound of the wood.

In the midst of that dark silence, I could only hear the wheezing of my agitated breathing. I stood still for a few seconds and managed to calm its rhythm. When I reached the corridor of the upper floor, I had to pass by the bedroom of the ex-wife, who was sleeping on her stomach, I opened the door and the children's decor of the next one pointed me to the little girls' room. They slept in beds separated by a bedside table, in front of them a large, elongated desk full of drawings and crayons. I had no desire to appreciate their art, but what I saw forced me to stop for a second.

In one of the drawings, the figure of a gentleman in a suit and tie was surrounded by four little friends, all painted red. The drawing was entitled *Dad and his helpers.* Very carefully, I took the sheet of paper, folded it into four parts and put it in my pocket. I wrapped the camera in a T-shirt to reduce the noise of its mechanisms and took a picture of each of the girls, who were sleeping like angels. I was worried that the *flash* might wake them up, but it didn't. I carefully put the camera and photos in the backpack, and stealthily made my way to the door, placed the plastic back between the slider and the frame, and closed it from the outside without making a sound. Everything went perfectly. I was already outside. As if I had never gone in there.

It was a little after three in the morning, and I had all night to wait until half past nine for the bus to pass. I followed the signs to the beaches and walked for quite a while. When I got to the sand, what was my surprise that the beach was already quite busy with travelers on the Camino de Santiago. Better for me, I wouldn't stand out among those people. I strapped my backpack across my chest, slipped the straps over my shoulders and went to sleep as best I could, with one eye open.

In the morning, with sand everywhere, I shook myself like a dog and went in search of a hot cup of coffee. I needed to clean myself up a bit; my stiffened face was full of salt and grime, and I think my breath was capable of killing a pack of rats. After an express wash, I was more comfortable. Sipping that piping hot coffee, careful not to be seen by anyone and sitting at that little bar table, I took out the photos to see them for the first time. They were perfect, just as I wanted. I took out the drawing and looking at it, incredulous, I told myself that those characters accompanying their father were who they had to be. At least one of the girls could see them too. I was no longer the only one in the world with that faculty. The developing, elastic and adaptive mind of those girls was not yet disconnected by synaptic pruning, nor badly influenced by adult denial of a parallel reality full of mysteries and unknowns.

That drawing made me feel more "normal".

Back on the bus, I couldn't resist sleep and fell asleep listening to the voices of the other sleepy travelers. As I arrived, I tried to stretch out as best I could, without being rude. My first such long trip alone, at the age of sixteen, and committing a crime of breaking and entering and, although I know that no one would miss that drawing, another crime of theft. The important thing for me was not to lose the final objective and not to cause any damage along the way.

I came home at lunchtime, and everyone was waiting for me. My uncle told me I smelled like a hobo. I wasn't going to argue with him, but I was amazed at his sense of smell. I took advantage of a few minutes before sitting down at the table and took a quick shower. There was only one topic of conversation at the table: my father's return. In a few days we would have him home; I was impatient to be with him, but more impatient to finish my task.

Despite the desire to take a well-deserved nap, in my line, disciplined, I went to give the classes I had committed to and after that I went to pound my body with elbows, kicks and punches. At the last minute I spent just enough time with Natalia, who did not understand what was going on and demanded more attention. I could do no more, I had to rest as much as possible to be at full capacity the next night. We kissed passionately, and before taking the train she told me,

"Sometimes I think you're a stranger, so much your own, I never know what you're thinking."

I kept my opinion so as not to go deeper into that matter. I hated talking about myself, because in doing so I always made mistakes with incongruous phrases of experiences not lived, at least not in that life.

I had learned by dint of incomprehension to hide my thoughts. My whole existence was necessarily a great secret. I analyzed others meticulously to say to each one what was most appropriate. Although with Natalia it was very different, she did not deserve a silence, but even less a lie. I felt guilty about it. Under no circumstances could I tell her the truth, although I swear I would have loved to. My reality was impossible to digest, it would simply be a breaking of schemes without any benefit for anyone. But Natalia, as an intuitive and strong-willed woman, was certain that I was hiding something from her and the rest of the world.

As I boarded the train, I gently let go of her hand, but she would not look at me. Without waiting for the train to close the doors and start moving, she began to walk down the platform, away from me. I walked down the aisle of the car dodging the rest of the travelers, trying to catch up with her in the vague hope that her deep eyes would fix on me and maybe a silent smile would say, "I love you," "I want you," or "You are important to me"; I would make up the message myself. But none of that happened. The train started in the opposite direction and I lost sight of her with my face pressed against the glass.

I had a feeling I was losing her.

I came home and my mother noticed my concern. She asked me what was wrong. Like so many times before, I told her nothing. This time we were having dinner at my aunt and uncle's house. It was Kingsley's big mouth who told her that he was sure I was like that because of that girl. Damn moment when he started speaking Spanish, and hearing me say that made me laugh. My mother and Kingsley looked at me puzzled, although they were used to my madness, as we walked around town on that pleasant summer night.

I decided to tell her. My mother listened attentively to the story I painstakingly described. She then gave me some great advice.

"You have to surprise her. She needs to feel you close. She thinks she's losing you. I'm sure she does."

"Mom, if you were her, what would you want me to do for you, a gift, a love letter?"

"How old you are, son. You should go to where she is and surprise her, the best gift is you."

"Yeah. So what do I do? -Shall I go tomorrow?"

"Of course not. Have a quick dinner and go see her today. Enjoy what you have together. You're on vacation. It's not all about teaching and training, son."

Puzzled, I took a moment to assimilate my mother's words and, at full speed, I answered,

"Okay, I'll listen to you."

"There are no parents in the world who have a more responsible child. Be careful with the bicycle, stand to the side if cars are coming, and if you are very intimate with it use pro..."

I had to interrupt her out of embarrassment, and she burst out laughing. She was happy for many reasons, with me, the family, with Kingsley and, of course, excited about the imminent return of her longed-for husband.

I had to translate a few things for Kingsley because, although he was getting the hang of Spanish, he still missed a few things. He was looking at me in amazement, as if to say, "No more leaving the window open" making thumbs-up gestures of success and nodding his head.

My paranoid mind began to wonder if my mother already knew about my nocturnal excursions, or if I was simply getting older and my margin of freedom was widening. Two nights away from home in a row was something unusual. In any case, I didn't think too much about it, I finished my dessert in a hurry and my uncle asked,

"Where are you going in such a hurry, Romeo?"

Damn, everyone already knew that.

"He's in love," Kingsley said slowly, almost spelling it out in his Nigerian tone.

Everyone laughed, including me. They wished me luck, asked me to be very careful on the road and not to forget my house keys.

I took a quick shower, alone at home. I combed my hair and dressed accordingly. The soft smell of my cologne blended with the sea breeze making a mixture that I still remember as if it were yesterday. I took the bicycle, but only to get to the motorbike. I exchanged one for the other, and again, very carefully, I erased my trail and made sure no one saw me.

I arrived at her house and rang the doorbell. I knew her father was away again, only a maid with little interest in Natalia lived with them Monday through Friday, and her job was not to watch her.

"Who is it?"

"Natalia, it's David. Come on down, we're going for a walk."

"But what are you doing here?"

"I needed to see you. Come on down."

"I'm coming," she said excitedly after a pause that seemed interminable. I could not lose her.

She opened the doorway dressed in jeans, Converse sneakers and a pink T-shirt with letters on it. She looked great.

"Put on the helmet."

"Where did you get this bike?"

"I borrowed it for today."

She put on the only helmet available, climbed on the back and hugged my waist. I caressed her intertwined hands and, looking straight ahead. I was glad to have her with me, together again. I started the bike, put it in first gear and accelerated a couple of times on idle before releasing the clutch, just like in the old days. I felt her chest resting on my back as we rode along that national road towards the Pimiango viewpoint. Twenty minutes separated us from there.

On the way, I caressed her thigh with my left hand. I wanted the trip to run along the waterfront; it was nicer and there would be fewer civil guards who might be surprised that I was riding without a helmet.

She told me she'd never been there before. It was a very special place for me. A lookout made of concrete, raised above the horizon, overlooking the sea as far as the curve of the land could see. The rotating lights of the lighthouses illuminated the dark immensity of the sea at times. Picnic tables made the place a good family meeting point where on more than one occasion we had all gathered for a picnic.

Up here we hugged, her skin was goose bumps. I took off my shirt and put it on her, but she wasn't cold. She was so thin that it was far too big for her. We started kissing and gradually lost control, undressing each other and fucking each other hard. She moved the reins of my passion at her whim. The clothes were an obstacle that prevented us from feeling our bodies and the dim light of a distant streetlamp became our stage light.

Without contemplation, we gave ourselves to each other, melting into one body. All my fear of losing her had disappeared, blurred by the fire of excitement, the harmony of our caresses and the whispers interrupted by gasps. I was totally in love with her. Natalia was setting the pace of our first time. She possessed me. We understood each other without speaking, looking into each other's eyes, crossing the expectation, the conventional borders of reality. Finding ourselves in a blurred bubble of secluded solitude, ecstatic to share our first surrender to love.

Exhausted, with the notion of time diluted, we lay embracing in the grass and stared at each other, aware of our connection beyond the physical. I could feel her heartbeat on mine, her crystalline essence. The beauty of her spirit surpassing affection, entering the walled fortresses of my heart. Inserting inside me the seed of an indelible memory.

I was afraid to let myself enjoy the feeling. I was free yet I was not. I stood up roughly breaking the magic of the silence and the slight rumble of our calm heartbeats.

"What's the matter?" she said softly, sleepily, looking at me.

"We have to go. Time with you slips like water through your fingers, thief."

I kissed her mischievously.

She sat up like a forced early riser, looked at me and smiled embarrassed at her laziness, stretching with a shy smile. Carefully, I helped her put on her helmet while she held her long hair in a bun on her head. I opened the visor and gave her an affectionate tap on the nose, closing it again. I started the bike and, enjoying the road and the dark landscape, we arrived at her house, this time said goodbye properly. I stayed in the doorway until I heard the door close on the inside of the landing and the light in the stairwell go out. Her room lit up, and this time it was I who left without looking back.

I felt torn in acknowledging my feelings, disloyal to Angie and clueless about my program. I had to seriously focus. Discipline was the word that kept coming to mind.

Inside me there were two colors, two loves, and all that was mixing; I could not allow it. Sentimental contradictions, mixed emotions.

I was a real mess.

Chapter 20
Liaison

Once home I almost entered through the window; habit, I guess. I had to turn around again. It was about two o'clock, almost three in the morning; my mother was waiting up for me, excited to see me. That made me think she knew nothing of my previous nocturnal escapades.

"Thank you very much, Mom, for letting me go out and giving me such good advice."

I noticed that my mother's lip trembled a little; excited, she seemed to relive love through me.

"You don't have to thank me, son, you're almost an adult. So, tell me, tell me, how did it go with the girl."

It was hard for me to open up and even harder to talk about these intimacies, but my mother had earned the confidence. I had to twist the details, omit my contradictions and, even with those, I almost escaped the motorcycle ride, letting it slip away. That's when I realized that to be a good liar you have to have a memory like an elephant.

We shared that time with a hot drink, and soon after I wished my mother goodnight with a big kiss. She let me rest at my leisure, and I was going to need it. I was scheduled to go to the Gallego's house the next night and nothing was going to stop me.

From the moment I woke up, I spent the whole day restless, nervous that the time would come when everything would be over. That morning I got up only a little later than usual, made my bed, asked my mother if I could help her with anything, and after that I went to the forest to check the order of everything I was going to need that night.

The afternoon was routine, I was a little absent-minded teaching class, and at the gym I tried not to overexert myself, I didn't want any annoying pains or stiffness latter. Not that night. I didn't even talk to Natalia; nothing should distract me. Back home, I was imagining what I would do; I had a more or less clear idea, but the unpredictable behavior of the moment might require me to improvise. Remembering the terrain and the escape routes was fundamental.

Finally, the moment arrived. This time I left as usual, through the window. Kingsley was awake, he asked me if everything was all right. Of course not, I was about to go to the house of an amoral drug dealer to risk my life. With a smile I told him that on Sunday we would meet a friend of Natalia's and spend the day at the beach, surfing, playing paddle, volleyball and water polo with the girls. He looked at me incredulously, but immediately knew that I was not lying and again that huge smile made us share a fleeting moment of happiness, living in our minds the illusion of that day at the beach.

I left the house and, on the uneven ground of the roadside, I walked to my hideout. I took the motorcycle and set off, on my way, determined to try to enjoy fighting against evil and helping, anonymously, Natalia and her father.

Once there, I unearthed the satchel and put on all the clothes I had bought for the occasion. I firmly fastened the buckle to secure the gun holster to my waistband, fed the magazines, chambered a round and disengaged the manual safety. With my finger parallel to the slide of the gun, I slid it into the holster. I anchored the knife, positioned it firmly on my belt, put on my gloves and balaclava, slung the black rope over my shoulder and tossed the kerosene into the opposite side pocket where I kept the photos of his daughters and the drawing.

I arrived at the observation point and kept an eye on Sideburn while he confirmed the security of the fort they called home. As usual, with punctuality, at a quarter past one he got into his dark Saab, started up and left.

"Good! They follow the routine," I said to myself, watching through the binoculars.

The next time I looked at the clock it was two o'clock. I waited patiently warming up my wrists, neck, knees and ankles. Once I saw him start to check the perimeter, I ran at full speed to the darker end of the fence near his sentry box. I figured that was a blind spot for the cameras, but I didn't really care.

I threw the rope over the top with a simple, wide gauze knot. The second time, it snagged on two barbs of those tall spears that guarded the passage to the interior. Aware of the adrenaline rushing through my muscles, I made an exercise of self-control to keep from making noise. I unhooked the rope, threw it to the ground and climbed down like a cat. I looked at my watch and quietly picked up the rope. There was no reason to be in a hurry, plenty of time to spare. I followed the watchman's steps, sneaking along the plants, blurring my silhouette with the surroundings, and I stopped next to two imposing Asturian chestnut trees that gave the estate that natural landscaped touch. They would serve as a support for the first phase of the plan.

I prepared some loops with the rope on the thick trunk of the trees and, having done this, I looked at my watch. In less than a minute the watchman was due back. With the pistol in my hand and my arm crossed over my chest, I waited patiently for his return. My heart wanted to escape from my chest, and I kept repeating to myself: "Calm down, calm down".

He was already approaching. He walked shuffling his heels at the beginning of each step, I heard him yawning and passing the trunk where I was waiting for him, hidden and impatient. I positioned myself right behind him, synchronizing my steps with his, and placed the barrel of my gun on the back of his neck.

"On your knees! I won't say it again!" I hissed at him in a low voice. A little nudge of the cleaved pistol on his flesh was enough to snap him out of his panic and make him obey.

"As you can guess, I must take the gun from you." As I disarmed him, I continued talking to him, "I want you to know that I have immense respect for your work: protecting people and putting your own safety at risk to preserve the safety of others is certainly something you should be proud of. If you don't do anything foolish, you will be able to tell the tale, and believe me when I tell you that you will not feel any remorse when you find out what kind of person is sleeping there peacefully, while you fear for your life."

I allowed some time for him to chew on what I was telling him and, without further ado, I continued,

"Strip down to your underwear," I demanded unceremoniously.

I didn't want to be cruel, but the psychological effect of nudity in that context would reduce any initiative and bend his will to mine. It was necessary. It was clear to me that before hurting that gentleman I preferred to abort my plan, everything depended on his voluntary collaboration.

I took the kerosene tablet out of my pocket, softened by my body heat, and asked him to spread it generously over his wrists. I made him put on his own shackles; clear orders, behind his back and with the locks facing his elbows. He knew why. I went over to check them and tightened them a little more without cutting off circulation. I pressed the lock buttons so they couldn't accidentally close any more. In the middle of that night darkness, for a moment I felt ashamed of what I was doing when I saw that older watchman in his underwear; it was a small moment, but I quickly got over it.

I went through all his pockets, removed his belt and checked his jacket. All his belongings I left on the ground out of his reach. I walked over to him and threw his pants in a heap on the ground next to the tree. I made him sit on them, with the handcuffs below his knees. With the surfing pad I smeared more grease all over his neck and placed the rope I had previously prepared around it.

Thanks to my father and the sea life, I was an expert in knots. He looked at my eyes between the holes of the balaclava. When I met his gaze, he immediately withdrew it, evading the provocation and showing submission, ignorant of the apparent concoction he had formed with the rope. He followed my movements as one who enjoys seeing the skill of the other. I placed the remainder of the rope towards the tree in front of me, holding tightly the revolver aimed at the watchman's chest. With one of his shoelaces I tied the rope to the trigger and explained,

"You are tied in such a way that if you move more than twenty centimeters you will trigger the revolver and cause your death. If by any chance of fate that should fail, which I completely doubt, the knot you have tied around your neck is tensile and, when you try to sit up or move, it will tighten without remedy, more and more, causing your death by asphyxiation."

"Why are you doing this?" he asked hesitantly.

"I have already told you, my friend, that you have all my admiration, even if you can't see it now, I assure you that we are on the same team. Don't kill yourself and don't try anything, everything you can think of in these hours I've been calculating for weeks."

I turned my head sideways so that he could see the expression on my lips and understand that I was serious.

"I hope you wore clean socks today." I took one of the ones on the floor, made a ball out of it and put it in his mouth, checking that he was breathing well through his nose. "Regarding your question, I do this because I can, because I must, and because it is the right thing to do."

I put his jacket over him without covering his legs and stood next to him for a moment, looking at the Gallego's house.

Walking quietly, I could see how my footsteps mingled with the low fog coming from the small jetty next to the night darkness, where only the animals interrupted the silence, and the calm stirred before the storm. "Let's go!" I encouraged myself. As I had seen during so many days of observation, the watchman had no keys to the house. It was up to me to pry open one of the sliding windows with a large spade screwdriver. In a matter of a second, it was open and my body was slithering like a snake's. I closed the window again, without completely locking it. I took a last look at the watchman, who remained motionless in the shadows of those majestic trees, just as I had told him.

I turned on the flashlight with very low intensity and a blue beam, I partially illuminated the room and I almost died of fright when I saw the image of an aggressive wolf coming out of the wall. There were hunting trophies everywhere: deer, wild boar and foxes. It was more like a cemetery than a living room. I preferred not to keep looking because of the love I felt for animals, but mostly because of the imperceptible wild bond with my guardian's protégé, my four-legged friend. I could understand hunting for food, but not for decorative purposes, that was too sinister.

I felt strangely calm, the dryness in my mouth and the accelerated pulsations had diminished. Something seemed to move behind me, and I hurriedly shone my light on it, bringing my hand to my gun in a reflex action. There was nothing. I guess the stress, the darkness and my alert senses were playing a macabre joke on me. It was clear that the servant would not bother me. This one resided in a small servant's hut, adjacent, but slightly separate. There was no reason for them to be an obstacle.

I had to find the hiding place, the place where he stored the evidence of his illegal and immoral activities. I started from the bottom up, and it didn't take long to find something. A flight of stairs led down to the basement of the house. A sharp change in temperature sent a shiver down my spine. The place was a cross between a meeting room and a spartan cellar. Suddenly, something moved in front of me, this time I was sure, I dropped my flashlight on the floor and it spun around, shining in circles on the floor and the lower part of the walls. I pulled my gun out of the holster as fast as I could resting my finger on the trigger, determined to locate my target. My pupils tried to adjust to the blackness of that elongated room, but I could see no one there; I wondered if I was going crazy.

There must have been no one in the house except Gallego; he must have been scared.

"Put the gun away," I heard in my head the order, so loud and clear that I immediately recognized what it was. In front of me, the elongated silhouette of three guards, almost as tall as the ceiling of the room, came into sharp focus. I put the pistol back in the holster, covering it with the safety bow, and breathed a sigh of relief. I stretched out my hand in greeting with the desire to touch my protector, our bond was totally spiritual, so I clearly distinguished it. He also reached out his hand to me. Contact was impossible, we belonged to very different dimensions, but

I felt that my shadow had missed me more than I missed it. I picked up the flashlight.

"What a scare you gave me," I said quietly.

"We are not the ones who frightened you. I'll let the guardian of the one you saw explain it to you," my shadow told me as I speculated in my mind about their presence there.

The questions kept coming to me: am I in grave danger, what are three shadows doing here, will they prevent me from continuing?

"I am the guardian of a spirit here present, using your language I could translate it abbreviated as a wandering soul in a state of denial."

And a dull space was made in the basement.

"I'm sorry but I need more explanation."

"Take your flashlight and walk to the back of the room."

I obeyed, while they did the same, moving their languid limbs.

"Open that freezer chest."

I did as he asked, shone the light inside and a person was lying inside in a fetal position. My first instinct was to try to get him out of there in the vague hope that he was alive; the hardness of the flesh, stronger than metal, was not enough to make me come to my senses. I had to be stopped by the guardian.

"No, I'll show you quickly; we'll finish sooner."

That guardian approached me, opened his huge hand in front of my face and, as in a first-person movie, but with all five senses, I could feel the last hours of that young man brimming with life. Now frozen and hard, his body blended with the surroundings in the form of inanimate and inert matter. The deepest sorrow slipped inside me.

That frozen man's name was Isaac. Twenty-eight years old, he had been planning to get married the following spring, he had a doctorate in Chemical Sciences, he had the whole future ahead of him and a past full of effort, sacrifice and eagerness to excel. His life was broken because Gallego threatened him, blackmailed him and forced him to work for him in the manufacture of a stable variant of adulterated cocaine. Then, without any regard, he killed him with a shot through the heart that same morning, and now that criminal slept peacefully in his bed a few meters away from the corpse of his victim. Fucking psychopath! Pure evil disguised with money and a small empire of power.

The communication with the guards was so real that for a moment I confused my life with that young man's; his pain and impotence became mine. I closed that chest without worrying about the noise and headed back to the stairs with the pistol in my hand, ready to kill that bastard and empty the magazine by disfiguring his filthy insolent face, so that he would wander through hell with his face in tatters.

"Stop! Where are you going? If we have shown you this, it is for your temperance and common sense, not for you to become one of them. You are the opposite! Violence is an impulse you should have overcome by now."

Gritting my teeth and enraged, I asked them,

"And what do you want from me?"

Now my shadow was talking to me.

"We want you, first of all, to take the variable of your emotions out of the equation when you do this. Never, ever, ever let those feelings lead you down the wrong path. Now I will show you what frightened you when you walked into this room and you couldn't see clearly."

He directed his open hands down the aisle toward the freezer, and I saw him standing there. At first, he was a small ball of light, what label connoisseurs call a rod. Gradually it grew into its former form, and I recognized it immediately as the spiritual essence of that young man, Isaac.

His guardian spoke to me. The poor man had no desire for revenge, he was still attached to his body because his family was devastated by his disappearance. His girlfriend, his parents and his siblings had organized patrols through the woods to find him, they clung to optimism like a burning nail despite the fact that the always responsible behavior of that young man foretold that something tragic had happened to him. Isaac refused to move on with his guardian to the next level, coupled with the pain and uncertainty of his loved ones. He had been robbed of a farewell, of a dignified funeral, of being known, of justice being done. That's why he remained clinging tightly to this reality.

I had my doubts about the third guardian. It didn't take long for him to introduce himself. That broke my mind completely. Although really it made sense. That third shadow, long and silent, I could almost say embarrassed, was the guardian of Gallego. I could not believe it. For a moment, everything became confusing and strange. Now the plans were changing. My priorities had to be different.

It was a short conversation, but I promised the guardians that I would make it.

More conscious, with a calmer and even more motivated temperament, I slowly climbed the stairs to the second floor. In the dark again, I reached the room where that monster rested, whose existence I was also supposed to protect. That bedroom was bigger than the living room of my house. In front of the bed was a high chest of drawers. I closed the bedroom door and turned on the light. It was unbelievable. That abortion of humanity continued to sleep; my eyes adjusted to the light. I opted to sit on the old chest of drawers, with my feet dangling and my gun in my hand. Without a second thought, I began to bang the frame of the pistol on the body of the furniture.

"Gallego! Hey, Gallego, wake up. You shouldn't sleep so peacefully, buddy. Wake up."

His eyes opened, sleepy; he looked around and, when he saw me sitting there, all in dark, with the gloves, the gun and the balaclava, he sat up like lightning with his hands raised.

"Please, please don't kill me. We can work it out, I'll pay you double or triple, whatever you ask, I have the money right here in that closet."

"I'm not here to make money, I'm here to make arrangements. It's very different."

"But you're a kid. How old are you, kid? And stop pointing that thing at me, it's probably a toy."

My voice had already broken, but it is true that to an attuned ear my timbre revealed youth.

"To begin with, I'll tell you that I'm older than you, even if I don't look it. And don't even think of patronizing me, you're in no position to do that. If you don't have your disgusting abnormal face full of lead with the mincemeat right now, it's because I've been prevented from doing so."

"Yes, yes, yes. Very good. Let's see, what the fuck do you want, kid?"

Without a word, he turned to the bedside table to reach for the pack of cigarettes and the lighter. I must admit that this made me lose my temper. I hurriedly put the gun back in the holster, jumped over the barefoot and standing on the mattress I gave him a strong kick in the chest while with my left hand I grabbed him by the neck and with my right hand I put the tip of my knife brushing against his lower eyelid. With my knees I held his arms preventing him from any movement. I saw no fear in his look, it was the forced resignation of a thug with airs of superiority and the expression of an inclement oath towards me with promises of pain.

"Have I given you permission to move?"

I pressed the blade harder on his flesh, drawing a little blood. Something inside me was begging me to inflict as much damage on him as possible, but I restrained myself. His bravado began to fade as he realized that I was really wanting to kill him, but that, for some strange reason to him, I might not.

"Okay. I understand. You're in control. You're in control. You call the shots."

He seemed to have gotten the message, because actually having him in front of me, his death and with it his total disappearance, seemed like the best idea at the time. I just needed an excuse to renege on the deal with the guards. I pulled the blade away from his cheek, flicked it with one hand and put it away again, took out the Beretta and put it in his mouth.

"Suck on the barrel with your tongue, do you smell that gunpowder scent mixed with oil? Look at the ejection window, look at the red dot and the subtle gold color of the sheath gripped by the extractor nail, does it still look like a toy to you?" He shook his head several times.

I took the gun away from his face and without taking my hand off the gun, I returned to the dresser and sat back down.

"I want you to listen to me carefully. What I am going to tell you is difficult to assimilate without the proper mental elasticity." I tapped the pistol a couple of times on the furniture. "I have to talk to you about supernatural matters." I snorted resignedly. "It wasn't part of my plan, it's probably a waste of time, but I've been convinced to give you a chance for a change."

I kept a moment of silence, quite usual in my way of speaking.

"It is important that you listen carefully and stop thinking of absurd ways out, about what is happening to you or what you plan to do when this is over. Pay full attention to what I am telling you, if not, it won't do any good, tell me if you understand."

"I'm all ears. I'm listening." His skepticism at the mention of the word "supernatural" seemed normal to me. I took the photos of his daughters out of my pocket and showed them to him. Do you recognize them?

I saw something twist inside him, now I could perceive his fear amidst the rage.

"Relax. I'm not showing them to you to threaten you with harm. I'm not like you. I want you to realize something that your daughter may have seen." I took out the paper and threw it to her. Can you tell me who are these four characters surrounding you in the drawing?

I motioned for him to respond.

"I don't know. But my daughter draws them a lot. She says they're my friends. Kid stuff, imaginary friends. Just a made-up drawing, nothing more."

"I don't know if it will be worth explaining to you. I hope so, although I have little faith in you, Gallego. That drawing is the vision of four beings that surround you, that are here right now. They are evil and feed on pain, anger, violence, immorality and evil deeds. In return, they seduce and deceive you by giving you luck, signs that guide you to get away with it and as far as possible prevent you from being caught by justice. But at the end of the road there is only one outcome, you will be another of them, your soul will stagnate and you will take their form."

"Let me get this straight. Are you saying I'm possessed or something?"

"Not exactly, but in part. You are part of an exponentially growing evil; for whatever reason, your guardian angel thinks there may still be a remedy for you, which I doubt."

"Oh, you also talked to my guardian angel?"

"And I've also seen Isaac in your basement. It's incredible, he doesn't hold a grudge against you, but he can't bear the pain his family is suffering and refuses to move on to the afterlife without resolving that. I have kindly awakened you to propose a way out; if you are not happy, your protector will leave you forever. This is your last chance."

A grimace was traced on his face holding back laughter, forcibly keeping the serious gesture. This had been a bad idea.

"Okay, kid. I accept what you tell me. And what do I have to do?"

His tone of voice offered me no assurance. He moved his legs and I heard the sound of an open clasp.

"Don't do anything foolish! I promise I won't hesitate to kill you!"

The quick movement of his hand from his ankle made me presume that the bastard was sleeping with a gun. The silver glint peeking through the bedspread confirmed to me that it was a small revolver.

"Stop!" I shouted.

I had already flushed the aiming elements, the rear sight and the scope were perfectly aligned to his head, my finger was about to be surprised by the shot.

Again that feeling that time stands still. The tunnel vision. It's a matter of milliseconds, hitting his head before he can even aim at me. My shadow appears next to me and Gallego's guardian. I hesitate and slightly ease the pressure on the trigger, I'm not going to be another victim of that criminal, I won't let him kill me, I don't care about the guards, I'll end up killing him because there's no solution. He doesn't want to listen. All that was going through my mind in that small lapse. I wouldn't feel guilty. There would be no remorse. That instinct of justice was begging me to do it now, I held it back for a moment.

At full speed, the criminal's guardian thrust his hand wide open into the center of the Gallego's chest and quickly removed it again. His body vanished, unconscious over the side of the bed and the small revolver fell to the floor, away from his body. Without wasting a second, oblivious to what had happened, I ran to grab it and remove it from his reach. I tucked it between my pants and belt, behind my back, and lifted that quilt, checking that it did not harbor any more dangerous secrets. As a reflex act of humanity, I could not resist helping him back to bed; I placed him on the bed and checked that he was breathing without difficulty, my glove was stained with the drops of blood that flowed from his eyelid.

That done, I looked back. My protector and his guardian stood in the bedroom, in full light, evoking an image so mystical and imposing that it took one's breath away. Near the window, the four reddish beings seemed impatient for something.

His guardian opened his hand and a small ball of light emerged from it. That luminosity remained suspended in the air. I was spellbound by the effect of light and color. The guardian brought his hands together and separated them diagonally. With that movement, that light adopted the form of the Galician; his face looked around in amazement, when he saw his body lying on the bed, he tried to go to him, but the power exercised by his guardian prevented him from moving away. His expression was the living image of panic and terror. That arrogant and haughty man, who seconds before maintained a defiant attitude, now crumpled like a frightened child. The reddish beings rushed at him claiming his essence, tugging at him to take him away, but he remained attached to his protector without any effort on his part.

It was clear that this was a terrifying experience. He looked into my eyes as if asking for help. This was as new to me as it was to him. The same man who moments before was ready to take my life was now pleading for his miserable existence. His guardian approached his specter and placed his open hand on his forehead; he seemed to relax and feel something extraordinary. He placed his hands diagonally again, but in reverse, and concentrated his soul again into a condensed ball of light the size of a marble. He closed his palm, deepening its light energy, and again pressed his limb into his protégé's chest.

An exhalation of air seemed to bring him back to life. He looked me in the eyes, shrank back on the bed and burst into disconsolate tears. I felt sorry for him. The protectors disappeared as fast as they came. I looked out of the window; I could still see that watchman, motionless and tense.

"Are you done crying?" Now I was the arrogant one. "I don't have time to wait for you to calm down. You didn't want to believe me and you had to see for yourself."

Between sobs and wiping her tears with the bedclothes, he made an effort to keep his composure.

"What should I do? Help me, please!"

"It is very simple. I have done exhaustive study into you and your crimes, I believe I had discovered enough, that added to what I would find here, could reveal a great part of your crimes before the law. You could appoint a good lawyer and fight, denying and getting around the deaths you have caused, the drug dealing, the coercion, the blackmail, etc." I said, pacing the carpet. "What your guardian is proposing is that you call the police right now, deliver Isaac's body to them so that he can have a dignified funeral, so that his family can find relative "peace", which I doubt. He wants you to acknowledge all the deaths you have caused and the activities you have engaged in, taking responsibility without qualms, and maybe so, and only maybe, if you strive daily to be a better person every day you can save your terrifying fate after this life."

"I give my word to you and my guardian. I greatly appreciate this opportunity. I will not waste it. I beg your pardon, from my heart, I have been blind."

I went to the closet and opened a backpack that was full of bundles of ten thousand pesetas. I took three bundles and put them in my pocket. I was no longer worried about danger; it was clear that this experience had flicked a switch inside him. In the meantime, I saw him pick up the phone, one of those old roulette phones, and dial a three-digit number. He was talking to the police, confessing to one of many murders, he gave the address of the place and hung up the phone.

"Take the photos and the drawing of your daughters, so that you don't forget that love is the only thing that matters in this life, and that everything else is banality." He looked dazzled.

"Thank you. I'm sorry." He caught his breath as best he could. I saw it. It was creepy.

He was really changed, what an instant transformation!

"Save your apologies for everyone you've hurt. By the way, now when you get dressed, give the watchman the night off; I don't want him to be here when the police arrive.

He nodded his head in confirmation that he would do so.

"Farewell, my friend. I hope that from now on you will be of the righteous; if not, I will remedy it."

I hurried down the stairs, turning on the lights I found on my way, and stopped at the front door. I turned around for a moment and headed for the basement stairs, I made it all the way down and felt that strong change in temperature again, I couldn't see him, but I felt Isaac's presence there.

"Soon it will all be over, my friend. You will be able to continue the transit. I am very sorry for what happened to you."

I still felt cold in my body, I could see the mist of my breath in front of me and my head shook, for a second, uncontrollably. His protector appeared before me again. With the characteristic voice of the guardians, that shadow approached me, with its impressive height always so striking.

"You have done more than could have been expected, we are both very grateful to you. As you said, it will all be over soon. There are only a few minutes left before the cavalry arrives. I am indebted to you, if the time comes I will be at your side. Thank you for being so; you are a "link"."

That word was familiar to me. I still had a lot to understand. I quickly climbed the stairs and went out the front door, which had the key in the lock. I ran through the garden to the watchman, who looked at me with such fear that he seemed to have seen a ghost. I forgot my masked appearance, armed and all in dark like a bank robber. I carelessly cut the shoelace that was attached to the revolver and the ropes that held his neck; he looked numb. He didn't dare look me in the eye. It was clear that this watchman thought I was a murderer. I took out the three wads of bills and put them in the pocket of the jacket that covered his body. I ordered him to lie down on the floor and removed his shackles.

"Get dressed quickly and accept this money as compensation for the bad time you've had. Your boss is going to tell you to leave; don't refuse and leave as soon as possible without asking questions." In your pocket there should be about three million pesetas, enjoy it with your loved ones. You have already guessed that you would not have died if you had tried to escape; I would never have hurt you. Now I have to go. Do as you're told," I snapped.

I shook his hand with my gloved one and helped him to his feet. He had to hold on to that tree to keep his balance; the poor guy's legs must have been asleep, and his distrustful gaze was watching me as if wondering what mental institution I had escaped from.

I ran to the guard's booth and with the flashlight I illuminated the control panel on the table, looked at the screen that was divided into several sections and quickly thought of removing that videotape. I stopped the recording and pressed the pull button. The VHS tape came out of the machine and I tucked it into my clothes. I pressed the button for the doors, and they both opened at the same time. I shot out of there and looked back for a second. Gallego was walking out the door, while I could see the watchman finishing dressing. I went up the side of the hill, disappearing. It took me a few minutes to reach my vantage point with my breath hitching.

I calmly gathered all my things and put them in my sports bag. A police car arrived in a hurry skidding through the streets with the lights on. In the distance I could see another car arriving with lights flashing. The guard had already left. I covered up the hole I had made, while the agents inspected the whole estate; two of them guarded him. It was after four in the morning. Time had flown. All the neighbors came out to see what was going on. I tied the backpack to the motorcycle, changed clothes, and saw police vans and another from the funeral home arrive.

Gallego kept his part of the bargain, he was detained. In the end, it was a better solution than mine, although I admit that I was about to see him off. To get out of there I took a different route, I did not want to cross any police vehicle. Paradoxically, I had to avoid the good guys. I considered myself as an ally in the shadows, although I worked outside the law, anonymously, without barriers, without explanations, without reports and, of course, without permits.

I started the bike and headed home, looking forward to celebrating with Natalia, and enjoying the promised Sunday at the beach with Kingsley. I put the bike away where I always kept it, still taking the usual care; I covered all my marks and walked back the last stretch. I extracted the magnetic strip from the tape and tore it into pieces along the way, tossing the casing into the trash can. I climbed through the window as usual. I took off my clothes and put on my pajamas, accompanied by my beloved solitude, tucked in bed, and with a permanent smile on my face.

I felt great. Exhausted but proud of myself.

Now it was my turn to savor the taste of tranquility, of a job well done, of my father's return, of my new brother's friendship and of the possibility of my trip to the United States.

It was my turn to savor life.

Chapter 21
Days of Light

Principality of Asturias-Madrid, summer 1996.

I returned the fantastic motorcycle to the Alberti family. It had been a faithful companion. That old couple never knew what a great favor it did me. Every time I passed by their house, I would stop to greet them and offer to help with anything; it was my way of repaying my debt to them.

I hid everything, clothing and operating equipment, in the hole in the woods, close to home. Completely hidden, away from any curious onlookers.

Without realizing it, I had added another firearm to the collection. As promised, this has always been one of my principles. Natalia could not have been happier. She kept her part and brought me the three hundred thousand pesetas. I would have liked to say no, that it was not necessary, but that amount of money was part of the alibi. It was not convenient to refuse and reject it.

On the other hand, it was a well-deserved amount and, in view of what I had seen, I did not know if I would need it. If it came to it, money could be a tool to act freely, without explanations. I was no longer able to predict what I would need in the recent future. I saw it as another means to an end. Simply and strictly, something "professional", intended for such corrective and unofficial activities.

That Sunday we had a great time on Toró beach. No classes, no gym, no more chores of my own, I felt totally light and carefree. Everything was pure fun. Natalia brought a friend of hers, Susana. When I had her in front of me, so cheerful, a sense of affinity came over me in a singular way. I liked her vibe, she seemed like one of those people you are destined to meet, though the feeling faded right away. It wasn't her, but the feeling came to me from the future. I didn't want to think about it anymore, it was time to enjoy life.

Susana had long red hair. Her petite face gave her an exotic beauty, and her large honey-colored eyes seemed to reflect a special glow when she first saw Kingsley.

It was clear that chemistry had developed between the two of them. They were both very similar in character: wild, cheerful and outgoing, not afraid to make funny faces. Best of all, although my brother had learned quite a bit of Spanish, Susana, with an excellent education, had a perfect command of English. Between the girls and us there was an evident social distance, an aspect of opportunities, of luck. Matters that with age contaminate the soul of many people; to ours and at that very moment, having a good time was the only thing that mattered to us.

People don't know it, but in my land the best days of summer usually fall between August and September.

Kingsley ran along the beach chasing Susanna. She, frightened by what was coming at her, let him do it, offering little resistance. He threw her over his shoulder and at the same time, she hit his back without force. They both fell plummeting into the water among the waves of the Bay of Biscay. They kept laughing, rolling in the strong waves of the shore. Now it was she who was chasing him. We were filled with sand running between the towels. Natalia and I kissed at our own pace, oblivious, unhurried. Indifferent to the hustle and bustle, as if nothing could disturb our connection. They shouted, "Excuse me!", laughing and going on about their business; but in the end, exhausted and exhausted, they had to stop.

Her skin was so pale that she had to apply cream every so often. Natalia saw me gesture to Kingsley with my hands, so that he would offer to help her. It was the perfect occasion to be gentle and tender. Susanna lay face down facing the other way. He looked scared, or maybe clueless, I don't know. His hands were smeared with that white cream and he looked at me without doing anything, blocked. I pointed to Susana's neck and back, arching and mulling my eyebrows insistently, so that he would move his hands with sensitivity and tact.

"I think I *look* like Mickey Mouse," he said suddenly, looking at the contrast of his white hands smeared in excessive sunscreen, chuckling at the taboo of his own joke.

The girls hesitated about whether to laugh too, but by half a second we all exploded in laughter at his joke.

It's very intimidating, we know that. You have to be brave to take steps with a girl. There is always insecurity and fear of rejection, but in a way, you also have to be suspicious. The signals are subtle, but if you are attentive you will discover them.

All in all, I decided not to interfere with Kingsley, I think I was doing him a disservice. He had to go that way on his own. And indeed he started to do so, but my goodness, what a mess, he looked like he had stumps! The amazing thing is that Susanna wasn't complaining.

Natalia was holding back her laughter as best she could, seeing him so focused on her best friend's back. He was squeezing her skin as if he was kneading bread with his knuckles.

"You're tearing me apart, Kingsley. *I declare war!*" shouted Susanna in such a wild way that it made all three of us gasp.

Maybe there was some truth to what they said about redheads, what do I know. She turned around suddenly, grabbed Kingsley's wrist and twisted it the other way past his thighs, passing her thighs around his neck, crossing her legs in a headlock. He was between her legs, but not in the way he would have dreamed. Immobilized, his wild eyes stared at us, not knowing what to do. I burst out laughing, watching his face change tone as she demanded,

"Beg for forgiveness! Beg for forgiveness! I won't tell you again! Beg for forgiveness!"

"Sorry! *Sorry!* Sorry!" he exclaimed in a choked voice, as she laughed in satisfaction.

"Do it right or it'll be your last minutes on the face of the earth, handsome."

She released his arm and stopped squeezing him with her legs letting out a childish giggle, winking at him in a charming and mischievous way.

Kingsley recovered his lost pride, hiding the force he had received on his neck, rubbing the back of his neck to see if everything was in place. He stretched out a towel smoothing out the wrinkles and Susana lay on her back. Natalia made a blunt gesture to me and we rose stealthily, leaving them alone.

She, with her eyes closed from the sun, and settled on the sand and towel, must have felt the mesmerized gaze of Kingsley, who gawked at her for seconds without doing anything. She wiped her hands on the towel and brushed back her coppery hair. She applied a dab of cream and caressed his face, sliding her fingers lovingly, following his magical lines. I think he noticed one of those signs then. It wasn't a visual thing, at least I didn't see it from a distance. It seems to me that he felt it was the right moment because she told him so with her heart. I saw them kissing, and I smiled with happiness, squeezing Natalia's hand tighter, walking along the shore.

It is difficult to distinguish the best moments in life. It is time that is in charge of telling it to you.

The day was coming to an end, we took a shower to wash off the salt and sand, resisting the absence of light to end the day. Half soaked, we went to get some sandwiches and soft drinks, drying off during the walk through the center of Llanes. We sat on the wall of the fishing port watching the waves breaking at our feet. It was as if the hand of a giant was trying to grab us with every beat of the sea. Natalia rested her head on my legs lying on the wall, closing her eyes, enjoying the musical rhythm of the tide. Susana copied her position, so that Kingsley and I were in the center and the girls were lying with their feet pointing in opposite directions.

I looked at Kingsley, grateful at our good fortune, while stroking Natalia's hair. For some strange reason, Kingsley seemed worried about something. My head went into alert mode, fearing anything. In a very low voice I asked him what was wrong. He just shook his head, I could tell that, despite the darkness of his skin, his face was completely red. Susana reacted quickly with an exclamation of fright. I made Natalia move away as a result of her reaction; instinctively, I took my hand where I should have the gun, which of course I didn't have it. False alarm.

I couldn't believe it, what an embarrassment my brother had to go through. Let's say that a part of his body had awakened from its lethargy, pushing hard on Susana's ear. We all sat up, except for him, who insisted on sitting there, crumpled and staring at the sea, and we couldn't stop laughing. He, with a look of circumstance, pretended to be crazy, while we all knew what had happened.

"I don't know what you're laughing about," he said, looking into Susana's eyes which only made the situation worse, because he was laughing even harder.

Apart from being funny, this harmless situation revealed my sensitivity to danger. Without realizing it, so many tensions were taking their toll on me. I had to calm down, although that was easier said than done.

Our perfect day was coming to an end, marked as always by the damned train schedules. Once again in that station it was time to say goodbye. First of all to Susana with a big hug and two powerful kisses. I wanted to tell her that, sincerely, I had loved meeting her. It was my way of thanking her for the wonderful day we had spent. I almost missed the train stretching until the last second the pleasure of Natalia's lips.

Susanna and Kingsley couldn't find a way to say goodbye, but in the end they gave each other a movie kiss. The door was closing and he didn't think twice, he interrupted its closing with his arm, the doors opened again and, like an opportunistic thief, he rushed down, grabbed her face with both hands and kissed her again. Taking advantage of his thinness, he slipped back in like a foil between the doors. She put her hands to her forehead, tossing her hair back, with a huge smile, full of illusion and surprise. It's those little things you never forget.

He started to do an African dance in the middle of that train carriage, as happy as he was crazy. When he finished, some travelers applauded the free show. After so much struggle, suffering and being such a good friend, I was overjoyed to be part of his happiness.

"David, hey, David, are you awake? -he whispered to me from his bed."

"What do you want, dude?" I asked, sleepily.

"I can't sleep. I'm going crazy. I keep thinking about her. I've been staring at the ceiling for three hours."

"Don't worry, my friend, that's normal. You like her a lot and your body is crying out for you to be with her, that's all. Try to sleep, tomorrow is Monday."

"I would love to do like you. I'd love to climb out the window, escape and join her."

"Do what you want. I'll cover for you. But it's late, better close your eyes and keep thinking about her, feel your weight on your back sinking into the mattress, and maybe you can dream about her tonight."

"Thank you, brother. I had a great time today."

"Me too, Kingsley."

I went to the Alberti's house before going to town and took care of an errand. I wrote down some things from the pharmacy and the market that they needed. I arrived with excruciating pain in my shoulders and fingers from the weight of the bags. I left ours on the kitchen counter and took their stuff over to them. My mother kept admiring my attitude, proud of my kindness. I was just trying to compensate, a little, the huge favor they secretly did me, and while I was at it, to take the cover off the bike and be able to see it in full light, without worries or paranoia.

"Start it up, if you can, and take it for a walk in the garden," said Mr. Alberti.

I climbed on top of her, pulled off and absorbed in my world, I felt Natalia's chest on my back again. I turned off the bike without moving it and carefully protected it again with its cover. Although no time had passed, I already missed my own adventures.

Tomorrow my father was arriving. My mother, as always, anxious about his arrival, seemed to suffer from hyperactivity. As always, Kingsley helped my aunt and uncle. The make-up exams were coming up, and that was the litmus test of my teaching the boys. Whether I wanted to or not, their passes were also mine. That afternoon I worked my heart out in the gym; it was my way of eliminating accumulated tensions.

The next day, my mother was busy making herself beautiful and kept asking me if she was beautiful enough. Everything looked good on her. She perfumed herself, put on her earrings, a necklace. Between my mother and my aunt, they did each other's hair. As custom dictated, that night we would dine out. It was already a ritual.

The Beluga arrived slowly, fully loaded. Its entry into the harbor and docking was a spectacle of skill to behold. At last I could see my father, concentrating on the perfectionism of the mooring. He gave the impression of not allowing himself to be distracted. Just for a moment, a small moment, he looked towards us, and his face lit up with restrained joy. I imagined him night after night, in the solitude of the sea, accompanied only by that dim little lamp, his inseparable pipe and cup of coffee on the coaster, fighting with his old boat against the resistant opposition of the tide, advancing mile after mile, without ceasing to long for the arrival of that right moment: the instant when he meets his family, and that now, with all that accumulated nostalgia and the fulfilled desire, he concealed, because he had been educated to be stronger than his emotions.

None of that stopped us from running to him, almost fighting to be the first to squeeze him against us in the warmest and most affectionate of embraces. His beard covered his face, helping him in the arduous task of feigning the coldness of ice, but his reddened eyes betrayed a feeling that fought to emerge, manifesting itself without contemplation. On this occasion, my father won the battle and was more powerful than himself.

That meeting could not have been better. I felt like the luckiest person on earth. Nothing can make you feel better than enjoying the company of family. What a great dinner, and not because of the food, which was also good: it was a celebration of togetherness, love and mutual affection. The best feelings floated in the air among anecdotes, stupid jokes, displays of affection and the best steak in the area. It was time for dessert and that old, varnished Castilian table shook like an earthquake, as my uncle slapped it. We thought he was going to break it, as he had done on another occasion. So brutish and corpulent, the poor guy had trouble measuring the intensity of his strength. It was obvious that something transcendent was going to happen because my aunt's complicit gaze was incessant. That fine crystal glass full of cider, raised on her hand, foretold the announcement of a news with a toast.

"We want you all to fill your glasses! We have something to say!"

I couldn't help but wonder: what's going on here, what's this all about, how come I didn't hear anything, what are they going to say?

We all obeyed, and I poured more orange soda into my glass.

"We have been thinking about this decision for some time." My uncle looked at the floor for a moment, uncertain. "Not because we were not clear about it, but because Matilde and I were afraid that there might be a misunderstanding. That it would be interpreted as if we were trying to replace someone irreplaceable. To begin with he didn't know what we were talking about. We had a hard time expressing what we were trying to say. Finally, we dared to take the step, explaining our purpose clearly, and above all trying to construct in words what our hearts were telling us."

I looked at my parents, and neither of them blinked.

"It was important that we were all together for this announcement, that's why we waited for you, Jemy."

He took a breath of air, looking at his glass and again looked up, clearly excited.

"With Kingsley's permission we have decided together that he will officially become part of the family, we have requested the right to adopt him, to become his legal guardians. That's why we want to toast tonight! To celebrate that we are now one more! And from now on Kingsley will never be able to say that he has no one left in the world."

And we all raised our drinks in a reflex action, following my uncle's example. Thoughts were racing through my mind. There couldn't have been better news. My father hugged my uncle, and this time he couldn't be so strong, he had to wipe his damp eyes with the sleeve of his sweater. He was excited because he knew well how devastated they had been to not be able to have children. I did the same with my brother and we hugged knowing that now we would be united forever, but I had to scold him for keeping the secret so well. Who was I to reproach him for that, though? The other diners in the restaurant knew we were celebrating because of all the fuss we were making, but they couldn't imagine what it was all about.

It was an unbeatable night, one of those whose memory remains engraved forever.

It turned out that my aunt and uncle had already arranged a room for him at home; the good Father Damián had mediated for them to expedite things, and with a couple of phone calls he got Kingsley a place at my school, of course, with the commitment that he would attend extra classes. He was going to need them to adjust.

Having my father at home was very fortunate. I tried to enjoy every moment with him as much as possible. Even the most insignificant things became important. But a couple of days after his arrival, he still had not made any statement regarding the test for my studies in Madrid. I had no special interest in doing those studies, I did not need to accelerate the obtaining of any degree, what I did need was to be able to travel to New York.

Finally my father talked about it. He asked me if that was what I wanted. I told him that of course I wanted to take the exams. He talked about homesickness, loneliness and distance and also about the thrill of prospering, of knowing new places, of discovering other customs, of building a better future for myself. He wanted to go with me to Madrid and he was thinking of taking the trip by car with my uncle and Kingsley. The appointment for my test was Saturday, September 14. My father was skeptical and was always wary of the unknown at first. He had developed that fear through experience and disappointment. I understood that perfectly.

I talked to Natalia about my trip to Madrid. I was totally honest with her, and she was honest with me. Openly, she told me that she wished with all her heart that I would fail the test, that she didn't want to lose me and that an ocean between us would drown our relationship forever. I couldn't deny that she was absolutely right, she looked enraged but restrained. On the other hand, she felt contempt for her own selfish thoughts and did not want her to be the one to cut short a better future for me.

I would have loved to have been able to tell him the truth. That I wasn't really interested in studying abroad. That I had a debt pending with my past, with the true love of my life. That love so anchored in me prevented me from giving her all my heart. I owed it to myself to search for her with all my strength, until my last breath. Every day that passed I felt that Angie was getting farther away. It was a race against the clock and the guilt grew inside me, it was like always walking with a stone in my shoe or a splinter stuck in my finger.

Meeting Natalia was the best gift this life had given me, even though it was accidental, that dragged remnant allowed me the possibility of feeling in love again, half in love. I knew that with Natalia I was trying to revive something lost, to bring back to the present sensations of memories with Angie. I wanted to be fair, but love does not obey rules, it does not obey reason, not even the slightest common sense. It is a free force, so strong that it is capable of bending the will, crossing time and breaking the most impassable wall: the border between life and death.

We left on a trip three days before my scheduled test; my uncle had to sort out hundreds of papers everywhere to put in writing the new responsibility he had acquired: with the Juvenile Prosecutor's Office, Government Delegation, criminal record certificate, shelter, notary, and back to the beginning. So many obstacles to do good. I reflected on this in silence, and I could not help feeling truly saddened by how hard it was to just try and do something good.

My uncle's patience, optimism and good character made all that ordeal go by little by little and step by step without losing an ounce of illusion. Although frustration with so much bureaucracy was beginning to win over my spirits.

The day came with hardly any progress from my uncle, and I was escorted to the rendezvous with my opportunity to fly to the United States.

Plaza de Castilla, 3. With the invitation filled out in his own handwriting by Don Manuel, with the seal of the university, the signature of the rector and the undersigned professor, we arrived punctually at ten o'clock in the morning. Only four other young people arrived. I was disturbed that one of them came with a violin. We were all more or less in the same age range, between fifteen and seventeen. To tell the truth, I was very distracted contemplating the construction work on two leaning towers next door.

I imagined its internal structure, the counterweights that must have been installed in the subway, the counterbalanced stresses in the cantilever, the quality of the steel, the central core, I marveled at such a work of engineering. A young woman's voice brought me out of my silent alienation. She was an impressive woman, tall, dark, with her hair tied back and dressed in a tight executive style, gray skirt, marking curves and attributes with an elegant and professional discretion. The exchange of glances between my uncle and my father confirmed her exuberant beauty.

"Candidates may follow me accompanied by their parents," she said, with a beautiful welcoming smile.

We were ushered into a foyer, more like a small assembly hall occupied by chairs with attached desks. A consent form had to be filled out with personal data, parents' profession and studies, average monthly income, property and signature. My father and another girl's father seemed to feel a kind of inferiority complex. The other girl's parents and the violinist gave the impression of being wealthy potentates, nicely dressed in tailored suits, coiffed and perfumed, and had brought their own pen to write with. We had a half-worn black Bic pen, but at least the cap was not nibbled.

My father and I looked quite out of place, even though we had dressed in our best clothes. Now I was even more amazed by the surprised look on the faces of those people at the entrance of the building. They didn't seem to understand what a little black man, a goatherd, a pipe-smoking Popeye and a redneck dressed in a shirt that was too small for him were doing there.

The elegant woman who was guiding us asked if we were all here and my father had to ask for one more minute to finish. Two parents looked at each other with malicious and mocking laughter because they had finished some time ago; only the father of one of the girls remained indifferent to that small nucleus. I was about to jump out of my chair like a lion for the jugular, but I realized that my father, so focused, had not noticed the detail. With his signature proudly finished, he handed it to that beautiful woman, and my father, as humble as ever, apologized for the delay.

Those arrogant conceits with pompous airs did not deserve a single word, let alone an apology. Although it must be said that the young lady picked up the pamphlet with sincere courtesy and kindness, smiling, kind and strangely enthusiastic. That very human and polite gesture gave me back my inner peace.

She told us all to follow her. We reached the elevators and another colleague of hers told all the parents to follow her to another room where the steps of the selection process would be outlined for them. We, the candidates, as we were called, rode up in the elevator with the beautiful woman carrying the documents in a blue leather folder. My ears were strange because of the sudden change in altitude.

The girls talked about their nerves, about the excitement of passing the test. The violinist moved his lips like someone praying, doing sums or reading in subdued silence. I had nothing to lose, so I was not nervous.

"Come into this room. In a few moments they will come to receive you. Sit wherever you like."

There was a huge table full of chairs. At the entrance, a symbol caught my attention: two spheres, one large and one small, one inside the other, just like that.

I could not resist. I approached the gigantic glass window at the back of the room, and all of Madrid could be seen from there. A man in his fifties entered the room. I thought it impolite to stand at the window, and immediately sat down in the nearest chair.

"Today we are going to give you a few tests. The first two you will do together and the last one will be individual."

At that moment, the woman who welcomed us entered the room pushing a trolley with thermos jugs, cups, pastries and juices. She placed the three trays on the table and said those French words when something is well finished: *et voilà,* again so happy to see us there.

"Before we begin, have a drink, get to know each other a little, and if anyone needs it, behind this door here is a bathroom," he said.

The girls were the first to help themselves to a glass of milk. I had already had a good cup of coffee for breakfast. I understood that this breakfast was intended to relax the tense ones. I got up again and continued to look out the window. I think you could tell I was from the village. But I didn't care. In front of that building there was another building, earth-colored, and some police vehicles were parked. I could not believe it, they were transporting people in shackles and almost all of them were accompanied by one, two, three or even more reddish beings. What was that place? It didn't take me long to understand that it was the Madrid courthouse.

I could not take my eyes off the immense danger the policemen were in, and yet they did not seem uneasy, quite the contrary.

I began to sweat at the sight of so much evil gathered together. "I'm in the big city, I must get used to it," I said to myself. I grabbed one of the napkins and wiped my forehead, I didn't want to look down anymore. My muscles and tendons tensed reflexively. One of the girls approached me; her features still retained all the essence of a close childhood, big, bright eyes, all of her exuded innocence. In her hands two glasses of juice, she gave me no option to refuse.

"We're going to do great; you'll see."

Chapter 22
One of Our Own

Without saying anything and with her beside me, I drank some of that juice, took a deep breath to recover from such a malicious vision, and we looked into each other's eyes in a skeptical parenthesis. There was something about her. As if we had seen each other before. Strange. I thanked her, and a voice on the other side interrupted our silence.

"Everything is ready. Follow me," said the charming woman.

They took us to another room full of desks each with a small lamp shining in the corner. I saw immediately that they had observed us! We were seated at separate tables, I had the lamp on the left and a pen on the right, but the violinist and one of the girls had it the other way around; they knew they were left-handed. No one else noticed that. The older man looked at me with sharp eyes and a half smile, he understood that I had noticed the detail. I pretended to be clueless and sat down at my post with the paper already in front of me.

The first test was to write an essay about the discovery of America, the 500th anniversary of which had been a few years earlier. I could have spent hours and hours writing non-stop on those blank pages. He gave us a five-minute warning before time ran out.

The next test was a personality questionnaire. There were two hundred short, multiple-choice questions to be answered in twenty minutes; effectively, six seconds per question, with two options, yes and no. I refused to take it.

Right away, I realized that I was very likely to make very serious mistakes, very compromising mistakes. I began to think that it had all been a trap. Anger took hold of me, and I asked myself how I had been so stupid. Immediately, I deduced that the purpose of the writing was to make a graphological study of us, without considering our knowledge of history. I stood up, visibly upset, apologized and told the man that I had to leave. Everyone froze for a moment, staring at me for a short time; then, like automatons, they continued in a hurry, six seconds per question. That forced me to vomit the whole truth, there was no time to imagine and lie, no matter how accustomed I was.

"But, son, how are you going to leave now? We've just started," he said softly and softly.

"I want to leave right now, this is not my place, excuse me," I told him so rudely and bluntly.

"Look, David, have a little patience, stay without doing the test, and then we'll discuss it, is that all right?"

He put his hand on my shoulder, calming me down. It was obvious that he had noticed my anger.

"Okay, I'll wait," I replied in a calmer voice.

I flipped through the test and it was full of dangerous questions, such as: do you always recognize yourself in the mirror, have you ever fallen unconscious, do you sometimes think you are someone else, are you afraid of death, does a voice dictate your actions, do you blindly believe in reality, would you kill someone, and again they asked the same questions in different words or with negative questioning. And again they would ask the same questions with other words or with negative questioning. Who did these people think they were to try to get into my head? Then there were other types of questions or statements, strange to say the least: "I prefer a thousand pesetas to a hug"; "I want to have and have"; "in a group of people, I want to be the best". Not to mention those that were somewhat uncertain and disconcerting, such as "when I cross a bridge I feel the urge to jump"; "I don't think drugs are dangerous if you control your consumption".

There I sat there, waiting, watching the candidates, crowded by the short time, revealing all the information of their essence. Politeness prevented me from interrupting that examination and quickly rejoining my family.

They collected the tests, mine was totally empty, and said they were giving us some time to rest. I got up quickly and asked if I could leave now, I didn't want to waste anyone's time. I was not jumping through hoops, so that was not my place.

"You, David, will be the first to do the interview. If you give us the opportunity, of course," said the gray-haired man, clapping his hands together, asking me for the favor.

"No problem. I will do your interview."

"Great, come this way, please. The rest of you can wait without raising your voices too much, take a break. Beatriz will be around if you need anything."

Everyone listened obediently. We walked down an elongated corridor, full of open doors with offices, meeting rooms, a kitchen, another bathroom, until we reached a very different office. It was a completely soundproof room, which closed behind two hermetic doors. Every step sounded even the tiniest sound, everything was amplified in there. That office was as big as two living rooms in my house, all white, no pictures, no windows; an air conditioning system could be heard very faintly. Next to the wall there were perfectly placed chairs. All very neat.

He took two chairs and placed them facing each other, a couple of meters apart.

"Please have a seat," he said, smiling and holding his hand out to the chair closest to me.

I did as he said, still wondering what kind of place that was.

"Beatriz and I are very happy to have you here. First, I will tell you briefly, without being able to give you too many details, the purpose of our organization: its nature, its objectives, what is expected of you and what we can offer you; always without any commitment on either side. It is a permanent relationship, favorable to all. If you don't understand something, you can interrupt me whenever you want."

"Okay. Thank you," I said more cooperatively yet I remained unconvinced of the intentions of those people.

"Good. We are a group of people with an international presence, which means that this center is one of hundreds of others around the world. You are here because of your outstanding talent for mathematics and its application to architecture, as you have already demonstrated. In short, because of your high potential, although you already know that. Throughout history there has been much speculation about our existence; we have been confused with many: Templars, Illuminati, Freemasons, the club, and countless other names. The truth is that we do not believe in labels. If you are part of this, you will refer to this organization as "we" and to another member, if you know him, by name, and if not, as "one of us"; it's as simple as that."

"But what do you do? What is the object of your activities?"

"Wait a second, one of our people has just arrived. I called her to give you a reading."

"Let's see, let's see, wait a moment." I lost my manners a little. "What's that all about?"

"Calm down, David, what are you so afraid of? No one is going to do anything bad to you."

Just then an intercom rang; it was Beatriz, saying that Paloma had arrived.

The gray-haired man approached the door, which was about eight meters away from me, and opened it. I was very worried, because nothing that man was telling me was completely transparent. He opened that door and an older lady, thin and energetic, appeared on the other side. She must have been about seventy years old, or a little older. She wore a blouse, a skirt and quality shoes, a scarf covered her neck, and various pieces of jewelry matched perfectly with her earrings, lightly made up without extravagance. They both began to talk quietly by the door; she looked away from him and locked eyes with me, I held her a little and she returned to focus all her attention on that gentleman. They closed, and both turned to me.

"Good morning, David. My name is Paloma and I'm here to get to know you a little."

She reached out her hand to shake mine. I hesitated, I didn't know what the right thing was to do, it was all so mysterious, a reading, what the fuck would that be, I wondered. At the same time, curiosity pushed me to know more. I shook her hand, and she gave me a wonderful smile and, naturally, I gave her one too, but it was one of relief because nothing happened. In my wild imagination, I thought I might detect something and that old lady would start convulsing. She looked at the interviewer and simply said,

"There is no doubt, he could be one of ours."

"How sure are you?"

"Sure of it all."

It turned out that the old woman had sensed something in me, I don't know what, but something. I started to get quite nervous, my hands got cold and sweaty; my rough tongue like a cat's almost sanded my palate. She took off the pendant she was wearing and began to twirl it in front of me with her right hand. Underneath that blue arrow-shaped stone, she placed her outstretched palm. Suddenly, she withdrew her forearm, and that pendant suddenly came to a standstill with the chain taut as a block, the pendant pointed at the end forming a forty-five-degree angle towards me, held irrationally by that thin chain. She put her left hand under the stone, again, and released the end of the chain, the chain falling naturally now.

"It was a pleasure to meet you, David. I hope to see you soon and learn from each other."

"Likewise."

Again, the host escorted her to the exit door, thanked her for coming and kissed her goodbye. She returned to the chair and sat down again; now her gaze was different, closer. Distended.

"What kind of magic trick was that?" I asked sincerely, because I didn't understand anything.

"Look, Paloma is one of us, she has several university degrees, but her special talent is that she is sensitive. So she can sense evil and goodness in people, among other things. We often tend to judge people by their appearance. Our minds are trained from childhood and in the early stages of socialization to label others by their appearance. So when we see, for example, a biker with long hair, a leather jacket, chains and tattoos, we tend to associate him with the fairytale monsters we were threatened with as children. Nothing to do with the truth of the reality in which we live. Normally, the worst people, and the most difficult to discover, are those with a kind face, flawless appearance and ordinary, even altruistic, life. They are the most detestable, because they deceive everyone they deal with, disguising their evil with the appearance of an earthly angel."

"So, have I passed the test?"

"With honors. That's why I'm being so honest with you. We want you to be a part of this."

"Yes, but you still haven't told me what you do," I insisted again.

"Well, I can't tell you everything, you will see for yourself. We are many and at the same time very few. Let me explain. Our goal is to try to make humanity a better community. We are not part of any government, but many of our people are secretly infiltrated in each and every one of the political formations. We are in every administration. There is always one of us in every important hospital in the world, in every construction project, in every engineer or architect. In every court, a magistrate; in every laboratory, a scientist. Commanders of the Army, of the Civil Guard; commissioners of the National Police.

"Top technology developers; weapons engineers; fire chiefs; aviation companies; tax inspectors. The list could go on and on. We secretly influence every aspect of daily life. We are the humblest of the elites. Our main objective is to take care of ourselves and to obtain the greatest economic resources. Not with selfish intentions, but to be able to develop our true purpose: to prevent the tyranny of those monsters we have spoken of from falling on innocent people. It is our duty to protect them, they are the only reason for our existence."

"Could you be more precise with an example?"

"As you will understand, I should not talk to you about specific issues, but I will tell you that we are the driving force behind the fall of the Berlin Wall, of a Europe of solidarity, where all citizens can move freely, enrich themselves culturally and share. We have promoted the eradication of illiteracy in Spain, making the Government invest in a minimum education for every child, who will be the adults of the future. In this sense, we are fighting to extend compulsory education to the age of sixteen, however much some of your friends may dislike that. There is no greater poverty than complete ignorance."

"And people like Paloma, what role do they play in all this?"

"My friend, you want to run before you can crawl. Just as you have the gift of applied mathematics, others of our people show intangible talents, usually associated with the occult sciences. Not everything is in the books, David, and not everything can be demonstrated. We do not close the door to any wisdom. That is why I sent for you, and you have passed the test favorably. There is no evil within you, after talent, that is what interests us most in a candidate. The question is, do you want to be one of us?"

"You said there is no commitment, didn't you, on either side?"

"That's right, that's right. But I'm telling you, you won't want to leave. Of course, there is no commitment, but there are conditions, obligations that you must fulfill."

"I am listening," I said, interested.

"No one can know anything about us; you could endanger yourself and the rest of our people. You will be required to perform and be disciplined. You will agree to study subjects such as etiquette, social skills, communication, values, and you will follow the instructions of the assigned tutor. You will only talk about us with one of our people, no one else."

"It seems acceptable to me. And now what?"

"Now I will continue with the interviews, and you will go home with this booklet and the stamped documentation. It is a more standard, legitimate and plausible explanation, in accordance with the law. Beatriz will take care of communicating the details to your father. Next Sunday, at three o'clock in the afternoon, a car will pick you up at home, as Don Manuel already told you; you will start your studies abroad. Be aware of that because in many cases the adjustment can be hard. You will, of course, be able to come back to visit quite often."

"Thank you very much for the opportunity; I hope I won't disappoint you."

"The opportunity belongs to both of us. By the way, a little birdie told me that you are working on a little family matter, about an adoption. An assistant will be in touch soon to expedite things. As you can guess, she's one of ours. Be discreet," he said in an authoritative voice. Celebrate with your family. I wish you the best of luck, and I hope we see each other again.

He accompanied me to the exit of that strange room, where, as I left, I saw Beatriz arriving with another of the candidates. She walked beside me to the elevator and went down with me.

"I knew you'd be in, you're already one of us. Congratulations."

Going down in the elevator, I looked at that brochure. It was a folder with children hugging in chorus and smiling old people; only unicorns and rainbows were missing. It looked like a classic hotel advertisement; there was a copy with my parents' authorization, the seal of the Ministry of Education and the emblem of the Spanish flag. It was clear that, at least in part, my education in the United States was paid for by Spain. It read: "The above-mentioned candidate has successfully passed the tests to benefit from the Avanza scholarship granted by this ministry, which with my signature I certify to all effects and purposes. Minister of Education and Science".

Briefly, because it had already been explained to him in that room where he had been, Beatriz informed my father that I had passed the tests, congratulating us again. She explained to my father that the trip to the United States was part of a state scholarship, and that they were in charge of ensuring its approval and development. She explained the details about my tutor there, his contact, and that I would be staying in a student residence. That I would be accompanied by a responsible person to facilitate customs procedures and my installation.

To my father everything seemed to fit perfectly, he was grateful to the system for working so well. But I could not tell him the whole truth, because he would not have liked it at all. It had more of a conspiracy cult feel to it than anything else.

Kingsley and my uncle were outside the building, restless and nervous. When they saw my father and me leaving, they ran to ask us questions. The passing of the test gave my uncle a breath of joy in the face of his disappointment with the poor agility and the obstacles he had encountered on the arduous road to adoption. I would have liked to reassure him and anticipate that from now on everything would be easier, but I couldn't either.

We looked for a good place to eat, while sightseeing in Madrid, and in the end, we went to a great Galician restaurant near the Plaza de las Descalzas. Everything was so good. When we arrived at the hotel, there was an envelope for my uncle José at the reception desk. The letterhead read: "Abogacía del Estado" (State Attorney's Office), as an announcement that it was something important. Briefly, it said that she was the lawyer with I don't know which number and that the Public Prosecutor's Office had assigned her to his case in order to complete the formalities, and that he had an appointment with her first thing Monday morning in her office. My uncle was delighted with the news, and exclaimed,

"Finally something is working properly in this country!"

I laughed inside, because it certainly wasn't like that. I know that no one wanted to impress me, that they had nothing to prove, but, without a doubt, that we were working like a Swiss watch, and it was only the beginning.

We were staying in an austere and spartan hotel in the Moncloa neighborhood. We took Sunday to go sightseeing in Madrid. The Royal Palace, the Temple of Debod, the Edificio España. I couldn't stop being enraptured looking at those buildings, which for me were true works of art. As night fell in Madrid, and Kingsley and I asked permission to wander alone in that territory of asphalt, concrete and strange bustle. Except for some guidelines from my uncle, we were not hindered. We went to the famous Retiro Park. I saw everything with different eyes. I imagined the way they had designed that huge artificial pond, so well framed in that natural environment full of plant life. It breathed forest, no matter how much they say about pollution in big cities. Despite the enormous differences, that beautiful metropolis did not fail to bring back memories of my real hometown. I didn't want to be sad, because soon my dream of returning to Brooklyn would be fulfilled and I would start looking for the true love of my life, relentlessly, among labyrinths of terracotta brick.

As we walked through the pedestrian streets of the Retiro, I kept feeling a strange sensation. As if someone was watching me or following me. I would turn around, but no one was there. At times, my brother Kingsley, more than used to my oddities, would ask me what I was worried about, but I was unable to tell him because it was just an impression, as if someone was calling me, thinking about me and wanted to see me; there are no words capable of describing it, or at least I can't do any better.

I made up my mind not to pay too much attention, because no matter how much I looked in the direction my intuition was telling me, I could see nothing. We stopped for a moment at the fountain dedicated to the fallen angel, that winged man, raised on a pedestal and at the same time trapped on earth, permanently punished and whose expression seemed to suggest that he had received unfair treatment.

As so many other times, I was left wandering in my thoughts, asking myself questions about the relationship between the extraordinary beings I could see, and that angel expelled from paradise. It didn't take me long to react, surprised, when next to me I could see that lady. For a moment, my breath caught. I recognized her immediately, it was Paloma. I was startled to find her there, by chance, I don't think so. She dressed in the same way, with her scarf, the beads, her prescription glasses and her smiling thinness. Her intentions seemed good, but, even so, I was frightened, I had no interest in exchanging impressions with that lady. I wondered to myself if taking the test was the best way to find Angie and remembered that sometimes it is better to skirt the mountainside than to climb it in a straight line.

Did you know that this monument dedicated to the fallen angel is exactly six hundred and sixty-six meters above the sea? Curious, isn't it?

"Good afternoon, Doña Paloma; the truth is that we didn't know it, it doesn't say it anywhere. Allow me to introduce you to Kingsley, my cousin."

They both gave each other two kisses, in a closer greeting than I had with her for the first time.

"What a coincidence, Doña Paloma!" I exclaimed, with ulterior motives.

"I would like to talk to you alone for a few moments."

My brother seemed to have misunderstood what she said, so I asked him nicely in English, although I always tried to speak to him in Spanish. Kingsley agreed and sat on a bench in that gazebo, listening to the street concert of a saxophonist who had a small crowd gathered there.

"Tell me, Paloma, how can I help you?"

"I want to ask you some questions about something I can't make any sense of."

I was afraid, because the rules of the shadows were clear: no one could know my secret.

"I have some questions to ask you too, ma'am," I tried to counter.

"Well, son, you start."

"How did you find me? Are you following me?"

The old woman laughed.

"You see, David, I don't have to beat around the bush with you, because I know you are also sensitive, and don't insult me by contradicting me. I found you because among my abilities I have a special one: it is an ability to follow with my instinct everything I concentrate on and I have touched recently, that's why I knew where you were."

So, that was what I had perceived, I could not believe it, this world is much more than it seems.

"Now it's my turn to ask. When I shook your hand the other day, I saw an immense overflowing goodness in your heart, pure and uncorrupted, but I also saw you shoot someone with a gun without any malice in it, can you explain it to me? Because you are only sixteen, seventeen years old?"

I was stunned, damn it, I was in a predicament I didn't know how to get out of. I had no use for a stupid excuse or an insistent denial, so I answered his question.

"Do you think there is evil when the police respond to a bank robbery alarm and turn their firearms on a criminal who threatens the employees with a knife? Do you think that this policeman, a real person with a family, sworn to protect life above all else, has the desire and the will to kill?"

"No, I don't think so. But you answered me with another question, and you don't want to tell me the truth."

"What truth? What do you want to hear from me? Do you want to know what I think? Do you want to?" I raised my voice in alarm, angry that she had breached my privacy without permission.

"Yes! That's what I want!" She shouted back.

"The truth is that evil is everywhere, masked in false smiles; in the envy of the friend who says "have a good time this vacation"; in that junkie who has turned his vice into a need, and the need into pure evil, willingly forgetting who he was; in that frustrated father who beats his children or his wife because they have sold him success in smoke boxes. I can't stand this world where being a good person is a handicap, do you understand?" I exclaimed with my eyes unfocused.

She came over to comfort me, but I had to tell her,

"No! Don't ever touch me again! Never again!"

"Forgive me, David, for the misunderstanding. I needed to know, even if I pay the price of your enmity. I had to be absolutely sure that you could be one of us, and I am convinced that you will be the most special of all. I want to teach you the way that no one can see anything inside you, if you allow me, and although I already know that you can see evil clearly, I want to teach you also to see the goodness in others. I have been waiting for you for a long time." This she said quietly.

"Accept my apologies, I think I have lost my manners. Right now I would like to be with my brother and return to our hotel."

"Logic. I had thought of applying to tutor you and teach you everything I know little by little in the United States, only if you don't stay mad at me."

I thought about it for a few seconds, although offended to the core, I understood that perhaps there were people with the same abilities that she had, and I had to protect myself from that. After all, she had been totally honest with me, and although I did not see her goodness, I found no evil.

"I agree, only on one condition," I said very seriously.

"I'm all ears." She began to smile shyly again.

"I'll need some freedom to do my own thing."

She understood right away, and although it was also about righting so much wrong, my real goal was to find Angie.

"Deal," she said, extending her hand to seal the pact, but immediately withdrew it when she saw the way I was looking at her. By the way, David, curious pendant. It is full of prayers and protections, which, no doubt, have been invoked by someone full of wisdom and power.

This lady didn't miss a beat. I'm sure that the vast majority of people who claim to have supernatural abilities are just charlatan con artists, but this elderly woman was one of those rare exceptions where the undisputed evidence inadvertently concludes in an irrefutable truth.

Finally, we said goodbye, without delving any further into the matter of the amulet. And I, at least, was partly relieved, because she did not mention anything about shadows or reddish beings. That meant that I could only see the material actions in others; it was something I had to meditate on in time and slowly.

Right away, I joined Kingsley, who was shaking his head and wiggling his upper body as he sat there, enjoying the live music. It was getting late and we had to get back to the hotel. We took the subway, which smelled of electrical sparks mixed with industrial grease, orienting ourselves like villagers in that spider web of a map at Atocha station. The day was coming to an end and we would have to get up early, but we still shared a short but a pleasant time on the small terrace of the room, all together, chatting while my father smoked his old and worn pipe.

We accompanied my uncle and Kingsley to the lawyer's office, which turned out to be in the Ministry of Justice, in the heart of the capital. We arrived a little early, with the car ready to leave for a trip later. At the door was a young woman in her early thirties. When she saw Kingsley, she had no doubt that it was us and came over to ask for my uncle José, staring at me from time to time, winking at me on one occasion. I, not knowing quite what to do, gave a half smile as a sign of gratitude. We were allowed to park in an area designated for official vehicles, and the three of us went up to the office. After more than an hour, which we took advantage of to have coffee in front of the office, my uncle and my cousin came down, smiling.

"We can go now. It's all settled now, it's a good thing, with competent people," said my uncle, visibly happy.

In his hands he held a folder with all the sealed documentation. Now Kingsley was, officially and in the eyes of the law, one of the family. We set off on the road to Burgos, bidding farewell to Madrid once again, although only for a short time. My uncle, satisfied and proud of having fulfilled his purpose, carried in his hands the most desired gift for his wife: the confirmation, in writing and with all the guarantees, of the adoption.

With my head leaning against the car window, and my hair blocking part of my vision, I reflected on the paths of life, on how strange and opportune coincidences cross between people; in short, the best gifts that The Order gives us cannot be measured with a price.

Happiness does not have it.

Chapter 23
To Run

Andrin-New York, late September 1996

The goodbyes began, with the hatred I have for them. I stayed at the gym until the last day. The teacher, a man with a steely character, wished me the best of luck, encouraging me to continue training wherever I went. My good friend Javier froze. So many afternoons together, breaks and weekends were too many ties to break; now the distance would become enormous. I said goodbye to the Alberti family, who with so many favors had grown fond of me, and I of them. I went to see, of course, Father Damian, who gave me such good advice and helped us so much. He prayed for a while by my side, and after that he blessed me holding my head, I closed my eyes expecting a slap out of the blue, but he didn't give it to me. I reciprocated with a big hug and a kiss on the cheek, he returned it to me sighing with sorrow disguised between encouragement and good wishes.

Sunday was approaching and the farewell with Natalia was inevitable. Nothing until then had hurt me as much as that moment. Although I wanted to put up a wall so as not to fall in love so much, some pretensions are never fulfilled, and seeing her for the last time, breaking up with her, broke my heart. We kept kissing each other hard, passionately, squeezing our bodies in embraces, with the impression that we might never again have the chance to feel that for each other.

As hard as I wanted to be, in my thoughts arose the reasonable doubt that I was betting everything on a past memory, but that pending debt did not stop hammering in my mind. It was stronger than any of my wills, but something also told me that I was being unfair to my present.

A discreet salty tear slid down my impassive face making my chin a spout over her shoulder. I tried not to let her know, but I don't think I succeeded.

"I'm sorry, Natalia, for having to choose. I'm so sorry, I'm sorry, I'm sorry," I repeated without pause in her ear. She remained silent. "There are so many things I would like to explain to you and I can't, I have so many secrets that it's as if I were carrying a huge sack of stones on my back."

"We can talk about it. What is it? Share the load with me."

"I can't." I had to lower my eyes, resigned. "It's forbidden to me. And even if I could, you'd think I was crazy. I just want you to know that, if it weren't for these crazy things of mine, I would never separate from you, I would never lose you."

She kept a straight face, trying to guess what I was talking about, although she was also already used to my strange rants, full of hidden and indecipherable signals that only I understood and that I needed to say to give entirely incomplete explanations, justifying myself only to myself to feel better about the decisions I had made.

"Well, David, will you call me from time to time? Will you tell me if that place is as nice as in the movies?"

"I promise, I'll call you and send you pictures of amazing places that are never in those movies."

She burst out laughing with her forehead next to mine.

"You talk as if you've already been there."

We promised each other that we would always be friends, and that, even if it hurt, no one else, no other person in the world could be "the first" as we were to each other. That memory, unique, would always be clean, illuminated and decorated on our soul shelf.

Back home again, and deeply affected, I tried to concentrate on everything I had to carry as luggage. I knew I could not take the weapons I had hidden in the forest, but nothing prevented me from taking a bit of that parallel and secret life, so at dusk I went to my hideout and threw in a backpack all my dark clothes, the black shirts, the flashlight, the binoculars, the gloves, and I was thinking about the balaclava, which I finally decided to leave in that waterproof bag together with the firearms, the knife and the magazines, all well organized and preserved in some cans and airtight food bags. I left everything as it was, burying the backpack with great care again not to leave marks on the ground.

That equipment was the first thing I put in my suitcase so that it would stay at the bottom. I could not run the risk of crossing the American border with firearms, and, on the other hand, getting another one in the United States would be a simple task. I had to go to Torrelavega, in Cantabria, to change the three hundred thousand pesetas into dollars. I went to several banks so as not to arouse suspicion among the employees, and then I distributed all the money in the pockets of my pants and jackets.

I admit that I may have been a bit paranoid.

On Saturday they phoned to confirm my pick-up time. I spent that last family dinner totally distracted and restless. I simply had a hard time getting away from my mother, my aunt and uncle, Kingsley, and of course my father, with whom I wasn't going to take advantage of his entire stay at home.

A driver came to pick me up in a black Citroën BX; it was a cab, but unmarked. The only thing that revealed the car's dedication was a small plate on the back, next to the license plate, which read PS, "public service". The driver waited patiently for the end of all the hugs, the advice of my father and uncle, the cries of my mother and aunt, the timely absence of Kingsley and my futile search as he watched me from a distance, sparing me the pain of a heartfelt farewell.

I was surprised when that driver, who was driving quite fast, headed towards Santander. I had imagined that we would go to Madrid by road; but nothing like that, there was a small plane waiting for my arrival on the runway at Parayas Airport, Santander.

I was not used to so much attention and I did not see myself capable of enjoying, without shame, such luxuries. That small plane took less than an hour to arrive at Madrid's Barajas airport. The stewardess of that small *jet* took me to the international departures terminal, where I met Paloma, who was also accompanied by two other girls and a boy, all about my age. Visibly happy, she came over to welcome me and ask about the trip. I couldn't get over my astonishment, I had arrived in Madrid in less than two hours. I was standing there, in the waiting room of that Iberia flight to New York.

We had to wait very little time to board. Our tickets were economy class, a detail that seemed strange to me compared to the previous flight.

I checked out the rest of the group, and only one of the girls, who was with me in that building in Plaza Castilla in Madrid, looked familiar. We sat together on the flight, not knowing quite what to say to each other, paired by that common experience of the previous week. It was clear that the other guys knew each other perfectly well, their conversation and confidence were fluid. I, on the other hand, with my classic intermittent asocial behavior, refused to talk about irrelevant trivia by initiating small talk. My flight companion looked at me slyly, not daring to initiate conversation either.

I focused on looking out the window of the plane, amused by the frenetic and orderly movement of vehicles and operators, until our metallic bird faced the exit and accelerated the engines to full speed to catapult us to our distant destination.

We broke the ice when the flight attendants, pushing that tight-fitting cart down the aisle, offered us dinner. She was a girl with curly light brown hair, medium height, rather short, slim, large brown eyes with green flecks, and a pretty smile; although I was sure her presence in the group was not motivated by her beauty. Something more prominent and noticeable would make her different from the rest. I barely exchanged a few words with her as we were served that miniature can of soda, and dinner in plastic containers.

So much pragmatism provoked too much artificial sensation, it was eating for the sake of eating, without decorations or pleasures. She, on the other hand, seemed to enjoy the taste and the presentation. Then they brought us a blanket and without realizing it, they reduced the intensity of the lights. Without asking for permission, she removed the central armrest that separated our seats, reclined the seat as little as she could and rested her head on my shoulder, having covered herself with the blanket.

I looked out the window at the black and distant ocean, which, below us, and oblivious to my observation, was swaying on the surface, waving trails illuminated by the moonlight. She seemed totally asleep, and I, uncomfortable as I was, did not know how to put myself so as not to wake her up. After a while, and accumulating a painful tension in my shoulders, I also reclined my seat, and very carefully raised my arm over her, who leaned against my chest, and with her forehead next to my lips I had the perfect position to kiss her. Somehow, that approach caused my body to ask for it, but the mind, always more powerful, prevailed.

I didn't know her at all, only from the other day. I had heard her name, I think, but I wasn't quite sure; Claudia, maybe. With that last thought, and absorbed by fatigue, sleep closed my eyes and made me forget the place, the context, my destination, my worries and my purpose.

I remember waking up almost startled on a couple of occasions, by some turbulence, I imagine; I removed Claudia's wavy, tousled hair with a caress, and felt her warmth on me, putting me back to sleep instantly. An intermittent ding woke me up fully; she and I were half lying and leaning against the window, hugging each other, she on top of me. Embarrassment took over and I had no choice but to wake her by whispering her name in her ear, louder and louder. She opened her eyes as if her eyelids were rusty and looked at me sketching a good morning smile, ran the sleeve of her shirt over her lips and checked to see if she had smeared drool, glad that she had not. She sat up naturally and checked that I was not far away.

We had missed breakfast, and we listened to the annoying repetitive sound telling us to buckle our seat belts. It was pitch dark, out the window a blanket of white and orange lights stretched almost as far as the eye could see, only blurred and interrupted by the presence of the water between the city. It was the outline of the Hudson River and Harbor Bay.

Fuzzy memories began to sprout in my mind, as if I had already experienced that same landing at JFK airport in Queens on many occasions. It was the first sign that awakened buried experiences, and never better said. Concentrating on bringing my lost past back to the present, I did not notice that Paloma had been talking to Claudia for a few seconds without taking her eyes off me, perhaps wondering what was going on in my head.

"You two seem to have hit it off really well. I'm glad."

And although I agreed with the silence, I still thought it was unusual to have slept in such an embrace after only three minutes of talking.

"I'm sure Claudia and I are going to be very good friends, but that's all."

Then she, in front of Paloma, kissed me hard on the cheek and added,

"I think we're going to be very good friends, too. I'm really glad we're in this together."

And she winked at me, sticking out her tongue a little, smiling, on the opposite side. The truth is that I didn't really know what she meant by that.

"Well, children, fasten your seat belts, we'll be landing shortly."

And Paloma turned to the other guys to give them, I guess, the same instructions. Once at the airport, we waited in the crowd for that metal mouth to spit out our bags, spinning on the conveyor belt. We headed for the checkpoint, with Paloma as our guide, and when we got to the police officer, she told him who she was and mentioned the name of a captain. That officer took the bundle of passports, stamped them quickly and opened a different divider, ushering us through and waving a firm hand on his plate cap as the rest of the travelers queued at another counter.

Although sore and tired from the trip, my senses were still awake. That airport was full of bad people, all accompanied, ignorant and unaware, of their corresponding reddish beings that helped them in, who knows, whatever misdeeds they were doing. I preferred to focus on getting on with my plan. It was almost six in the morning, and in Spain it was not long before noon; I had to adapt my body to the new schedule. It felt like being hungover.

We had a few days to settle in and adjust to our residence, an old, refurbished school in the Newark neighborhood. It was brick, with white wooden windows and seemingly fragile glass, its own fenced courtyard, basketball court, library, game room, movie theater, assembly hall, dining room and, of course, the dorms.

They had let us organize ourselves as we wanted, but Claudia left me no choice and took it for granted that we would share a room. It seemed strange to me that at our age they didn't put those kinds of limitations on us, but later I understood that they knew that, whatever happened between us, the fact of sharing or not sharing a room wouldn't avoid it. In fact, prohibitions could have the opposite effect; however, despite the permissiveness, mixed rooms were very rare.

Our room had peeling red bunk beds, two old oak desks with drawers, a coat rack, a metal wastebasket to match the beds, four small oak shelves and a couple of lamps. Best of all was the huge west-facing window looking out. At the end of the corridor, separate bathrooms and showers for boys and girls, and, on the other side, a wide staircase to go up and down.

Our room was located on the second floor. Those who had been there for a long time moved to the upper floors, with better views and fewer people passing through the staircase. For me that second floor was a gift of chance in my plans to go in and out as I looked for Angie, as always in complete secrecy. I couldn't wait to find a moment of solitude to head to the old factory, our warm industrial home in the Brooklyn neighborhood, and start looking around.

All the newcomers, about thirty young people from different countries, were summoned to the assembly hall. A man in his forties, wearing a gray suit, no tie, straight hair, rectangular, thin-rimmed prescription glasses, a thin face and a prominent nose, was waiting for us all to begin. In the front row were, besides Paloma, other older people of various ages, who must also be the tutors of the rest of the classmates.

"Good afternoon, everyone."

"Good afternoon," we replied in unison.

"I am Edgar, director of this center, and I am here to welcome you on behalf of our community. First of all, you have been given a brochure with what you should say about this place and why you are here. The brochure spoke of a residence for high-achieving students and elite athletes. But, as you were told at the entrance exams, our organization has a greater purpose. It is vitally important that this information remains confidential only among us; our personal safety depends on it, it is not a trivial matter."

Behind hum was a folding white screen and an overhead projector.

"I am going to show you some slides; we have selected the least shocking images, even so, I hope they do not offend your sensibilities. Friday, February 10, 1989. A young gunman enters a university biology class, and starts shooting indiscriminately, especially aiming his weapon at the girls in the classroom. Among the dead, one of ours; we know that she was the target of the attack. She was on the verge of finding a cure for HIV and made the mistake of sharing her findings with her professor, who, of course, was not one of ours; a man of no malice, who told a businessman friend in the pharmaceutical industry; this in turn to another, until one wanted to look after the interest of continuing to sell antiretrovirals. As difficult as it may be for you, you must protect your talents with silence and discretion, avoiding standing out too much."

We were shown the image of her lifeless body together with police metric witnesses.

"Only among ourselves can we be free to express all our knowledge and abilities and develop advances with confidence. Because, as Nicola Tesla, the great Yugoslavian inventor, said,

'When a genius invents something, and wants to know if it will succeed, he should not ask himself who it benefits, because it will fail. He must ask himself whom it harms.'"

Edgar had a great power of communication, he moved around the stage dedicating seconds of his gaze to each of us without ceasing to gesticulate, projecting the message he was sending us, although, of course, I was eager to find the moment, selfishly, to begin my search and did not pay much attention to his sermon.

"That is precisely why your tutors and I are here. We are now all part of humanity's hope to improve little by little, and to close the gap between the elites and the rest. Whatever gifts you have proven to have are as useful as those of anyone around you. Here the airs of superiority are forbidden, we promote self-confidence, which is something very different, determination in decision making, emotional intelligence, conflict resolution, empathy and assertiveness, social skills, the use of different registers in communication, and all with one goal: to achieve the benefit of a human group that will never know it was your work, but that, without a doubt, you will improve their existence."

The speaker approached the lectern and took a calm drink of water, continuing with his speech,

"We have been promoting this purpose behind the scenes for decades now, and we are proud to say that we have succeeded in improving the world, not as much as we would like, but we are getting there one step at a time. We have abolished slavery in this country and everywhere else. We have fought for fair labor rights. At times we have had to defend the indefensible in order to infiltrate and influence from within, operating as advisors to the worst and most tyrannical leaders. Our radius of action knows no borders, ideologies or greed. We are against anyone suffering abuse, and war is the worst of our fears.

"The messages of love in almost all the songs is not the result of chance, it obeys an educational intention of respect and affection between people, but we already know that this is not enough to stop evil, which many times and unconsciously is introduced into the minds of people disguised as false unhealthy competitiveness, materialistic eagerness, and desire for success and power. That is why here you will live in an austere and spartan way; I am sorry for those who come from wealthy families, you will have to get used to scarcity, despite the fact that our resources are practically unlimited."

I didn't care about that, I came from a lower-class family, but I could feel the discomfort of some students.

"This way of life is part of the education that is intended to be instilled in you, so that no one loses touch with the reality of the majority of the world. You must begin to see money as a tool, and not as an end. Excess makes us weak, causes harmful temptations, alienates us from human coexistence by making us live in huge isolated and lonely houses, and is an insult to those born poor, who find true happiness in human relationships. Don't worry, you will understand little by little."

He paused, walking across the stage with his hands clasped behind him, giving special emphasis to what he was about to say.

"That is why you are asked to pass your exams properly, and to be very careful about standing out too much, that is what your tutors are here for, to guide you properly and ensure your well-being and safety. Finally, it must be said that you will be provided with timetables for unofficial subjects. You will be given classes in Negotiation and Manipulation, Communication, Socialization and Self-Control, and in the case of some you will be taught in a somewhat special subject. That's all, guys. Finally, I welcome you and tell you that my office door is always open for anything you need."

Afterwards, Paloma and the rest of the tutors talked for a while. Claudia and I went out to the courtyard; she kept talking about the girl and how sorry she felt for her. She was frightened by everything she had heard in that presentation. I, more and more distracted, kept thinking about how to get out of there and start my own thing. That place, that strange secret community with cult-like overtones, Paloma, Claudia, Edgar…, all those people didn't matter to me. I had moved away from my parents, from my uncles, from Kingsley, from my whole life, for a reason, and that reason was not them. I heard Claudia's nervous and excited voice in the background; I interrupted her by resting my hand on her shoulder.

"I'm going to the room to change my clothes; I need to go for a run. I'll be home for dinner, in case anyone asks."

"How? Well, I'll go for a run with you, I don't want to be alone here."

"No way, you won't be able to keep up with me."

She looked at me with eyes of slaughtered lamb and good girl face, insisting.

"Please, please, please, please."

"All right, I'm going to change, tell Paloma we're going for a run, and I'll wait for you at the exit. I'll be warming up. Don't get too warm, or you'll get the seven evils, okay?"

"Thank you, thank you, thank you."

Uncontrolled and excited, she gave me a kiss on the cheek and went into the auditorium to tell Paloma.

I quickly changed clothes, left the others lying on my bed and wrote her a note on her desk: "I'm sorry, Claudia. I need to be alone. I didn't mean to lie to you."

I rushed out the door, jumping three steps at a time up the wide old staircase, crossed the perimeter waving to the janitor and started running in the opposite direction of the assembly hall. As I rounded the corner, a strange feeling came over me. Wisdom brought me to my senses, I hoped I wasn't too late. I turned around and went back to the room, heard footsteps on the stairs, crumpled up that stupid note and slipped it into my pocket just as Claudia appeared, smiling and in a hurry to put on her tracksuit.

"I'll wait for you downstairs, hurry up, otherwise I'll leave without you."

She took off her sweater and threw it at me with all her might, I closed the door to protect myself, and suddenly I knew I had done well to go back and not leave her lying there; it would have been unfair and treacherous. We warmed up and I immediately started running; she complained that it was too little warm-up, but time was running out for me.

I realized that no matter how much I wanted to, and even if I had gone alone, I could never have covered the nearly twenty-five kilometers that separated the residence from my former home. We reached the Hudson River, and in front of us was an incredible and classic Hollywood Manhattan skyline. That same image, which I remembered as mine when I saw it in the movies, was now in front of me. It was right there, just a stone's throw away, so close and yet so far.

We had to go back so that no one would worry about us. But that didn't stop us from lingering for a few minutes contemplating the hustle and bustle of ships, lights and frenetic lives. To get to the old Brooklyn factory, we still had about fifteen miles to go. It was too much, and the ferry schedule ended at eight o'clock in the evening. I saw that Claudia was resentful of the effort, my haste to move forward made me force the pace. I proposed to her to return to the residence by taking the subway and her face was filled with relief after so much running. I asked one of the locals where the PATH train station was, because I knew we were close by, and sure enough, the station was two blocks away.

"And you, how do you get along so well around here? It's as if you know everything, have you been here before?"

"It's just that before I came here I was memorizing maps and stations in the library, so I know where I'm going. You have to do your homework, Claudia," I laughed and pretend scolded her.

Getting back to the residence on that railroad took us only ten minutes, but it made me realize the enormous distance we had traveled; that explained why Claudia was sitting in that train car like a used rag. She looked at me knowing I was thinking just that, she was laughing at her lousy appearance, but she wasn't doing anything about it either.

We were leaving the Newark station and right in the main lobby I froze for a moment. I had seen other reddish beings there before, but never anyone accompanied by so many. I could count twelve around them. A tall, thin, yet broad man. Caucasian. With a bony face and a shaven head. He could not have been more than forty years old. I was struck by his big feet encased in shiny brown shoes and his ivory-colored trench coat. Holding his hand was a little girl of about eight years old. She walked stiffly, almost shuffling. Something dark and evil was happening in front of me, disguised as a familiar archetype.

"What's the matter, David? Are you paralyzed?"

Claudia tapped me on the shoulder with her fist to get me out of my lethargy. I didn't know what to do, I had never intervened directly, in public.

"Stay here. Don't move, and no matter what happens, don't even think of screaming or coming near me."

I shook her by the elbows so that she would confirm that she understood, because now she was the one who was surprised and immobile. She stood there still without knowing what I was talking about. Her feet frozen to the ground and her gaze with those big eyes kept scaring me, because I knew she was very serious.

I partially covered my face with the black sports bandana that I fortunately wore around my neck, imagining my appearance as that of a remote stagecoach robber, intercepting the strange couple as they passed and opening my arms in a cross, preventing them from continuing in a straight line. I could see Claudia, worried, watching me from the window outside the station.

"I don't know what you plan to do, but I'm not going to let you do it."

The girl wanted to free herself from the rough and sinewy hand that deprived her of her freedom, but the bonehead squeezed her tightly. The reddish beings went into alert mode; I saw them clearly doing their job, I was almost unfocused watching them. Through one of the corridors a couple of policemen were arriving, but something did those beings to call their attention from the other side of the station. Not even the passersby noticed the atypical scene, the reddish ones diverted the attention of every possible candidate to witness something while my pulse was accelerating more and more. I, helpless and improvising on the fly, stripped of the advantage I had always had in making a plan, didn't know what was going on or how it would end. The girl was pulling hard with both arms to get rid of him, but the man was squeezing her small hand, to the point that the little girl exhaled a howl, shrinking suspended in the air. She couldn't wait any longer, enough was enough.

"Let her go!" I shouted at him with all my might, noticing that he was putting his hand on the back of his belt.

He was going to hurt me, but I, who already had experience from the gash I took from that thief in Gijón, reacted quickly considering that I already knew he was right-handed. A low and forceful kick to his right leg, he instinctively bent down, almost bowing, and the hand he was going to use to wield a weapon was brought to his knee to mitigate the pain. The girl let go of his hand and stood there paralyzed, I could see her that small instant. I leaned on the bent leg of the bony man, who now bent over matched me in height, and jumped on him kneeing him in the chest. He was trying to get up. I was about to elbow him, but I saw that I didn't have to. It was a matter of seconds before he understood that he had nothing to do.

Now yes, the whole station was watching the show; the girl ran out, I shouted at her,

"No! No! Wait! Wait! Wait!"

But, frightened, she ran out of the door opposite Claudia's. I looked at her to tell her to grab the girl as I grabbed him by the neck. Claudia's hands rubbed across her unhinged face denoting her anguish. And, suddenly, I saw a large group of reddish beings coming down the same corridor.

I couldn't believe it, behind them the same pair of policemen from before were coming after them. One of the agents took out from his belt a long black leather fender and the other one a Taser electric contact weapon. The way they looked at me it was clear that for them the bad guy was me, and they were going to show no mercy using both instruments. There were about twenty meters to go before they reached me. I felt around the bony man's trench coat and found what I was looking for, his wallet. I took it in my hand, released the tension on his neck while the police officer raised his Taser, ready to strike.

With both of us lying on the ground, I kicked out and then jumped up as best I could, narrowly escaping a beating.

"He's the bad guy! He's the bad guy!" I shouted at the top of my lungs, so that even the echo was heard in that big station hall.

It was obvious that, with my face hidden behind a handkerchief, strangling the man and carrying his wallet in my hand, I was not the most convincing person; even so, I tried. I was the victim of a reflex action to help that kid.

It gave me time, a microsecond, I looked at Claudia but she was no longer there. A hollow sound brought me back to my situation. The police officer, a young, short, athletic man, with that plate cap on his head, dropped his fender to brandish his firearm with both hands.

"Don't make me shoot you, kid! Don't make me!"

It's funny how our senses act in stressful situations: I had time to see that the policeman was wearing a wedding ring, I looked into his eyes and I could understand that his intention was not to hurt me, but to stop me, not to mention that my shadow did not show up at any moment. I didn't hesitate, I turned around, taking the risk, and started to run.

I pushed with all my might against the heavy solid door of glass and metal, and I could feel the bustle of the city outside. I turned around just for an instant and saw the police officer chasing me. I looked around at lightning speed hoping to find Claudia, but I didn't see her. I started running at full speed; I was going so fast that I almost fell down. A man tripped me when he saw the scene, I started to lose my balance and without any remedy I was already lost, falling face first to the ground. There, lying on the asphalt, I could see that the reddish beings were following me in the distance. They were influencing me.

I got up as fast as I could, picking up the wallet again, and without feeling any pain I kept running, the agent's footsteps and relentless pace felt closer and closer. It was a long-distance race, but in the first few steps I made the mistake of pushing too hard. I could hear him behind me shouting over the radio the streets we were crossing. At a short distance I heard sirens, and suddenly that scarf was suffocating me, I uncovered my face and repeated the words of my shadow: "It's a matter of effort".

I began to take longer strides, to deepen my breaths, to throw my head back a little to catch more air. It was working, I could feel it getting farther and farther away. I rounded a corner and saw an open dumpster. I jumped over it and jumped in like someone jumping over a small fence. Between garbage I held my breath so he wouldn't hear me gasp in exhaustion as he ran past. Red and blue lights illuminated all the facades I could see.

"He's got to be around here! Look in the doorways, under the cars! Comb everything!"

I could not forgive myself for having been so stupid, impulsive and foolish. Hundreds of thoughts were racing through my mind at once; I knew the experience well, what explanations could I give for what had happened? They would lock me up in a mental institution and throw the key into the sea. The light of a flashlight oscillated wavering around me. In one of those luminous swings, closer and closer, I doubted if it was my imagination or if what I was seeing was a hallucination of what I wanted to see. In front of me, the familiar imposing silhouette of a guardian. I saw his shoulders turn toward me and his elongated forefinger raised to his face, totally dark and featureless, clearly indicating to me....

Silence.

Chapter 24
I Am Not Alone

New York, October 1996

Rarely in my life have I felt so much relief that I was not alone. Someone was climbing the container and the light of a flashlight peeked out. I was in a fetal position with my eyes wide open; my body wanted to explode with tension. One of the officers shone his light directly into my face. Right next to him, that guardian with the outstretched, still hand, almost three feet taller than him, was covering me in some strange way.

"He's not here!"

"Don't stop looking in every nook and cranny! He must be here somewhere!" shouted the voice of a policeman who must have been the chief.

"You have to get out of that dumpster, time is running out and I can't stay here long," said the guardian with that deep and penetrating voice that characterizes them.

"But there are police everywhere, and all the neighbors are looking out for me," I said, skeptically.

"I have come to help you because I am indebted to you, but my stay here is limited. Do as I say and no one will be able to see you."

I held my handkerchief tightly over my face, and making as little noise as possible I climbed up and out of the large metal garbage can full of bags. The shadow walked behind me with hands and phalanges outstretched. Cops crouched down looking under cars, opening and checking all the doorways, focusing their flashlights on the trees meticulously, and me, walking beside the officers with shrugged shoulders, fearful and incredulous, almost on tiptoe. I arrived at the corner, where I saw the policeman who had just moments before had chased me down. The officer was sweating profusely, describing to a superior officer what had happened.

I would have loved to apologize to him, to be able to explain things to him at length, to clean my image in his eyes. But I passed by him, protected, like an anonymous and cowardly spirit. On his chest, under the coat of arms of the NYPD, it read "Harris".

Already a couple of blocks away, far from the police siege, sensing that he was leaving, I asked the shadow,

"Do we know each other? You said before that you were indebted to me, how so? Whose are you?" I heard him laugh for a few seconds.

"Since you are a liaison, I will tell you. Most never get an explanation, eventually everyone ends up intuiting how The Order works. I am the guardian of Doña Isabel, the lady you helped in Gijón. Although I induced her to walk quickly and made her feel the danger, if you had not been there, it could have ended very badly. When a person helps another person in any trouble, especially when he is a complete stranger, a bond is created between the two and his guardian will always remain indebted and will return the favor when he is nervous, worried or frightened, as was your case just now."

"How did you do that?"

"We are beings of light, we can manage it as we please. Light and the slowing down of it, and therefore of time, is an example of our power. There are many people who sometimes need to cross a border, or soldiers surrounded by enemies to escape without being seen, for example. But we can also make someone stand out, shine in a theatrical performance, make the best impression in an interview. Favors acquired by doing good to a fellow human being. They are little winks, tricks, that only another guardian in your debt can do for you. They usually invoke our help by imploring, pleading to the cosmic universe, or simply with the anguish of an important problem. Your protectors, normally, only come to you on a fatal occasion of life or death, unless you have also helped another of their protégés."

At that very moment, I remembered the wolf.

"What's that about a link? You have already told me more than once."

The guardian maintained a long silence, the way one acts in the face of an uncomfortable question.

"I thought you would know this from your protector. I will explain quickly because my presence on this plane is very limited. A liaison, or link, is an individual who should have already left the physical spectrum and advanced his progression along the path of light, becoming a guardian. That is why your reality blends with ours."

"And why do I go on like this? Why did I come back again? Could it be because of love?" I asked in a rush, aware that time was running out.

"I would love to tell you that yes, and that you will leave happy and content because another soul joins you to this confused world in whose atmosphere pain and pleasure, innocence and evil, selfishness and altruism are chaotically mixed, but it is not so, David. You have returned here because in the last instant of your past existence, when you were about to finish your journey, you did something totally contrary, something really contrary to your destiny, but don't ask me about that because I don't know. What is clear is that this is the reason why you can have contact with both types of entities, with our plane and the opposite one.

For you to understand it in a more understandable language, the time you have in your current existential manifestation and the concept of purgatory are a reasonable comparison, roughly speaking. Although I must tell you that, at the moment, you seem to be doing very well."

I listened attentively to his explanation, while little by little all my schemes, my project, my illusion, my courage were crumbling.

"When you need us, think of us and someone will appear, don't drag it out so long. I must go." His figure disintegrated in front of me, letting in the reflection of the light of a Victorian building with a long staircase enclosed by two beautiful old and well-preserved railings.

"I was so blind, so deluded, so stupid!" I reproached myself on the way to the residence, smelling of who knows what.

In that phase of internal mourning, it was all the same to me. It turns out that my strange and unique existence was an opportunity, a last test of effort to categorize myself between being a shadow, a servant of protection, or a reddish being, whose existence is fueled by injustice, tyranny and malice. I felt like the biggest idiot in the world, believing that my memory and abilities were due to the unraveling ties that bound me to Angie.

Step by step, reflecting, understanding and speculating, I found myself emptier and emptier with every meter. Absent-minded, I no longer cared if I found the police, the wallet I was carrying, what had happened with Claudia or where that small girl was. I was only focused on myself, my circumstances, and the pitcher of cold water with which the shadow and his ambiguous explanations had soaked me.

Like a little boy, I arrived at the wall that delimited the residence, sliding my hand over the rough bricks worn away by time, enraptured, engrossed, almost in *shock*, I refused to accept the new reality. The Order didn't care about my particular desires, the love I had carried from another life; I was only here to conclude what I was going to become when the time came, that final moment that comes to all of us.

Shouts brought me back to reality.

"David! David!"

With my head down, I looked up; it was Claudia, she was running towards me. She crashed against my chest in an embrace, kissing the lower part of my cheek, as far as her height would allow. I, sad, apathetic and indifferent, remained still, with my arms and body unusually relaxed by the blow I had received. Claudia grabbed my face with her cold hands.

"Are you all right? Are you all right?" she kept asking me.

"No, I am not well. I want to go to my room."

I continued walking, leaving Claudia behind me, with a rude demeanor. She just stood there, with her huge eyes full of sadness and concern. Almost at the entrance I stopped, the guilt of being unfair did not let me move forward. I turned around and she was still there, motionless, disappointed. I walked slowly back to where she was. I took her by the hand, without interlacing my fingers.

"Forgive me, Claudia, my soul is a mess."

I gently tugged on her hand, and she began to walk beside me, I put my arm around her shoulders and gave her a lingering kiss on the temple, apologizing for my nauseating odor. We opened the door to the room and, sitting on the bottom bed of the battered bunk bed, was Paloma. Hearing our footsteps, she jumped up.

"You had me worried. You took too long. This is New York, everything happens here, don't you see?"

Unwilling to do so, overexerting my mood, I justified myself for both of us.

"We went for a run and accidentally got lost; it took us a little longer than we thought to find the residence, we apologize."

"No. It's okay, guys. Put yourselves in my place, I know you have to scout, but always have money on you so you can at least call from a pay phone, call the tutoring section, okay?"

"I promise you, Paloma, it won't happen again. We lost each other."

"And how was the race, how did you like the city?"

Discreetly, I hid the wallet behind the elastic of my sweatpants, covering it with my T-shirt.

Paloma said goodbye but not before giving us some ill-received messages about sexual protection, I went ahead and made it clear, also subtly, that our relationship was not of that type.

Sticky yet dry, Claudia wanted to talk about what happened.

"First of all, I'm going to take a shower, and we have to have some dinner. We'll talk about it later."

I grabbed some clean street clothes and jumped into the shower. The light from the study lamps was leaking from under the doors of some of my classmates' rooms. The girls' and boys' showers were separated by an incomplete wall of a little more than two meters high, there was a gap of about twenty centimeters to the ceiling, so Claudia took advantage of that space, and threw iced water over me from her shower, laughing. Suddenly, the strong uneasiness I had felt because of what the shadow had told me was diluted by Claudia's lively enthusiasm, who happily passed on her energy to me.

It was past dinner time, so when we went down to the dining room there was no one there. They always left something to eat in a two-door American refrigerator for these cases: cold cuts, cheese, milkshakes, juices, bread, things like that. We grabbed something and sat down by the window. The dim light of the school's lamps merged with the orange of the ones on the street, illuminating the worn solid wood table in two tones. Claudia insisted on leaving the dining room light off, she liked the ambiance the gloom offered us.

"Well, David, may I ask how you found out about the girl?" Straight to the point, without preamble.

"First you tell me what you did and then I'll explain it to you, as far as I can."

"Okay. When you started all the fuss, I thought you were crazy, but when I saw the girl running in terror, running away from that man, I knew you were right about something. As I saw that you were coping well with the guy, I thought that the girl should not run around alone. I needed to know what had happened to her."

"The girl's name is Margot; it took me a few minutes to gain her trust, but finally she told me that a while before, when she was playing in a park a few streets away, that man tricked her by saying he was going to show her a puppy he had nearby; and then, when Margot realized that something was wrong, he told her they were going to a place where she would be with many more children, playing all day long, without classes and eating sweets. Suddenly, she felt afraid because she started to remember the things her mother had told her: not to trust strangers, the bogeyman, all that. The little girl insisted that she wanted to go back to her mother, and then that man threatened her and said that he was going to kill her and her whole family if she didn't obey him."

"But then?"

"Then you appeared and as soon as she saw the opportunity to escape she ran away. As there were so many police in the area, I stopped a patrol car and told them that the girl was lost, that she was very scared, nothing else."

"Clever", I thought.

"I went back to the station, but they had the perp being treated in an ambulance. Everyone was saying that he had just been mugged, what a pity, and stupid things like that. I asked a witness if you had been arrested, but he said no, that the bastard had run away from the police. That's why I came to the residence to wait for you. I know you're not a robber or a bad guy, but I don't know who you are either."

"Actually, I am a mugger." I threw the black leather wallet on the table. Claudia was surprised and didn't touch it. "I took it from him in the struggle.

"We have to tell Paloma about this. We have contacts in all branches, don't we? She will help us."

"Whatever you do is fine with me, Claudia. But I don't want to know anything more about it."

"But how can you say that? What if he abducts Margot or other children again? Won't you do anything?"

"He's not going back for that girl because he's not stupid, and I've risked enough."

Claudia was clearly angry at me.

"What the hell happened to you today, David? You don't look the same!"

I wanted to be reasonable with her. She was my roommate and my only friend there.

"Look, Claudia, you are here to study medicine, and I am here to study architecture. The us you are talking about is not here to pay attention to small, specific issues; we are part of an organization that operates on a large scale. They try to prevent wars, to make sure that water reaches drought afflicted regions of Africa, that a large part of humanity has access to sanitation, things like that, but they will not conscientiously take care of Margot or her abductor; at the most, they will give responsibility to some police chief, and he will take care of that as well as everything else. That's the impression I have of this place."

With each of my words he seemed to get angrier and angrier, but now it was because she realized that I was probably right.

"Well, we have to do something, David! We have to do something! There may be more children in danger!"

"Keep your voice down!" I whispered, "We did it! We've stopped him from taking that little girl! We've done it!"

"Well, it's not enough!"

Her fists were clenched on the table betraying her pent-up frustration.

"Claudia, you are an idealist. Although you already knew that. But the world doesn't work like that, we are eternally surrounded by evil and injustice, and even if you avoid something today, a few meters away there are other things just as bad or worse, and your good intentions, although noble, are not enough to eradicate all that cruelty."

"So, answer me this question: why did you intervene at the station?"

I stood there for a while not knowing what to say.

"It was an impulse, an impulse to do the right thing. But it could have cost me dearly. The policeman pointed his gun at me, I had to hide in garbage bags and everyone thought I was the criminal."

"That's what I mean, to do the right thing. You have to finish what you've started and that's the way to do it," she said, staring at the wallet on the table, timidly illuminated by the light from the window. Something tells me it's not the first time you've done something like this."

"You don't know anything about me!" Now it was me who did not control the volume of my voice. "Nothing!"

"I know more about you than you know about me. I know that in addition to being secretive, you are inconsiderate. You haven't even bothered to ask me why I'm here; you don't know anything about me."

In the darkness of that dining room, we both remained silent for a few eternal seconds.

"Look, Claudia, I don't have an identity conflict, I am the way I want to be. I'm sorry you don't like it, but I have no other choice. I'm going to turn the page, focus on organizing everything to start my studies, and I would like not to talk about it again. I'm going to bed."

I picked up everything I could from the table expecting her to come to the room with me, but she didn't. Her expression was a mix of calm, anger and disappointment as she remained seated in the night darkness, alone in that huge dining room where my steps were duplicated by the echo of the emptiness.

I put on my pajamas and got into the bed. Again that feeling after the tension, that heavy tiredness pulled me to the floor causing me to fall into a sleep from which it is difficult to escape. Suddenly I woke with a start, I sat up with a jolt. I looked at Claudia's bed, but she wasn't there. Barefoot, I hurried to the dining room; worried, I reached our window table and she wasn't there either. I had never felt so angry and worried at the same time. An unfamiliar pit was getting bigger and bigger in my stomach. Another cold sweat broke out on my back, fearing the worst, and my sense of guilt only increased by the second.

I hurriedly opened the drawer of a cupboard and grabbed two equal, sharp, medium-sized knives. I returned to our room and silently took my gloves, put on my black clothes and T-shirts, the belt with the flashlight, a navy-blue Yankees cap and the bandana around my neck; finally, I slipped both knives into the belt at the sides of my hips.

My heart wanted to burst out of my chest, I was ready, but I had nowhere to go, Claudia had kept the wallet and I was sure I was going to do something crazy. I stood for a few seconds in my room, I wanted one of the shadows to come and help me, just as she told me before. The fear that something would happen to her, the feeling of responsibility and the helplessness of not knowing what to do, brought my body down; I fell to my knees on the wooden floor. Desperate and bleary-eyed, I whispered,

"Please, somebody help me! Please, somebody help me!"

I looked up, suddenly feeling that I was not alone; the room was full of crowded shadows. The strange sight shook me, the appearance of so many together could be frightening to the untrained eye; to me, however, tranquility came over me, and that image suddenly, without knowing why, seemed familiar, something *déjà vu*.

"Thank you! Thank you for coming!"

I would have loved to give them all a hug, but I knew it was materially impossible.

"What can we do for you?"

I could recognize, I can't explain how, maybe by his voice, his energy, I don't know, but I had no doubt: there were Gallego's guardian, the one of the boy in the freezer, Isaac, Natalia's, mine and an unknown one.

"I need to find Claudia. I'm afraid she's in danger, I think she's gone after a criminal."

The unknown shadow stepped forward.

"I'll take care of it."

Without a word, all the other shadows, so thin, tall and dark, faded away, allowing the soft, warm light from my desk to pass through. The unknown guardian raised his hand, in the space between the bunks and the wall. A light from his hand created a parallel reality in front of us. Claudia was riding in one of those yellow cabs, a beat-up '87 Chevy, as she looked at the photograph of the abductor.

Just what I was afraid of: she was going for it.

"I need to get to her before it's too late."

The sharp image disappeared as he lowered his hand.

"Follow me."

Chapter 25
Superhuman

New York, October 1996

And suddenly, it disappeared from the room. An unfamiliar feeling told me that the shadow was outside. A fleeting glance through the window of the room confirmed its presence outside the walls of the remodeled school. The thick darkness of his figure stood out in the night, the street was deserted and his immobile, patient posture accelerated my haste. I had to get out of there as soon as possible, inconspicuously and quickly. Fortunately, since we arrived at the old school, I had done nothing but keep think about that possibility. I had not imagined that the moment would come so quickly and now I had to put it into practice.

I turned off the lamp on the bedside table, left the room and without running, but taking long strides, I walked as fast as I could, sticking as close as I could to the wall so that the old wooden floor wouldn't creak under my feet. I arrived at the laundry, my escape plan. I looked at the hatch and, indeed, a very large tubular square descended vertically about three meters to a container full of sheets, tablecloths, and towels, all stuffed in transparent bags. Regretfully, I took a bunch of sheets from the shelf, clean, scented and starched, and tied them together at the diagonal corners. Three were more than enough to cover the height.

I couldn't go out the front door because a janitor was guarding the perimeter from the access control post. Word around the residence was that he was armed, but I certainly had no desire to confirm the rumor. And, although the drop to the bags was only about five meters, I had to think about the return. Finally, I tied the end of the sheet securely to the firm steel pole of an industrial mop, pulled the makeshift sheet rope through the metal conduit and it went all the way down. I hastily soaked the sheets with mop water; this is the only way to guarantee a strong resistance of the fabric.

As I went down that gloomy passage, I remembered my father, all that I had learned from him and how he was helping me.

At full speed I got out of the container and ran around the back of the residence. A little further on, I distinguished the long shadow of the guardian waiting for me; he disappeared, and instantly emerged about fifty meters further and further away from the residence. I was becoming disoriented by the moment with so much haste, nerves, and anxiety. On that last occasion he did not vanish. With his elongated arm stretched out and tipped by his index finger, he pointed to a van next to us, in front of a plumbing company.

"On the right rear wheel are the keys," he said in his deep voice.

Without hesitation I ran to get them. I opened that old Dodge Ram, sat down in the driver's seat and moved the seat forward a bit as it started up. Accustomed to European cars, it took me a few seconds to pull the knob to unlock the handbrake and to place the automatic lever to start the car. Valuable seconds I couldn't afford to waste.

I accelerated to full throttle. The shadow guided my way, appearing and vanishing every hundred meters or so. I saw the guardian on the right side of a street and turned in a hurry. He vanished and reappeared a few meters ahead, but this time in the middle of the lane, his hand open, signaling me to stop. I slammed on the brakes; a little further on there was a *stop sign*.

"Wear your seat belt, drive slowly, respect the *stop* sign and then go straight ahead."

I did as he told me and, as I passed the intersection, I could see a police car with its lights off, stationed on that corner. I narrowly missed having them chase me again. Then I went full throttle again, squeezing all the speed that old van could offer.

Moments later, almost oblivious to the journey, I faced the majestic Brooklyn Bridge, as flamboyant as the last time I saw it. I crossed it in the blink of an eye.

"You're nearly there. Claudia is around the back of that bone-colored house." His tone sounded like a farewell to me.

"Don't go yet, please. I need you; I can't do this alone."

"Just because you don't see me doesn't mean I'm not there."

I put the van in neutral, and turned off the lights and the engine, letting the inertia move the van a little away from the house indicated. I stepped lightly on the brake pedal, took a deep breath, put on my bandana and pulled my cap tight. I immediately recognized the area; I was in Carroll, a former Italian immigrant section of Brooklyn. I got out of the van, left the keys in the ignition, and carefully screwed the door shut. Arriving from the corner, I paused for a split second to contemplate the facade of that little single-family house, etching its image in my mind, its dimensions, and recreating its supporting skeleton. It was like a mania that I could no longer shake, whatever the situation.

Small narrow hallways separated the structure from other similar cottages, leading to a backyard. With great stealth, I reached the back and found Claudia crouched down, looking out a small basement window from which a faint orange light was emanating. She was tapping gently on the glass with her knuckles. I assumed she would want to break the glass and do something crazy that would put her life in danger. In complete silence I stood behind her, totally distracted, and whispered her name:

"Claudia... Claudia."

She turned around with a dumbfounded expression, accompanied by a hasty and unhurried inhalation of air. She did not expect to see me there. I placed my finger on her mouth.

"Shhhhhhhhh. We're getting out of here."

I took her by the hand and pulled her gently. She refused, offering strong resistance. For an instant, I was filled with rage at her refusal. She insisted that I look through that little window. I squatted down and looked out. The first thing I saw was the figure of a reddish being staring at me while shaking its head from side to side, like a threat through that refusal.

In that immaculately white room, lit by an old kerosene lamp, two little girls were tied to beds by their wrists. Next to them an eyedropper was injecting something into their veins. One of the little girls was struggling against the heaviness of her eyelids, trying in vain to open her eyes fully. The poor thing was struggling to raise her hand to get our attention. The deepest sense of pity does not do justice to the feeling that moment conveyed to me.

Recently, I knew I had become prone to impulsive behavior. I restrained myself from being foolish.

"Claudia, we're going to do this right. You know medicine, don't you?"

"We have to call the police, very strange things are happening here," Claudia said.

"You're not focusing and you don't see the situation in perspective. I told you in the dining room to leave it alone, to go to sleep, and you can't think of anything else to do but come here to investigate what's going on, or did you come to return his wallet?"

"Not knowing something does not imply that it does not exist. It was you who pretended to look the other way. Now that I know what's going on, we'll call the police and they'll take care of this madman."

"It's too late now, Claudia! You don't understand anything. The police are insufficient, don't you see? The bad guys don't abide by rules, they don't respect norms, nor rights, nor principles. They always play with an advantage, and this criminal is not just any bad guy, he is someone who is very lucky."

"What does luck have to do with it? The police will know what to do."

"The police are guided by strict protocols. They can't enter the house unless someone's life is in clear danger. Even if a patrol car looked out that window and saw that girl, he could justify that it was someone sick, a relative, a friend's daughters, I don't know. And they wouldn't be able to go in and check anything. So let it go, Claudia, we are here and we know that this guy is dedicated to doing evil. Now I ask you a simple question: are we in this together with no matter the consequences? Yes or no?"

With her gaze lost to infinity for a few seconds, she fixed her eyes on mine again.

"We are together, David. I know what I've learned about medicine myself. But in this case, it is easy to know that he are administering an opioid sedative with a morphic active ingredient. The frequency of administration is long, and the dose is very low, probably so that it does not cause tolerance and inhibit their respiratory systems, but, as you can see, it is a sufficient dose not to escape from a deep sleep."

"So, for the time being, their lives are not in danger. The first thing we will do is try to get the girls out of here. That is the priority. We will try to do it without being seen. I'll climb this tree and try to sneak into the house, go down to the basement and take this little window out of its frame, because, as you can see, it's secured by a lock. You will go in and take the dropper from them; then you will go back outside, I will pass you to the girls, drag them a little, if necessary, slowly so as not to make noise; then I will come out to help you. Outside, to the left, there is a white van labeled with a drawing of a smiling tap with eyes. It's open; we get them in, start up and get the hell out of here.

"What about the guy? Is he getting away with it?"

"We don't even know if he is in the house, if he has an accomplice. None of that is important right now, our priority should be the girls; revenge doesn't suit me. If we stick to the plan, it will go well. Put your hair up so none of it falls in the room, and if you touch anything use your shirt as a glove so you don't leave fingerprints. You must be very meticulous with these instructions. Take one of these knives in case you have to defend yourself; keep it in a safe and accessible place."

"It is obvious that you have come well prepared. I, on the other hand, am a disaster."

She took my hand when I was already turned, ready to go up.

"Be very careful," she said. I nodded.

Immediately, I was climbing the sturdy tree, which had grown strong in that small, dark courtyard. I reached the second floor without difficulty. There was light coming from a window and I could hear footsteps upstairs. I turned on my flashlight with the green filter so that I could plan the climb and memorize the branches to hold on to, then immediately turned it off.

I was getting closer and closer to the top of the tree and stability was being compromised centimeter by centimeter. In front of the second-floor window, the shape of my body mimicked the dull branches, and the blackness of my attire camouflaged me in the thick darkness. Fleeting like a star in the firmament, I could see our guy pass restlessly down the corridor.

Suddenly, he turned on the light of the room whose window was in front of me, closed, but without the curtains drawn. My camouflage no longer gave me so much confidence, I could only remain as motionless as possible so that nothing would attract his attention. With my face covered and my cap on, I kept my eyes half-closed, wishing to remain as unnoticed as possible by the outside environment.

He opened the drawers in a hurry without closing them again, taking out effects from inside, he hastily put them in an old brown leather suitcase. Everything was going well, nothing outside caught his attention, I controlled my breathing and maintained my postural discipline with integrity. On the bed, he put his chest on top of the suitcase and with his hands ran the zippers on both sides to close it. He was in a hurry, a big hurry. He was in a hurry. Until the unthinkable happened: one of the reddish beings, if not the same one from downstairs, I'm not sure, entered the room.

He lifted the suitcase off the bed, relieving it of its weight and recovering its usual shape. He was leaving the room loaded, ready to turn off the light and continue with his things, when the reddish being, staring at me in front of the window, began to slowly move his finger on the glass. I began to hear a creaking sound. I could not believe it. One of the square portions of thin glass cracked causing a sharp and brief sound, at the same time that miserable and evil being held my gaze, giving me away.

The kidnapper immediately stopped under the doorway, dropped the suitcase and headed for that old-fashioned sash-opening window. Actually, I had already sensed that everything would go wrong when I made the plan in Claudia's company. In any case, I preferred to take on the danger myself, and I needed to stay focused on the unforeseen events that might arise.

Selfishly, I did not want to worry about her safety.

Now I regretted having doubted myself, questioning my own commitment, that obligation acquired voluntarily to defend ethical justice and that a few hours ago, in front of Claudia, in that dining room, I betrayed myself. I went-back on the promise I made, all because of a strange disappointment. Because nothing seemed to be as I imagined. Worst of all was that, because of my indifferent and irresponsible attitude, lacking empathy for the victims, Claudia had had to take the reins and lead me back.

There perched on that branch, like an absurd giant bird, while he came closer to see me, I reflected on my stupidity, on my indirect "participation" with evil and injustice by evading the fulfillment of my duty, and on how doubt puts us in danger. A chain of danger.

He approached the window. He noticed the small square shard of broken glass and looked out. I stood motionless as the leaves and thin branches fluttered in the light New York breeze. He lifted half of that window all the way up and I myself felt the air change direction going into the house. He leaned out and looked down; I did the same to check if he was able to see Claudia, but fortunately the thickness and abundance of that tree prevented him from doing so.

Several of the reddish beings began to crowd around him; there were more and more of them. Now he sensed that something was wrong, and that something, which was me, was barely five feet from his nose. He was so tall that his face was flush with the upper frame of the window. The prominent features of his face and that empty expression, almost devoid of humanity, accompanied his countenance trying to decipher the fault that he could not see.

His big blue eyes, the same ones that once belonged to a child without malice, now reflected the coldness of a slightly frightened man, obstinate and at the same time perverse. I wondered where and when this turning point occurs. What is the trigger that allows one to accept oneself as an active cooperator of evil, pain, suffering and anticipated death. Those beings who accompanied him, all in rigorous silence, pointed their fingers at me. Then he directed his hand to the wall and turned off the light in the room. He stared at the branches, the ones closest to the trunk. I watched him sharpen his eyes among the foliage, stretching his neck a few centimeters. It was a matter of seconds. I opted for the surprise factor.

I caressed that tree, thanking it for having hidden me, begging its branch to hold me without breaking. I took a couple of steps forward and I could feel the fright he felt when he saw me in front of him. From my initial position and the long jump I took, it must have seemed like a gargoyle attack. Except that I am an ambassador of good and righteousness, and I am not made of stone.

With the strong leap, I rushed into the room, landing on the elongated and malnourished body of my now victim. We both slammed into the furniture. He crawled backwards leaning on his hands, helping himself with his heels, while I was still recovering from the wretched blow I gave myself in the back with who knows what piece of wood. The fact was that something was wrong, not only because I had gained the upper hand in the fall, but also because the appearance of my shadow in the room. Once again, I had everything at stake. With no other possibility to act in my protection, I was gifted with the slowing down of the present, as always, in slow motion.

He pulled a firearm out of his pants. Everything was so slow and my consciousness so awake that I myself demanded more speed in my movements. The exaggeratedly elongated barrel of his semi-automatic pistol confirmed to me, at the first shot, that it had a silencer attached. That room, in total darkness, was illuminated with each incandescent shot. I clambered over the furniture to my left side, his right, hoping that the inertia of his haste in drawing the gun would direct the shots to the opposite side. Thanks to the extra time offered by my guardian, I was spared death.

Without warning, everything went back to the frenetic rhythm and propelling myself over the wall I jumped on him holding my insteps with my hands to drive my knees into his chest. He was clutching the gun as a survival resource trying to point it at me.

He was so tense that he still held the trigger of the last shot firmly depressed. I grabbed the gun by the burning sound suppressor feeling the intense heat through the glove. I was trying to pin him down with all my weight on his body, but he was resisting with all his might to let go of the gun. With my knee on his neck, he struggled not to lose it. I squeezed his forearm and bent his hand to the limit; it was his decision, either he would let go or the first thing to break would be his disgusting, elongated and protruding index finger, followed by a brutal dislocation of the wrist.

Naturally, he loosened the tension, a victim of pain, and gave up the pistol. Without thinking, as if in a reflex action, I threw it out of the window. I don't know, made me part with it, perhaps the fear that I'd resort to using it myself.

He was panting in an endless, arrhythmic fashion, the brief exertion had left him exhausted and he was getting weaker and weaker. With his head on the soft carpet, I stood up in the dark, dull room. I checked that my face was well hidden by the bandana and fastened the cap to my forehead so that only my eyes and my straight, rather long hair peeked out from its edges. I turned on the light, and without taking my eyes off him I put my hand out the window with my thumb up so that Claudia would be reassured and know that I was all right, although I wasn't sure she could see it.

Both exaggerated fear and overconfidence put us in danger. Taking something for granted, underestimating the scenario, thinking that one has the situation under control is the same as selling the bear's skin before it has been hunted. The prelude of the glass being broken by a reddish being, something unusual and never seen before, should have made me think that the union of so many of them gave them a special power. An announcement that foretold something bigger and worse.

"Are you in a hurry, are you going on a trip?"

He sat up slightly, still choking with shortness of breath and a dry throat. On his wall there were numerous titles: degree in Medicine and Surgery, title of medical specialist in cardiovascular surgery. "You should eat more. And exercise a little, doctor, you should know that better than anyone. I don't know what business you have with these girls; nothing good, I'm sure of that. What there is no doubt about is that you have tried to kill me. But don't worry, I don't bear grudges and I don't believe in the law of retribution."

By telling him that, I swung and caused an unwanted effect.

"Well, you're wrong, because I'm going to kill you, kill you, kill you, kill you and... kill you! Who do you think you are? Who are you, you little shit?" he shouted uncontrollably, with all his rage, in the middle of that silent night.

"Keep your voice down, Bones! I don't want to hurt you!" I threatened him.

I kept seeing all those reddish and evil beings next to him. They were giving him that security that seconds before I had snatched from him. He was growing by the minute, by leaps and bounds. Now I was the insecure one. Of course, a controlled and submissive situation would be ideal, but people influenced by the evil ones do not reason easily; they are robbed of their own dominion, of their sanity. I pulled the knife from my belt, on guard, holding it firmly, just as I had trained in Asturias. The blade jutted forward; my fist clenched. I needed him to cease his defiance.

"You'll have to kill me! You'll have to get blood on your hands!"

Leaning on the carpet he stood up and, although thin, his height was imposing, but above all that look full of anger, malice and hatred conveyed to me that he had nothing to lose; he was going to go all the way, and damn the consequences.

Having someone in front of you who is willing to die killing you is hardly desirable.

"Sit down! Sit down! Don't make me do it!"

His eyes looked teary, almost bloodshot. His jaw squared and clenched tightly. The veins in his neck and forehead were swollen. All those signs foreshadowed that nothing I said to him would stop him.

My hope was based on hitting him with a blow that would knock him out, then immobilize him while he was unconscious, and with everything under control, think about the girls and a decent solution. With his face crazed, opening his mouth and baring his teeth like a beast, he advanced towards me. I concentrated on hitting him with all my strength, smashing my fist, stuffed with the handle of the knife, against the side of his face, gaining momentum in a leap forward.

It didn't work. On the contrary, I lost the advantage of distance. He grabbed my neck with both hands, squeezing all the way to the back of my throat. The pain was unbearable. I gave him a very strong kick, but nothing would break him. Then I saw what was happening. Those reddish beings, one by one, were slowly entering his body, endowing that elongated and malnourished man with superhuman strength.

I didn't have much air left in my lungs and I felt my eyesight fading at the edges of my vision. My chest was burning, I had to act and fast! Something deep in my soul refused from the beginning to use the knife, I never wanted to wield it to inflict wounds, but now the situation was becoming desperate. I began to throw slashes tracing an arc against his torso. It was useless, his arms were much longer than mine, which made it impossible for me to reach him.

I felt my life begin to weaken, my legs began to fail me and stopped supporting my weight, I looked for the last time at the face of my killer, his expression unhinged, and joyful frenzy seemed to smile between evil grimaces. I was suspended in the air. The Bony One, now showing enormous strength, slammed me against the wall, still squeezing my neck harder and harder, dragging my back up the wall. My abdomen and legs spasmed uncontrollably. I heard knocking, I think it was coming from the floor below. The fleeting image of Claudia came to my mind, at that very moment I stopped feeling pain, my body relaxed, gave up. "One more effort, one more effort, one more effort!" I heard from deep inside me. I squeezed the knife with the little strength I had left, and with a muffled cry I began to cut his sinewy arm between elbow and shoulder. He wouldn't let up, one last cut on the inside and the knife dropped to the floor.

I felt my neck lax; it was the end, my mind was leaving my body, I was unconscious. An immense sense of peace, absent of pain, made me happy. I was no longer in that room in the Brooklyn neighborhood, I did not miss anything, everything mundane was indifferent to me, I did not feel material. It was something different, it was as if I was now part of a whole in which you can be in different places at the same time. And it was dark, but nothing worried me.

A beautiful multicolored light appeared before me in the distance. It was so beautiful that going towards it was irresistible. I was immensely happy, and I was not alone, I was welcomed.

They had come to look for me; they were the shadows, the guardians who had helped me so much. For the first time, I saw them illuminated by the majestic bright light. Their bodies glowed, overflowing with thousands of colors at the same time.

"Let's go home."

I was walking surrounded by them. Curiously, I still looked the way I looked, I looked at my hands and tried to feel myself, but I could not. None of the recent events occupied my thoughts anymore. I was being led toward the light and it grew larger and larger, I was feeling more and more intensely the infinite love that flowed from it. My illusion had no earthly comparison.

Then, in front of me, I could distinguish among all the shadows my guardian; his hand was holding me back as I passed.

"It's not your time yet, you have to go back."

"No! I don't want to go back!"

"You're not ready! -Not yet!"

Something was not right because the guards were very worried. They were watching in all directions warning of imminent danger.

"Your body will wake up! With you or without you!"

"Let me go on, let me go on."

That place was so attractive that not my family, Kingsley, Natalia, Angie, Claudia, nothing was reason enough to return. That dark and indeterminate passage was the final stretch to reach absolute happiness. Then I felt a strange presence in that place, something very different, something opposite. I looked up and they were the reddish beings, crawling along an invisible ceiling hoping not to be seen.

The worst scare in the world, I did not expect it. Their image, which, unlike on Earth, was always somewhat blurred like the heat of the asphalt, was now presented in a crystal clear and sharp manner. Their bodies were hideous, bloodied, with incurable scars; skin scaled with scabs, brown nails, disheveled hair, rotting teeth and exaggerated tongues. Like a hybrid of wild man and monster. I deduced that, as on the other plane, they could not see each other.

"The reddish ones are here! Take me to the light!" I shouted to my guardian.

Several of the reddish ones jumped on me. Even the hardest scratch or the deepest burn didn't hurt as much as the contact with them. It was terrifying to the core. They were taking me to the opposite side, where there was only darkness, emptiness and the smell of sulfur. I had no way to stop them; I was a wimp, a rag doll attacked by rabid dogs.

I had never been so afraid; it was the definitive end.

I wanted to resist with all my might. It was in vain. I was getting farther and farther away from the dreamed light. With the distance from the brightness, the fear grew greater. Horror took possession of me. My guardian returned to my side.

"The Order does not allow you, for the moment, to go towards the light. Your time of mixed existence is not over. You have only two options, and one of them is worse by far, but the decision is yours."

As the dreadful creatures dragged me further and further into the unknown abyss, that wonderful light was fading into that strange horizon. I longed for it without having been there; despite being completely terrified by those creatures, its brightness and color was still hypnotic.

"Please get me out of here, take me anywhere! Don't let these beings take me with them!"

My shadow approached me, defying all the laws of physics, in that strange tunnel whose norms were not governed by natural rules. With his hands gleaming in a thousand colors, as I had never seen them before, he brought them close to my head and we both came into contact. The stinging disappeared instantly;

peace returned to my soul. The creatures, dissatisfied, screamed with high-pitched screams. I watched them with pity and at the same time with curiosity, because I knew that once upon a time, they had been normal people, neutral souls whose weakness succumbed to the pleasures facilitated by evil.

A breathtaking speed transported my essence accompanied by my loyal protector. I felt vertigo and deep shock when I suddenly returned.

Again, the pain. I felt my body again. I had returned to the starting point of what was supposed to be a journey of no return. My back numb against the carpet, a sharp discomfort in my chest. I had never thought carefully about death; it was not that I believed I was immortal, it was simply something I saw far away, something that happens to others; however, that experience made me reflect immediately on the fragility of life, on the importance of my actions and the need to earn the final entrance to that wonderful place.

As always in earthly existence, something bad and something good intermingle in a potpourri of contrasting flavors. Soft, tender lips pressed against mine, quenching the burning in my lungs. A breath inside me, unmistakably sensitive, brought my breath back.

I coughed non-stop, I felt as if the walls of my lungs were overlapping, peeling off with every effort to catch my breath. Hot and cold at the same time. My eyes had been watering in my absence.

"Don't die, please. You can't die."

Claudia gave up, kneeling beside me with her brown hair in front of her face. I think the color of my skin had turned violet and funereal. I opened my eyes. They felt doughy, but at least Claudia's features reminded me that this world also harbors beauty.

"Tell me you're all right. Tell me you're all right," she repeated, shivering with relief.

She threw her arms around me, kissing every inch of my face like a madwoman. I hugged her back with one hand resting on the floor. I couldn't speak. Suddenly, I remembered everything that had happened and another troubling fear put me on alert again.

"Claudia, where is he?" My voice came out broken. My throat hurt like hell.

She looked at me with an indecipherable expression, with a certain halo of sadness and concern. Next to Claudia was the pistol with silencer, and that made me think the worst.

"He's in that hallway. I think he's dead. There's blood everywhere," she said in terror.

Chapter 26
Dustin?

New York, October 1996

I got up as quickly as I could and went as fast as I could to see the body. Weakness was taking possession of me. I followed the trail of blood until I reached his body. In my mind I recreated the scene of Claudia shooting him down.

"How many times did you shoot him?" I asked, ignorant of myself.

"None. He was lying like that when I came up. Both of you were lying on the floor."

I, stunned and shocked, accepted the situation with reservations.

"He must be saved! You're the one who knows, help me!"

Without even asking, nor fearing it in the least, I turned him over to make an assessment of his wounds. He had numerous and varied cuts on his arm, one of them next to his armpit, from which a lot of blood was gushing out. Claudia put her ear to her mouth.

"He's still breathing! So, he has a pulse. Let's turn him on his side and hold his arm up; I'm going to get something to pack the wound with."

"Shall I make a tourniquet with your belt?"

"No! The blood is dark, so the artery has not been severed." – She took some clean T-shirts from the open drawers.

"Keep pressure on the wound and don't separate them at any time."

Claudia ran downstairs in search of something, leaving me alone with him. I was convinced we were doing the right thing, but a part of me, a small one, was struggling to surface to insult me for my stupidity. I didn't want to listen to it. Immediately, I noticed Claudia coming up the stairs at full speed. Bandages, iodine, adhesive tape and scissors in her hands, on which she wore giant latex gloves. That made me ask her, worried,

"Claudia, have you been careful not to touch anything with your hands?"

"I have been careful at all times; you can rest assured."

The gloves confirmed this.

She was telling me how to help her to stop the hemorrhage. As she asked me, I placed a chair in an anomalous position, with the backrest in an upward diagonal to support his legs and to help blood circulation. Or so she explained.

"I have to immobilize him, all we need is for him to go crazy again, is that okay?"

"That's fine with me, but what are we going to do now? -I wondered in fear."

"Have you seen the girls? How are they?"

"They are sedated, but they are fine."

"Let's leave him like this," I said to Claudia as I tied Bony's feet to the chair with the laces of his own shoes, reinforcing it with his belt.

After that, I tied his wrists, apart and high, to the legs of the wrought iron headboard, with plenty of adhesive tape. Next, I explained the plan to Claudia, while she tucked him in with a thick quilt from the bed so he wouldn't lose body heat.

I picked up the knife and the pistol with silencer. I looked at the ammunition. There were only two cartridges left, one of them in the chamber. Enough. Claudia had spent a few to smash the lock on the entrance. I made sure that neither Claudia nor I left anything forgotten there, we couldn't leave any traces. I needed fresh ideas, and she came up with a great plan. I asked her to give me back the knife I lent her so that she wouldn't walk around armed with it on the street.

I took the phone from the bedside table and with the wheel I dialed 911. Claudia did everything just as she said. She put on a scared little girl's voice with a rag on the receiver.

"What is your emergency?"

"Help! Please! Help! Help my father!" she said in a magnificently trembling voice, almost in panic.

"Hey, sweetie, what happened?"

"My-my-my... daddy has fallen and he's bleeding, he's not moving! I'm so scared!"

"You're doing great, where do you live, honey?" asked the operator in an affectionate but urgent tone.

Claudia answered between feigned sobs, giving the address.

"An ambulance is on its way; it will be with you in a few minutes. Don't hang up on me, tell me if your father..."

"My dad is shaking! she shouted, so as not to stay on the phone.

"Daddy, Daddy!" Her voice trailed down the stairs as she ran into the street.

The plan went as we hoped. In the soft, warm light of that room, I remained sitting squatting, keeping an eye on him, who kept breathing harder and harder; I hoped he wouldn't regain consciousness in the meantime.

The ambulance arrived, without police. Claudia was in charge of leaving the door wide open and, in their haste, the paramedics did not notice the bullet impacts on the door. Loaded with metal suitcases, they shouted,

"Hello! Hello! Have you asked for help?"

In the entrance *hall*. Without taking my eyes off him, I left the room, taking special care to cover my face well, and stood at the end of the hallway with a direct view of his legs. I kept reminding myself of him every time I swallowed saliva, because it was as if I were passing a handful of nails down my throat. Dressed in blue and attracted by the light from upstairs, one of them went upstairs without a second thought, followed by a female companion. Another, perhaps more intuitive, warned his companions that something in that house was not to his liking.

"A wounded man! What the hell is this?" exclaimed one paramedic.

The paramedics observed the scene trying to guess and reconstruct the facts. The wide-open cabinets and drawers, pictures lying around the room, some broken furniture and the bullet impacts made them think that he had been the victim of a robbery in her own home. One asked:

"What about the girl who called? We must find her!"

It was time to intervene. I slowly approached the room, while with a pair of scissors they were about to cut the ties and his shirt.

"I wouldn't do that, lest he wake up and you two have a serious problem on your hands," I said in a sincere tone, gripping the gun with both hands, keeping the barrel flush to the ground.

All startled, and visibly frightened, they dropped everything they had in their hands and raised them. It annoyed the hell out of me to cause fear, I really didn't mean to, but on the other hand, I didn't feel like dealing with any misguided heroes either.

"This man is a very dangerous criminal, do not be fooled by his wounds and his respectable appearance. Do not untie him without the presence of the police." They listened to me without blinking. "In the basement there are two little girls, he kidnapped and sedated them. Just yesterday I prevented him from taking another little girl, and by stealing his wallet I found him today. Yesterday I had to escape from police officer Harris. I would like you to remember his name by extending to him my apologies and admiration." My voice cracked with pain.

My little speech was interrupted when I saw how, now from his body, reddish beings came out without stopping, abandoning him to his fate without looking back.

"Did you see that?" I asked while they looked at each other skeptically obviously worried about having a madman in front of them. I can see that they didn't.

"As I was saying, this man has a deep cut on the inside of his arm, I think I have partially severed the humeral vein, but, in principle, the bleeding has stopped. Do not let him out of your sight until the police arrive; then the girls, who are well, will confirm what I am telling you. Thank you for your work, you are true angels on earth," I cleared my throat uncomfortably. "It's time for me to go. I insist, contact Agent Harris."

Not one of them moved a muscle; only when they saw that I was leaving could they breathe a sigh of relief.

I snapped the pistol into my hip belt. I hurried down the stairs and ran out. The ambulance lights flashed amber, red and white on the street. I looked into the windows of the adjoining houses and no one seemed to be gossiping. The absence of the ambulance siren helped with that. The paramedics had respected the rest of the neighbors, and that favored my escape without witnesses. I ran to the corner where I left the van, looking everywhere, almost paranoid. The guardian's voice surprised me.

"No one is watching you; you can leave peacefully; the police will be here in a few minutes."

"But who are you? I don't know you."

"I am Margot's guardian."

Now I understood, it was as if he too was seeking justice for what had almost happened to his protégé. I opened the van door and got behind the wheel.

"Claudia?"

"I'm here!" she answered, hiding among pipes and junk in the cargo area.

"Sit with me, we're leaving!"

I started the van and after a couple of crossroads I turned on the lights. She was trying to move forward through the cargo area, between gadgets and junk, but she kept falling over, wheezing with effort. I stopped the van slowly, turned around and we stared at each other, very serious. She looked like a spider, holding onto the ceiling with her legs bent. She was angry with me, her eyes were devilish, from the stumbles she'd taken, but then we burst out laughing at the same time. I was shaking my head as she was shuffling through pipes, stumbling and stumbling all the way to the seats.

"Don't say anything. I forbid you to laugh." She demanded with a raised finger, but I laughed again, and she with me.

If it weren't for those moments, life would be meaningless.

We had covered a little less than a kilometer. Again, the guardian's voice burst into my head.

"Park the van and turn off the lights!"

Meanwhile, Claudia asked me,

"Did he wake? Was he still alive when you left?"

I swerved to the right, turned off the engine and lights. Seconds later, a police car cut across the intersection a little further ahead. Its blue flashes illuminated Claudia, who looked frightened.

"But how did you know?" she asked, impressed.

"Well, didn't you see the reflection of the lights in that window?" I thought to say.

In less than a minute, the police car was driving in the opposite direction, slowly, watching the cars in its path with a hand-held spotlight. We, hidden, felt it pass. Again, it stopped at the next intersection. Apparently, the cops call it 'doing the cage.' They cut off streets in an elongated radius from the scene, and little by little they close the circle, well-coordinated. Every car they saw was stopped and checked quickly, taking extreme precautions.

Peeking out of the dirty back window of the old van, I could see the police moving forward another intersection toward the house we had just left. Other police cars were reinforcing the surveillance with mobile patrols. Without the guardian's help it would have been impossible to get past the checkpoints. Slowly, and with the blue lights getting farther and farther away, I got back behind the wheel. I started up and continued on my way. Less than four minutes were enough to reach our destination.

I felt my soul sinking; a strange and unknown vertigo affected my heart. My little old Brooklyn textile mill, renovated as a home, stood before me as a desolate and neglected ruined building.

"Wait for me here, Claudia, I'll be right back," I said, feeling crestfallen.

"But where are you going? Where are we?"

"I ask you please, give me some time to be alone, will you do that for me?"

She had the gift of reading eyes. She moved her hand to my hair and, pulling back the bangs from my eyes, concluded by caressing my cheek,

"I owe you much more than that, David."

I got out of the van. In front of me, a makeshift fence from New York City Hall was intended to prevent entry. I only had to push it aside to gain access without any difficulty. The metal gate, ajar, made me wonder whether to enter or not. I expected something else. I expected to find our rooftop garden as manicured as ever, with the flowers impatiently waiting for the morning light. I expected to find the heart we always drew on our window, where we took turns every day to leave each other a message of love. I hoped to see that old salvaged light bulb that we always left burning. But most of all, I hoped to find my Angie. Anything from her: some clothes, a photograph, her name on the mailbox, anything. But no. Someone had taken everything.

Nothing was left in the kitchen. With the flashlight I could see cat food on the floor, and motionless in the corner, on a dirty cushion, the gleam in the eyes of one of them looking fearlessly at me. I climbed the stairs and reached our room, knocked on the window and looked around, reliving our happiness for a few moments. I had to accept that it was all in the past. That nothing is forever. That I was left with only blurred memories. I felt like crying. I kept wondering what the fuck happened to me when I was Dustin and why I didn't remember anything about my ending.

I went into our bathroom. Only the dirty tiles were left. No sink or anything. Leaning against the absent doorframe, the memory of Angie in the shower came to mind. Her long hair soaking wet. The beauty of her nakedness illuminated by the natural light from a skylight I designed myself. Her smile as she saw herself being watched by me when she kept her eyes closed because she was complaining about the shampoo. Reliving it, I smiled for an instant. The return to reality wiped it off mercilessly. Now, dirt, dust and mud were accumulating on the floor where only the drains full of bushes remained.

I turned off the flashlight and threw it on my belt, sore from the vision. I was giving up. Back to square one. Why did it have to be so hard? Now I questioned whether everything that was happening to me was a blessing or, rather, a terrible curse.

I was getting ready to go back to the van, walking down the stairs. I saw something move out of the corner of my eye. As if in a reflex action, I placed the bandana on my nose, and with my right hand I pulled the gun from my belt. With the rear sight and rear sight perfectly flush, I walked slowly with my arms semi-flexed close to my eyes. It's funny how when you're on alert you can hear every crack of the ground amplified.

Without taking the gun away from my directing eye, I took out the flashlight again. I could see nothing. Maybe extreme fatigue was playing a trick on me. Shining the flashlight was the same, there was nothing strange. I began to speculate on the presence of a small animal or cat, although I had the impression that I had seen something bigger.

For some reason, my own explanations did not convince me, and my body did not obey the tranquility. Without taking my aim off, I preferred to go back the way I had come, backwards. As I reached the staircase again, it revealed itself. I was about to pull the trigger with all my might. But it would have done no good. A reddish being was emerging from the back of what was once our living room. On the one hand, I was glad that my senses had not lied to me. I put the gun away and, without paying any attention to the reddish wanderer, I set out to descend the stairs at once, even angrier at the thought that my house, now, was also frequented by those repulsive beings. I had not even gone down three steps, when his voice paralyzed me.

"Dustin! Dustin Sanders?"

The voice was so shrill that it was annoying to the ears. I went back up the steps slowly and stared at him, surprised, because I never heard the voice of one of them and because it was the first time someone mentioned my real name. A few silent seconds, both of us remaining motionless, gave us time to stare at each other. A long shiver ran through me from head to toe, and I don't think there wasn't a hair on my body that didn't stand on end.

"We need to talk, Dustin." The voice sounded like fingernails tearing chalkboards.

Scratchy nails.

Chapter 27
Nearby Universes

New York City, October 1996

The silhouette of the reddish, incandescent being glowed in the darkness. Among the debris and cobwebs, the dust and the smell of homelessness, that being walked step by step approaching me.

"Back, evil one!" I ordered him with energy and decision, still with the fresh memory of the tunnel of light.

Instinctively, I reached my hand to Kingsley's amulet holding it tightly.

"Don't be afraid, I mean you no harm," he said in his squeaky voice, or so I thought I understood.

"Don't come any closer. Who are you?"

"It's me." He sounded distant and metallic. His voice was distorted in the air, and I struggled to decipher the sound.

"I can hardly understand your words. I'm having second thoughts and I'm not interested in what you have to say."

I turned around again, still clutching my pendant in both hands, and started down the steps. His voice was getting louder and louder and also more intelligible. That confused tone sounded like the desperate, halting cries of several people. I shuddered, but I did not stop moving forward; only one word, almost distinct, stopped me.

"Angie!"

Paralyzed by the name, I resigned myself to thinking. I was trying to make some sense of his presence in that ramshackle place, that place I once called home. I won't go around with presumptuous manliness. I was afraid. Those despicable beings feed on people, ruin their lives with happy shortcuts that pay dearly. I hesitated, but Angie's name coming from its lips, from its disgusting existence, was the freshest clue I could grab hold of.

"Sindade, Sindade." I couldn't quite make out the words. A gesture of his hands and body made it clear. He wanted me to sit on the floor. Bu then, "Get out... get out," he kept repeating, every second it seemed like a worse idea to just sit there.

I felt helpless, but at the same time I had the strange feeling of being in front of someone I knew.

With his hand outstretched in greeting, he offered me help to get up. I let go of the amulet and took a chance. I tried to take his hand, uselessly, and stood up again.

"No! No!" the reddish being repeated incessantly, shaking his head from side to side.

I sat down again because he asked me to. It was strange, because every second I spent with him the fear was getting more and more diluted.

He wanted to teach me something, and his constancy combined with my clumsiness only obeyed to a tiring process of learning, trial and error. He had to repeat it several times until I could understand him. My question and his affirmative confirmation made it clear to me.

"Do you want me to leave my body?" -I asked, more than skeptical.

"Yes! Come out, come out."

He held out his hand to me again. His gaze, blurred, but with a sincere expression. His demeanor, strangely kind. And what he conveyed to me. Everything made me, oddly enough, be able to trust him. There was something familiar about him. My instinct was pushing me to keep calming my nerves. He knew who I was. I had to take a chance.

I needed to know.

I tried to take his hand, but mine went through it like a thick red fog. He was gesturing calmly to me, as if he already knew it was a slow process. I watched him strain. Consuming energy as he spoke.

"Find my hand, feel it."

I liken this moment to the sensation one has, for the first time, when one can see a figure in three dimensions on one of those chaotic drawings full of spirals and strokes, apparently without sense.

I found his hand, moved the dial of my perception and found it. I squeezed it and he felt it too. He helped me to sit up and then I realized what I had done. A loud thud echoed behind me, the noise echoing in the old factory because of the echo. Alarmed by the sound, I turned around. What was my surprise to see the source. My body lay on the floor, eyes open, apparently unconscious. My understanding broke into a thousand pieces, leaving me paralyzed. The word "panic" does not do justice to the sensation I experienced. At that critical moment, my most pessimistic visions seemed to come true.

"Easy, Dustin, easy. I know it's a shock the first time, but calm down."

Now his voice was perfectly clear, and he addressed me with great tact and understanding.

"What have you done to me, you filthy creature?" I shouted.

"I have done nothing to you. You have so much more to understand. I thought you'd be further along by now. I'm going to step away for a while, so you can take it in. When you're calmer, we'll talk."

I looked at my body lying on the floor. I saw it breathing amidst the filth of the floor, which was littered with dirt, pigeon feces and garbage everywhere. Seeing myself like this, I felt truly sorry for myself. My self-respect prevented me from looking at myself as a corpse, alive but absent. I admit that I felt the most atrocious fear, uncontrolled hysteria.

"I don't want to be here! Make me go back to my body! Make me go back or I swear...!"

"You kept your secrets, your abilities, your gifts from me. What we are doing, this meeting, everything, is a past consequence. I have been waiting for you for more than seventeen years. Years of sacrifice, of pain, of injustice, of bounded eternity."

I was listening to what he was saying, but my consciousness was analyzing the whole situation in general. I was mentally accelerated. Worried.

"Answer me! How do I get back to my body?" I demanded, terrified.

"Your body always pulls you, no matter how far away you are from it, you will always find the connection. I have spent all this time learning how reality works, how these realities work. Relax and you will come back, just let yourself go. You will get the hang of it. It's innate to you."

It was true; I concentrated on my physical state and my essence returned with brutality. Suddenly, I was back to occupying my body, to feeling the pressure of my rib cage, of my face against the floor. My eyes were so dry that they seemed to stick to my eyelids. I breathed hard, relieved, coughing, but master of myself. The reddish being had its back to me, far off in the distance, amassing patience, or so it seemed. I swallowed saliva in the hope of hydrating a very dry throat.

"Forgive me, I got really scared. I don't know if I want to continue with this."

As he listened to me, I could detect the frustration in him, the hopelessness. His hands over his lowered head and his restless walk made it clear. I stopped to think sensibly for a few seconds. Seventeen years... Then I understood. I had inhabited my body since conception. Seventeen years plus nine months of gestation. And you say that all this is a past consequence? I had a moral obligation to listen to him, to give him a chance to explain himself. I needed to understand what the hell he was talking about and... why did he know who I am? The mystery was more powerful than the risk.

I leaned my head against a corner and closed my eyes, ready, again, to leave my body.

"Eyes open," he repeated several times until I could understand his detuned words.

With the sensation still fresh in my mind, I soon repeated the operation, this time unaided. The experience was so natural that I could hardly distinguish that I had escaped bodily limitations. Calmer this time, and more conscious, I investigated this new dimension. The creature in front of me now appeared clear again. His face, though haggard, was very familiar to me, as if we had met before. I had to listen to what it had to tell me.

So far I had just learned something really unusual, the out-of-body experience.

"What is this place? Why can I be here? How do you know me? What do you want from me?" The questions kept coming to this reddish man I couldn't remember.

"You're in shock, obviously. I'll explain it all to you, although it's too much information to take in at once. I'm your best friend. Sorry, I was Dustin's best friend and, as far as I can see, there's not much of him left in you. Anyway, we met at a congress, where I and other scientists presented to the world discoveries and hypotheses related to a new field of research: quantum physics."

"What do you want from me? What did we have together?" I insisted rudely, bored by the beginning of a biographical monologue.

"I will try to summarize. You introduced yourself at the end of that conference. You were full of enthusiasm and convinced, no doubt, that I would find your virtues more than interesting. At the beginning, you only asked questions; quite enigmatic, by the way. In the end, as time went by, we became friends and you proposed me to join a group of people whose number was growing. The entrance requirements were commitment, kindness and knowledge. You met one of the leaders of that small society, nicknamed 'Us'. Among the faithful, a motley group of personalities, with a great capacity to contribute: politicians, jurists, scientists, journalists, businessmen, all with the power to participate, with creative and, in many cases, sensitive capacities. You were the discoverer of the great threat to humanity. The one who confirmed the most feared suspicions, hiding at all times our small society, and for this you were persecuted to death."

"Threat?" I asked him, surprised.

"From the way you question me, I deduce that you don't know what I'm talking about, do you?" I shook my head, "That means that your plan came out half right. It was clear that we had to recruit young talents of kind essence all over the world, thus ensuring the increase of followers for the fight, but also the return of the lost ones, among them you."

My face must have been transparent, because the reddish one realized that it was certainly a lot of information all at once. I was overwhelmed to have someone in front of me, albeit a creature from another spectrum, but someone, after all, who knew my secrets. A part of me felt liberated.

"There's something here, my friend, that doesn't add up. If you were really one of us, it's impossible that you would have ended up being the creature I have in front of me."

"You really don't remember? I'm Daryl! -Your friend Daryl!"

Hope and frustration mingled in his expression. He sat on the floor with his elbows resting on his knees and his hands holding his head. He looked dejected.

"I'm sorry, Daryl," I said in a sympathetic voice. Something inside me tells me I know you, you're very familiar, but you must excuse me. My memories are very buried and sometimes they are slow to surface.

"It's not your fault. It's me, I'm desperate. Finally, the long-awaited day has come, and I am aware that you are no longer exactly the same."

"I need to understand. How did I get out of my body, and how can I share space with you and see you clearly?"

"I'll explain it to you in a nutshell, without too many technicalities. Have you read anything about string theory, parallel universes? Don't look at me like that, I know that your thing is architecture, at least it was. Or has that changed too?" I subtly shook my head.

"To make it easy to understand. It's as if in the same space, let's say, on a plot of land, a building with several floors is constructed. On each floor there are several inhabitants. Among these neighbors there is a very special one. A neighbor of mixed nature. Material and spiritual at the same time. The inhabitants of that floor want to live oblivious to their neighbors, although he can sometimes hear and feel them, above and below. He is too busy with its material needs to pay attention to that unexplained, mysterious, ignored and, why not say it, feared. But the true reality is that that spiritual half of which the human being in your dimension is composed is, on a daily basis, influenced by all those neighbors, good and bad. Are you following me, Dustin?"

"I think so. I've already heard something like this. Tell me more."

"You have that gift. Your essence can tune into all energetic, spiritual manifestations, which, after all, is the ultimate identity of a living being. As you told me, more than twenty years ago, you are a..."

"A link," I interrupted him, finishing the sentence.

"Exactly. You have more transcendental awareness. Spiritual. Whatever you want to call it. That's why I was hoping one day you'd come back spinning your memories. That's why you see the guardians. That's why we can be chatting right now."

"Since you seem to know me so well, what about Angie? I've heard you mention her."

My apparent best friend couldn't help but restrain his sense of discomfort. An uncomfortable grimace came over his face. He turned away from me, like someone looking for time to avoid the subject, but knowing it was impossible. His human aspect surfaced more than at any other time. His eyes were full of sadness, pain and melancholy. I saw them as he turned around doubtfully.

"What is it, Daryl?"

He stared at me. I noticed that he looked sorry.

"It's complicated, Dustin." He looked down at the floor.

"Complicated? What are you talking about?"

I started to get a little nervous because he wouldn't look up. Fear was growing in me. The silence between the two of us was shaking me inside. I understood that I had to calm down. I was about to lose control and treat him badly. But that would only make things worse. I looked around for a few seconds. I thought about the long journey I had made to get there. I saw my body sitting on the ground. Eyes open. Inexpressive. Like a rag doll. Yes. I had come a long way.

With the calmness that came of much training, and at the same time with a knot of nerves in my heart, I told him firmly, looking him straight in the eyes,

"Tell me, Daryl."

"Angie," he rasped shakily, "Angie died with you."

I felt the greatest emptiness I could ever remember. My whole existence seemed to be diluted. Each time he repeated his words to me, I felt more broken. Broken. Defeated. Completely defeated. How unfair this world was, I cursed silently. With all the good I had done, and fate still had a kick in store for me.

It was such a hard blow that I felt the very foundations of my being shift. I was dismayed. I refused to accept it, although I did not doubt him. I was not lying. Order was once again merciless with me. It crushed my only desire.

"What happened, Daryl? Tell me now! How did she die?" I was suddenly going through all the stages of grief: denial, anger, grief. I sighed, calming down. "Please don't beat around the bush anymore."

"I must explain a few things to you first. Things that you obviously don't remember at all and are key," he said in a more confident, imperative tone.

"No. No. No. No. No! How did she die?" I demanded uncompromisingly.

"It's not the right thing to do. Let me explain. Everything has a reason. Let me tell you," he insisted in a brotherly tone, and it was that same tone that made me fear the unthinkable. "You must calm down, Dustin."

Nothing he said diverted my attention from my question. I was overwhelmed by the need to know.

"Tell me!" I shouted as loud as I could in that alternative space, that parallel reality.

"I killed her! Are you happy now? I killed you both!"

And emptiness filled the entire ruined factory. A library silence remained between the two of us. I fell plummeting. The reddish one seemed very affected; I could feel his pain. Inside me a feeling of dismay surfaced. Disbelief. Incomprehension. Skepticism. And again silence. Absolute silence. That thin line of solitude and intimacy was broken by a mechanical interrogation.

"What?" I managed to articulate in a dying voice, "Are you telling me that you, my best friend in another life, killed me? Me and the one I loved the most?"

"It wasn't supposed to be like this! I betrayed you, Dustin. I was driven by greed. They offered me something no one else could. Access to absolute knowledge, self-realization and abundance. I couldn't resist and succumbed. Now I have to carry the weight of my actions, turned into this filthy being you see before you. And you know what the worst thing is? That this is not over. I betrayed you then and I must betray you now. For that is my punishment and also my fate."

I needed time to digest something so extreme. It was complex, because his words spoke of death and betrayal, but his non-verbal language showed that lingering and unmissable ember of humanity. There was still love left in him. Out of the darkness in which we were immersed, a pleasant, familiar voice emerged. It interrupted our talk and my eagerness to know more. To remember.

"David, can you hear me? Is everything all right?"

Cautiously, Claudia entered the ruins of that place, once a factory and then a home. With a worried voice, she interrupted my pain.

"I must return to my body."

I stared at Daryl. I knew I knew him, but I couldn't seem to rescue the memories.

"We will talk. But remember, you're in danger. That's all I can do for you. You can't trust anyone. No one."

"In danger?" I said, surprised.

"I must tell them that you are here. That you're back. Now go away if you don't want that girl to be scared to death seeing you lying there. And stay away from all your loved ones."

"To whom?" I asked hurriedly. "Who are you talking about?"

"I have warned you. That's all I can do for you. I owe you. Get away from it all."

He turned away from the conversation, without answering, leaving me with more questions than answers.

I returned to my numb body. I felt rusty. The pain in my back was worse when I was at rest. My eyes felt dry again. And heavier than before, I started down the stairs. I stopped in the middle of the flight, watching Claudia. She stood there on the landing, petrified, aware that she had disobeyed me. She had broken her word, her commitment. The only thing I had asked of her until then and yet she had not respected.

All of her exuded a sense of guilt. I walked down the stairs without saying anything, staring at her, resigned. I headed for the van. I ignored her, immersed in my thoughts. She, more slowly, followed my footsteps, got into the van and remained silent.

The night was getting darker, and the fog was gaining prominence over the lights of the streetlamps. I started the van and set off. The way back was my chance to reflect, but also, for a few moments, to let my mind go blank. The night air, the apocalyptic solitude of the early morning, Claudia's company, the unhurried driving and the James Taylor song playing softly on the dirty old boom box directed my body towards the residence.

That strange sense of peace invited me to make the route a little longer. I needed to observe the city. I needed to find myself again. To remember. In spite of everything, you can't escape the present, and Claudia moved her lips silently, following the beautiful lyrics of that song, *You've got a friend,* looking at me from time to time with an air of apology. She was a disobedient person but also my only friend. My best friend. I smiled at her insistence with my gaze, and so did she, hiding it with her face to the window.

I drove slowly over the Brooklyn Bridge. I took a detour into the life of the Lower East Side, the dangerous neighborhood of fire escape facades. I crossed the Hudson River. I breathed the humidity in the air, the smell of the machines at rest, of the tireless boats that crossed from one side to the other. Then Jersey, and its colorful buildings. And, without wanting to, I had completely disengaged myself from Claudia. She was biting her fingernail, looking nervous, visibly uneasy. I looked at her to say something, catching my breath, but she stepped forward.

"David, I have a bad feeling," she said with conviction. "It started when you went into the old factory. Ever since then, I've been worrying about something. Crazy, isn't it? That's why I came in looking for you. I felt something wasn't right. I beg your pardon, but I was so scared."

"Calm down, Claudia. Don't apologize. It's been a very hard night for both of us. I shouldn't have left you alone."

"No. It's not that. It's something else. Something that distresses me and grips me. Silly, isn't it?"

She gave a nervous laugh and immediately went back to biting her finger with a serious look on her face. I pulled the van over to the side of the road, set the brake, and did what we've all seen so many times in the movies. I put my hand on her knee, she turned to me and, without taking my eyes off her for a moment, I told her in a firm tone,

"Everything is going to be fine."

As we finished the sentence, a small sound distracted our attention. A crow had perched on the hood of the battered van. It looked at me, shaking its little head, like a messenger, as if making sure it recognized the one in front of it. Then it began to caw. Needless to say, both of our hair stood on end. Then it flew away, leaving behind a mysterious coincidence that only added to Claudia's fears, and which we both reserved our comments.

I started talking again, unable to hide the contagion of worry.

"Give me a hand, Claudia, keep your eyes open. You never know."

From there, I took the shortest way to the residence and stepped on the accelerator. I parked the van in front of the small plumbing store whose emblem was identical to that old van. I pushed back the seat to leave it just as I found it. Shining the flashlight into the cargo area, I stressed to Claudia how important it was that no one knew we had taken it. Not to leave anything behind. After the exhaustive check, and verifying that the mess of cargo was irrelevant, we got out making as little noise as possible. We locked it and put the keys on the same wheel as I had found them. We then walked back down that dreary street to the rear of the residence.

Claudia couldn't resist asking,

"And how did you know the keys were there?"

Before she could finish her question, one of the guardians appeared in front of us. So slender, thin and elongated that he competed in height with the lamppost whose light illuminated his shadowy silhouette. I stared at Claudia to see if she noticed anything - he was right in front of us - but she kept walking, shivering at times in the damp night chill and waiting impatiently for an answer.

"Observation and vigilance, Claudia. Just that," I said in a quiet voice, slurring my words, distracted.

Something was not right. And suddenly the guardian vanished, his appearances always so fleeting. I tried not to dwell too much on that, nor on the raven, nor on Claudia's hunch, nor on everything I had talked about with Daryl.

We got to the laundry garbage can and the knotted sheets were still there, soaking wet. We had to climb up the chute to get to the laundry, but Claudia seemed to be having a hard time. She began to have an untimely fit of giggles. I no longer knew if the laughter was robbing her of her strength or if she really couldn't do it. The fact is that, despite my discouragement, she infected me with her laughter and the two of us, like drunks, could not stop laughing for a long time, laughing non-stop under our breath.

"Come on, now seriously, get up! -I shout-whispered. She tried and fell back on the dirty sheets, like a clown, still laughing, "Keep it down, we're going to get caught!"

It took a few minutes for our imaginary drunkenness to wear off. I warned her that the janitor was on night watch and that we couldn't make a sound when we entered. She tried again, but this time I wound up lifting her up by her ass as my feet sank through the piles of bagged clothes.

"Hey, watch it or we won't be able to resist each other!"

Chapter 28
The Enigma

New York City, October 1996

She stood motionless holding onto the sheet rope, and then I realized that she was indeed unable to climb. I prayed that the improvised invention and its anchorage with the mop would support the weight of both of us.

I positioned myself underneath her with my feet tightly together and my head between her legs. As I began to climb, I indicated to her that she really had to work with me. She was still laughing, but when she saw the effort I was making she finally took it seriously. My biceps were burning, and my legs were shaking with tension but we made it. Once upstairs in the laundry room, I had to take a few seconds because my heart was working like a jackhammer.

I quickly gathered up the sheets untied the knots, stuffed them all into a bag and dropped the bag down the chrome chute. I put the mop back in place, checking, in detail, that everything was as I found it. Then, in case the janitor was making the rounds, I told Claudia to go to our room. A few minutes later I would follow her.

Slowly, discouraged and tired, I walked after her, but not before passing by the dining room cupboard to return the well-cleaned knives. I opened the drawer gently, and then the guardian resurfaced behind me.

"They're coming for you. You have a few minutes before they arrive. You're in danger. Run! Run away!"

I realized that he was Margot's guardian.

"What are you saying? Who is coming for me?" I knew he was serious because suddenly more guards appeared in the dining room. Then the raven, the feeling, it all made sense. I didn't ask any more absurd questions. "How much time do I have?"

"Three minutes, at the most."

The guardian looked nervous. I picked up the knives again and ran, oblivious to the noise, to the room. When I entered, the first thing I did was to turn off the light.

"What is it"? asked Claudia, puzzled.

I hurriedly opened the closet and took the money from the pockets of my pants.

"You haven't seen me all night, okay? Get into bed and pretend you're asleep. I have to go; they're coming for me!"

"But who?"

"Please, Claudia, pretend to be asleep. I will find you." As I said this, that last sentence, I had another *déjà vu moment*. "I will find you." That was the last thing I said to Angie.

Then my own guardian appeared in the room. In his deep, gravelly voice, he shouted the same to me,

"Run. Now!"

And I came out of my reverie at full speed. Without thinking about it, I gave Claudia a kiss on the lips and as I was leaving the room I repeated the order,

"Pretend to be asleep!" It was a forced goodbye.

I ran at full speed down the hallway. My sneakers rattled across the varnished floor like drums and squeaky hinges. I held both the knives and the gun so as not to lose them in the race. I reached the laundry room and without looking I threw myself down the shaft. I fell on the bags and felt the blow I had got early resurfaced with more force.

"Come on, come on, come on," I said to myself as I jumped over the frame of the container.

I ran and ran and ran. I jumped over the huge fence into the darkness of the small park, next to the residence. My lungs were burning, my whole body was screaming in pain. Two huge Chevrolet Tahoes were parked next to the north corner. From the first, a woman and a man emerged. She was tall with platinum blonde hair. He was about thirty-five, burly, broad-backed, firm-shouldered, Caucasian, tough-looking. Both dressed entirely in black.

Watching, I tried to catch my breath. Four men got out of the other SUV; heavily armed, a full-fledged tactical group. They were equally equipped: a bulletproof vest, a gun at the level of the abdomen, another holster with a pistol on the thigh, helmet with a night vision device, gloves. All completely dressed in black. The woman motioned to them and at full speed they got back into the car, completely hidden behind the tinted windows.

I had been discovered. They were coming for me. I had nowhere to run. Ideas were crisscrossing my mind at lightning speed. My life was falling apart; it was all the fault of my uniqueness. It was a curse. A ball chained to my ankle that I'd been dragging around since I was a child. My heart wanted to burst out of my chest, it was an uncontrolled locomotive. I crouched down in the brush and crept closer to the fence. There was no sound of the classic police radio station. The man and woman stood motionless, cautious and extremely calm.

The fine mist and the deep darkness of the night created an eerie, almost gloomy atmosphere. The woman opened the back door and out of it came an older lady, about sixty years old, slim and tall. Long, curly hair, as black as shoe polish. Dark clothes, covered by a fringed shawl. Her face conveyed disgust with the situation, professional serenity and also malice, a lot of malice. In my case, detecting that is not something subjective that could be due to prejudice. As she stepped outside, a huge number of reddish beings appeared next to her. One of them caught my attention in particular.

This did not fit with the police. Something very strange was going on.

"Who are these people?" I kept asking myself.

It was clear that the young woman was in charge of the group. She was the one who gave the orders with a military and disciplined attitude. The young woman asked the old woman, in perfect Spanish with a Mexican accent,

"Is he here?"

She replied,

"Yes, ma'am, he is close."

The young woman smiled. Did they mean me? I couldn't believe it! I was confused. On the one hand, I thought about going out and showing myself to them. Let's see how that would go. I was also armed, and I had already faced death recently. On the other hand, I wanted to escape, to get away from the threat, and avoid all of this. Neither one thing nor the other. I stayed there crouched, hiding. I had to gather more information.

The man in black opened the other rear door of the car and pulled out a medium-sized briefcase. He opened it on the hood of the Chevy. From it he took out large glasses which the man and the young woman put on. A bright light, the color of fire, streamed from the small suitcase. The strange couple looked toward the residence. Two glowing balls emerged from the suitcase, suspended in the air. At full speed, the small, coconut-sized spheres began flying around the residence in different directions, combing all the windows of the building. Lights in the house turned on. I had to be sure of my suspicions. I repeated the extracorporeal operation. I could clearly see all the reddish people and my fear was confirmed: among them was Daryl, looking ashamed, repentant.

I immediately returned to my body. One of the spheres stopped checking the perimeter and began to widen its search. It stopped in mid-air, over the laundry container, about a hundred meters away from me; it seemed to follow the trail of my footsteps. Slowly, it began to head towards the park where I was hiding, the other incandescent sphere joined and both descended in a straight line. I acted like a coward. I was afraid of the unknown. The guardians suddenly appeared around me. They all stretched out their hands toward me. I think they were trying to hide me. To make me invisible.

"Run!" shouted one of the guardians.

I started to run as fast as I could. I looked back and the reddies had spotted me. They were pointing out my position to that old woman.

"He's over there!" cried the old woman in a sharp tone, pointing her elongated finger at me.

The armed men got out of the vehicle and began to chase after me. I heard the cars start up and the screeching of the tires as they accelerated. I had never witnessed a chase like this before, and the target was me.

I did not understand anything except that my life was in danger, now more than ever. The guards appeared and then vanished ahead of me, pointing out an escape route. I noticed silent impacts on a tree in front of me. I ducked instinctively. They were shooting at me. This was all serious. I pulled out my own silenced pistol and cursed that I only had two rounds left.

"Shoot there!" advised my guardian, pointing to the flying spheres.

Fate and its ironies, again. Two cartridges for two spheres. I could not miss the shot.

The gun sounded like a blowgun. Two quick shots between them, the incandescent balls did not even flinch. I was about to throw the gun to the ground but I thought better of it and put it away again. The footsteps of the armed men now sounded more cautious. They knew it was not going to be so easy to catch me, that I was armed.

"This way!" said another of the guardians.

Crouched behind a tree, with my bandana and cap tightly fastened, I hesitated. Adrenaline made me believe I could take them on. I came to my senses. If I had to face them, it would be life or death, and I did not want death, neither for them nor for me. Shooting at the flying coconuts had not been a great idea, but at least it offered me the opportunity to deceive the enemy, to slow him down.

I threw a stone to the opposite side. I heard the four men aim their weapons toward the sound. I ran back in the opposite direction.

"Follow me!" said a guardian.

The others stretched out their hands over me. They hid me in the darkness, blurring the sound of my hurried footsteps. He pointed me to a manhole. I opened it and climbed down the concrete duct ladder. From inside I pulled the cover back on and climbed all the way down the ladder. I turned on the flashlight. A narrow corridor ran parallel to a subway stinking stream.

The bandana over my mouth and nose helped me cope with the nauseating smell that flowed beside me. I walked at full speed, always in the same direction. I passed some forks, and tried not to deviate from the course, without losing the direction of the current. No one was following me. They had not seen me escape into this fetid underworld. Safety is in the movement, I repeated to myself; I have to continue. Down there, among rats and Jurassic cockroaches, one loses track of time and space. The gases were affecting me, it was time to surface. I went up another duct and came out to the outside world. Pure air!

I never thought I could say that in New York. The night was reluctant to leave the city. Tiredness was getting to me. Some coffee shops were already open. I didn't recognize where I was. A man in a suit got out of his car next to a newsstand. He had left the car started, with the headlights on. A dark Lincoln. The opportunity was there. All I had to do was get in and drive away. Instead, I just stared at that careless, naïve, happy man. He got back in his car, now with his newspaper, and drove away.

My ethics prevented me from taking the car even though I was in a critical situation. I continued walking. I could feel my feet dragging. Branch Brook Park; I planned to lie on the grass and sleep in the bushes as long as I could. But the night still had one more errand in store for me.

Nothing in this life is a coincidence.

A woman was screaming inside a car, in the lonely and dreary *parking lot.* My body was triggered again. I approached slowly, without making a sound. A sweaty, thin, short-haired man, visibly restless, was pointing a gun at a young woman, who was raising her hands inside the car, in the passenger seat. I approached him, pulling up my bandana again, with the gun in my right hand and a knife in my left.

"You're going to do it for free!" he said as he unbuckled the belt of his pants.

I put the barrel a few centimeters away from the back of his neck and I opened the hammer of the gun, making him hear that characteristic sound, unmistakable. He froze. I even heard him swallow saliva.

"How does it feel? If you want to live, take the gun with two fingers and give it to me," I said with the serenity of a gangster.

Now such a situation was presented to me as a simple task. I didn't even feel nervous. He obeyed without complaint. I put the knife away and took both pistols.

"Get out of the car!"

The young woman was trembling with tension. The thin, sweaty man was licking his dry mouth, wiggling his jaw in a strange way.

"Her clothes!"

He looked at me silently for a few seconds, with his hands in the air, his whole body trembling – probably coming down from something.

"I'm sorry, man. I'm sorry. She's your girl, right? I'll pay you and it's settled, okay?"

I looked at the pistol I had just taken from him, removed the safety catch and shot by his foot. The noise woke up the birds, which flew away. The thin man curled in on himself with his hands over his ears. He looked like he was crying and yet I felt no pity for him. On the contrary, an enormous contempt was growing inside me, so strong that I was finding it hard to tame it.

"The clothes," I demanded again, in a calm voice, almost a whisper. The woman was standing in her underwear.

"Are you okay?" She nodded nervously. She wanted it to be over, and I don't blame her, I knew that feeling.

"I don't think so." She understood immediately and stood in front of us as she came into the world. "Put the clothes in the trunk and close it again."

When she had finished, I looked coldly into her eyes, with a real desire to fulfill my promise.

"Hands against the car!" Do you have a lipstick?"

"Yeah. Yeah, sure," she said hesitantly.

Still aiming at his head, I wrote, vertically, on the center of his back *"free sex" and* drew an arrow pointing to his buttocks. He kept begging for forgiveness and that I should not kill him, that he was taking care of his mother and other nonsense.

I'll give you a ten-second head start before I shoot you. One, two...

He ran so fast that it took him no time to lose sight of him. I got in the car, started it up and we drove away, with that stranger by my side.

"Where do you live?" I asked, uncovering my face.

"In the southeast Bronx," she said, almost embarrassed.

I headed for the George Washington Bridge. It took us half an hour or more to get there. We got to talking. She told me that she was doing sex-work out of necessity. She was only nineteen years old, and her father had kicked her out of the house two years earlier. Everything pointed to the fact that she had had a very difficult life. The life of a survivor. And yet, even with that, her eyes conveyed kindness. I could feel the gratitude in her eyes. I introduced myself to her as Dustin. She told me her name was Chloe.

"What do you do, Dustin, besides being a hero?" And she laughed with a mischievous look on her face.

"I fight every day to get ahead. I try to be fair. That's all," I told her sincerely.

"It's what we all do. That's what life is all about, isn't it? Fight or surrender. Fight or die," she repeated with a sorrowful face, looking out the window at the first rays of the sun.

"And how can I repay you for what you have done for me?"

"She looked at me fiddling with his finger and lips, mischievously."

"To tell you the truth, there is something you can do something for me," I said, ignoring the unspoken offer. Do you live alone?"

She nodded her head in affirmation.

"It's a dive, but it's my dive."

"Could I take a shower and sleep for a few hours? I'll pay you." She thought about it. "I need it. I'll leave tomorrow."

"No problem. The cops are looking for you, aren't they? Is that it? When you grew up on the streets, you smell the runaways. I know you're a stand-up guy."

I kept silent and let her assume it was so. I liked the paradox of "being legal" and at the same time "wanted for justice".

She indicated her block. I left the car windows down and the keys in the ignition. I opened the trunk, grabbed the clothes. In his pants pocket was his wallet, three dollars and his papers. How did he plan to pay? I put it in my pocket. I closed the trunk and threw the clothes in the garbage can. The car would be taken care of by the neighborhood thugs.

"Follow me, Dustin. It's this way."

In front of us was a huge four-story apartment block of exposed brick. The doorway was wide open, and the mailboxes were crumpled at the entrance. A charred car by the curb served as a signpost. Sneakers laced together over a high-tension cable also sent their message. A drug addict staggered as if in a slow dance. He looked asleep but was actually moving. We climbed the stairs to the fourth floor, door 11. She opened her full bag to take out her keys. I stood for a few seconds on the landing of that long hallway.

"You're not a neighborhood punk, you're like one of those polite stiffs," she laughed again. "Come on in, man."

I went inside and closed the door.

"I won't trouble you. I promise."

"I know, Dustin. I have a good eye for people."

She showed me to the bathroom. I left the guns and knives on a small table in the living room. The rest remained in my pockets. I went into the bathroom. It had no lock. I took off my clothes and got in the small bathtub. There was no curtain. I couldn't wait to take a shower; the smell of the sewage still clung to my body. She walked in without saying anything. She saw me naked, but nothing changed in her look, she didn't care.

"Wow, you're *ripped*. Here's a towel for you. There's no curtain because I like to pretend I'm rich." She winked at me. "Oh, your back!"

"It's nothing. It will heal."

I showered trying not to splash, limiting the flow in the shower head. I finished quickly, put on my underwear and T-shirt. She began to fill the tub, small and rusty, but very clean.

"You can sleep on the couch, it's not much, but it's comfortable," she said. She had covered the couch with two sheets that smelled better than those of a five-star hotel.

"Now it's my turn," she said, referring to the bathroom. I gently took her hand and turned her face away from me. I gave her a lingering kiss on the cheek. It wasn't a romantic kiss, it was a kiss of gratitude.

She smiled excitedly, unaccustomed to affection without double intentions. She blushed, despite her job, or maybe because of her job. She finally went into the bathroom, and I lay down on the sofa and my tired soul sank between the cushions. I collapsed, exhausted. I fell asleep instantly.

I woke up suddenly. Very frightened, I took a huge breath of air. It was as if my body, asleep, had forgotten to breathe for long seconds. I sat up with a start. I looked around and for a few moments I couldn't remember where I was. I did not recognize the place. It was a passing thing, but at that moment between sleep and consciousness, I felt very lonely and lost. I uncovered myself from the sheet, which smelled of intense and pleasant lavender. The blinds were down, giving the sensation of night, but the street bustle blurred that illusion.

Without making a sound, I hurriedly got dressed, concealed the pistol in the front of my pants. I put the other behind my back, ready to open fire. The knives were on my hips. I put my cap on and bandana around my neck. My long hair covered my eyes. I looked at the documentation in the wallet of the wannabe rapist, Samuel, born in '72. I opened the ajar door to the only bedroom in the apartment. Chloe was sleeping peacefully hugging a rather large teddy bear. With the light streaming through the slits in the blinds, I could see several others crowded together on the shelves. It seemed to me that it was meant to construct the absence of a childhood taken away. I left five hundred dollars on the little table in the living room next to a note: 'Thank you from the bottom of my heart, Chloe. You have been another angel in my path. I look forward to seeing you soon. Your friend, Dustin.'

I carefully closed the front door and left the apartment block. Samuel's car was gone. It was almost two o'clock in the afternoon. I passed some thugs. Some of them stared at me, with territorial eyes. I went into a store and bought some second-hand sunglasses, almost square, with dark frames and lenses. In front of me was a defaced telephone booth. I picked up the phone and rubbed the receiver and microphone with my clothes; it gave a signal. I put in the change and dialed a long phone number.

"Yes? -Yes?"

I stood quietly listening to his voice. A police car was driving slowly along the curb. It stopped a couple of meters before the booth. The two officers had their eyes on me.

"Hello? Hello!"

"Father Damián," I said in a defeated voice, barely keeping my composure.

"David? What's wrong?" he exclaimed, alarmed.

"Father, I need help."

Chapter 29
Hitting Bottom

New York City, Southeast Bronx,
October 1996

"What can I do for you, son? What has happened?" I could tell he was worried.

"Father, you need to talk to your boss, I need him to give me a hand. I'm in a difficult predicament."

"Tell me, my son," he answered just as any priest in confession would do.

"I can't, father. I can't tell anyone." I sighed, in forced loneliness.

"Well, look, David, listen to me carefully. The first thing you must do is to expel discouragement from inside you. A good attitude in the face of difficulties is the determining key. When faced with a problem, you must change your approach. You must take the active and persistent decision to solve it! You must be convinced that it will not be able to defeat you! Because you are capable of solving your own problems! And then nothing will defeat you!"

At that moment, the two officers got out of the patrol car. They walked towards me with an exaggerated calmness. One of them was chewing gum, wearing aviator sunglasses, he was blond with rosy cheeks. This one walked with his right hand resting on his pistol. They were both tall and strong. The other, the dark-haired one, seemed less arrogant, simpler.

"Excuse me, Father, but right now I have two policemen in front of me, and I think they want to talk to me."

I was scared, I was carrying two bladed weapons and two pistols. But I was also mentally defeated, tired of running away, of hiding. I put the headset on my shoulder and took off my sunglasses, out of politeness and so that my face would be clearly distinguishable.

"Good morning, officers. What can I do for you? Do I need to hang up?" The blond stepped forward to question me.

"No. Don't hang up. Hold on. We don't know you at all. You're not from around here, are you?" he asked rhetorically.

"No, sir. I came to see a friend, I live in Newark," I told him honestly.

The dark-haired policeman stared at me, hesitating. Then in perfect Spanish, albeit with a Latin accent, he addressed me.

"Who are you talking to, young man?" His serious and authoritative voice carried in the air his distrust and at the same time a great self-confidence.

"I am talking to Father Damian, a good friend of mine who is in Spain."

The dark-haired policeman laughed and repeated what I said to his partner in English; they conferred among themselves, making fun of each other. I guessed they figured me for a liar. The blond's badge read Douglas, and the dark-haired man's badge read Sanchez.

"May I speak to your priest?" he asked as he grabbed the handset from my shoulder without permission.

I stepped to the side, knocked over by his corpulence. The policeman spoke up. The skeptical tone stood out. They must have been used to being lied to and mistrusted by everyone.

"Good afternoon, am I speaking to a priest?" I am Officer Sanchez of the New York Police Department.

Silence. Sanchez's partner and I watched and listened intently, both with the curiosity of an expectant child.

"I don't have to assure you that you are talking to the police, it is up to you to prove to me that you are a priest."

Policeman Douglas stared at me. I immediately understood the silent message in his gaze, he was asking me for a simultaneous translation, and so I did. I was glad I did, otherwise he might have thought to search me.

"I never really thought about it," I translated for Agent Douglas. So you think the phone numbers for calling the police, both here with 911 and there with 091, might be based on Psalm 91?"

"The truth, father, is that I don't know what you are saying." Again, there was a brief gap. "If you would do me the favor, I would be grateful to hear it."

Agent Sanchez listened with a strange expression that little by little his face changed, he became almost excited I would say.

"Come on, boy! Do me a favor, take out everything you have in your pockets and put it on the hood."

Agent Sanchez raised his index finger above the others, ordering me to wait, took some coins from his pocket and inserted them into the slot in the booth. Unbeknownst to me, Father Damián was saving me from a serious problem.

"Thank you very much for your blessing, Father. I'll put you with my partner right away," I translated literally. "Douglas, come here! Get on the phone," ordered Agent Sanchez.

I noticed that the badges on his shoulder were different, more overloaded, that's why he carried the voice of command. His partner made a hurried, grumbling gesture, as if wanting to refuse, but knowing he had no choice. Agent Douglas picked up the handset.

"Yes?"

I remembered that Father Damián spoke English very well, and I remembered that he had been a dedicated missionary traveler, a man of the world, a tireless and humble helper throughout the five continents. Only the expiration of his body, manifested in old age, made him give up his travels, because according to him he received more attention than he gave. Agent Sanchez turned to me, while his partner conversed in a respectful tone over the phone.

"The priest told me that you have received an important scholarship. That you are a genius in mathematics and architecture. Well, I think that's all fine and dandy. But listen to me carefully, because I'm the expert in this field. If you continue to frequent this neighborhood, you'll find yourself in trouble. Here, life, crime and death dance together and the song is not slow. This is no place for a naive young outsider, whose principles and values, far from being an asset, are a weakness." He looked at me sternly. "Don't forget that."

"Excuse me. You think there are no good people here?"

"Oh, not at all. The best men and women in the world have often come out of neighborhoods like this one. But they have had the mental fortitude to make themselves respected, to be a chameleon, to endear themselves to the good and the bad, and to learn from the mistakes of others. To make the most of their scarce opportunities. In short, to reinvent himself. So don't insult the good people of my neighborhood, okay?"

He tapped me on my chest with the tip of his index finger. It was more paternal than policing.

Agent Douglas was saying goodbye on the phone, thanking Father Damián for his blessing. He slipped some coins into the booth and handed me the phone.

"In this district, any protection is welcome," said the policeman, lifting my cap and tousling my hair with his hand. And they got back into the police car and drove off without further ado.

I felt relief, but also discomfort: the uncomfortable feeling of being an imposter.

I unburdened myself by talking to my dear friend, Father Damián. I told him that now I had some problems that only I could solve. I told him that I was going to be disconnected for a while. He insisted on knowing what was going on, but I had no answers for him. I told him that I could not return to the residence, that I was in trouble. I told him to reassure my mother if she was called, hat I was trying to get the situation under control. I asked him to pray for me. And, hardest of all, to tell my aunt and uncle, Kingsley, and my parents that I loved them very much.

Father Damián became more and more concerned with each of my statements.

"I have to hang up, Father."

"No! Wait, David! Calm down, tell me the details."

"No, I can't, Father. Forgive me for asking you this bitter favor. Take care of yourself."

And I hung up, with the haste of a coward.

I walked aimlessly and arrived at Parkchester subway station. The deafening rattle of the trains and the noise of their brakes pervaded the whole atmosphere, the convoys were running in the open air. I entered the concourse and made my way to the toilets. The smell of urine mingled with the smell of spilled bleach. I closed the door and held it shut with my back. There was no toilet, just a hole in the floor and two stencils in the shape of feet, like in a fairground booth where I could aim. I went about my business. I counted: a little over sixteen hundred dollars. I left one hundred and thirty dollars in my pocket and the rest I stuffed in my underpants. I stopped to think about what to do.

I bought a backpack, a sweatshirt, a couple of T-shirts, socks and underwear, toothbrush and toothpaste, deodorant, razor blades, a comb, and then I kept a few dollars loose in my pocket. It was urgent to find a place to be, especially before nightfall. Paranoia began to take hold of me and dominate my thoughts. I didn't dare go to a hostel. I didn't dare go to a bus or train station. Whenever I came across someone well-dressed, in a suit and trench coat, I stayed well away. Hunger and thirst were making an appearance, but I wanted to avoid public places and crowds. I entered a small grocery store. I bought a yogurt smoothie, a loaf of bread, water and a couple of bananas. That would be my dinner.

The sun's rays were fading in the firmament of the big city, and the night again claimed its time. I sat down in a small indoor square, away from the traffic, away from the police, away from people, and began to eat my dinner. There is nothing sadder than eating alone. I tried to put my thoughts in order, to take into account all the details, but nothing made me understand what these people wanted from me.

A disheveled and dirty man was pushing a shopping cart full of blankets and items. Behind him, a small dog looking proud and happy followed him animatedly. As he passed me, he greeted me with a smile, saying good night. I returned his greeting by forcing a gesture of joy. His little dog approached me, put his paws up on my knees and with his tongue out, wagging his tail, barked for my attention. His master continued on his way without looking back; only when I stroked him for a few seconds he was satisfied and returned to the nomad.

Moments of kindness.

It was getting later and later and I still had nowhere to go. A group of thugs were passing through that square accompanied by their reddish invisibles. Workers were also passing by. Gradually people thinned out and I was left all alone, in semi-darkness, just sitting there. I went into survival mode. I told myself that I wasn't going to fall apart, hat I would get out of this and that the so-called order would not turn its back on me, because I had always tried to do good, and destiny would help me. I took courage and then I took action.

I took out my knife that I'd hidden in my new sweatshirt, and cut the central part of the smoothie container, obtaining a small square-ish tub. I washed my hands and the plastic, trying not to waste water. In front of me was a wrought iron gate, rusted and tarnished. Its glass was cracked, badly patched and held together with pieces of tape that had once been transparent. With my backpack over my shoulder, I slung the sweatshirt over my right forearm and tucked the plastic into the crevice between the door and the frame. From above I slid it down until it reached the obstacle I was waiting for, the latch. I spun the piece of packaging around on itself, pushing, and the door opened as if by magic.

I went up to the top floor and lay down on the access landing to the roof, where no one would pass. I fell asleep, sitting with my back aching and leaning against that metal door that peeled with contact. The cold at night gets into your bones. I awoke to put on all my shirts at once, but, even so, I did not remedy the shivering or the chattering of my teeth. It's funny how, at any given moment, anyone can get caught in the spiral of necessity.

I slept little and poorly, and that impaired my ability to reason. The whole next days slipped away from me, solving the most basic human needs. Food, hygiene, rest and my safety became daily stony tasks that took up all my time. Man is a creature of habit and how true it is. Every day I went to the same places, avoiding crowded places. At night I would climb up to the fifth floor of that landing, but now I did so with a couple of pieces of cardboard for the floor, a shredded paper bag as a pillow and a newspaper to warm me. I would tear the sheets from the staples noiselessly and tuck them between my T-shirts; I did the same in my pants and the hood of my sweatshirt. It was simple, but very effective against the cold. A hamburger cup became my portable toilet and day by day, my money dwindled.

As I did every night, I tore the pages out of a newspaper. A headline inside stopped my nightly ritual for a few seconds. It read:

> Dr. Fraud, so nicknamed by the police, was arrested thanks to the help of an anonymous and mysterious citizen. The doctor was dedicated to kidnapping minors to sell their organs to families in the United States and Canada. The ignorance of the desperate families favored the payment of a large sum of money, making them believe that the origin of the vital organs came from an independent association of donors.

I was perplexed reading the page and, for a moment, I felt pride, especially in Claudia. Then, I put myself in the shoes of those families, shattered by the trials of this life, and I felt very sorry, I could understand their pain, and their involuntary and incorrect complicity.

Almost without realizing it, the days went by. When I went into a store to shop, the salesclerks watched me closely, a clear sign that my appearance was not at its best. Some refused to let me in with my backpack, but it was just a pretext. Others were more direct, inviting me to leave the establishment with subtle pushes and threatening whispers in my ear, while in front of their neatest customers they showed the fakest of their smiles. Marginality was taking over my identity. Every day I trained for a couple of hours using street furniture as a makeshift gym.

I often thought of all that I had gradually lost, and I was no longer so sure that The Order was taking care of me. One way or another, circumstances, fear and destitution were making the world turn its back on me, and I, seemed to accept this state of affairs. I had thrown in the towel.

Analyzing it now, the reality was quite different. The truth is that I was just a boy with old memories, strange perceptions and a lot of fear. I had thought repeatedly about the words the reddish man and I shared, but, as it turned out, nothing was reliable. I couldn't hold on to any of it. The only valuable thing I had, safe and tangible, was my people. The ones from Asturias, Spain and the ones from here. I missed family meals. I missed going to the port with my mother, my aunt and uncle. I missed, he days of happy girls on the beach with Kingsley, boat trips, conversations with my father and his silences with his gaze fixed on the horizon. And now I also missed Claudia, who had unknowingly helped me so much. I missed her friendship, her character, the calmness of her company, her silly follies, her strong and tender style. But the most powerful nostalgia of all was for someone from another life. It was an unfinished business. An uncomfortable feeling of something remaining. A promise to keep. And it didn't fade with adversity. Never.

I lay down as usual, on that landing where the cockroaches circulated, like a stowaway and fugitive, thinking about all that. A tear slipped out. I did not wipe it away. And for the first time I asked The Order, the universe, God, whatever it was to help me.

I was fast asleep. A familiar feeling startled me in the middle of the night.

"Watch out!" It was the unmistakable voice of a guardian.

I woke up with a start. My eyes widened, trying to adjust to the light from the staircase. Then I could make him out. A fat, tall, gruff man in boxer shorts and a tank top was wielding a baseball bat in his hands.

"You're going to wish you never slept here!"

He raised the bat over his shoulders, as a lumberjack would, and tried to hit my legs with all his might. I jumped at once, and the thump sounded against the ground like the roar of a cannon shot. I pulled both pistols out of my pants. I heard him swallow, taking steps backwards.

"Dude, dude, wait."

Calmly, I put the pistols in my backpack. I felt the heat of adrenaline, the pumping of my heart. Still, I forced myself to cool down. I took off my sweatshirt and T-shirts, dropping the papers on the floor.

"Don't worry. I'm not going to use weapons against you. Just my fists, elbows and legs. You can keep the bat if you think it will do you any good."

My muscular body was full of dirt, blackened by dirty clothes transferred from the floor and grimy cardboard, dark from training and wandering the streets. The fat man, cowardly, threw the bat to the ground and refused the challenge. In a hurry he rushed into his house, locking it. Filled with rage, I picked up the bat and started banging on the door with all my might.

"You're fucking trash, do you hear me?! You trash, you have no shame!" My tears were flowing with impotence and rage. "You have no heart! What do you know about me, huh? You have no soul!" I could hear him sniffling inside me.

I threw the bat to the ground. My hands were shaking. Tears streamed down my face, down my neck, mingling with the sweat on my chest. I turned around and the landing was invaded by elongated shadows, by immobile and mute guardians. I could feel them taking pity on me. They faded away almost at once.

I put on my clothes, my cap, my bandana, and grabbed my backpack. I had to get out of there. As I walked past the landings, in the dark, I could see the shy light from the curious and expectant peepholes of the neighbors. I apologized, saying "I'm sorry" at each one.

The cold, early morning air was blowing through the streets of the Bronx. It was just after two o'clock. A cab stood on the corner, its interior courtesy light on. I approached it walking slowly; I thought to myself, "If it's still there when I get there, I'll try to catch it." I noticed that the closer I got, the slower and shorter my steps became. It was as if I didn't want to keep my pact with myself. I stood in front of the cab driver, who was passing the cloth over the dashboard. My eyes fixed on him seemed to warn him of my presence. He stopped wiping. He stared at me, very serious, guessing my intentions. His black eyes were reminiscent of the depth of the sea at night, and his stubby, rounded nose decorated his face with an air of kindness.

I must have had the face of drama. Grief with legs. Suddenly, a giant grin from him made me look like a light bulb turned on.

I was taken aback; lately, no one wanted to be nice to me. He started waving his hand, signaling me to come closer. He got out of the cab and continued to signal for me to follow him, looking as if he had a secret and mysterious treasure. I hesitated and for a few seconds I stood there motionless, facing the old Checker. The cab driver opened the trunk and leaned out of the side, with that expression that rascally children wear.

"Come on. Come on, let's go."

I approached apathetically, keeping a little distance. But he made me smile. He had a large thermos of coffee with milk, plastic cups and a small tray with pastries.

"Boy, come closer. You and I are going to have a cup of coffee together, are you up for it? Aha, you laughed. I hope you like it strong."

And he started pouring the glasses. He brought it over to me and sat down on the trunk bay.

"Take one. They are the best Italian *ciambelle* you can find in New York."

I took one of those doughnut-like buns, and it was delicious.

"Why?" I asked the cab driver, referring to his invitation.

"Because I have coffee and buns to spare, and you're just in time. It's as simple as that."

Defensively, I still felt incredulous at this act of kindness. I had lost faith in my fellow man, I no longer believed in the good of others. In the selflessness of a good person.

"I need to go to Newark."

The cab driver arched both eyebrows, somewhat surprised.

"-I can fix it, it's not a problem. By the way, my name is Flavio." He extended his hand to me.

"You don't have to fix it, Flavio, I can pay." I took a few bills out of my pocket to prove it to him. The cab driver continued to eat the roll, his eyes fixed on the ground, as if I had ruined his chance to help me a little more. "Forgive my arrogance, Flavio. Tonight, before going to bed, I said a prayer for help. And now that I have crossed paths with you, I begin to believe that it has been heard."

"You exaggerate, my boy. I'm just a humble cab driver on the night shift. Nothing more than that. Come on! Anytime, we'll throw miles to Newark," he said, clapping his hands in the air, rubbing them together from the cold.

"Can I ride up front?" I asked respectfully. He made a quizzical face.

"In this neighborhood they have asked me for everything. Even if I carry them in the trunk, how can I not want you to stand next to me? Those trunk people, after a while, they get out of the trunk, putting on the-the-the..." his own fit of laughter interrupted him, "the suit and they would ask me: 'Do I look elegant? Who knows what shady shenanigans they were up to."

Flavio couldn't stop laughing.

I wanted to laugh with him, but I could not. I felt devastated.

Chapter 30
Controversy

I was on my way back. Returning to the point of origin. On the way to danger, to that reality that I had refused to face, hiding behind forced destitution. Flavio did not stop talking, the journey was long and for him silence was an uncomfortable companion. Halfway there, a guardian suddenly appeared. I did not know how to react or what was happening. Flavio continued telling his anecdotes. I played along as best I could, but I couldn't ignore the presence of that guardian sitting on the back seat of the old Checker.

Oblivious to the conversation, he watched the landscape through the window. Again the deep, hoarse and predominant voice of the guardian revealed itself. Reflexively, I glanced at the back seat behind Flavio's seat.

"You have to give him a message for me. He knows I've tried, but he's always been afraid, so now that you're here, I need you to do me this favor."

"I hid as best I could, staring straight ahead, at the road."

The guardian explained to me, at the same time that good old Flavio continued to talk enthusiastically. My hair stood on end, and a knot in my stomach grew with each of his words. What his guardian was begging me to do was simple and at the same time very difficult.

"Hey, Flavio, forgive me for changing the subject but I need to ask you something. I see that you are a good, caring and kind-hearted man..."

"Thank you for the compliments; you seem to be a nice guy too. Go ahead and ask."

"Do you think being good should be rewarded?"

I wanted to steer the conversation to my ground, but also to know his opinion on the subject. He didn't hesitate for a second, but I could feel him selecting the words cautiously, they seemed to be rushing from his lips.

"Of course. Nothing comforts the soul more than doing good for others. To be honest. To be just. Reaching out. Sit next to someone, as an equal, without judgment, and share a good time with something as simple as a good conversation. When you do good, even for a bad person, they feel the need to be better to you. Maybe not good, but not so bad. I don't know if I'm making myself clear."

"And how do you know you're doing the right thing? I mean, spiritually, with the hard decisions."

"Spiritually? He paused for a few seconds to give me a simple and authentic answer. Doing the right thing is what makes you happy and doesn't make someone else unhappy. But sometimes this world is very complex. Once, in that same seat you see in the back, two boys, a little older than you, were dividing up the proceeds of an armed robbery. They were celebrating by counting the money, while bragging about how stupid their victim had been. They were so happy and immersed in ecstasy that they didn't even notice that I was taking them straight to the police station. I parked at the door, which is always forbidden, and as expected, several policemen came out to scold me. I locked them inside and explained everything to the officers. Did I do the right thing? Yes. Did I make them happy? I hope so, at least in the long run. I gave them a chance to change. To apologize. To correct. To improve."

"This question will sound strange to you. I don't want you to think I'm crazy or anything like that. Have you ever witnessed an apparition? Something mysterious, unexplainable?" I noticed he was changing the subject. He made a gesture with his head, like a kind of tic. "If you don't feel like talking about it, we'll drop it. I don't want to make you uncomfortable, Flavio, although your reaction gives you away."

"Why are you asking me this question? Have you ever seen anything, ever?" he replied in a defensive tone.

"I asked first," I said, arching an eyebrow to relieve tension.

"Well, it's funny you should ask, because I recently had a terrifying vision. I think I saw a winged being from the underworld, demonic almost. It scared me so much that I ran for my life. I did some research on these paranormal phenomena and discovered that what I had seen was the Mothman."

Again, that resounding, deep voice eclipsed all sound.

"It was me! Explain it to him! What moth? What does this man say? It was me, the one in Central Park at dusk!"

"Okay, Flavio. Let me explain and answer your question. I've seen something too. Often, in fact. What's more, right now I'm seeing your "moth"."

Flavio's face seemed to unhinge between fear and anguish, and then transformed into the expression of one who thinks he is being played a joke. The strong voice of the guardian complained.

"I don't like being called a moth!"

I laughed with pleasure, because for once I seemed to have some control of the situation, and I found the guardian's anger comical.

"Flavio, it's not a moth." Flavio unbuttoned a button on his shirt and pulled out a Crucifix. "It's a guardian angel. He told me you saw him in Central Park at dusk. Is that right?" He slowed down so much that we were almost at a standstill. "He wants to give me a message for you. About your father, Lucca. He says he's very sick. He wants to take him away, but he refuses because you don't want to see him off in peace."

Flavio began to cry. The wrinkles on his unchanging face became discreet tributaries of pain.

"He says to gather the family, all together, and for a valuable time your father will regain all his splendor, all his vitality. The guardian will take care of it. Take the opportunity to tell him everything you feel and how much you love him, and keep in mind that for a person like your father, death is the beginning of a much better existence, a prize. Now he thanks me for having acted as a go-between and tells me that when you go the wrong way with the cab, don't get angry, that it is your guardian who provokes it to protect you. Never change the way you are." I clicked my tongue. "He's fading away, Flavio. It's going away. He's gone."

He stopped the cab at the curb and got out of the car. He walked a few steps. He wiped his eyes with the sleeve of his shirt and sat down on a metal bench, staring up at the sky. Every now and then he glanced toward the cab, checking to see if it remained there, trying to comprehend what I had told him. We weren't far from my destination, so I left the fare money on the speedometer and got out. The door creaked open and sounded tin-hard when I carefully closed it. Flavio jumped up.

"Please let me give you a ride. Get back in the cab," he insisted with a pressing sense of unfulfilled commitment.

"We're so close, Flavio. I'm sorry to hear about your father and I'm sorry that our jocular conversation has turned to sadness. Anyway, it has been a privilege for me to meet you. You must be someone very special for the guardians to reveal their existence to you, we are an exception."

Still glassy-eyed, he took my hands in his. I noticed the contrast. Flavio's were smooth, clean and immaculate. Mine were covered with dirty scabs, with the edges of the nails blackened. I saw his intentions. He wanted to kiss my hands. I prevented him with a brusque, almost rude movement.

"I'd rather we had a hug, if that's okay." It meant a lot more than it might seem. Appreciation. Mutual help between two strangers united by adversities, by the mysteries of life, and who, without uttering a word, wished each other luck and strength to face them.

I slung my backpack over my shoulder and walked in the direction of the residence. I walked to the unknown, towards fear. I was only a few minutes away from my destination, but I didn't want to expose myself too much. When I arrived at the residence, from afar, everything seemed to me to be in order. Nothing was out of place. The tinkling light of the streetlamps illuminated the perimeter absent of those SUVs, people dressed in black, and orange balls flying through the air. At the entrance to the residence, the icy white light of the neon tubes illuminated the interior of the access control post, where the guard was probably taking a nap.

In front of that entrance, slightly tilted, was a phone booth. I removed my bandana from my neck, used it to loosen the light bulb on the ceiling, and darkness fell. I tossed in a few coins; the signal rang continuously through the receiver, but I couldn't make up my mind to dial. The tone cut out and I had to hang up. I took a breath and inserted the coins again. This time I dialed the number of the residence. I could hear the buzzer ringing at the checkpoint, almost in front of me.

"Newark dormitory," answered a gruff, masculine voice. He insisted, "Who is it?"

"Good evening. I am David Fonseca. I know it is very late, but I would like, if possible, to speak with my tutor, with Paloma."

"Boy, is that you? You've got half the world in an uproar; the big bosses are here. Here! Can you believe it? Everyone's looking for you. Where are you?"

"It doesn't matter. I have to talk to Paloma. Is it possible or not?"

"Paloma is no longer your tutor; I have to notify another external department. You have to tell me where you are. Apparently, it's something serious, but nobody tells me anything here."

I began to get nervous and questioned whether this was a good idea.

"Leave it. Thanks anyway."

I had already separated the receiver to hang up, when I heard the voice of the janitor.

"I'll put you through to Paloma. Don't hang up. She'll know more than me, because nobody tells me anything. Let her take care of it," he said.

The seconds passed eternally, marked by the telephone tone in my ear. A light was coming on at the top floor, the third floor. Now all my thoughts were focused on what I would talk about with Paloma. I was still a slave to my secrets, a slave to lies. And in my head, at that moment, there was only space for made-up excuses and hollow stories and shame for being forced to defend my uniqueness with deceit.

"Hello?" Paloma's rusty voice sounded startled in the middle of the night. An extra sound caught my attention and made me remain silent. "David is that you?" she asked again.

"Silence, Paloma. I think they're here. How stupid I've been!"

"Where are you? Where? Tell me! You're close, I can feel it!"

I covered the earpiece with my hand to listen to my surroundings. Again, my heart was fluttering uncontrollably in my chest. I unzipped my backpack and hurriedly pulled out a pistol. I made sure it was ready to open fire. The noise was getting closer and closer. I dropped the phone, which fluttered in the booth with the steel cable taut, swinging like a pendulum.

"I'm in the phone booth! I have to go, I don't know what these people want from me," I exclaimed without attempting to hide my fear.

I was about to leave the phone booth, holding the gun firmly in front of my eyes, when the sound of footsteps revealed his identity. I reacted immediately, without even hesitating, there was nothing to think about. I hid the weapon *ipso facto* behind my waist.

In front of me was a little girl, no more than six years old. Her attention was not particularly focused on me, but she seemed distracted playing a fantasy hopscotch game on the pavement. I did not understand what was going on. What is she doing here at this time of night? Why was she alone? I stepped out of the booth and stared at her, unable to believe my eyes. She was wearing a white dress, simple, with some light embellishments on the shoulders and a bow at the waist. A small purse. Clean, shiny little shoes. Her blonde hair was held back by a headband, all matching.

"Do you want to play?" she asked me with the sweetness and innocence of her age.

Simultaneously, I could hear the voice of the telephone hanging from the wire. Something was not right. The loud noise of a window opening violently diverted my attention from the girl. It was coming from Paloma's room. My guardian appeared next to me, just as a sedan car on the other side of the residence pulled up to my position. My senses were collapsing with so much information.

"Escape, David! Run, go away!" shouted Paloma from her room.

She seemed to know something I did not.

The situation was confusing, and the real danger, that speeding car, was the threat. Conflicting feelings argued within me. On the one hand, the suspiciousness of the girl in that context, and on the other hand, my innate obligation to protect her. Doubt is always a great weakness.

"What should I do?" I asked my guardian. "I'm tired of running away!"

"I can't make decisions for you, nor interfere in that regard. But you will never be alone, you should know that."

"We have to go; this place is not safe. Come on, little girl! We're leaving!"

I took her by the hand and with my right hand I held the gun. The girl could not keep up with me, so I pulled her up with my left arm and began to lose myself in the surrounding streets. A dog rushed against a garden fence, barking aggressively and furiously. I continued to run, still looking at the sky, in search of that orange ball that, fortunately, did not appear. With the kid on my hip, my biceps stiffened; it was painful, but I ignored it.

In that situation of imminent danger, I still had a moment to feel bad for staining the girl's precious dress with my dirty homeless clothes. Little by little it seemed that I had thrown them off; then, in the distance, I heard the revving engine of the car that was looking for me. I saw curtains were flapping out of an open window, I took out my flashlight and peered inside. On the other side, the living room of a small house was lit up.

"Wait for me here, don't move," I said very softly, placing my index finger on my lips as a sign of silence. She remained standing, still and obedient.

I entered that small room with the help of my flashlight. It looked like an old lady's house, but I had to check it out. It was an elderly woman was snoring contentedly in the room at the end of the corridor. I closed her door and placed a vase in front of it, so that if it opened, the noise would alert me. I also closed the living room door and looked out the window, stretched out my arms and picked up the little girl to bring her into the house. I looked out and, in the distance, I could see someone running across the street. The car pulled up next to them, they exchanged a few quick words and continued on their way. I closed the window and pulled the curtain.

"Listen, princess, this is like playing hide-and-seek, we can't turn on the light, understand? We have to be very quiet, so we don't get caught. We have to win, okay?"

Suddenly, my guardian appeared in the hall; behind him there were others. I began to worry; I feared the worst, that someone had followed us. I discreetly looked out the window, still holding my gun, but I could see nothing outside. I looked around the cramped room to find a place to hide the little girl if necessary. Then the little girl spoke up.

"You know? You are very lucky. It's definitely you. It's true. You're the one who can see beyond the visible."

I let go of the window curtain and turned to her. She was standing perfectly still, her hands behind her back. She retained all that angelic image that only children can convey, except for one nuance, her gaze.

"I'm sorry. What-what did you say?" I stammered nervously, my throat dry and my voice trembling.

"I will introduce myself. You can call me Saya, although that's not my real name. I will be straightforward. You are the reason for my presence in this world."

I stood with my mouth open, and a shiver ran through my whole body. I felt cheated, and behind the sweet and childish image I could see the enemy in front of me. I wanted to know more but I was scared and wished this could all stop.

"I don't understand anything. But go out and tell your friends not to bother this poor woman."

The girl began to clap her hands smilingly. It was not cynicism, but rather condescension.

"That doesn't suit me. I came alone today. Those men are on your side. They belong to that collaborative community of yours, the one whose name cannot allude more profusely to the atavistic and individual need of belonging and group acceptance, the one you call Us."

"Are you with those who chased me the other time?" The girl, with disturbing seriousness and coldness in her face, nodded.

"Who are you? And what do you want from me?"

"I gather that your people do not know who you are. Questions will be answered in due course. If you wish to join me, we can share our knowledge. There is no need to be enemies. I will show you the riddles of your civilization. I will provide you with whatever you desire: abundance, power, whatever you need to achieve what you call happiness."

"I was very calm before I met you and I would like to stay that way. You don't inspire confidence in me."

"He's here, isn't he?"

She was looking around with a satisfied smile and a restless look in her eyes.

"Who? I asked.

"Your protector," she said, this time looking at me and turning her head slightly, as a sign of assured confirmation.

"Get away from me!"

I pointed both guns at the girl's head. We were only a few meters apart. The sound of the porcelain breaking did not divert my attention from the girl. The old woman's footsteps were undoubtedly coming down the corridor. Damn it, we had woken her up! One more ingredient for that cocktail of madness.

"You cannot kill that which is already dead. Shoot and see for yourself," she said, opening her arms in a cross, palms up and without altering her icy gaze.

"What kind of creature are you?" I asked with contempt for anyone who would camouflage themself in the body of a small child, and lowered my weapons.

"I could kill that old woman and you wouldn't be able to stop me. Unless you give in and come with me. And, who knows, maybe you can find out more about what happened to you and Angie. That was her name, wasn't it?"

I looked at the guardians with apology in my eyes. I would have fought against everything, but I didn't want to measure the certainty of their statement, that lady was not to blame for anything. And selfishly, I admit, I needed to know about Angie.

"Don't hurt her. I will accompany you."

I held the doorknob to prevent the lady from opening the door. Saya, as she said her name was, opened the window and pulled back the curtain.

"You first," she ordered.

I let go of the door and went out quickly, but not without suffering from the tastelessness that haunts those who are making a mistake. Once outside, she ordered me to disarm myself by throwing everything on the floor, checked I had done so and told me to hold tightly two small spheres that looked like metal. An immense light was shining from the sky in the closed night; I tried to look at it, but it was blinding. At the same time, I felt a force pulling me upwards. I heard the dog barking. And suddenly, almost without realizing it, I was suspended in the air, rising above the treetops. The vertigo was overwhelming, a cramp ran up my legs from my belly. Mixed in with the excited barking, a recognizable voice shouted at me from the ground. There was no doubt about it, it was Paloma, who, anguished, was screaming at me repeatedly,

"Find a way back, David! Find a way back! Come back!"

She fell to her knees, and pounded the ground with an open hand in an act of helplessness and frustration. It was confirmation of my fateful mistake.

Trial and error, the eternal trance of learning.

Chapter 31
Other Forms of Life

Somewhere undetermined on the ground,
November 1996

Instantly the atmosphere changed. Paloma's screams could no longer be heard, nor did the barking continue. Silence became chaotic inside that structure. I kicked the floor but got no sound. A warm, changing light began to gradually flood the room. Every inch of the place was iridescent. I clapped my hands and it sounded hollow; it was so disconcerting that I repeated the action.

A female voice caught my attention. I immediately turned around. A young woman, in her early twenties, stood before me calm, confident and smiling. She spoke perfect Spanish. She was blonde with straight hair, a small, upturned nose, fair complexion and rosy cheekbones, she was wearing tight black pants, shoes with a slight heel, and a black sweater with a white shirt peeking out from the collar. Over it, she wore a tailored blazer.

"Be welcome. Come with me," she said with a gesture.

"Just a moment. I want to talk to Saya." A tender smile appeared on her face; I mean that endearing expression girls get when they see a litter of puppies. She was surprised at my innocence.

"What's wrong?"

I replied, "What is this place?"

"Patience, dear friend, patience. Relax, there is no need to be tense. I am Saya, only with a different appearance. A body more in line with your mental parameters. I do not intend for our communication to be distracted by this rational incongruity."

This surprised me and I dropped the two spheres that had brought me there. However, the ground absorbed them without making the slightest sound, like raindrops in the ocean. Saya watched my face, and on it my frustrated expression of incomprehension and fear. She raised her hand in a vertical motion and a door opened. On the other side the light was constant, warm and familiar, without the strange movements of the undefined and unsettling room we were in.

I think my subconscious made the immediate decision to go in there. I was much more comfortable. Behind that door was a large, 1950s-style kitchen, worn but in good condition. In the center was a table with four chairs. Through the window you could see the darkness of the sky and a large field lit by the silvery moonlight. Nothing made sense, it was very artificial.

"Please sit down. How do you like your coffee?"

Somewhat shocked and overwhelmed, I complied by sitting in the wooden chair. My hand rested on the table touching the surface and I noticed my fingertips tapping. The anxiety needed to come out. I examined the rounded refrigerator, the flowery wallpaper, the curtains halfway up the window, the huge ceramic sink, the beautiful, worn lines of the cabinets with those simple handles, and one question kept haunting me, infuriating me. I took several deep breaths, calming myself; I decided to play the game, I had only one other choice and it wasn't smart.

"With milk and a teaspoon of sugar, thank you."

She moved freely around the kitchen. She opened the silverware drawer. The cup cupboard. And so on. I stopped for a moment and looked down at my hand whose fingers were still dancing on the table. They were black and gnawed with dirt. I felt ashamed of my condition.

"Is there a bathroom to wash my hands?"

"Of course! At that door."

I stood up, turned the knob and reached for the switch. A small chain, hanging from the lamp, turned on the bulb. I scrubbed and scrubbed, and kept scrubbing, and the sink grew darker and darker with my grime. I ran my hand over it with plenty of water to clean up the mess and leave it as clean as possible. In any case, dirt persisted on my skin that did not want to come off. I dried my hands gently, not wanting to stain the towel too much, and returned to the table.

The pleasant smell of coffee flooded the kitchen. How much I missed that aroma and clearly my predisposition to drink it was conditioned by a positive memory. Extracts from memory, from other experiences, always in good company. This time it would be different. I sat down at the table. I crossed my arms, sitting comfortably, looking at her with an inexplicable security. I watched her remove the cups from the tray and add the sugar.

"A teaspoon, right?"

I stared at her, my head cocked to one side, I felt the involuntary pressure in my teeth; I have never nurtured hatred, that was not the point. It just seemed like a big farce that we both had to put up with.

"Yes, a teaspoon. Thank you very much, Saya."

"I know you have a lot of questions. I want us to establish this relationship as a partnership between you and me. A mutually beneficial friendship. What you call symbiosis in your science, right?"

I took a sip of that coffee, which was delicious. My first thought was that it might have been poisoned. I put the thought out of my mind because it was obvious that I was at the greatest disadvantage. I'd be dead by now if they wanted me so.

"You have my undivided attention, because I honestly don't know what this is all about."

And I pointed to her first, and then to the realistic set.

"You are not the first person with whom I have had this conversation. I will try to be brief. You have before you a specimen of another civilization. A very distant one, specifically thirty-seven light years."

I definitely questioned my own sanity for a moment, questioning my mental health. It was too much in one day.

"It seems like a long trip, doesn't it? I don't doubt you, but you don't look like an alien to me either. Our original appearance is not too far removed from yours. Cosmic nature follows a very similar evolutionary path throughout the universe. It finds the same biological solutions to complete the vital functions. However, if you wish, I can show you what I am talking about."

Clearly, it was a rhetorical question. A few seconds later, the doorknob of the kitchen door slowly turned, and the door opened. I sat up properly in my chair and involuntarily tensed. The door was wide open, and behind it the orange lights circulated through that strange and undefined structure, and now, yes, an anthropomorphic body entered the kitchen closing the door.

It was instinctive, we tend to react in an irrational way to what we do not know. Fear. I stood up and moved away from that creature that was walking towards me. Then it stopped. It was no more than five feet tall. Huge, black, oval eyes, without eyelashes or any hair. Small mouth and big head. Elongated, sinewy neck. Very large hands, four fingers on each. He wore a kind of metallic-colored cloth and, most characteristic, his skin was gray. I later learned that, for this reason, a small part of humanity that knew of their presence nicknamed them the grays.

"He just wants to shake your hand. That's your peace symbol, isn't it, that you're unarmed?"

I took a few steps forward and offered my hand, the creature embraced part of my forearm with its fingers. I admit that I was both fascinated and horrified in equal parts. He didn't say a word, nor did any gesture appear on his face. He turned around, looked at Saya and went back to the door through which he had entered, as if the demonstration was over. The feel of his skin was thick, but soft at the same time.

"Wow, my goodness, what was that?"

Saya started laughing.

"I'm sorry, but I wasn't prepared or prepared for something like that."

"However, you are one of those who have reacted the best. It is obvious that this is not your first contact with other entities."

I reserved my thoughts. I didn't want to add anything to her statement, but neither the reds nor the guardians had ever provoked such a feeling of strangeness in me when I saw them for the first time. I deduced that, whether we can see them or not, all of us, and I mean human beings, sense that they are there. They accompany us. We perceive their latent presence. But these beings from another world, from such distant frontiers, are something very different. That's what I thought.

"And you? Why do you look so human? And what do you want from me? I don't understand anything."

"Relax, David, we were doing fine, don't worry. In reality, none of us has a fixed body. We overcame the body barrier a long time ago. That was our great breakthrough, but also our great failure. We thought we knew everything and, on the contrary, we still had a lot to learn."

Saya stood up and leaned on the counter in front of me. It was as if talking about the matter cost her.

"Our technology was advancing in all fields. The development of our artificial intelligence had reached its peak, but even so, no matter how hard we tried, it lacked an essential virtue for progress: creativity. The solution we devised was hybridization. Eventually we found a way to extract individual consciousness from our bodies. Thus, our civilization split in two. The majority of us evolved towards technological and immortal eternity, but there was also a minority who, respectably, rejected the idea, perishing in union with their organisms, with their natural expiration.

Saya took a long drink of her coffee and continued with her explanation:

"At this point in our history, we were completely unaware of the energetic eternity of each being. We learned to duplicate the body of other biological beings, regardless of their chemical base, although your species, based on carbon, is one of the simplest. Therefore, by means of DNA we duplicate a selected body, and we advance in its maturity progress for the desired time, introducing our consciousnesses inside it. That is how you can see me in this or any other aspect, human or not."

"And what do you want from me? Why did you force me to come with you?"

"When we made that evolutionary leap, we were extremely pragmatic. Although thousands of years ago we had theistic beliefs and worshipped deities, they were all the result of our ignorance. We see ourselves very much reflected in you, just as until recently you called Thor the god of thunder, Ra the god of the sun. All this current of thought is nothing more than a consequence of the intellectual beginning, of exploration and the restlessness to understand.

She looked at me briefly with a melancholy muteness. Saya looked stricken, but continued:

"When the turning point came, of which I have spoken to you, we never thought that there was life after life. It was only after observing among a multitude of living beings and from different planets that we understood that an energetic pattern outside the individual was repeating itself. It first manifested itself at conception, then during extraordinary events in life and finally at death. That energetic imprinting was more pronounced in some individuals. So, for some reason, they were able to contact more firmly what you call the source. We became aware that by separating forever from our bodies, without intending to do so, we had broken one of the major rules of the universe. We lost touch with that energy. That infinite energy that manifests itself in the form of metaphysical entities, in cycles of creation and destruction. We need to contact it, and that is why we need you."

"I have already seen you do it. That woman put evil beings at your service. You don't need me for anything."

"These entities are anti-energetic, source vampires, beings who have not properly transcended after many opportunities and have been trapped in a parallel reality. I am referring to contacting the protectors. Your guides, your custodians. I am not wrong about you; I know you can communicate with them."

"And what do you want from them? I cannot call them at will. I prefer not to get mixed up in this. I do not trust your intentions; although I have no soul, I sense evil here."

A sardonic, uncontrolled laugh took hold of her for at least half a minute, then she frowned, and her face became more serious than ever.

"If we had not arrived in time, you would not even have been born. You want to give me lessons in ethics when your civilization almost destroyed itself in its enthusiasm for the mediocre division of the atom. We arrived to prevent it, presenting ourselves with clear pacifist signals, your act of kindness was to treacherously shoot down our offering ship. Does New Mexico ring a bell? Of course you didn't actually kill any of us, but that primitive gesture made us realize how underdeveloped and violent you can be, and you dare to talk to us about evil? You know, we had to explain to your peers what the new rules of the game were. That unfortunate incident made us rethink our strategy and certainly we do not feel any need for any human individual to stay alive, especially those who are not cooperative."

"So anyone who disagrees with you is dead. That is pure evil, as well as a direct threat."

"You don't seem to understand. Nothing that is alive dies at all. The vital energy that occupies a living being always remains. It changes places, it is something immutable. It simply travels, it evolves"

"I am understanding it perfectly. If you intervened to prevent our self-destruction, it was not for altruistic purposes. You want and need something from us. You want to understand the mystery of life because you have been dead for too long. You are only matter in motion, am I wrong?"

"We are very much alive. We won't hide the fact that we lack connection, but with your help we will recover it, whether you want it or not."

"At last we are getting to know each other; we take off our masks."

And right at that moment I realized that something in me was not working properly. Regardless of the true identity of these beings or their intentions, I myself was feeding the worst in me: arrogance and contempt. Without looking for it, like a natural call, I could feel a seemingly unjustified shame. Something deep and subtle was exclaiming, "Judge less and listen more." Labeling them was putting me on the spot and, worse, diverting me from my own essence. Between thoughts a gap in time was made, filled with skepticism, broken by my remaining voice. A shared reflection.

"I beg your pardon, Saya. I respect your search. Human beings live with a maxim internalized since childhood: "Every stranger is evil until he proves you otherwise"; that's why since childhood all parents insist that we never talk to strangers. As you can see, we are a species accustomed to dealing with evil, maybe that's why I am being both victim and executioner of that premise."

The atmosphere relaxed and I could see Saya, again, content to have me where and how she wanted me. We both took a sip from our cup of coffee, now lukewarm, but still.

"For coming from so far away, your coffee is not bad at all."

I gave laugh at my own joke and took another sip, smiling, rediscovering my lost social tact.

"It is an exact reproduction," she said with a didactic air." In our world we have other things, but no coffee. That's true, though. Tested from your sense of taste, once you get used to it, it's pretty good."

And we laughed again, me because of how crazy it all sounded, and she, well, I don't know.

"Reproductions and reproductions. This whole kitchen, the crockery, the floor I'm walking on, you, is that all that? Reproductions?"

"I intend to be a diplomat and a good ambassador. Our worlds are very different. This ship is programmed to emit in its interior the light of our sun, whose luminosity is quite different from yours because it is a red dwarf. You will understand that my appearance and this environment are an effort to make you more comfortable. Over time, we have become adept at duplicating any material, any living thing; it's just a matter of arranging the particles in the right order."

"And how can such unevolved beings like us help you?"

"When we first made contact with your leaders, we succinctly addressed the issue of protectors. It was a failure. Most of them were completely unaware of the virtue some individuals, such as yourself, may possess. Their entire concern was to negotiate over their hydrological, fuel and mineral reserves. We felt sorry for them with their base worldly needs. We explain to them that we possess all kinds of resources, that the universe is full of matter. In short, only a few rulers, and curiously from the countries that you contemptuously call Third World countries, had some knowledge, however, very distorted. We quickly understood that we should ignore your leaders. We would not ask permission. We would avoid any hostile threat from your ground, air or sea forces, civilian or military. We would blend in discreetly without attracting attention. By the way, the remains are kept in that military complex with such fervent secrecy that, in the end, it has the opposite effect to the desired one. I believe that they will never be able to decipher our technology, you need more than a thousand centuries of progress. This is an unquestionable fact."

"So, Roswell really did happen?"

"Those of us who are here are a very small portion of our civilization, a research group, one of many in the universe in search of the same goal: to reconnect with the original energy source. That is why we do not hate you. We need you, but we understood that, when the time comes, we must also be implacable with you. That is why I had to be firm with my threats when we were at that old woman's house. I hope you understand that."

"Well. Having overcome and clarified our differences, here and now, and without rancor, what can I do for you?"

"We need you to establish contact with your protector, or protectors, if you have gained the favor of others."

"But what's the point? If you are basically immortal, I don't know what they can do for you. You don't seem to suffer from the troubles of life. You seem to have everything perfectly controlled, measured and calculated."

"I have already told you. We thought we were conquerors of the natural limits, and yet, along the way, it is true that we gained much, but we lost even more. We lost that link with the source, that singular energy that you call soul emanates from there. Now, only those mysterious entities can help us reconnect."

"I understand. And I am very sorry for your situation, but I cannot control those presences at will, quite the contrary, they are the ones who guide, help and lead me through the intricate paths of existence."

"We know there is a way to summon them." Again, there was an awkward, reflective pause. Then she continued, "You are going to have to suffer. We will try not to cause your death. That is why I want to reward you first. We have understood that we must be fair to our guests for there to be acceptance. A deal.

"Suffering? Compensation? Acceptance? What are you saying? Are you kidding me?"

"Not at all. We are confident of getting what we want from your protectors, but if they abandon you, it may be too late and there will be nothing we can do to save you."

"I want to get out of here. Right now!"

I began to get nervous, looking at the ceiling, the window, the doors, desperately searching for the way out that I already knew was not there.

"Think logically, I can't allow it. Take the opportunity to negotiate with me, because, whether you like it or not, at this point in the process, there is no turning back. We must continue."

"Negotiate a deal? What's the point, if I can lose my life? Everything you say is crazy."

"Believe it or not, most of the "intervened" manage to survive, and we can do things for you and also for your family."

"I'm not interested. I repeat again, I want to get out of here, let me out!"

My clenched fists, well, actually my whole body was unable to hide the feeling of injustice that was growing inside me, and at that moment Paloma's words kept echoing in my mind: "Find a way to come back! Come back!" The kitchen door opened with that orange glow in the background. Without stepping over the threshold of the door, the strange alien creature emitted a high-pitched, undefined sound from its modest mouth, and closed the door again.

"You see, David, we have found that the uncontrolled resistance of the "intervened" is very detrimental to our mastery of the energies. We are getting closer and closer to achieve what we need, that's why we ask you to help us in this and we guarantee you that we will do everything possible not to take your life. We know that killing for the sake of killing is the worst and most unforgivable act. It is a fact that alters all individual transcendence and that, although we are not connected to the source at the moment, our actions can be registered in the victim's experience."

I opened the first kitchen drawer, but it was empty. I had been left alone with the clothes on my back. Saya understood that I was looking for a way to defend myself. Any sharp object would have served me well. But the whole thing was a *prop*. A successful recreation of the human environment.

"Inside this space we can eliminate you just by thinking about it, but you, however, even if you had a weapon and managed to kill this body, I would reappear in a few seconds through that door, with this or another form. Truly, try to relax and weigh your options. I offer you abundance and excess for you and yours, and, in addition, something I believe you have been looking for some time: to hear from Angie."

My whole being was in that familiar survivor's switch, in that fight or flight phase, but it is true that, hearing Angie's name, thinking of a route to find her and the option of being able to see her again, and being able to have her in front of me, relaxed my agitated state.

I began to think about her. Imagining it mitigated that nostalgia that gripped me since I was reborn. Just remembering her was a balm for my inner fire. Even so, I should not let myself be carried away by my longings, I knew it was not convenient, I needed a strategy, but, confused by all the information, the stressful situation and the hope of being able to find her, I was feeling blocked.

"But what have you become?" I asked with some pity.

"Information. We are only information that can travel from one body to another or remain in hibernation in a database. You, however, like us before you, are pure active energy mixed with a physical medium. But the protectors, they are our real unknown. The point of union with the original source, the trace that we have yet to discover. The longed-for obverse of matter. And, honestly, I don't want to spend more time on this, will you help us?"

"Answer me what I want to know, and I will collaborate with you. How do you know about Angie?"

"As you have already deduced from your experience, you know that some of your species work for us. They feel that their talents are really useful. For example, as you mentioned before, the woman who came with us to look for you. You know, she was subsisting on the few unhappy customers she picked up in an advertisement for words. She is what your society calls, as if it were an anachronism, a sorceress. It took us a while to find her, but it was worth it."

Damn! Precisely at that moment, I became aware from a wider perspective and drew instant conclusions. I was in grave danger in there. I listened to her without stopping to think.

"Like us, some of your species, as in your case, you carry information, memories that you should not keep because they simply go against the natural order. She made the gesture of quotation marks with her hands. What we do not know is what the purpose of this recurring anomaly is. We do know, however, that all these memories become an obsessive fixation for the bearer. Thanks to this, we were able to locate you after such a long time. We can help you clear your doubts... if you help us first."

"Let's see, because I'm not clear, and I'm a bit confused; explain to me what you mean by "locating me after so long". What does that even mean?"

Saya looked up at the ceiling for a moment, regretting her words. A grimace of displeasure shone on her face making it transparent; even so, she answered my question without elaborating on details.

"We tracked you down more than two decades ago. Back then you were Dustin. As far as we know, you grew up like any normal boy. You never missed a day of school, helped out on the farm in the afternoon, and studied late into the night. You were a credit to the Sanders family. Not without effort, your parents mortgaged everything to enroll you in college. You graduated with honors. You and architecture were made for each other. However, your secret lived with you in the most absolute secrecy. Only your mother, in the period of your childhood, listened to you talk about the protectors as if they were playmates. She took you to a doctor, and the latter, ignorant like so many others, played it down, saying that you were an only child and that such imaginations would disappear with maturity. But it didn't, and to your mother's concern, you learned that it was better to keep your visions to yourself and hide them."

I listened attentively, nodding without meaning to, because her words were clearing the cobwebs from my memories.

"We would never have known of your existence had it not been for your unexpected and bizarre arrest when you were twenty-six years old. You spent four months in prison surrounded by the most dangerous criminals. That's what I call survival. Correction, the correct thing would be to talk about providence. I'm sure you remember. Yes, yes, yes, yes," she affirmed, reinforcing it with a clenched fist and tilting her head with an empathetic grimace, knowing the injustice of that past penitence. Such an abrupt trance leaves its mark forever, doesn't it?"

I, however, crestfallen, not out of insecurity, but meditating, I entered the distant depths of my clouded memories. A dreadful shiver ran down my back, like a reappearance of that insurmountable fear.

Like a sudden reoccurrence of lost memories.

Chapter 32
Findings

The event Saya was talking about came back to me as fresh as if it had been a few moments ago: now I remembered it with absolute clarity.

It all happened on a cold autumn afternoon. I was coming out of the library, where I'd browsing books on classical architecture for an upcoming project. I bundled up as much as I could and unclipped my skeletal, narrow-wheeled bicycle, removing the lock by touch rather than sight, my eyes only half-opened due to the force of the wind. I jumped on my bike, in a hurry, like someone escaping from an invisible enemy. I was returning to the student apartment I shared with some classmates. It was Thursday, and I was preparing to present my ideas for the important work. A lot was expected of me, and I was trying hard to live up to it.

That's what I was thinking about, riding hard to try and beat the weather. The road home ran, for the most part, parallel to the tracks of the Inter-City train that covered the Boston, New York, Philadelphia and Washington DC passenger route. Many of the streetlights along the way were in need of maintenance, some tinkling in their effort to gleam, and others, simply defeated, rested unlit. A knot formed in my stomach. I automatically stopped pedaling, only moving now by the embers of inertia.

The vision in front of me stood out from all the others. The bicycle's sprocket rattled to the sound of the wheel. Meanwhile, I, frightened by the vision, by the announced omen, was unable to take my eyes off those train tracks. I got off without a care in the world, leaving the thing lying on the ground. I ran towards the clearing, crossing metal cords anchored to posts. I slowed my pace. Solemn and atavistic respect dictated it. Along the tracks stood hundreds of guardians, like long, sharp shadows in the night, all with their faces turned in the same direction.

"What's going on here?" I asked hesitantly, mingling among them without getting an answer. They remained unmoved. I stumbled over the sleepers of the tracks as I hurriedly questioned all the guards. Nervous, frustrated and accelerated, I shouted at the top of my lungs and with all my strength to those presences,

"What are you doing here?"

After a few seconds, one turned his attention away from the track layout, noticed me and, in a prominent but taciturn voice, stated,

"We are here, waiting for doom. We took our people with us." Without further ado, he turned his gaze to the rails, which seemed to get lost and melt into the night darkness.

I understood the gravity of the situation, what was to come. In a hurry, drowning in anguish, I went through the metal barrier, tearing my jacket through the wire. I stopped on the sidewalk, looking all around, looking for a phone booth. I had passed by it dozens of times, but I had never noticed the details. In front of me, a small, semi-detached, single-family house shone light through the windows. I knocked insistently on the door, as a madman would. A gray-haired man pulled back the curtain behind a thin pane of glass.

"Quick! Call 911! There's going to be a serious train accident! Call 911!"

His skeptical gaze scanned the path where the trains were to pass and nothing caught his attention, he just watched empty and calm, the usual from his window. Now his droopy, prejudiced eyes rested on me without a shred of credibility. It didn't take him long to wave his hand in the air commanding me to get out of there and stop bothering.

Stubborn, I kept knocking on the door.

"Call 911! Call 911!"

I heard a door open two houses away. A woman in her robe, braver and more supportive, perhaps also more foolish, was visible under her small porch, alerted by the sudden commotion she was making. I ran towards her in desperation. I saw her backing away, frightened. I controlled myself as much as I could by lowering the torrent of my voice.

"Help! Please! They need help!"

I know my expression was unhinged, my eyes wild and my hair disheveled from holding my hands to my head.

"Soon there will be a tragedy right here, there will be many victims, accidents... Deaths! Hundreds!"

The sentences were incomplete.

"And how do you know? Everything is as usual!"

At that moment, a child of about six years old was babbling in fear of my unexpected intrusion. He claimed the natural protection of his mother behind her door. The boy's guardian made an appearance prompted by the apparent sense of danger.

"You tell him!" I ordered the shadow, who, without being able to say for sure, affected, understood the reason for my despair before the chatter of his fellows.

The woman looked at me astonished, because behind the line of her door there was only a coat rack and an old photograph of a man with a beard.

"The boy's name is Solomon, like his grandfather. I had to come to his aid when he was drowning last winter, in his aunt and uncle's pool, he was about to leave. It wasn't his time yet," the guardian said in a thick voice, giving me this precious information.

I repeated, literally, everything the shadow told me. The woman turned to the photograph with emotion. For sure, it was her father, the boy's grandfather. She wanted to understand that it was he who saved his grandson. She took her son in her arms, gave him a motherly kiss and with her other hand reached for the receiver of a telephone that was hidden from my view behind the wall of the hall.

I grabbed the phone like a madman and dialed in a hurry. Dialing felt as if it took forever. I was glad that the number was only three digits.

A woman took the call. She asked me for the address. Rushed, I had to ask the mother standing next to me. I asked to bring as many ambulances as available, firefighters and to warn the hospitals about what was about to happen. A strange, suspicious silence made me think they weren't taking it seriously. That pause, with the faint crackling sound in the background, was interrupted by a final statement.

"I confirm that we have already sent out the call," said the operator in a clear radio tone.

Then I only heard an intermittent beep. She had hung up on me. I did not understand anything. I heard a car coming, but I couldn't make out its lights. It was coming with its headlights off. I only heard the creaking of its doors. I looked out on the landing and could see an impeccable Plymouths with police plates. Two officers were interviewing the gray-haired old man, who now, out of the house, indicated my position. The officers hurried to catch up with me. I stood still and raised my arms, not knowing how to act.

Without saying a word, and at a certain distance, one of them would point the barrel of his revolver at my chest.

"Don't move! Don't you dare move!"

His companion searched me, dragging his hands along the contours of my body, holding a huge flashlight the size of a stake under my armpit. Unaccustomed to being searched, I gasped as he reached a certain part of my anatomy.

"Clean!" shouted his companion.

It was then, and only then, that they holstered their weapons and began to be polite. I didn't have time to feel offended; something more pressing was occupying my thoughts. One of the policemen was talking alone with the woman. He was very calm. She was fidgeting, infected by my anguish. The other one was asking me to please give him my personal documents. It was useless; I handed over my identity card. He compared the photograph with my face several times, satisfied.

"Late," I said aloud to myself.

A golden light galloped from the distance increasing its brightness in the darkness. The train was approaching. The sound of its power mingled with the clanking of metal. For a few seconds, I stood motionless, guilty of not doing enough.

"It's coming!" -I managed to vocalize.

I ran across the street, ignoring the orders of the agents who instinctively chased me. I crossed the rusty barrier and from inside I turned around. I stepped on one of the wires with all my weight and lifted the other. I waited for them to come in with me, as if we were a makeshift team. The agents watched me transfixed, pondering how to proceed. They fleetingly crossed their gazes as if having a conversation in a secret, telepathic language. Without articulating a word, and careful not to tear their uniforms, they entered with me. The dark, lanky silhouettes remained motionless.

"Don't go any closer!" I said to the agents, holding them with tact and respect. "We need to call for reinforcements! Ambulances!"

I don't know if it was a product of suggestion or if they also sensed something. The fact is that they remained attentive to the train, trusting that it would continue on its way after passing that slight curve, unable to anticipate events on their own. Now the track offered us a side view of that gigantic metallic snake. Its side, full of luminescent windows, was approaching.

The disaster sounded as deathly wounded animals do. The locomotive overturned dragging its load of souls with it. The wagons squeezed and crowded together, making the steel scream. A mingled set of shrieks shook us. I ran to the spot before that metallic beast came to a full stop.

The mixture of dust, sand and ballast hit me violently. Something hit me hard in the head; I felt no pain, it didn't stop me. My worst predictions had come true. Suddenly, a sepulchral silence, implausible. The policemen took a few seconds to react. One of them hurried to the patrol car, I suppose, at last, to ask for medical assistance over the radio. I, with his partner, was entering the horror of the tragedy. The friction of the materials gave off a bitter smell of burning. The flashlight was moving very fast, in all directions, illuminating a succession of terrifying snapshots. I stopped for a second. I felt like a victim of panic. I was trying to grasp the impossible. I finally listened to my instinct, to that unique part of me that I had renounced all my life.

Stifled, I turned to the officer. I contained my nervousness and looked him in the eye.

"Please turn off the flashlight for a moment, officer."

Surprised, accustomed to being the one who gives orders to the citizen, he maintained for a few moments an internal dispute. Something inside him made him trust me and a few seconds later, his thumb disconnected the switch. It didn't take long for my eyes to adjust. In the air, above the carriages, small wisps of light floated, disappearing with their guardians. I focused all my attention on those who remained at the side of their protégés, those who were still here, those who were still in this life.

"This way!"

I hurried to run ignoring the first car that was fused to the locomotive in an impossible turn. There were no survivors.

The policeman's disciplined personality pushed him to attend to the locomotive and the first carriage, engaged in a methodical exercise of orderly checking. I grabbed him, this time with force, by the arm.

"Listen to me. There is no one there to help."

He pulled away impetuously. His anger was not for me, the circumstances were overwhelming.

"How do you know?" he shouted at me, skeptical and helpless.

"I know, and that's it. Just as I knew this would happen." I noticed that he was breathing deeply, as if in an unconscious act of professional self-control. "We must help the wounded. This way," I insisted."

We made it to the second car, moving through broken glass, open luggage, twisted metal and bodies. Dozens of guardians were waiting for help for their protégés. Among them there seemed to be an invisible communication, a consensus of priorities about the victims. They made me ignore the plaintive cries of pain. Some of the more seriously injured people couldn't remain conscious. The little flashes of silver light kept hovering in the air, disappearing, losing their glow in the night. With each of them so did an elongated dark silhouette.

"Help!" exclaimed one of the shadows, who was crouching with his hand on someone. When it saw us coming, it stood up. "Joel must survive!" I grabbed the policeman by his jacket, who was looking around in confusion. "We must get Joel out!"

We approached, in the dark, clawing at each other, cutting everything in our path. The spotlight of the flashlight illuminated a child lying down. Actually, I deduced that he had been thrown down the center aisle, hitting everything in his path. He ended up against the door separating the cars and, although it was true that he was lying down, his body lay in a complex posture, painful to the eye.

The policeman and I were overcome by the same feeling of desperation. We were paralyzed by fear of failure and hesitated for a few seconds as we tried to figure out to how to rescue the boy. The guardian brought us out of our lethargy.

"Help him!" We reacted in unison, as if the agent had also heard the voice of the guardian.

"Careful with his shoulder, he has a glass shard stuck in it. I am keeping him unconscious so he doesn't suffer pain." I relayed the information. "Agent let's be careful, we can't see it from here, but the boy has glass lodged in his shoulder."

He looked at me, accepting the information without question, but with that spark in his eyes, the expression of perplexity. It was clear that he would ask me for explanations when everything had happened.

"Call me Billy," he said with a refreshed air.

"Let's go! On the count of three. One, two and..."

We carefully pulled the boy out, holding him by his legs and arms, and sure enough, when we turned him over, a foreign object emerged from his shoulder, a red-tinted shard of glass. I prepared to separate it from his small body, but Billy stopped me.

"No! He could bleed to death. Let's take him to the street! Hurry!"

And running, but carefully, we retraced our steps all the way. Billy's companion was running towards us, choking and pale. Behind him, some neighbors followed, willing to help. Billy and I handed the boy over to him, who with the help of another man carefully carried him to the vehicle area. At that moment, Billy's professionalism, or rather, police talent, came into full force. Wrapped in a cloud of leadership, he strode decisively into that small crowd of men and women who, anonymous and disorganized, were flocking to the disaster.

"Listen to me. Repeat my words to everyone who arrives! There are no survivors in the locomotive and in the first car! I repeat, there are no survivors!"

Billy paused for a moment to look at me. His eyes calculated just the right amount of complicity intermingled with silent pain. Without reservation, it was clear that he trusted me.

"What you are about to see is very sad! Don't let yourselves be carried away by grief! There will be time to cry. Now it's time to help. Dustin and I will guide you to find the wounded." He said this leaning his hand firmly on my shoulder, with a double message.

One obvious one, to grant me a certain authority before those people, and another hidden, more intimate and secret one: "Don't fail us". It never ceases to seem strange to me that it is in the most difficult and dramatic moments that the best of humanity comes to the surface. Solidarity is something universal, a stamp imprinted and inherent in each and every one of us.

In a matter of minutes, my relationship with Billy had taken a radical turn. I went from being held at gunpoint to becoming his trusted ally. Something mysterious and irrational was pushing him to put logic aside and surrender to the unknown, to the invisible. With his flexible and deeply pragmatic attitude, Billy was living up to the police emblem of "Serve and Protect".

Dozens of firemen and policemen joined the rescue. An orderly maelstrom of professionals arrived to pull out the injured. The ambulances were overcrowded. They flew through the streets and the sound of their sirens echoed throughout the city. Neighbors took mattresses and pillows out of their homes, creating an improvised field hospital on the sidewalks, it was almost a military scene. Towels and blankets were stained a vital red as they wrapped or pressed against bleeding wounds. The sweet and ferrous smell mixed with gasoline and nerves.

I lost track of time a bit, as exhaustion set in. During those hours, Billy and I were inseparable. He, uniformed, somewhat gruff, charismatic and with a powerful commanding voice, led the entire evacuation with me at his side. We enlisted the help of firefighters to dig out and pry metal from an overturned railcar. Beneath a myriad open luggage and twisted metal, the guardian of a young woman insisted on her presence. She was one of the last living victims to emerge from that accidental trap.

Having opened up enough space, I entered the overturned wagon. I had become accustomed to being observed by volunteers and professionals in complete silence; some of them uncovered their plate caps or helmets as a greeting, an enigmatic sign of respect for what some of them baptized miraculous findings. They did not understand my inexplicable intuition that led to the survivors.

Like an unstoppable arrow, I followed the directions of that young woman's guardian. I dug through shoes and clothes and removed heavy leather suitcases. I remember the special gleam in her exhausted eyes. Dull. She had become almost voiceless, overcome by her first frightful shrieks during the derailment. Now when she saw me, she was smiling slightly, relieved to share the loneliness. Her face was dirty with sand and soot.

Her guardian told me she was fine, just a few bumps and bruises. I brushed the tears away from her cheek. We looked into each other's eyes for a frozen eternal moment. She was babbling something, and her tears were getting heavier and heavier. I soothed her.

"You're going to be fine. Let yourself go and don't let go," I insisted, concentrating on putting an end to her nightmare.

She hugged me with all her strength. Tears, sweat and blood mingled on our skin. I carried her to the open hole. I walked with her along the side of the wagon, avoiding glass, window openings and debris.

A pleasant warmth surrounded me with her. Her panting breath hitched in an effort to tell me something. I paused for a few seconds. We created a moment of calm in the storm. I looked into her eyes again, going so deep into them that I was overcome with vertigo. We felt the touch of our souls. There was an infinite sense of well-being together. A spark of magic.

The shouts of firemen throwing a rope brought us back to reality. Finally it came close enough to my ear. A soft, feminine, raspy, earthy voice affirmed,

"I know you. I've seen you in dreams."

Very weak, almost faint and tied now to the thick rope of the firemen, she rose up in the air face up, with her eyes closed and her body sagging, exhaling the air with fatigue. I held her carefully, watching to make sure she didn't hit anything. She reached for my hand and squeezed it as hard as she could, endlessly repeating my innocent command:

"Don't let go of me. Don't let go. Don't let go. Don't let go."

She was a complete stranger. My sudden attachment had no explanation. I didn't hesitate. I climbed over the seats like a wildcat. We put her on a stretcher, and I took her by the hand.

"I'm not going to let you go."

I knew then she was special.

—I won't leave you either.

We were rushing her to the gate to put her in an ambulance. By now she was having trouble breathing. I held her head by the stumbling road, taking the opportunity to pull her bangs out of her eyes. She placed her hand over mine. Closing eyelids hid those infinite eyes.

"Nearly there," I dared to say to fill the void. "My name is Dustin."

She swallowed with difficulty, in an attempt to clear her throat. "Angie."

His fingers caressed mine.

We put her in the ambulance. I looked at the mess. There were no upright shadows left. There was no life left. She was the last survivor.

"I'm going with her."

I set out to accompany her to the hospital.

"Get in the front. There's no time to lose," the driver told me, but I didn't listen.

I helped close the ambulance doors while an attendant strapped her to the stretcher; the ride would be bumpy.

I asked the driver for a second. I wanted to say goodbye to Billy and his partner. However, something strange was happening. They were meeting with other agents, some of them in full dress and brimming with medals on their chests. Billy was holding my documentation, the one I had given him hours before. He was slapping it against the palm of his hand, distressed. His partner was arguing loudly. Something was wrong. The triumphant and profusely decorated policeman was warning him something, threatening. My new friends looked at me in awe. I couldn't understand what was going on.

Another big, burly policeman, who had just arrived, grabbed me by the shirt exclaiming mockingly,

"Don't worry, I'll do it!"

In his other hand I saw a pair of chrome handcuffs with a fine chain. Billy burned with anger and, without thinking, gave him such a push that he almost knocked him down.

"Take your hands off him!"

I still didn't understand. The ambulance activated the lights and siren and hurriedly began the transfer. Without me.

Billy and his partner approached me.

"Dustin, we're very sorry, but you have to come with us."

Petrified at the abrupt turn of events, I asked,

"Am I under arrest?"

His call of forced "due obedience" bellowed shame from every pore of his skin. The invisible made me responsible. My gift became a curse. It was unnecessary to ask for more explanations. My ordeal began.

That's how it all started.

Chapter 33
Grays

*Rikers Island, 1977-Over
an undetermined point on the map, 1996.*

That was the turning point. The moment when I stopped looking the other way. The moment I began to pay attention to that inner voice, to be brave, to be consistent, to take risks and to help others. Even if I had to be punished for it.

Billy did all he could. He wrote a favorable report extolling all my goodness, my good conduct, my commitment to rescue. But even so, it was totally insufficient. They always look for a scapegoat. Without any medical interview or previous study, I was diagnosed with hero syndrome.

My lawyer explained it to me without even looking up, reviewing other cases that piled up in his tightly packed folder. I was shivering with cold in that concrete cell, peeling, damp, and so dreary, making an effort to concentrate on the lawyer's explanations.

They accused me of sabotaging the railroad. In short, of causing the accident and then presenting myself in society as some sort of savior. A strange pathology, but well known. In their invented logic, everything fit perfectly. I have always tried to face my problems from an external, objective point of view, that is, as if it were happening to someone else and I were called upon to offer the best of my advice. On this occasion, I had a very, very hard time.

Indeed, I lost everything. Family reunions, the future of work, enjoying friends, the simple joy of a walk in the park; but, above all, I lost that magical, special and unique contact, that new discovery that invaded my mind like a catchy song, and that made me smile making my imagination fly in the lowest hours: Angie.

They removed me from the world, taking away my freedom.

Those early days at Rikers Island, New York's maximum-security prison on the East River, did not do justice to its infamy. It was even worse than they said. I followed Billy's advice: don't look, don't talk, don't look weak. But no matter what, it was hell on earth. Reddish beings everywhere watched me hungrily, but something was holding them back.

You never get to know the workings of that parallel universe, that world of invisible beings, but I did perceive the caution of the reddish ones and, therefore, of the prisoners. They all sensed that behind me a powerful energy was protecting me. In street slang they called it respect. But it was not that.

On the fourth day of being there, everything changed.

"Sanders!" shouted a huge African-American guard. I jumped from the top bunk alarmed by his tone and stood up, firm and disciplined like the military man I had been. "Come with me. The warden wants to see you."

He placed hand and foot cuffs on me. Both were linked by a central chain. I tried to keep up with him. The guard dragged me by the shackles, but my feet wobbled like a penguin's. I didn't think of complaining. It didn't occur to me to complain. I tried jumping, but I was never good at sack races. Without saying anything to him, he became aware and slowed his stride.

We passed through corridors guarded by armored doors. The atmosphere and decoration changed slightly for the better as we walked. The doors began to be made of wood and pictures decorated the corridors. Lamps with opaque lampshades hung from the high white ceilings. A fresh, sweet, feminine scent greeted us before we reached the warden's office. It came from his secretary, a young woman, who, upon seeing us arrive, alerted the warden to our presence through an intercom and immediately moved away from us, unable to disguise her fear.

The scene seemed ridiculous to me. She looked at us as if we were two beings from the underworld that had emerged from the depths. Two beasts. The giant escorting me did not even flinch, he was more than used to it. He shunned eye contact. I thought it was odd, but then, thinking it through and putting myself in his shoes, I understood.

"Listen to me, Sanders. I don't know, nor do I want to know, why the warden sent for you. What I do know is that if you go even the slightest bit too far, I'll squash you like a cockroach." He slapped his big fist with his opposite palm. "Do you understand?"

I nodded politely.

The guard knocked on the door calculating, now carefully, the two taps of his knuckles. A voice from inside called,

"Come in!"

As we entered, a strong natural light invaded our senses, collapsing my sight.

"Good morning, Mr. Warden. May I have your permission?"

"Go ahead."

An immense glass window exposed before us the imposing living image of New York City. Manhattan, Brooklyn and Queens lay before me like an urban carpet full of detail and glittering activity. The massive back of a swivel chair concealed the figure of the man who moments before had ushered us in. One hand peeked overhead with fingers raised to the ceiling in a gesture of authority.

"Guard, leave us."

"Are you sure?"

"I am."

The burly warden stared me straight in the eye ensure I understood his previous warning. Punching his own palm, he mouthed the word "cockroach." Then he pointed his finger at me.

I didn't know how to react. It was clear that he was very serious, and I was partly intimidated, but without knowing clearly why, I almost burst out laughing. Thank goodness I restrained myself.

"Mr. Warden, I'll be right here if you need me."

The guard left the office. The secretary would be uncomfortable again, I had time to think.

"Sit down, Dustin."

I approached one of the armchairs, dragging the chain and making more noise than I wanted. I pulled out the smaller chair apart both hands and took a seat.

Finally, he turned his chair around, revealing himself to me as an obese man with two double chins. He must have been about fifty years old, and he wore gold-rimmed glasses. He must have been short, because his feet barely touched the floor. He seemed intent on raising his seat above the rest in an act of pompous preponderance. A tight-fitting brown suit matched perfectly with the dull cigar he held in his left hand.

"Are we treating you well?" he asked the air.

Immediately, I was hit by a deluge of images. Me spreading my buttocks open during prison intake. Doing squats naked, shaving my hair down to zero, enduring that icy shower spray. Sticking out my tongue while an arrogant, latex-gloved guard explored my mouth after diving into someone else's ass. I found myself covered up to my head with a tattered, lousy blanket, the same one I promised not to use. Eating that mashed rice pudding mixed with hot water, muddy and stringy, psychedelic soup they called it. It didn't take me long to respond.

"Yes, sir. They are treating me very well. Thank you."

I lied as best I could, trying to appear sincere and grateful.

"I'm glad," he said, satisfied. He opened the drawer of his desk and took a metal lighter, one of those with a lid, and lit his cigar, taking his time. He stood up; and yes, he was a short man, although he still had that halo of high office.

"One of the people upstairs has taken a great interest in you. They have asked us to make an exception for you," he waved his fingers in the air looking for the appropriate word. "They insist that you are someone very important and that you should be kept separate from the rest of the inmates. That we give you a good bed. Hot water. Reading materials. Radio. That we allow you to receive visitors. Well, the list is long."

His rage seemed to take hold of him little by little in increase.

"Why are you so special? Can you explain it?" he asked me as if I were not me, or as if he were asking himself, I don't know. In spite of everything, the answer came out of my lips like a sharp arrow.

"I am innocent, sir," I said coolly and calmly, without intending to offend.

However, prejudiced skepticism glowed in his eyes as embers do in the campfire.

"No. No, Mr. Sanders. You are guilty. Guilty like everyone else. Guilty. Guilty. Guilty. Guilty! Guilty! Guilty!"

He began to rant and rave in an escalation of madness. I looked down at my shackles, landing with a jolt on my pitiful situation. The door opened and the huge African-American guard leaned out, but he ordered it closed again with an implacable gesture, continuing:

"And do you know how I know that?"

He looked at me with a cruel grin.

"No, sir," I said, resigned and respectful.

"Because you are here," he affirmed with open arms, emphasizing with his circular gaze that this place was a prison. As if his statement responded to an overwhelming and irrefutable syllogism. I was getting more and more uncomfortable. Now you are going to meet with a civil servant. She's an errand girl, and I want you to tell her what you told me. I want you to tell her how well we are treating you. Do you understand me?

He looked at me seriously, taking a long drag on his cigar, and then looked like a steam locomotive.

"I am very grateful to you and all your officials. I could see on his desk a black, leather-covered book with gilt lettering. Holy Bible. It was stained and traveled, but it occupied an important place on the table. I swear it by Our Lord Jesus Christ," I swore without taking my eyes off the book.

The warden's face softened. For an instant, I could see his humanity behind the shield of tyranny.

"Get up. Gary will take you to the visiting room."

Although he still radiated a commanding voice, a certain softening was noticeable.

As I passed through the office door, I met the huge jailer with a cold and watchful countenance.

"To the visitors' room," he said, as if sending a suit to the laundry.

The giant nodded obediently, grabbing me again by the shackles.

"Gary!" said the warden behind us as we left the *hall*. Treat him well. Tell everyone.

The jailer held his gaze with the warden quizzically, although he did not hesitate,

"At your service."

He released his hand from my shackles and for a few seconds my arms followed in front of me out of inertia. Gary stood behind me, and without touching me, he led me through the maze of modules and corridors until I came to a gray-painted pinewood door that announced in black letters: "Visitors".

The room was empty. All the chairs and tables were fixed to the floor with industrial fasteners. It was a monochromatic, bland, joyless room. So neutral that it was sad.

"You have fifteen minutes."

At the back, in the corner that I couldn't see from the door, an elegant, slender woman in her forties or fifties, wearing an ankle-length floral dress and an off-white cardigan, was waiting. On the metal table, she had binder crammed with sheets of paper peeking out from the ends. Behind her, a transparent window with another watchman standing guard.

Unsure, I approached the woman who scrutinized me with her gaze as a market appraiser does. I felt ashamed to wear the uniform of a convict and to appear chained. I looked dangerous, uncontrollable or unpredictable. It looked bad. She took the last steps. The ones that, in those few days in prison, I had learned to guard.

"Lawyer," I said to myself.

"Good morning, Dustin. I'm Paloma and I'm here to get to know you and a little bit about your case."

She extended her hand to me. Like a mirror, I brought mine closer, wrapped around that abnormally pale and fragile hand, but also warm. She placed her other hand on mine, a small gesture of affection in this cruel place. An alarming acoustic signal, like an out-of-tune and annoying ringing, sounded from the speakers installed in the corners of the ceiling. Immediately a voice, just as unpleasant, boomed:

"Contact is forbidden!"

I looked up and could see the official's lips speaking into the dirty microphone in the adjoining room. His gaze was fixed on me like a piercing dart, loaded with a message. I withdrew at once. She stared down at her hands. She was amazed. I didn't understand anything. Then, I thought: "She is not a lawyer, such strange behavior is typical of a psychiatrist". Everything was coming together. They would send me to a psychiatric hospital. My mind was boiling and racing with thoughts, making uninformed guesses.

"We'll get you out of here, Dustin, I give you my word. You'll go back to your old life as if none of this ever happened to you. But better than all that, you won't have to pretend or run away from your gift." She looked at me as if she knew something I hadn't told her. "You will be one of us."

All that memory, rescued from the insurmountable frontier of time, emerged lush, full of nuances. Vivid.

Now Saya was examining me with renewed interest. She was trying to glimpse beyond what her eyes would allow, although you could also guess her frustration.

I played innocent. The months in prison and everything I remembered from my other life made me understand, at that moment, that my existence was interconnected. Destiny and certain clues were making their way to connect the unfinished, I understood it perfectly, it was not casual. I denied the flowering of those memories and made it clear that my gaps were even more murky and opaque than they were.

Now, despite finding myself in that otherworldly artifact surrounded by mundane *props,* I felt stronger, more myself. A lot of information, intuited and unraveled, was reorganizing itself in my head; piece by piece, the puzzle was taking shape. Without intending to, Saya had unraveled more than she would have liked.

Visibly displeased, and with a certain arrogance, she pulled me out of my reflective loop.

"Come with me. I'm going to show you something." Her words were an angry breath. She opened the kitchen door and again the disturbing light made me look away. Put this on. I don't want you to miss anything.

She gave me something very much like an elastic, flexible plastic eye mask, kind of sunglasses that you put on like a blindfold. She put on another one. I imitated the way she put it on. The kitchen looked bluish and duller; however, the light behind the door was no longer painful.

"Where are we going?"

"We call it the room of knowledge."

In my innocent imagination, I had devised a sort of futuristic library where they gathered all their knowledge. The tour of that floating construction did not leave me indifferent. They did not use straight lines. Not even the floor was completely flat. The surfaces were warped and oval, there were no right angles. When I arrived, the light had a different, paler, whitish color.

"Here we are."

The place was quiet. So much so that it was eerie. I could hear our breathing. The light in the room was dimming softly, like the theaters at the beginning of the show. The wall in front of me began to glow. At first, I could only see blurred figures moving. The image became sharper and sharper until it became crystal clear. As I made out what was happening, a sudden acid burn traveled from my stomach to my throat. I had unintentionally become too relaxed, or too confident. In that chaotic silence I could hear the hammering of my wild heart, even the blood rushing through my veins.

Four gray beings were engaged with a human being. A male in his forties, American, relatively athletic. They had him on a horizontal platform. The place was spotless and conveyed a strong aseptic component. All the walls were televisions, where moving signs and headings appeared. Their language, I assumed.

I could see the man, but I deduced that he could not see us. His face was the living image of the most ancestral terror of the human being. Black lines blended on his naked torso. He looked around at those apathetic and insensitive creatures. I saw him screaming, tied with something invisible to that horizontal surface, but was unable to hear the roar of his screams. I had to help this man.

"Let him go! What are you doing?" My voice sounded strange in that place.

"You're going to miss the best bit. Watch."

"Let him go!" I shouted so loudly that I could hear the pain in my voice.

The black lines on his torso converged at the same point, at the level of his heart. At that moment, indifferent to those beings, his guardian appeared. As on other occasions, time became more elastic. That shadow observed the place and those creatures. He seemed to weigh that the death of his protégé might be imminent; then I saw him looking at me. He could see me through the wall. Now, time was running at two speeds. Ours and that of those otherworldly beings.

"What is this place? What are these machines? Who rules them?"

"They are beings from another world."

"They are not beings. They are something else. They want to kill my protégé. Help me save him."

"What can I do?" I asked, constrained by the limited options and the staggering scenery.

"If you give me your permission, I will enter you and we will try together."

Like an exhalation, my friend Javier's remote fight in the schoolyard came to my mind.

"Of course. I am ready."

I did not finish the sentence when I could see the silhouette of the guardian become vaporous and, like a swift mist, compressed in my thorax. It was a great injection of energy. Instantly, I felt different. My senses were more acute, and not only that, but I could also perceive other stimuli from the environment, as if in an inexplicable way every molecule in that place transmitted touch and vision to me. I try to describe it, but I cannot find the exact way. Of course, now the connection with that terrified man was absolute. The guardian and I became one. Someone new and powerful. There was no conflict over who was in charge, none of that human trivia. A perfect blend. I was me, but also the guardian. Complex and simple at the same time.

—Let him go.

My voice became different. Deeper and deeper. I felt that my body was stronger. Faster. My intuition, my ability to process information, the surge of ideas. Everything in me had been amplified exponentially.

"At last you show yourself," said Saya, smiling with satisfaction. The grays paused, as if amazed and surprised by the encounter, by the contact with a guardian through me. As you understand, it is necessary to hold the sword of Damocles. Otherwise, I know you will disappear immediately. Understand that the reason for going to such primitive and grotesque trouble is to force your visit."

The grays snapped out of their surprise and, again, as if in a rehearsed act, turned their attention back to the human. One of them picked up a cylindrical instrument which he held in his disproportionate four-phalanxed hand.

"What do you want?"

Despite the power conferred by the alliance between me and the guardian, the outcome of a conflict was risky and unpredictable.

"We want the connection. Open the door to the other side. We want to get there, to penetrate, to transcend and return. All of it." An ambitious gleam glittered in her eyes. We have already reached the limits of this universe. For our civilization, moving forward is imperative.

At that very moment, one of the grays was driving the cylindrical instrument into the flesh of the terrified man's stomach. No contact, except for the tip glowing with an electric color. His flesh began to open in two, revealing the inside of his abdomen. A Dantesque mixture of entrails, of striking purplish, pale colors, peeked through the incision. The man seemed to collapse in excruciating pain. However, a robotic needle prevented it. In a flash, it quickly penetrated his shoulder, injecting some stimulating substance, prolonging the suffering and multiplying the aberrant anguish.

"Don't hurt him!" I demanded with a desperate cry.

"That's not up to me." Her calm and detached tone obviously reflected inhuman temperance. Take us to the other side and we'll bring him back without a scratch. Strong as an ox.

At that moment, the incision on his torso extended from his navel to his throat, and showed a vivid, crackling image of his organs. Eerie. His wild eyes, overcome with trembling terror, begged for a quick end, a dignified death.

I could not consent. Not in my presence. Not a second more.

I hurriedly approached the strange wall that separated me from my fellow man and began to hit it again and again. It was a very hard surface. The skin on my knuckles cracked from the impacts, spurting blood that mixed with the dirt on the back of my hand.

The gray alien, who wielded the cutting device, paused for a moment over the throat, switching off the blue glow of the instrument. The unknown man stared at me, as if he could somehow now see me hit that division of space. Time froze briefly.

Other dark lines concentrated on the same point above his heart, and suddenly a spasm ran through his body, arching his back in a painful contortion. The strange alien symbols and signs, which moved along the walls reminiscent of hospital monitors, immediately stopped drawing a fixed, motionless imprint. The guardian stepped out of me and slowly approached his protégé, as if not giving credence to all this nonsense. His chest was no longer inflated, exhaling an exhausted sigh, a last gasp.

Suddenly, a small ball of light sprouted softly from the dissected body of that stranger, rising a couple of meters. It waved up and down, rocked by a non-existent air. I turned to Saya.

My eyes burned with anger.

"I will eliminate you!"

My teeth gnashed together and my hands, bloodied, folded in on themselves so tightly that the fibers of my forearms looked like guitar strings. Saya stepped back a few paces and held out her right arm with an open palm, like a *stop* sign.

"We still have time to save him! We can bring him back! It's up to you to get him back!"

I put my hands to my head, pulling my tousled, unkempt hair to the nape of my neck. In the chambers of my heart I had never left room for hatred, but these beings, calculating and ruthless, made my mind turbulent with an invasive collapse of vengeful thoughts.

"Show us the other side!"

"Saya, you don't understand. The guardian is no longer with me. He's going with his protégé. You have failed."

Her lips contracted hiding their pink color. She was angry now. I was comforted to see the displeasure on his face.

"Not at all," she said haughtily.

Chapter 34
Irreversible

Somewhere on the map, 1996

The body of the half-naked man jerked again. It was as if he had received an electric shock from the surface. Again, another jolt made his limbs contract and suddenly the characters on the walls moved again in a repetitive cycle. Now his rib cage was expanding with each breath. His body was still wide open, like a cracked watermelon.

His guardian was there, next to him, but the small luminous sphere continued to float above him like a spun balloon. The stretcher folded slightly into a concave shape, pulling the man's shoulders and arms closer to his trunk. A contraption from the ceiling released a thick, milky fluid that thickened into a rubbery blanket.

The device returned to the retracted ceiling and the four gray beings removed the sticky blanket. The stretcher was horizontal again. Now the man's body was no longer incised. From my distance, not even the slightest hint of a cut could be seen. I had to remain silent for a few seconds, fascinated by the reversed process.

"Why doesn't he come to his senses? What is the protector doing? Where is he? I demand to speak to him!"

That barrage of words brought me out of my reverie. The guardian was still beside the man's body, and his soul, reduced to a shifting glow, was still wavering over the living body. I don't know why I answered. It was as if I had the need to tell her, to share that scene never seen before.

"He is next to the man. He has not left, but neither does her allow him to return to his body."

Saya stroked her chin thoughtfully, sorting out her thoughts. The guardian walked, languid and calm, crossed the hard transparent wall and stared at me.

"I'll take him. Thank you for helping me, but I can't bring him back."

I never ceased to be amazed by the husky, deep voice emanating from the guardians.

"No! Bring him back. He's been cured. Look at him!"

Saya's stunned expression quickly made me realize that, first, she was only listening to my side of the conversation and, second, that they had never gotten this far in an encounter.

"I can't do it. He has suffered too much. Even if he has been put back together physically, his mind will always be scarred by insurmountable terrors."

"You will find a way. Don't separate him from his life. I'm sure he has family, friends, projects, dreams. Don't take them away from him. Don't take him away!"

"I can bury this memory deep, but even so, this episode is indelible. He would never be the same. He would be tormented by inexplicable fears, frightening nightmares, night terrors, phobias. Little by little he would fall into madness and constant pain. There is only one way to erase it forever, and that is what I am going to do. I insist on thanking you for everything you have done for us, we are indebted to you."

"Ask him. Let me explain to him what's going on." Even I wasn't clear what I meant at the time. But what I did know was that this man was clinging to his life, that he was willing to fight for it.

"I'll tell him everything I know; he'll be able to cope. I'm sure!"

"Goodbye, my friend. I'll be back whenever you need me. Provide a burial for him. A place where his loved ones can visit his memory."

"No, please. No. No! No! No!"

The guardian ignored me, walked left the room. The grays stared at the walls, oblivious to his presence, invisible to them and intent on interpreting the changing information. The elongated shadow stopped at the foot of the bed. He placed his hands on the feet of his protégé's body and the color of his skin paled. His feet, bluish with cold, infected the rest of his body, which a few seconds later shivered with subtle cramps.

Saya reflected a palpable restlessness. A growing frustration was tormenting her and the grays. It seemed illogical. It was like having a good car in front of them, serviced and in perfect condition, with the engine running and ready for the trip, except for one small detail: there was no driver.

The elongated shadow of the guardian began to blur, taking with it the bright floating light and disappearing altogether after a few seconds. The body stopped breathing, and, despite all the greys' insistence, it was impossible to revive it. Electric shocks, more and more intense, ran through the man's body with no effect. Injections and all kinds of devices joined forces to return him to an irreversible state.

The guardian had disconnected the body from the source. So I understood.

They tried for a long time. So long that it was beginning to exceed the limit of human respect. Stunned, perplexed and discouraged, I remained engrossed with my infinite gaze lost in the scene, observing how the blue subtly climbed up those legs faster than I had imagined. The veins confirmed the old phrase of our elders, death comes for the feet, revolting me with the macabre coincidence.

Finally, they gave up their efforts, covering the body with a kind of white sheet whose relief was even more unbearable for me.

"We didn't mean for it to end like this. It's the first time it's happened to us. Everyone else endured the trance."

"You killed him!" I shouted at Saya, pointing my finger at her. "What did you expect?" I was so furious I didn't recognize myself. "You are absurd! Underdeveloped! Cruel! Filthy, savage, unjust!"

Saya endured my string of expletives with her head down, immersed in her own confusion, in her guilt.

"I have no choice but to do it. Experiment. It is our obligation."

"Shut up!"

My eyes were burning, and all my muscles were twitching.

"We must accumulate knowledge. Know more about the other side."

With her eyes straying to the floor, she seemed to justify herself.

"It's collateral damage," she said with a sigh.

"Collateral damage?"

All my trained self-control, my eternal patience, my calmness and intelligence. All that suddenly vanished. In its place, an explosive energy took over me.

"Murderers!"

An unbearable visceral heat made me take off my jacket and throw it on the floor with all my strength. They would not be human. Maybe they would be immortal, as I claimed, but, of course, in their eyes at that moment there was only fear. A fear that grew as much as an uncontrolled, nocturnal and forgotten terror.

She took a few steps back. A bright light, the size of a doorway, opened behind her, cut out by the swarming entrance of four burly men, uniformed in a black suit, matching tie and white shirt, dressed just like the day I escaped from them. I looked into the operating room where the man was, and the grays had gone. Maybe it was them, maybe it wasn't, I didn't care too much either. For a moment, I cursed the life I had to live, my uniqueness, the constant rot I had to deal with, and finally, like a cornered wild animal, I found no solution but to fight.

The four men overtook Saya and lined up in front of me. Their expressionless faces had their eyes covered by a mask like the one they gave me. It wasn't thirst for revenge that stirred me inside, it really wasn't that. I understood that they would hurt me, that I meant nothing to them, that behind that false diplomacy there was nothing, only pain and death.

I would not leave without a fight, and if I succeeded, I would not leave without fulfilling the guardian's order. The body of that man would be buried. It was a forced decision, made in the heat of the moment, unrealistic and with no other purpose than to rebel against tyranny. They would kill me right away or, worse, torture me mercilessly. I could already see myself suffering unimaginable pain at the hands of those grays, cut in two, mutilated and disemboweled. A drop of cold sweat ran down my back. I caught my breath, closed my eyes for an eternal instant and, without commanding my body to do anything, my arms intertwined, lifting my bent knee, hitting the ground hard as I planted my foot. I was on guard.

Unarmed yet ready. The internalization and incessant training of *muay thai* acted by inertia, like an innate reflex. Although I was outnumbered, the idea circulated in my head that at any moment some kind of projectile or strange technology would stop me without a fighting chance. But that was not the case.

One of them took the first step. His hands were open, one in front of the other. My heart was pounding, and the space that nature had allotted it in my chest felt too small.

I did not know how prepared they were, but at first glance, as he approached, he did not convey any known technique to me. It was more like he was trying to grab me and throw me to the ground, but, of course, I couldn't take anything for granted. I quickly grabbed the front hand pulling him toward me. His six foot two inches of flesh yielded to the thrust and a full force shiver impacted against his temple. At full speed, I regained my footing. His stocky body slouched with relaxed limbs and absent gaze. In an impulsive act, practiced thousands of times, I took impulse protecting my face with my forearms and plunged my knee on his chest with a sharp and swift blow, accompanied by a warrior shriek used to channel the energy and recover my breath.

The suit was projected a few meters backwards and fell on his back, like a badly demolished building. His body lay sprawled on the ground like a rag. He was breathing heavily, semi-conscious, the victim of a knockout. I raised my knee again and resumed the initial position. Saya looked perplexed, as if no one had ever stood up to them.

"Next!" I exclaimed, full of rage, with the present memory of his cruelty.

Two of them stepped forward at the same time. Saya leaned over the suit on the ground with some pity and concern in her eyes; something I had not seen for the guy on the operating bench. Not allowing them too close, I gave one a front kick to the knee that placed his leg in an impossible and unnatural posture. He tried to keep his balance with small hops of pain on his intact leg. His partner was no better off, taking the blow of my elbow and knee at the same time to his head and face.

The leg guy collapsed, writhing on the ground in pain. His companion, completely stunned by the elbow, wandered drunkenly backwards in pain, holding his nose, from which a copious flow of blood emanated. Only one suit and Saya remained. They looked at each other as if a mute language crackled between them.

Saya rose to her feet and stepped forward over her wounded companions with a confidence worthy of an Egyptian authority.

"Let me out of here! I've had enough," I demanded, pointing to the body of the deceased.

"You are wrong. This has only just begun."

Her posture expressed tranquility in front of me with her feet together and her hands clasped behind her waist.

"You will have to kill me. I will not help you in any way."

"You're right about one thing." A disturbing smile broke out on her lips. "We'll kill you, but we'll do it slowly. And you'll help us, whether you want to or not."

Saya made a quick movement with her hands. I was a little more than two meters away from her. She threw something at me. They looked like small marbles, translucent ball bearings. I tried to dodge them as best I could, but there were too many; I don't know how many hit me, but in doing so the little spheres became hard elastic cords that wrapped around me tightly. The more I struggled to free myself, the tighter they tightened. I couldn't move my legs, every inch I lost I was unable to regain. My arms ended up with my elbows stuck to my trunk.

The last man rushed at me. I tried, uselessly, to make use of my limbs. I was entirely wrapped up now. Still, when I got close enough, I jumped as best I could, smashing my head into his face. I hurt him, but not badly enough. In a few seconds, I found myself face down on the ground, stuffed with those strange spheres, immobile and at his mercy. I contracted as best I could, expecting to receive a collection of kicks and blows for my audacity, but nothing of the sort happened.

They left the room helping each other, leaving me there alone. I turned on my back, I was staining myself with the blood spilled on the floor. As I turned over, I had to close my eyes; my blindfold had moved, and the light was disturbing. However, a puff of laughter suddenly invaded me. I had hurt them. My emotions were traveling on a roller coaster and dozens of ideas wandered through my mind crumbling with each one the same fateful outcome.

My uncontrolled laughter merged with a painful wailing, drawing in the air a crazy continuous melody of laughter and crying.

I knew I was dead.

Discipline, discipline, I told myself over and over again. I tried to calm myself by controlling my breathing, although in my soul I could already feel the fierce scratch of the claws of pessimism. Dejected and strapped down, I was hyperventilating on the floor. I had realized that the more I forced my restraints, the tighter they tightened, compressing me with every urge to break free. I remembered everything that had been instilled in me especially my father's sage advice, "Calm in the face of the storm, never lose control."

I felt guilty, everyone would be worried about me and for a moment, a very brief one, I felt ashamed of myself. Lying there, covered in my own and other people's blood, tarnished by the dirt clinging to my skin, my clothes tattered and my hair disheveled. That image was far from that of a student enjoying an international scholarship. It was a moment of fragility. A natural weakness. With the fresh memory of my parents, I caught my breath, cleared my mind and the sadness drifted away embraced by loneliness.

"I am not alone. We are never alone," I said to myself.

Like a flash of lightning, I remembered the meeting in my old house, the longed-for old factory and that conversation with Daryl, my friend transformed into a red. That dialogue that

I preferred not to remember and that had sown more doubts than answers. However, I could escape from the strange leash that bound me using his teaching of parallel universes. It was a small possibility and, although I had not repeated it since then, I had to try.

My own smile made me reflect on destiny and free will. I dragged my face on the floor to replace the mask, opened my eyes wide with my gaze fixed on an undefined distance and tried to regain the light sensation of that state. First, I felt heavy, sinking into an imaginary well, falling down a free descent to nowhere, and then suddenly the sensation of floating freedom. I was outside. I called it an out-of-body escape, but in reality it already had a name: remote viewing.

I had escaped from the physical limitations of my body and now no barrier was an obstacle for me. By inertia, the first thing I did was to go to the next room, where the man's body waited in its eternal rest. Covered by the shroud, like an empty vessel, I silently apologized for what had happened, knowing that he was already far away from there, in a better place. I understood that the pain remained here, like an ember difficult to extinguish, and that his loved ones would pick up the baton of the immense pain.

I continued on my way into the unknown. The light no longer bothered me and my senses behaved differently. In a strange way, I could perceive the nearby presences, I felt and heard them marking me the direction with perfect clarity, like the call of a light for a moth. I can't pinpoint the distance, but it was very short. At one point, I entered another of the rooms where the suits and Saya were. I heard them talking and was a bit puzzled, because I thought they would use that strange high-pitched squawking language; however, that was not the case. I deduced that the human body was not capable of communicating in that way and they had no choice but to communicate like humans when in our form.

"The contact has been amazing. It has been a long time since we had a conversation with a protector."

"I hate these bodies. I have never known a being in the universe that feels damage and disease with such intensity," complained the first who had attacked me, from whose lips a strange concoction of saliva, blood and stomach reflux was spilling out.

It's not nice to think it, let alone say it, but I felt satisfied.

"We must transmit what happened in order to receive instructions. Maybe this time they want to do something different."

There was a certain discordance in Saya's words.

"We must not disturb the board with a regular check. The orders are clear and unanswerable. We shouldn't even be talking about this. Do you want us all to be suppressed?"

The suit stared at Saya, whose unchanged countenance remained steadfast in its conviction.

"There is nothing more to talk about, then. We'll continue with the procedure. I have a bad feeling about this specimen, though."

Immediately, Saya seemed to regret her words biting her lower lip.

"Sentiment? Don't make me laugh, you've been among them too long. You should stop watching their TV shows. Maybe the board should be made aware of your sudden identity crisis."

The other suits burst into derisive laughter, only interrupted in some cases by the painful awakening of the wounds inflicted.

Once they lay down, a series of lights circulated over their bodies like the needles of a matrix printer, making their bruises, scars and contusions disappear. Surprisingly, their costumes were also restored to their original neatness. They were millennia ahead of us technologically, that was indisputable.

As the suits concentrated on their restoration, Saya began a monologue for her companions, as if she were musing aloud.

"We know that killing a midwayer is contrary to advancement, the protectors have warned us. On the contrary, locating a link is extremely difficult, arduous and laborious, at least on this planet, and when we do it we have orders to subject them to physical, chemical and psychological tortures to contact their protector and gather information. We must experiment with them until they are reduced to nothing and, of course, without being seen, without attracting attention, without arousing suspicion. However, and for some time now, this group of organized humans has been offering us resistance, I know it is minimal, and sometimes even flattering, as in this case, but resistance nonetheless."

"We don't communicate that to the council, we only show the reports with positive results, eliminating those incidents that call into question our objective. But the truth is that they are getting harder and harder to capture and, most worrying of all," here he made an intentional silent pause, "they are getting stronger and stronger. You only have to look at yourselves, you look pitiful. The most disturbing thing is that with this specimen we have not even reached the energetic area. We will see what happens. That's what's bothering me. Sentiment? No. Intuition? Neither. Probability? Yes. Not much, but yes."

The less injured suit sat up refreshed, hands tense on the flat surface, looking around. He gave a disappointed sigh.

"They are filthy creatures. We have talked about it a thousand times. Their natural selfishness prevents them from collaborating as a unitary society. They are disloyal, arrogant, ignorant, envious, driven only by greed!"

"I know! But there is something different about the members of this resistance. They are not the same! Don't you see! Don't you see?"

"I suggest you limit yourself to following orders. I won't say it anymore. You should be watching the guest."

By now the suits all stood, freshly uniformed. Their appearance was reminiscent of the presidential escort of the secret service.

Saya and the suits were heading back to the room where they had left me. My body pulled at me like a powerful magnet clearly pointing the way back. It was like dropping me on the bed. I gravitated with such force that when I regained my body I gasped for air, frightened by the vertigo. My eyes felt dizzy. My eyelids were regaining their lubrication after the time without blinking.

After a short while, they came into the room looking for me. They grabbed me like a sack of potatoes. The more I resisted, the tighter those damn straps tightened; I felt like they were cutting off my circulation. I knew my fate, an insurmountable and grotesque torture to force the presence of my guardian.

I was placed on one of the adjoining stretchers. Fear was growing like a snowball falling down the hill. To my right, the body covered with the sheet foretold my future. I tried to free myself, but it was impossible.

Saya contemplated the scene, letting her companions do all the work. Our eyes met a couple of times. She could have spared herself all that explanatory theater in the kitchen, I thought, but in her eyes I could see a small doubt of sadness, some sincere compassion, something pure that was lacking in her fellows. "Her cruelty has been confirmed, sometimes we see what we would like to see," I reminded myself.

I struggled again to escape from the straps, clenching and wriggling with choked cries and bellows of helplessness.

When I opened my eyes, my first impression was that they had lowered the intensity of that annoying light, but that was not it. Instantly, I stopped struggling. I was shocked by the image in front of me, a shocking image that evoked that recurring *déjà vu,* the one I had not quite rescued from the back room of my memories.

Surrounding the stretcher stood, erect, dozens of guardian shadows. They were so many that they prevented the passage of light, their silhouettes left me overwhelmed, immobile with hope.

"I think his guardian is already here, he has arrived before his time," said Saya, letting the sentence sail in that troubled sea, now flooded by a mysterious silence.

"It would be the first time. I don't think so, not before time," disagreed the suit.

I concluded that he was referring to before he started to slit me open. I admit that I relaxed when I saw them. There were so many shadows. The number was uncountable. I recognized guardians from both lives: Natalia's, the freezer boy's, Gallego's, the girls kidnapped for their organs, all the guardians of the train victims and many more.

All the shadows of the people I had helped had come to my aid. An inexplicable sense of peace enveloped me. Saya, though more awake than the others, was mistaken in thinking that only my guardian had arrived.

She was completely wrong.

Chapter 35
Betrayal and Pain

Somewhere in the world, 1996

A choking sensation came over me. That vision, surrounded by elongated shadows, so expectant, awakened a sleeping monster that emerged madly from the deepest part of my memories, like an elephant stampeding through a junkyard. I said that image was familiar to me. It was the same one that surprised me before I died.

My heart froze as I relived it. My lips exhaled an involuntary mouthful into the air as I rescued those moments.

I was beginning to understand.

Brooklyn, New York, August 1979

That last Friday, at the end of the month, was completely ours. As if fate had given us the opportunity to say goodbye with a few wonderful hours of absolute happiness. It was a magical evening. The theater highlighted Angie's beauty. The actors and the stage brought out that childlike and curious sparkle in her eyes. Expectant and absorbed in the plot, she seemed to fly into that virtual world like a dazzled observer. I enjoyed watching her enjoy herself.

The sweltering summer heat hit us on our way out and we decided to dine at The Corner Stop restaurant; no reservations were required and it boasted an enviable terrace. At night, it had one of the best views of the dark and enigmatic Hudson River. On the way home, in the cab, we gazed at each other, impatient to arrive and unleash the hurricane of desire that was in us both. Her skin glistened covered with a thin layer of moisture that multiplied the scent of a thousand flowers in her perfume. I could already see myself sliding down every section of her body, gaining centimeters of ground, winning the battle of caresses and kisses. I imagined myself merging our essences in an agitated rhythm of breath and passionate sweat.

Just unfulfilled dreams, dreams that would have to wait. My countenance changed suddenly. Daryl was waiting at the door of our old factory. He paced from side to side with a disturbing impatience, a nervousness that made me fear the worst. The warmth of plans was turning into an unpleasant, uncomfortable embarrassment.

"What's going on, Daryl?"

The voice in my dry throat cracked. He leaned close to my ear, visibly nervous, and whispered words that chilled my blood.

"The foreigners have discovered you. They know about you. We have to leave here immediately."

My confidence in Daryl was unquestionable.

"How do they know?"

Angie didn't understand the problem, nor did she know what we were talking about. She was my haven of peace. My happiness. I just wanted to protect her, to keep her from getting involved in that crazy world. I wanted her to live in peace and not be under constant threat.

"They know, period! They could arrive at any time! There's no time to lose!"

"Dustin, what's wrong?"

Angie put her index finger to her mouth, biting her fingertip. Whenever she was nervous she did that. It was her escape valve for handling stress.

"Don't worry, love. It's just work stuff, but we have to leave right away. I'll explain it to you."

Everything that had happened to me since the train accident had become a confusing gibberish that was very difficult to explain to regular people. My attention focused on Daryl, I grabbed him by the arm and pulled him a few feet away, out of Angie's reach.

"Do any of the nine know?"

The nine. That is the number of people who make up the leadership of our secret society. They represent the highest authority of the organization. They are its government, and they must always be aware of pressing issues, especially those related to the "foreigners", pseudonym for our four-fingered friends.

"Of course! Where do you think the orders come from?"

"Go get in the car. I have to go in the house to get some things. If you see anything strange, leave immediately."

"You don't need anything from home. Money, passport and everything else will be provided for you. But she must not come. You will put her at risk."

That statement surprised me but coming from Daryl I didn't think anything of it. Blinded with confidence, I let my guard down.

"You're kidding, right? I'm not leaving Angie here. Come on, it takes longer to argue than it does to get things done. Start the car and if you see anything strange, honk the horn. I won't be long."

I opened the factory door, just enough to get in. I ran up the stairs, into the bedroom, straight to the closet. There was the shoe. I pulled out the last, and behind it I found what I was looking for, a small box with trim. I put it in my pocket and ran downstairs as fast as I could. I slammed the door shut and hurried to the car.

The purring of the engine began to accelerate intermittently, as if it wanted to show off its power. Immediately, I thought that Dodge Monaco wasn't the best tool for escaping from anyone. Daryl was squeezing its power at full throttle and Angie was clinging with both hands to the roof handle, struggling not to fly from side to side in the rear seats.

"Daryl, slow down."

He remained focused on the road, braking just enough at every *stop sign* and traffic light, without fully stopping. The Monaco wiggled like a flan and the wheels squeaked on the asphalt like bad chalk.

"Daryl! Daryl," I had to yell at him. Finally he lifted his foot, "Keep calm! If you drive like that, you'll draw attention to us, and that's the wrong thing to do."

I lowered my visor and scanned behind us. Nothing suspicious. I looked up in search of anything strange above us, and nothing either. I felt Angie's expressive, skeptical gaze boring into my neck.

"Is anyone going to tell me what's going on?"

I turned around to reassure her. I had never seen her so angry. She had had to take off her heels to brace herself against the floor of the car and was now straining to find them in the dark demanding answers. Daryl answered by throwing out an explanation, which, in hindsight, I now found loaded with meaning.

"It's business. Some investors will go to any lengths to get Dustin's firm. The architectural firm is dealing with some bad clients, and their boss asked me to warn you and get you to safety. They couldn't find you and there was no way to locate you. They're going to meet us on the outskirts, in an industrial building they own, and we'll see what happens there. The important thing is to stay away from familiar places and think of it as just that, business."

"I don't understand anything you're saying. Why haven't you called the police?"

I admit that I let Daryl hand out false explanations and I was more concerned with making sure that no one was following us. There was a calmness in the air that was too unsettling. All is well, I said to myself.

"You see, Angie, the police suggest you file a complaint for threats. But, of course, they haven't really said anything serious, nor can we provide any proof. In the end, it all comes to nothing, and don't think they're going to put you under some kind of police surveillance to protect you, as if they have nothing better to do. The only sensible option left to us is to avoid confrontation and see how the mess sorts itself out. I assume the board of directors will have some strategy thought out in these cases."

He winked at me, but I was paying him just the bare minimum of attention as, dazed, I searched for anything suspicious on the ground or in the air. Everything seemed normal and I began to relax a little, letting Daryl lead us. Kilometer by kilometer we were taking shelter from a terrifying and unknown danger; however, it turned out to be quite the opposite.

If I had paid attention to the details, maybe and just maybe, I would have been able to get a glimpse of what was coming. Daryl was very nervous, too nervous. On the road, theoretically out of danger now, he was still breathing heavily and over-explaining, not to mention that he was incessantly drying his hands on his pants.

We entered a dark and winding industrial site. The perimeter fence showed clear signs of abandonment and the old metal signs exhibited a tarnished patina of rust. The buildings fought stoically against time, confirming that everything from the past was tougher and more resistant. The branches of the trees, illuminated by the moving headlights, traced on the walls a tremendous specter.

Angie's hands rested on my shoulders in search of a physical and comforting connection, while Daryl took more turns than a madman's signature. Finally, he stopped the vehicle more than a hundred yards from a grizzled gate. A giant sign, peeling from the weather, read Simon & Sons Storage. Its yellow letters stood out against the green background. We all fell silent for those long seconds. Behind, a haze of red smoke, visible through the taillights, mingled in the night with an eerie silence, as Daryl struggled with the decisive step of his betrayal.

A stifled sigh made him re-engage the gear and rush into a considered decision.

"Is this it, Daryl?" His forehead was glistening with sweat and transparent beads of sweat were trickling down the collar of his shirt. "Is everything all right?"

"It's going according to plan, although I'm finding it more difficult than I had imagined. I guess it's the education we've received."

"Dude, what are you saying? Sometimes you're weirder than a cat's butt!"

He nodded, forcing a nervous, sad smile.

There were only a few dozen meters left to reach the gate and several guardians suddenly stood in the way.

"Get back! Danger!" I heard a guardian with his piercing, deep, guttural voice. His slender stature spanned the entire dimension of that huge gate.

"Stop the car, Daryl! Stop the car! Turn around!"

He didn't obey one bit; on the contrary, he stepped on the accelerator even more as that giant metallic door opened to swallow us. Straight into the mouth of the monster, into the mouth of the unknown.

A dust floated from the ground in unison with the high-pitched screeching of brakes. The interior of the empty warehouse was illuminated by the amber headlights of the idling car. It struggled through the layer of suspended dust, trying to focus on the charged air. Several men, smartly uniformed in black suits, ties and matching hats emerged through the haze with their hands in their pockets. They looked relaxed and cool.

Their posture reminded me at that moment of the Sicilian mafia in the movies. They were accompanied by an attractive blonde woman, too well dressed for the setting. A sharp knock echoed repeatedly through the echo. They had closed the grayish gate again, securing it with its pins and adding a chain whose links were perfectly distinguishable, bumping into each other and ending up linked by a padlock.

The discreet, humble click of the lock diverted Daryl's gaze on me with a message colder and guiltier than any verbal explanation he could have given me. Just then, I understood what was going on. My best friend had handed me over on a silver platter, and although he tried to prevent Angie's involvement, he hadn't tried very hard. Countless thoughts came over me at once. I couldn't believe it. Not coming from him. I guess that's why it worked.

Several reddish beings were swarming around a thin, pale, middle-aged woman in a tight black dress that was as black as her hair and as dark as her eyes. Her slow walk impregnated the environment with a cadaverous atmosphere.

My unheeded warnings to Daryl and the bad vibes that woman was giving off were enough to convince Angie that something wasn't right. Of course, no one else was seeing what I was seeing: guardians and reddish creatures mingling in space without noticing each other.

"Why, Daryl, why are you doing this to me? A lump in my throat prevented me from swallowing non-existent saliva."

"You don't understand. Nor do the nine. Nor do any of us." he said, referring to our secret society. "They want an exchange of knowledge. They are not what we have been told. They dress weird, but that's all. They're not bad, man. They just want to ask you some questions, something you know. In return, all of humanity will benefit from unprecedented progress."

An accusing finger shot out of my hand, pointing at him with compunction.

"You don't listen, Daryl. You don't trust your own. Despite your immense scientific intelligence, you are ignorant. You have fallen into selfishness, thirsty for knowledge. You are one of those who need to burn to prove that fire does indeed burn. How could you do this to us? Now the three of us are in danger."

"You and your mystical gifts that you never talk about. Can you see the future? Contact the dead? What?" Now Daryl was venting his frustration, reproachfully and without restraint. "Of course you can't. You're nothing but a silent charlatan. With your secretive hermeticism you want to feed a hollow legend. Even the outsiders have believed that you have something special, but I don't care about that, because they will comply anyway, and I will spearhead scientific progress that will really help mankind. Don't you see, Dustin?"

I held my hands to my face, defeated by his full-throated defense of a misconception. It was even more exasperating because he had never argued with me about it, right up until that moment. Suddenly I felt a new alarming presence. Behind Daryl, a guardian never seen before emerged; it was his.

The blonde woman watched my reactions. I watched her as she scanned the surroundings, looking for the threat that loomed over her. It didn't take me long to spot it. The older woman was pointing a small revolver at Daryl. It was hidden in plain sight, but in the middle of the night darkness. She wielded that gun with disconcerting firmness. It was not her first time. Her pronounced cheekbones and the black shading of her eyes gave the false but eerie illusion of empty sockets. It was as if Death had grown bored with the scythe and, for today, wanted to try something new.

"It's too late!" The piercing, hoarse voice of my guardian boomed in my head. "You will die if you do anything!"

"Daryl, look out!" I shouted to alert him. Everything was going slowly. Very slowly. He's my best friend. I couldn't let him die.

As quickly as I could, I stepped over Daryl just as my ears rang from the detonation of the revolver. The flash illuminated my friend's face for a few brief moments. Hundreds of reflections circulated through his pupils at once, all stemming from disbelief, regret and terror.

I succeeded. I managed to get in the way. In front of us, dozens of guardians were lined up, making a strange movement with their hands. They were trying to deflect the trajectory of that projectile. An incandescent, spinning projectile. Deadly.

Time was not passing; it was almost at a standstill. It had put the guardians in a serious predicament. The deep sound of their voices bounced as they all shouted the first vowel of the alphabet. Of course, it was a bellow that only I could hear. The bullet was aimed precisely at the left side of Daryl's chest, but now I was inserted like a shield between the two. I had my gaze riveted on the skinny woman's empty sockets. Of death. At first, I only felt a small bite on my arm, below my shoulder. I didn't even think anything of it.

"Before you hurt him, you'll have to kill me first! Did you hear me?"

I clenched my fists with all my might, enraged by the injustice.

"Now there is no doubt. He is a link," affirmed the older woman, who turned to the blonde younger woman who was watching the scene unfold.

Something viscous and warm oozed between my clenched fingers. A thick fluid dripped from my left hand. The fabric of my shirt began to stick to my skin.

"I'm sorry, Dustin. I'm sorry!"

Daryl's words sounded strung between sobs.

"I screwed up, buddy. I screwed up good," he kept repeating more to himself than to anyone else.

"Now don't worry about it. We'll get through this."

I turned to look for his eyes, which were lost on the floor in a crestfallen pose. I lifted his chin so that he would stare at me.

"Do as I say. This is no time to be hard on yourself."

I looked over at Angie; I wished she hadn't been there, I thought. Motionless and frightened, she didn't understand who these people were, what they wanted, or why they were determined to kill. I seemed to be rocking in a bad dream of strange and incoherent information. Lies and truths.

Action had to be taken, and fast.

My guardian guessed my intentions. I hurriedly ran towards the woman holding the small revolver pointed at us. The shadow entered her body, paralyzing her completely, assuming the risk it entailed for him. It was easy to snatch it from here, she was not even able to blink. I gave her such a push that her thin body fell violently to the ground, blending in with the prevailing darkness.

I felt a sharp burning in my arm. The pain demanded my attention. I gritted my teeth to avoid a choked howl and nervously waved my revolver at all those people.

"Angie, come! Honey, come on! Get behind me. We're getting out of here."

She was in shock. Her body was responding to me, but I could see from her eyes that her mind had retreated for its own protection.

"What is this?" She looked at her hand in mine, searching the air for the light from the car's headlights. "My God! Dustin, you're bleeding!" Hier words sounded like a feline howl.

"It's just a scratch. Come on, get in the car," I said in a calm whisper.

Daryl hurried to get in the car and turn on the ignition. I kept pointing the gun at those strange people who, unmoving, watched us intently, with their indecipherable gazes. The car started the first time.

"Jump in," I told Angie, protected behind my back.

There was no time. Daryl, in a panic, and I would like to think that, driven by a primal instinct for survival, accelerated to the maximum with the steering wheel crossed, turning the car on itself and facing the grayish gate at high speed.

Angie and I could not believe our eyes. Without a second glance, he was gone, leaving us in the lurch, alone in the face of danger. Instantly, an orange sphere, the size of a soccer ball, descended through the roof of the warehouse, cutting through the metal like butter and hurling pieces of roofing and glass across the floor, all accompanied by a trail of dust. It drew a withering elliptical trajectory until it hit Monaco. It entered through the trunk of the sedan like the cannon fire of a pirate ship. The car continued its march without the roar of the engine, totally mute, only moved by inertia, accompanied by a whistle and tinkling headlights, like a ghost ship cradled by the swell of a closed night.

It slammed at low speed into the gate without managing to knock it down and the ball of light disappeared.

A lump in my throat prevented me from breathing normally. The situation was serious. I searched desperately for the presence of Daryl's guardian. I found him among his peers, and for a few brief seconds I was reassured to think that all was well, that he had not been harmed. I was dead wrong.

A huge number of reddish beings ran euphorically towards the car claiming a long-awaited belonging, a prize, an equal. Blurred and in the shadows, they looked like lions fighting for prey, until, with lively violence, a new reddish creature emerged from the driver's side writhing in visible pain. Incredulous, I returned my gaze to its guardian. A few moments of silence preceded his words.

"He cannot be brought into the light. His destiny is marked."

Accustomed to the depth of sound in those voices, I could make out the tinge of enormous regret in his terse explanation.

"I'm no longer here for him, but for you. Run away!"

"Which way? We're trapped!" I shouted.

"We will light your way, but you will have to leave everything behind."

At that precise moment, I was unaware of the scope of that last sentence.

The gate was still writhing with metal shrieks in its own struggle to regain a lost form. One of the hubcaps rolled freely in concentric spiral circles. Without releasing my grip on the revolver and ignoring the excruciating pain of the shot, I grabbed Angie's hand. I could no longer do anything for Daryl, who at that moment seemed to be writhing in some sort of horrific rebirth. Fleetingly, I wondered how many evils he must have committed to suffer such a tragic and undesirable outcome.

The rush of events had me bewildered, there was no time to sort out my ideas, but a crystalline premise flooded my thoughts: save Angie at all costs, no matter what.

The guardians positioned themselves at a distance of approximately ten meters from each other, with their hands open in front of them and slightly bent downward. The prevailing darkness disappeared for me. They illuminated an exit that was lost in the distance. Blindly, I began to run, pulling on Angie's arm, who was resisting moving forward in the thick blackness.

"Run, honey, run. Don't be afraid."

The sound of pounding feet began to flutter in the air. They were stalking us. I took a quick glance back and could see those men in black chasing us and at least one was carrying something strange in his hand. Angie was running barefoot through all kinds of debris scattered on the ground. Her strength prevented her from complaining. We ran past old metal shelves, abandoned pallets, iron columns, broken pipes and a myriad of obstacles that stood in our way.

"But, Dustin, how can you see anything?"

The lack of training sapped my endurance, and fear made me hold my breath during the endless meters of the escape. The truth is that I had no breath left. I stopped for a second to catch my breath. I remember that her skin glowed beautifully in the light of the guardians; however, a grimace of pain was reflected on her face. She lifted her right foot to avoid contact with the ground, keeping her balance by leaning on my shoulder.

"Dustin, something's wrong with my foot. I think I cut myself. I'm scared."

A thick piece of meat hung waving from the sole of her foot, reminding me of a badly cut steak. I shuddered with a stinging cramp that made my hair stand on end. I cursed under my breath. The footsteps of the suits clattered on the hard floor with a multiplying sound. But, in spite of everything, I could discern that they were separating out to look for us. My guardian walked a few paces into the luminous circle of another; I suppose one of those I helped in the train rescue, I couldn't quite remember, nor was there time for it.

The elongated, tall, long-armed shadow was transformed by that light into a being of a hundred bright and changing colors. It had a serene countenance and gray eyes full of wisdom, mystery and the past. He gave off an aura of peace; I would have liked Angie to have seen him. Behind him, more than a hundred meters away, another orange ball took advantage of the previous hole to penetrate the warehouse with a cunning, stalking slowness.

My guardian observed me looking at that spherical threat with panic in my eyes. Without looking at it, he made a gesture with his hand in its direction, and the rest of the guardians also pointed theirs towards that strange floating ball. An explosive and luminous flash burst from it in all directions, and it fell to the ground making more noise than expected. The ground shook beneath us, and I couldn't help but wonder how much that little thing weighed.

"The light is ours," my guardian asserted with disdainful suspicion.

A few seconds of thick silence reminded me that we were still fatigued from the race.

"She must be left behind. We can't protect her. It's the rules. I have seen several outcomes. Despite this, the decision is yours and must be made."

My head vibrated dull, skeptical. I couldn't comprehend what he was telling me.

"No! She's coming with me! You have to help her!" I whispered under my breath, full of disbelief and false arrogance.

"Who are you talking to?" asked Angie.

Then it dawned on me that I had used audible communication, driven by fear, nerves and habit.

"We have to keep going. Lean on me and don't dig in your heel. We'll get through this."

She pouted and clutched at my shoulder, limping hurriedly. Mixed feelings pecked at my heart. I was proud of her, of her perseverance, her intelligence, her self-control, her mastery, her courage; but I was also burdened with guilt and worry. I had gotten her into this mess, and I had not even been honest. I never shared my secret. The rules again. The damn rules.

We ran roughly between the path of guardians. Mine got in the way,

"You will not leave here with her."

I ignored him and took her in my arms carrying her delicate body, still stumbling and running in pursuit of a way out. My eyes began to bulge through my eyelids and the summer heat was pooling in the stale atmosphere. You could chew on the suspended air, trapped there for years. My guardian insisted and stepped in again a few feet away. I refused to accept his ruling, and stubbornly, immersed in childish behavior, I ignored his presence, his warnings. Suddenly, he placed his hand on my head and at once I could see, in a strange and fleeting way, different final versions of our escape. Only one of them showed me the way out, but it wasn't me. I mean, I wasn't there. It's hard to explain. It was just a vision of a path I would never walk, because I would never leave Angie.

I paused to think for a few moments. Angie was grateful for the break like an elixir of relief, though she felt the urgency in her breathing. I was terrified, she bore the anguish and pain with an unrelenting steadfastness, worthy of admiration. Then another of those phrases, more true than false, came to my mind. It belonged to my paternal grandfather, a forced farmer, who opportunely emphasized: "Each person has his hour. And when the time comes, it is neither early nor late".

Chapter 36
Alliance

Weighing the wise words retracted in the *flashback,* with a certain calmness, I decided to be grateful for the advantage given and I got off the stubbornness cart. I looked all around, in search of the door that the guardian had shown me and upon locating it I walked slowly with the intention of propitiating a calmer atmosphere.

"Let's go this way, honey. We'll hide. They won't be able to find us if we're quiet."

I worked hard to ignore my fear and tried to focus on my last moments with Angie but of course, it was almost impossible.

As we walked the length of that long corridor, lined with empty and abandoned offices, I could see how two guardians were solemnly guarding the inner path. Their presence would conceal the door, blurring it with the walls of the long corridor making it undetectable to our pursuers and maybe even a refuge of intimacy for us.

"I don't know how you can see anything, Dustin, I can't explain it."

I kept quiet but at the same time I swore to myself that I would never hide anything from her again if we got out of here. I knew this was also not the time to offer up explanations though. The guardians towered high above us and despite the rust and abandoned feeling the place gave off good vibes, as if the jokes, laughter and joy of the workers were also part of the indissoluble greenish patina that sweetened the atmosphere.

A doorless doorway at the end of the room led to showers, whose intermittent dripping seemed to mark the rhythm of time. Another small room, smaller, offered a bunk bed. A yellowish wool mattress rested on a slatted bed base; the mattress was illustrated with arabesque lines that traced the unmistakable lines of dried sweat on its fabric.

The pain in my shoulder was becoming unbearable, intense and sharp, and I felt weaker and weaker. My strength was leaving me with every drop of blood accumulating on the elbow of my shirt. That bed, rusty, filthy and yellowish, felt like a gift from heaven. With extra care, I laid Angie down on the mattress and sat at the foot of the bed.

She seemed drowsy and I was caught up in my own thoughts. Self-absorbed and meditative, and as if it wasn't enough with the incessant pain, something else was digging into my thigh. I reached into my pants pocket and pulled out a small box. Dumbfounded, it took me a few seconds to recognize it, so absorbed was I in my worries. Nothing is casual. Nothing.

A faint dim light was coming through a fan mounted on the wall, highlighting the moving blades that still rotated, moved by the subtle current of air that traveled in the night. Angie was swallowing with visible difficulty and she shaking from the effort of suppressing the pain in her foot; however, no complaint came from her lips.

"What have you done to make these people so angry with you?" Her voice sounded like a settled snore.

"Nothing, honey. I don't know them at all. I've never hurt anyone. You believe me, don't you?"

She reached up slightly to caress my face with the back of her hand.

"Of course I believe you. There is no better person than you."

In an automatic movement, my hands rotated the small box I held.

"Dustin! Dustin!" a male voice chanted my name mockingly.

It made me jump to my feet and the little box fell to the floor. The voice sounded close, very close. My guardian made me stay calm. I never thought his tone, so low and deep, could placate me.

"Don't worry. They'll never find you."

Upright and without saying a word, I turned to the shadow; to the tireless and loyal guardian companion who always took care of me.

"Do whatever it takes, but please get us out of here. She must live, it can't end this way."

Its elongated silhouette loomed blacker and more silhouetted in the darkness.

"It's not up to me. You could get out of this, if you wanted to, because you have won the favor of many protectors, but she does not. She has only yours, and you will not allow her to suffer what awaits her at the hands of these creatures."

"But can anything be done? It's not fair! I'll fight them! With your help I'll get rid of them!"

"You're not ready, Dustin, it won't work. You have to know how to pick your battles."

Again, my name sounded like a whistle rocking in a ringing melody, a menacing tic; the man in the hat was calling me.

"Dustin, my friend, Dustin!" I didn't get distracted. "You're protecting her, that's the biggest sacrifice. And every sacrifice has its reward, but also a consequence, don't forget that. You've made your decision, accept it and make the most of your time."

With bated breath, and in absolute silence, the incessant pain in my shoulder completely passed and gave way to a more unbearable and powerful one. My heart shrank in on itself and I began to sob quietly. I remained motionless and reflective for a few eternal seconds.

"I think you dropped something on the floor." Angie's voice seemed changed; she had regained some lost vitality.

As I turned around, I could see her guardian resting his hands on his head, acting like a magic elixir. I bent down to pick up the little box and told myself that I had to take strength from wherever I could. I wiped away my tears and cursed under my breath. We had thousands of things left to do and those wretches were taking everything away from us.

"Well, my darling, my move," Not without effort, I tried to strike an amused tone. "I had hoped for Paris, but now that I think about it, this cool little bed is pretty romantic, don't you think?"

Laughter escaped her as she covered her mouth with her hand like a naughty child afraid of being detected. I sat next to her in search of those wisps of light that sparkled to the rhythm of the fan.

"Come out of hiding!"

The man's voice sounded far away, in another part of the warehouse but we heard footsteps that seemed close by. The heel tapping sounded higher and slower. Undoubtedly, women's shoes.

"You'll come out sooner or later, like rats do! We're going to burn everything!" called the male voice in the distance.

The nearby footsteps interrupted me, and I left the box on the mattress, next to my beloved. I walked back down the hallway and stood in front of the door, which was still open. In it, the two shadows stood guard with impeccable posture. Peeking out of the side, I could see that elegant woman walking down the narrow corridor, entering the offices and pulling up the blinds. She returned to the corridor and looked back at the guards.

With the blinds up, framed photographs of the business in full swing could be seen, some of them twisted as we passed by. On the floor, a trail of fresh blood revealed our recent journey, like the famous breadcrumbs. It was all under control, the guardians had camouflaged the trail by blurring it with the dominance of the light. She, not seeming entirely satisfied, came a few more steps closer.

Now she was barely a meter away. My heart was pounding violently, feeling the strong current of the pulsations in my shoulder. The beautiful woman with the blonde hair, was inspecting the corridor unconvinced.

I looked around and I found what I was looking for. Hanging inside a rusty metal box that might once have been red, an axe awaited its premiere. I grabbed it with both hands. The woman's clear eyes scanned the hallway with a glint of suspicion. My breathing was quickening, and all my strength was clenched in that wooden handle.

"Don't do it, Dustin. Don't do it. Trust me," my guardian implored without leaving my side.

I was afraid, very afraid. Terror puts us in tunnel mode and prevents us from seeing reality with perspective. The truth is that I was untrained. I was unable to control my emotions. It was the first time I was faced with a fighting situation. My legs were shaking and I was weak, but in my imagination, and with my hands pressed against the axe, I saw myself emerging glorious from the false wall. Spectral and surprising as a ghost, I would strike accurate blows.

But it would not happen like that, at the moment of truth, and betrayed by my own moral and ethical values, I would only go out to scare her, praying that she would spread the fear to the others and leave us alone.

I listened to my shadow's words and glimpsed a more realistic expectation of myself. I was incapable of harming anyone. I reflected for a moment and decided to be a victim rather than an executioner, since really, I was incapable of being the latter. I swung the axe in the air with a clumsy movement and laid the thick, sharp metal on the ground. Unclipped from the weapon, I felt relieved, while secretly watching the woman. The voice of the singing man was also approaching the corridor and at last entered my field of vision.

He carried a red carafe in his hands. As they met in the hallway, they whispered to each other. She wasn't pleased, although it didn't sound like the man in the hat was in charge. I concentrated on listening to them, but the shattering torrent of my guardian's voice prevented me.

"Take a good look at them. Look at them carefully, something is missing. Take a good look at them."

With his words, the guardian launched a riddle. They had eyes, feet, mouths, hands. I did not understand what he meant.

"I don't get it. I'm sorry, but I don't follow."

Meanwhile, the man in the hat began to spill the fluid on the floor and into the offices.

"They have no aura. Look at them again. There is nothing in them, they are empty. The aura of people can be seen when you look through their bodies. It is more or less iridescent, depending on their goodness, but it must always exist. It is the imprint of the soul."

I returned to Angie. She was breathing calmly, and her face seemed to be wearing a slight smile of satisfaction, a little mischievous. I looked through her as the guardian told me, and indeed, a kind of colored optical illusion covered her outline like a small aurora borealis, caressing her body.

"Last chance! You'll get out by hook or by crook!"

The footsteps were moving away now.

"What are you laughing at, you rascal?" She opened one of her eyes shamelessly, falsely pretending to be asleep. That was the kind of nonsense that made me fall in love with her. I know you're awake, you little liar.

And I started tickling her sides. She began to laugh, and I asked her for silence, without stopping the tickling.

"Sssshhhhhh! We're going to get caught because of you."

She was wiggling around covering her mouth to keep from making noise and her eyes were sparkling with life. I enjoyed seeing her this way. She uncovered her lips with suggestive slowness. Drawn by a sensual energy, I approached her slowly without looking away. Her eyes were the showcase of a vibrant essence. We melted in a long kiss, full of affection, tenderness and love. Locked in our brief parenthesis, our eyelashes caressed each other as if in a rehearsed choreography.

I sighed and brought us back to reality. Her eyelids slowly unfolded like the first flight of a butterfly and, again, her crystalline eyes mitigated the pressing pain. She was everything to me.

"I have hidden it inside a locker."

She pointed to the nearest lockers, without specifying which one. Absorbed in a thousand things, I wondered for a moment, not knowing what she was referring to. She noticed and clarified,

"We'll do it right. Don't worry, it's well hidden. When we get out of here, we'll go to Paris, and you can ask me properly."

And she hit me on the wounded shoulder. I gritted my teeth drawing a creepy smile, like that of a macabre clown, vaguely trying to conceal an unbearable pain. She noticed the sticky wetness of my blood and sat up quickly. She covered my face with kisses, repeating:

"Sorry, sorry, sorry."

I laughed, aware that pain was the least of my problems. The voices of our enemies took center stage in our little nest of solitude, although I tried not to let Angie pay any attention to them.

"We can do it another way. It's risky." The blonde woman in the hallway opted, loudly, to change the course of things.

"We have already made the decision together. Don't worry, Saya. They will come out. You'll see how they'll come out." Their voices were getting farther and farther away, and she seemed to be still arguing with her colleagues, but their voices were already distorted in the distance.

The air in the room began to move as if sucked in by a giant. It escaped through the door at great speed leaving a vacuum absent of oxygen. A subtle rumbling sound echoed through the floor at high speed, increasing the revolutions of the resurrected fan. It sounded like a thriving beast with a voracious appetite. Fire. It stopped at the entrance without breaking the vigilance of the guards. The open windows of the adjoining offices fed it, orange tongues growing and growing, licking the walls up to the ceiling.

"Come out and you can live! You still have time!" called the male voice.

I promised myself that I would have justice, sooner or later. And I regretted not having been more prepared. I would have liked to inform our society, all of our people; we were making serious mistakes and we had to correct them.

I was aware that our end was near, but I did not want to go through my journey with a backpack full of anger, resentment and hatred. A brief prayer made me beg for another chance, one to become a better person, more trained and skilled, more sensitive, more committed; in short, stronger. I longed to be the hammer of change, but my time was running out. Life was fading away.

"I think I'm ready for what's coming."

Her guardian did not leave her side. His passive, calm presence conveyed to Angie an immense sense of peace, a familiar sensation that she had already experienced during her harrowing rescue from the train wreckage. She knew all too well the caresses of death but this time there was nothing I could do.

I looked at her guardian, caught his energy, his imprint, and thanked him for his presence with a slight bow. It was a secret message between him and me. Partners in the same cause.

"Let me lie down next to you. I want to hold you. Feel your skin. Taste your lips. Look into your eyes. Hold hands." She looked at me with an indecipherable halo, an intimidating intensity charged with feminine emotions. The kind of enigmatic strength that cowers the bravest man.

"I want to be with you, love."

Thick smoke began to drift across the corridor. The blackish cloud grew thicker and thicker. Lying next to her, on the dirty old mattress, I stroked her silky hair, taking in her fragrance. I concentrated on her scent placing her face on my chest, trying to stay strong, hiding my tears.

"Get out of here. Find a way out and call for help," Angie's voice sounded weak.

"Listen to me. I will not leave you alone. Never. I love you. I will love you always."

I pressed her tightly against my chest unable to stop an uncontrollable hiccup of weeping from taking over my whole body. The heat of the approaching fire glued our clothes to our skin like a wet, soft film.

"I love you too. I love you so much, Dustin. I'm going to miss you." Her tone was becoming more and more subdued. I gritted my teeth, unable to forget our killers. "I'm scared. I'm afraid of dying."

The toxic air, which filled the entire room, seemed to gradually lull her to sleep.

"Don't be afraid, sweetheart. You're going to be fine, I promise."

I looked at her guardian for a hundredth of a second, like someone silently closing a contract. His appearance at the foot of the bed was implacable.

"We'll be together, honey."

"Promise?"

The thread of her voice became more and more of a whisper.

"We will be together until the end, my love. In this life and in the next. I will find you. I promise."

His body was increasingly drowsy. Fragile. The hot, unbreathable air made us cough between fleeting moments of lucidity. She hit me with two soft punches in the ribs. The effort to open my numb eyes seemed Olympian. Again, two more punches to the stomach brought me partially back to consciousness.

"It's my grandfather. Look, Dustin, my grandfather is coming for me."

I opened my eyes, looking in the direction she indicated, pointing to the bottom of the bed. There alone stood her guardian, erect to the ceiling, dark, dull and elongated. It seemed to be preparing for the ritual of accompanying Angie on her final journey. However, she was totally convinced she saw her grandfather. She was vehement. Without a hint of doubt her dead grandfather, to whom she had been very close, had come for her.

Her face was filled with optimistic nostalgia. She was excited about this reunion. She only saw this relative who came to look for her from the other side, as a sort of exceptional emissary.

She was paradoxically happy, so much so that her own dramatic situation took a back seat. The bed was completely surrounded by guardians, whose translucent eyes covered the cloud of smoke simulating a vaporous starry sky.

A constellation of protective gazes.

My strength was leaving me. Extreme weakness gripped my body, but something inside me refused to give up. I was too attached to life. I had a lot to fight for, but not without Angie. One last glance to say goodbye. My eyes orbited in an uncontrolled cadence resulting from exhaustion and the absence of oxygen. One figure stood out among the others. A reddish-colored one. Good heavens, it was Daryl! There. My guardian claimed all my energy, but an intelligible voice emanated from that new creature, the one who, until so recently, I had called my best friend.

He kept insisting in an indecipherable voice. I finally figured it out. Dying and exhausted. Daryl, persistent to the point of exhaustion, called out,

"Forgive me, Dustin. Forgive me, Dustin. Forgive me."

A glow of light emerged from Angie's body gently picked up by her guardian. My throat burned and my lungs worked like a bellows without air.

"I love you, honey. I'll find you!"

My voice was breaking with that last effort.

And that was the end of it. That's how I was separated from the love of my life. So unfair. Remembering it, my body overloaded with an enormous energy. Trapped between strange straps, immobilized inside that damned ship. Held and imprisoned in the home of my tormentors. Deceived again, against my will. The time had come for justice, and this time it would be different.

Very different.

Chapter 37
Atlantic Blue

At some undefined point on the map, 1996.

A force inside me grew by the second as I relived the clear memory of my murder. It was a volcanic energy waiting for the right moment to explode, but an intelligent opportunity overcame my desires. I scanned the constellation of expectant gazes of the guardians. They were waiting for some initiative from me to help me, to safeguard me from danger. Their mere presence acted like a balm.

I examined and analyzed, one by one, each guardian.

"Let's start with the procedure. We are tired of incomplete results. This time we must go one step further."

I felt danger approaching. Pain was coming. Time was running out and I could not find what I was looking for. If I didn't react soon, I would be hurt and everything would be over, because wounded I would be vulnerable, weak. The feeling of not finding it, coupled with the imminent danger, filled me with frustration. It would all be over for me, but I did not plan to give up. Because giving up was the same as living without life. It was not a considered decision, but rather an uncontrollable impulse.

"Where are you? Because I can't find you! Without her I'll let myself die! This is the end of everything for me! I can't go on! I can't go on! This is my limit, show yourself! Without hope I can't go on!"

The contraption slowly descending toward me stopped for a moment. Time began to travel at a different pace, slower again. A guardian was making his way among his peers, approaching the stretcher where I was tied and immobilized.

"I am here, and I have come to help you. I am not hiding."

His voice, recognizable, penetrated my head. It was like a gift from another life.

"It's you! Tell me, how is she? I need her. I have to find her. I beg you."

The words spilled from my lips.

"Overcoming does not understand limits, it is something independent. That is the strength of life; even if you perish, you have to live fighting to the end. That's what it's all about. Overcoming expectations. Overcoming trials is what makes you different. That's the purpose of this whole invention; you should know that by now. If you give up, you'll never find what you're looking for. If you let yourself die, there will be no second chance. Without courage there is no reward. The effort and the decision depend on you, no one else."

Lying on the cold, hard stretcher, and pressed against myself, tied with those strange straps, I stopped for a moment to think about what I had suffered since I was four years old when I realized I was different. I thought about how my parents had fought to bring me up, to give me the best, even if they had to endure the distance and uncertainty, giving up so much.

I thought about all the fights I had fought, looking for my enemies along the way. I thought about my defeats, my fears and insecurities. But suddenly, I also began to think about my successes. All those people I had helped in one way or another. I thought, smiling, of my travels, of my uncles, of Kingsley, of Paloma, of Claudia, of all the good things I had and all the good things to come. I realized that a defeat begins with a thought, and I promised myself that I would never give up again.

My muscles began to tighten, and with them the straps became tighter and tighter against my skin. Behind the reigning darkness of the shadows I could see Saya's worried face. For some reason, she had something different from the others; she was, how shall I put it, more intuitive. She sensed the subtle differences that her companions overlooked. The more force I exerted, the tighter the straps tightened. I felt my veins swelling and my muscles congesting to the max as I strained with all my might to free myself from their bonds.

I breathed to regain my strength again and again, I did not give up, I kept trying to free myself. Until, at last, the guardians were convinced of my will. Of my firm decision to fight. Of my will to live. To return to the battle. To find myself again.

It is difficult to explain, but I will try.

The guardians were disappearing from the room, from my sight, but not to leave, quite the contrary. One after another, or all at once, I do not remember well, they joined me, as if they were lending me their strength for what was to come. They did not speak or give their opinion, I barely perceived their presence; however, I knew they were there, a part of each of them was inside me. They had delegated all their power, as if they were certain that I would use all that potential correctly. They knew that they could yield it without a hint of doubt, without a shadow of suspicion, without fear of making a mistake.

"Let him go! Let him go!" Saya shouted unheard.

Then, the same straps that had seemed indestructible gave me the impression of transforming into paper chains. I sat up on that cold, horizontal surface, observing those individuals with calm serenity. My restlessness had disappeared, the nerves, the fear, the anxiety, the stress, the high pulsations. All these interferences were no longer part of my state. I was surprised by this new reality, energetically calm and controlled, and it seemed that my hosts also perceived this security.

I got rid of those oppressive straps like someone who gently dusts off his clothes. I felt my muscles were denser and more compact than ever. It was a strange sensation, especially when coupled with a new clearer awareness of my surroundings. I looked in all directions making a mental map of that flying structure, more than that, it was as if I could understand its functioning, acquiring with the presence of the guardians a knowledge that until then had been denied me.

The suits and Saya looked at each other, undecided how to act, surprised by the ease with which I had broken free of their restraints, but mostly by the chilling serenity of my gaze.

"Don't try it. It should not even cross your mind. You have mercilessly killed a creature connected to the source."

My thoughts were expressed in a voice much more powerful than normal. I felt the strong vibration of my vocal cords, and, in addition, my thoughts were now being expressed in a different way.

"I will tell you what is going to happen, as I see it. You are going to leave me near the house of this man, the one you have murdered. Here we pay tribute to life with a dignified funeral. It is the minimum for the family of a good man. Then you will be gone forever. You will never go near any living being in this world again, and you will inform whoever it may concern that this place is no longer of interest to you. You can invent the most reasonable excuse you can find. It is the kindest offer I can give you. If you refuse, you will simply not have the capacity to regret it."

They exchanged looks again, worried and unsure. One of the suits stepped forward. His countenance was impatient and displeased, just the kind of reaction he did not want.

"We can kill you in less time than a finger snap and still learn something."

The suit looked around the room with a haughty air, boasting that he was on his home turf and bragging about his advanced technology.

"I would like to ask a question."

I pinned my eyes on Saya and the other suits.

"Does this individual decide for you?"

Uncertainty was palpable in the air. They were facing the unknown, and yet they could not shake off that unbearable, unbridled arrogance. Only Saya tilted her head negatively, subtly, so as not to be seen by her companions.

"One last warning. I want you to know that the rules of order prevent me from killing a fellow human being, as long as it is not strictly unavoidable, but I must inform you that you do not officially fall into the category of the living; you have no aura, that is, you are literally heartless."

I burst out laughing, hearing my own words, and seeing how I confused them. Several fire-colored balls appeared; I suppose with the purpose of neutralizing me without having to move a muscle. They soon became aware of the power the guardians had bestowed on me when the spheres dropped to the floor as if they were crude toys. I barely had to devote a thought to snatch all the light from those hostile devices. Worry was now beginning to show on their faces. I wasted no time.

I spun on my heels, rapping my knuckles on the face of that foolish suit, the same one who dared to approach me, the same one who seconds before had been threatening to kill me. I could feel the crunch of his facial bones, and then he crumpled to the. I raised my fists watching how the rest of the suits would react, waiting for a response from them.

I also had to keep an eye on the one on the floor, to ensure he did not get up again. The eyes of the others were still fixed on him but none of them seemed to want to come to his aid. Then, a gasp caught my attention. I let my guard down for a moment and looked at my defeated opponent. He was struggling to breathe. I shuddered, though it passed as I remembered who they were.

Observing him, I could perceive a subtle glow behind his tie, at the level of his sternum. I gawked at him for a few seconds. I was aware that the guards had also influenced my ability to perceive reality, as I was used to. It was as if the light I could pick up had been amplified a thousandfold. That brightness shot to the back of the room, and that body stopped breathing. That was when I understood.

The faint glow that shone from my adversary's chest was not natural, precisely the opposite. Now I understood that flesh and artificial technology were annexed through some kind of mechanism placed in that body position. I looked at Saya and the rest of the suits, all with mute expressions and who were also absorbing what had just happened. But that was no longer of interest to me; I discovered that this glow was a characteristic common to all of them. It was then when, without expecting it, the creature entered the room.

It was very similar to one of the four-fingered beings, but with obvious differences. It was Atlantic blue, a shimmering blue. It was faceless, I mean, without lips or prominent eyes. Everything about him was smooth, without any creases. He oozed a premiere shine, all of him looked metallic and crystalline, like a freshly polished car, although, yes, one thing he had in common with all the others: that slight sheen in the center of his chest.

His arms and legs were thick and well-set. This being conveyed the impression of superhuman strength. He walked smoothly, straight-shouldered and fully erect; he seemed to reserve his potential for later. The rest of the suits regained their calm, as if they had restored all their lost confidence. He bent over the inert suit lying on the ground and began to stroke its head. Saya looked at me with a piercing pity in her eyes, like someone who knows something terrible that cannot be shared.

"You know, of all the humans whose DNA we have collected and thoroughly examined, this specimen is, of all of them, my favorite and, although it is true that we can recreate as many replicas as we want, I have to admit that seeing it lying here gives me a certain feeling of unease. I think you call it, correct me if I'm wrong, anger. Obviously, the scales were somewhat tipped in your favor, or it was a stroke of luck. I don't know. In any case, I will take the license to correct it.

I looked at him and listened to his words not with fear, but with expectant curiosity. I understood that the light that shot out of the pectoral of the deceased was nothing more than coded information that traveled through the air to be deposited in another body, another container to manifest itself in our reality. Like *software*, or, better said, as if a driver went from a passenger car to a fighter *jet*.

"Quickly now. I recommend you all replace your current bodies with the hardest and strongest you have if you wish to face me. Or, of course, surrender, there's still time."

I stared, one by one, at everyone present and, although they were not so human, the disturbing skepticism was once again on their faces.

"This is what our creators looked like before they took the technological leap and plunged into the abyss of decadence. They were hopelessly weakened by neglect. The only difference is that this is a version a thousand times more powerful than the strongest organic version."

I had no intention of listening to any more bullshit, let alone having to face the same opponent a second time.

"Stand up and let's get this over with. I'm done listening to you."

With a calculated slowness he sat up and stood in front of me. He was about six inches shorter than me, but much broader in the shoulders.

"We keep this copy only for cases of extreme urgency. As you will see..."

He wanted to keep talking, but my patience ran out and I started the fight. I kicked him with all my strength, and he moved backwards a few meters without falling. It looked like he had hit a concrete block. I regained my position and that's when, without touching the ground, he moved horizontally towards me with a strange glow in his right hand. I was able to dodge it, but just barely. I gave him an upward punch in the abdomen followed by a low kick. I barely noticed him tremble.

I didn't even see him coming, I just found myself flying across the room from his blow. I got back to my feet, but I couldn't see him anymore. That's when he grabbed me by the neck from behind and started choking me; I bent down, grabbed his leg, and sat on his knee. He was trying to keep his balance, but eventually we fell to the ground. I stood over him and threw a punch that he dodged. My fist slammed into the ground, a gaping hole opened up, revealing a complex maze of titanium-colored ducts and materials.

That strange being could levitate with a kind of swift weightlessness, rising above me to attack from above. From his forearm, small spheres emerged again. They were orange projectiles that shot out. I moved at full speed to avoid them. I remember thinking that it wasn't fair, that it wasn't a just fight anymore. New perforations and chunks of material were splattered on the ground from their impact. He was levitating at a height of approximately two meters off the ground.

"If it weren't for the uniqueness of your existence for our study, you would be dead by now,'" he told me, like someone who has already sold the bear's skin.

That was not a living being as such, it was a war instrument from another world. I caught my breath and as I did so I coughed, a sputum of blood falling on the floor. I don't know if it was because of the strangulation or the vicious fall. I was looking forward to the end of the struggle, to being victorious and to finally be able to talk to Angie's guardian. It was then, remembering her and reliving for an instant how it felt to be with her, that my body experienced a renewed injection of strength.

For the first time I began to understand something I had always overlooked, a universal truth. I thought of that poor man tortured on the alien stretcher, but not in the spirit of revenge. I imagined his family giving him the last farewell. I knew that in that final ceremony they would be able to recall the love that united them, that indelible feeling that would always remain between them.

With every pure, righteous, evil-free purpose that sprang from my mind, my body was fed with energy. I stopped hating. That flying entity was nothing more than a harmful interference to achieve the goals of that invisible force, my strength: love.

"Today you will cease to exist forever. No one will miss you. You will be a sterile and aseptic memory that has traveled astronomical distances to end up forgotten."

He bowed his head assimilating what he had just heard, unable to dispute my omen. His four-fingered hands began to glow again. He landed with such force that he dented the ground, and the vibration could be felt coursing through the entire structure. A barrage of punches and kicks, of unimaginable force, began to be directed against my body. Almost all of them I dodged or negated by protecting myself, but his fists burned like red-hot metal against my flesh.

With one of the blows I could feel my dirty, tattered T-shirt transform into a burning goo that stuck to the skin on my shoulder. Enough was enough. It was time for a counterattack. I kicked him in the side with all the strength I could muster, accompanied by a fierce scream. His body did not recover its original position, it remained curved, as if something had broken inside. I rushed over and grabbed his long-phalanxed hands, which burned hotter than a coffee pot puffing the last drops.

"Everything that has light belongs to us."

My voice sounded guttural, like that of the guardians. It was his power that he was now going to use to the fullest. His hands stopped glowing and his matter began to fade away to become large ashes that fell to the ground like black feathers. He took a few steps back, almost staggering, doubled over, and stopped to contemplate the place where his hands should have been. Something more than concern could be breathed into the atmosphere. You could smell his real fear, even though his face was devoid of any expression.

I needed to put an end to all that as soon as possible. The desperation to know anything about Angie was driving my rage and desire to deal with this weird and almost unbelievable adversary. I gave no respite, crashing my elbows, knees and shins all over his body. The blows I threw caused wounds to my own body. My skin was splitting in two and soon, blood began to ooze from my flesh. My arms and skin blackened with stray dirt began to turn a dark red.

Soon, he fell limp, but not before trying to hit me. He was still moving, there on the ground. My shoulder was stinging from the burn, and I knew my body was bruised and bleeding. But, overall, I felt okay. Very sore but fine.

I looked at the rest of the suits and Saya. They were petrified.

The bright blue android stopped moving and the glow in the center of its chest became present and shot outward. I interrupted its journey, like someone catching a fly on the fly. Now I was holding that light in my aching hands, and something told me that the personality of that suit, turned blue android, wanted to escape from there to resurface in another body. I was not going to allow it. It was obvious that those present were unable to see what was circulating between my bloodied and trembling hands, but they didn't need to. Using the power of the guardians I undid each photon, shattering that glow and extinguishing it forever, thus fulfilling my omen.

The rest of the suits swarmed at me. Saya watched the scene sensing something that her companions had missed. One of them pulled a revolver from his pocket.

"It's not a good idea. We've done enough damage to the ship, and we need him alive. Put that away!" the others said.

"No! He must be killed!" said the one wielding the gun.

Then I came up with the idea of hiding in the light, more than that. I left the light of my still image where it was and started to move around invisibly. The suit was still pointing at my body, they were still arguing with each other. It was time to act. I made myself visible. It might have been stupid and wasting a tactical advantage, but as a martial arts fighter I found it dishonorable to fight on the sly. So to them the effect was as if I could move around the room at unimaginable speed. I grabbed the revolver wielder's arm and dislocated it over my shoulders, forcing him to open his hand.

Another one of the suits hit me in the back and finally the revolver was thrown to the side, sliding on the ground and spinning on itself. The one who was carrying the gun before started throwing punches wildly; I easily protected myself while still feeling the repeated bruises on my back. Soon I began to hear them choking from the effort, trying to catch their breath. It was my turn. As I stood on guard and saw that they had failed to reduce me, despair overcame them. I lifted my knee and brought my foot down hard on the floor and stood against the wall as I saw them half crouched down breathing, trying to catch their breath.

The first one that approached me I smashed his leg; immediately, he curled up into a ball on himself. I jumped on him and used him as a catapult, impacting my knee against the head of another suit, holding it from behind to increase the effect of the blow. The one left standing was throwing punches at me wildly, with no control whatsoever. I dodged them with a certain calmness, until I hit his knee three times in a row, noticing the crunching of bone underneath his flesh.

Now everyone was crawling, or simply lying motionless on the ground, grunting in pain. I looked around and then I saw her; Saya was holding the revolver in her hands. Bang, the detonation sounded like a bomb. The smoke from the gunpowder could not hide the gun's trigger, pointing the barrel towards the ceiling due to the recoil. Instinctively, I looked down to check myself, just in case, in case I had been shot. I hadn't.

On the floor there was a growing pool of blood next to one of the suits, who was wielding a large dagger in his hands. The light of that body burst from the chest, towards some central point of that ship. I interrupted its journey and, just as before, made it disappear forever, while I thought about what Saya had just done.

However, I did not want to face the same opponents again and again and again.

I said to myself, "There they are." I

The negotiations never came to fruition, there was too much arrogance on their part, but now Saya had completely thrown me off.

"What have you done, Saya, have you gone mad?" shouted one of the two remaining suits, his voice breaking with pain.

"Shut up! Shut up! Don't you realize that this is beyond us? He's killing us one by one!"

"We'll talk about it later. These bodies transmit more pain than any we have ever inhabited."

"No! Don't do it or he will end your existence forever! Haven't you noticed that the others haven't returned?"

Lying there, one with a broken leg and the other on his back holding his belly, they had a moment to look at each other, writhing in pain, and realized it was true. Saya could be right.

"So, if that were true, you helped him eliminate Trock. You helped him, do you know what that means? You will be judged by your behavior."

"Will you stop thinking about him now? This one will wipe us all out! All we can do is beg for mercy!"

"Never that. Behaving like these filthy creatures do? Begging in tears? No! We cannot!"

He stood up as best he could with his arm tucked over his belly, limping awkwardly, his breath choking, approaching Saya and reaching out for the revolver.

"Back off, I tell you! Don't make me do it!"

The suit with the broken leg stared at the scene in horror, wondering how they had come to this situation.

I analyzed the behavior of both, unable to guess the outcome.

"Back, I beg you! I don't want to!" "Haim! Haim, tell him to get back!"

She wielded the gun firmly, gripping it by the hilt with all her might, aiming it at the suit, whose face was swollen and disfigured from the fight.

Haim, who must have been the name of the suit with the broken leg, stared into my eyes, paralyzed in my memory. His eyes were glazed over as if he were about to burst into tears. I told myself that it was not like that, that in that body there was no soul with feelings like ours, it was only a physiological reflex to pain. Shortly after, his words confirmed it to me.

"Traitor! Traitor! Traitor! Filthy traitor! What are you doing?"

I saw her pressing the trigger.

"Don't do it, Saya. Don't do it, I'll handle it," I said in a calm, but firm voice.

She looked at me strangely. Now she felt like an enemy to everyone.

I approached the suit, whose face was almost unrecognizable. He was shuffling his feet, and with each of his steps he complained more of a hellish pain in his abdomen. He turned around awkwardly and still drew energy to try to throw a punch at me, slow and erratic like that of a centenarian grandfather.

Saya lowered the gun and placed her finger on the barrel of the revolver, escaping with a sigh of relief that she could not conceal. I dodged her blow with ease and without thinking I punished her abdomen with three consecutive kicks, so that she too fell to the ground and her eyes orbited uncontrollably looking in all directions, like someone who is about to lose consciousness. I leaned over her and offered him the best advice I could give,

"When you lose consciousness, which you will because of the acute pain, do not think of leaving this body or you will suffer the same fate as the previous ones. I will give you a chance because I have seen something in you, Saya. You have something different from the rest, no matter how much they now insist on calling you a traitor."

Her chest began to glow with that orange hue that came to them when they were about to emigrate.

"Remember that I have warned you. I will not fight you again today." I looked at the suits so that they would get the message and take the decision they wanted, freely. "Take me to the place where this man lived; I must deliver him to his family. I have promised."

Saya made a slight affirmative motion, her finger slid down the luminous wall drawing a squiggle, and a sphere the size of a large watermelon descended vertically from the center of the room. It was dark, with glowing sparkles inside, like a dense, filled bubble. She approached it and began to move her hands in contact over it. The color changed. It was getting larger and larger. I saw very clearly that it was a live terrestrial map: the clouds, the sun's bath, artificial lights in the darkness. Symbols appeared on the spherical screen. Saya pressed and manipulated it, until she had confirmed our destination, the place of origin of the unfortunate tortured man.

"We'll get to Raymond in a few minutes. I'll help you get him down."

Her brief embarrassed words broke the noisy silence of agonized breaths and controlled moans.

"Raymond?"

Although, after all, the location was the least of my problems.

—He was a native of Raymond, Washington State. We'll drop you as close to town as possible. I'll help you get him down. Follow me. As I told you before, we travel very fast. We're getting there.

Only a few minutes had passed, and we arrive at our destination. From where, I wondered. We were coming from New York at the very least, and I didn't feel even a slight movement.

But at that point I wasn't too interested in it either.

None.

Chapter 38
Internal Debate

City of Raymond, Washington, 1996

"It's this way."

The wall opened out, and I remember thinking that I was no longer bothered by all that light.

"Don't try to play me," I said to Saya holding her by the arm, looking at the two suits so that they would understand that the message was also for them.

I picked up the lifeless body of the tortured man and threw it over my shoulder. The walls opened to our passage in a straight line. The internal structure of that flying contraption was flexible and could be cut off by creating a straight corridor.

"We have arrived. We'll go down to the ground on this platform. Then we will say goodbye for the last time, and I will pass on your message to my people. At least, I personally will not bother you again." She took a deep breath, taking in everything that had happened. "You have my word. It is the only guarantee I can offer you."

With the weight of their victim on my shoulder, her words did not seem comforting, and I made a strong exercise of self-control to simply remain silent upon receiving her promise. The floor beneath our feet unlocked with a sound similar to that of a glass jar being opened for the first time. Suddenly, the air began to have nuances that I had unknowingly missed. Our descent was silent and unobtrusive.

It was night, but the last rays of sunlight were still visible on the horizon, and the atmosphere mingled the smell of vegetation and the flowing humidity of fresh water. The platform levitated above the ground, and when I looked up, I could only see a large dark spot in the sky. I put my feet on solid ground and walked towards the place from where the intermittent and scarce hum of road traffic was coming. I heard Saya's footsteps behind me. I breathed in to recharge my patience and paused with the intention that the silence would insult them more than any curse. Saya gently grabbed my forearm. In the distance, the lights of a pickup truck flashed past, indicating the narrow road I was to reach.

I got away from her, but I kept hearing her footsteps behind me.

"I lost too! You know?"

Her voice sounded broken. I grabbed the corpse's legs with my left hand, and with my right hand I grabbed her shirt, pulling Saya tightly to me.

"You don't know what it's like to lose! Tell that to this man's family! Come on!"

Despite the darkness, I could see Saya's features were alight with a senseless and incomprehensible rage. Orange lights shot out from above toward us as the circular platform, which lowered us to the ground, ascended at great speed. I dropped the man's body to the ground to, with both hands, stop the energy with which I was again attacked. Saya stood behind me resting her face on my back. I was scared beyond belief and gasped uncontrollably in panic. The ship fired again those small incandescent spheres and I had to work again to neutralize them and, without further ado, the lenticular ship shot into the sky at an irrational speed, leaving no trace of its presence.

"Now do you see? I too have lost everything. I have been confined to this world, with this mortal body. I must act quickly or they will hunt me down to kill me for high treason."

I picked up the body from the ground and put it back on my shoulder, walking towards the road, where, from time to time, a solitary car passed by. Saya kept following me at a short distance. The undergrowth was clearing and the ground was hardening. In the distance, amber lights were slowly approaching. The five bulbs over the cab told me it was a truck. I signaled from a distance, and the driver turned on the high beams and overhead lights. The roar of the brakes and the blowing of the boilers added to the titanic sound of an ancient and enormous gasoline engine.

The cab light illuminated inside and the sturdy metal door opened. The truck driver stepped out with a crowbar in one hand. He had a face covered in white whiskers. His belly was fat and he was wearing green overalls. He was sucking smoke from a curved, picturesque pipe, which immediately made me think of my father. Saya, without any permission, walked ahead of me.

"We need you to turn this body over to the authorities."

Immediately, an elongated shadow appeared behind him and watched me closely. I raised my hand slightly to greet it, and it leaned over the truck driver to say something in his ear that would ring in his head louder than a thought of his own and he would never know where it came from. He released the crowbar he carried in his hand and hurried to help me with the man's body.

"What happened to you? Were you attacked by a bear?"

Certainly, my body was full of bleeding wounds, disheveled, dirty, with tattered clothes, and I guess I looked as if I had come from the forest.

"Help us, please. Help us," I implored him, as he bent down to take the body from me.

"But, boy, this man is dead! Come on, there's no time to lose. Hold him for a moment." He jumped nimbly into the back of the truck and returned with a tarpaulin, which he unrolled." Get up! Let's get you to a doctor!"

The truck driver turned around with several sharp maneuvers, jolting the entire driver's cab, which we clung to from behind. It was like an agitated carnival attraction. An auxiliary spotlight on the platform remained on. I held on to a metal handle protruding from the front of the truck. Saya came up beside me and opened the toolbox and rummaged around inside. She discarded items until she found what she was looking for. I had planned to get out of the truck as soon as it slowed down, but the man's body could fall to the asphalt at any moment and I had to hold him down.

Saya leaned her back against the metal frame that separated the platform from the truck cab and stripped off her black sweater, beginning to unbutton her shirt. Firm, round breasts were hidden behind a white bra. Distraction prevented me from seeing that in her right hand she held a retractable-blade box cutter firmly in her hand.

"But what are you going to do?" I shouted overt the mechanical noises and the wind that enveloped us.

"I must remove tracking device or they will find me, and then it will be all over for me, forever. I told you I have lost too!"

"What are you talking about?"

"You'll see, if I don't faint!"

Her hair fell around her face as she picked up a dirty grease rag and stuffed it into her mouth. She bit down hard and it was obvious that her small nose was not enough to channel the air she needed. She drove the blade down the sternum making a slit, a few centimeters deep. A tear slipped from her eyes. She set the box cutter aside and a channel of blood gushed out, flooding her navel, over her jeans. A fleeting thought made me ponder the existence of that navel.

There were too many questions and not enough time. She dug her index finger into the open wound, and slowly pulled it out as she gritted her teeth biting down the filthy grimy rag, until she spat it out letting out a terrifying shriek of pain.

"Help me get it out. I won't be able to do it alone." Her eyes, so human, softened my resolve. Pull here until all the string comes out, and get rid of it or they'll find me."

Her finger had pulled out a small translucent duct. She looked at me without blinking.

I looked into the same eyes that years ago, in the corridor that led to the room in which Angie and I hid, participated in the fire that killed us. Now, thousands of miles from nowhere, years later, I was debating whether or not to help my enemy.

Resentment told me not to help but when I listened to my conscience, I saw another way. Maybe it was a mistake, maybe not, I didn't know then but what I did know was that I was suffering, and that, honestly, I think she had made an effort to talk to me, to make me understand, to mediate on my behalf as if she were a negotiator, divided between our two worlds, disagreeing with her principles, and at the same time having the duty to go with the flow. And the truth is that, pushed to the limit, she decided to break with her roots. She had decided to strive to be a little more human. She decided to risk living and dying, knowing that her death would be literal. Eternal.

So I pulled on that thin flexible wire, and centimeters and centimeters began to emerge, branching out in six rows. Three up and three down, and in the center, behind the rib cage, a solid lump flickered with a light glow. All that tangle was coming out of her chest as she writhed in excruciating pain.

Finally, she lost consciousness and I took the opportunity to extract all the filth that invaded her extremities. I threw it to the gutter. I took the box cutter again and ripped her shirt in the cleanest area and pressed the wound to stem the blood flow. We were entering the city and the truck driver was running a red light honking the shrill horn of his old beast.

The gigantic size of the trees prevented me from seeing the blue lights of the police car. I panicked at having it so close, and again another dilemma gripped my mind. I looked at Saya's unconscious face and wondered, "Is she worth it?" the rational answer was a resounding no, but a strange hunch or an inexplicable inner duty encouraged me to protect her, as if we were united because of our secrets, a sort of invisible code never written between enemies.

"Jerry, thanks for coming! Blessed CB station! Anyway, they're in the back, the young man is badly hurt."

The policeman rushed to us with his flashlight. He uncovered the corpse and when he saw our wounds, Saya unconscious and our clothes stained with blood I think he could only think that we were victims of a wild animal attack. He didn't even ask, he ran as fast as he could inside the modest hospital returned with nurses at his side and a trolley for Saya.

"You'll be fine, we'll take care of you," the policeman told me.

In the eyes of the police officer, we could see sadness, camouflaged under a professional and methodical countenance as he focused on our transfer.

Saya was carried away on the stretcher, and Jerry put my arm around his shoulders to help me inside. His spotless uniform was stained with my blood, and I wanted to pull my arm away to avoid it, but he wouldn't let me; he almost dragged me, and although an illogical shame oppressed me, I must also admit that I enjoyed the pleasant sensation of feeling cared for.

The doctors cut off all my clothes. I gripped the amulet tightly with both hands so that no one would even think of touching it. Just by lying on the spotless hospital bed in my underwear, I noticed that my skin had transferred, in addition to fresh and dried blood, part of the dirty patina accumulated during weeks of living on the street.

A nurse smilingly approached me with a basin and a sponge, and then, at that very moment, I felt more embarrassed than I had ever felt in my entire life.

"I must wash you to look at all your wounds. But how many days had you been in the forest?" she asked

Next to me separated only by a curtain, I heard the doctors assessing Saya's wound, and my nurse noticed my concern.

"Is she your older sister? Your aunt, maybe? And how come she's not that dirty? Did you go hiking? What the hell happened to you? Is the other gentleman your father?"

The string of questions felt endless and the nurse's voice gradually faded as I retreated into my thoughts, weighing whether or not helping Saya was a good idea. I listened to the doctors prepare the materials to stitch her wound and how they set to work.

My nurse kept asking me questions, and from time to time she would say,

"This might hurt a little."

I had reached a point where I could hardly feel the pain, or rather, it had stopped bothering me.

I knew Jerry was close by because I could hear voices over his police radio. I had to do something and fast. The nurse was finishing dressing my wounds. I noticed that they had stuffed our clothes into blue knotted bags under the beds. Jerry walked over to the nurse and peeked in to see me; I had to pretend to be asleep.

"Nurse, I need to ask him a few questions." The agent's voice sounded authoritative and impatient.

"He is exhausted and unresponsive. Tomorrow morning you will be able to talk to him, he needs rest now."

"We must wake him up. For the safety of the population, I must know what has happened."

The doctor who had just stitched up Saya approached the policeman and in requested him to forget about interviewing us for the night. Jerry stood firmly in front of us for a few seconds. Despite the coldness of his gaze I could sense he just wanted to help protect the population from whatever had attacked us. His skepticism was also palpable, because I think a lot of things didn't add up for him. I wanted to keep him from exploring his doubts.

The lights went out and we were left in near darkness with a dim light. In the background, we could hear the sounds of monitors and, from time to time, the beep of the police radio station. I pulled back the curtain and looked at Saya, who was resting peacefully with a drip at her bedside.

I got up, and got dressed again in my dirty, now ripped clothes; the T-shirt was just tatters and I left it there. At the head of my bed was a huge window; I checked that it could be opened quietly and made sure we were on the first floor. I peeked through the curtain that led to the central hallway of the room. The first thing that caught my attention was the presence of guardians in front of the beds. One of them saw me watching him and approached with his languid walk, blocking with his lanky height the scarce light that bathed the room.

"It is very sad and at the same time gratifying to see that there are still links, although you are becoming more and more rare. Do you know that there was a time when all people could see us? In fact, we were drawn hundreds of times in the caves, accompanying early humans on the hunt, taming wild animals. It was a time when communities helped each other, saved each other, respected and loved each other. It was the only way to survive in those times. Now humanity has gone astray. True strength is not intellectual. It is spiritual. But they have forgotten that.

He bent his face over Saya and watched her carefully in silence, resting his hands on her forehead.

"I see darkness within her, many regrets tormenting her. But there is hope, for an imprisoned light struggles to emerge and prevail. She does not belong here. She has no guardian. The Order does not know of her existence."

Again, there was a prolonged pause, and then he said,

"Tell her I'll keep an eye on her. We'll see."

He didn't even give me a chance to say anything before he returned to his protégé. I removed the IV they had put in Saya, and made the intermittent sound of the machines coincide with the pulling of the adhesive tape. They had covered her body with a thick white sheet. I looked for her clothes, not even sure if Saya was capable of waking up. In the bag under her bed they had only left her shoes and pants. I guessed the police had the rest or maybe they had thrown it away because it was torn. I approached her ear and called her name.

"Saya. Hey, Saya, wake up. We have to go."

But she would not wake up. On her finger was a white clamp connected to a monitor. It showed the pulse rate and other values. I put it on mine and saw that the parameters were almost identical. I went around the bed and stealthily slid the next curtain. A lady was sleeping peacefully. I placed the clamp on the lady's finger and no alarm went off. That was it. It was time to leave.

I pinched Saya's ear, but she did not respond. Seeing that it didn't work, I squeezed her hard behind her earlobe; it's a known sore spot, and only then did she start to come back from the dream world. She finally opened his eyes. I commanded her to be silent with my index finger over my lips and plugging her mouth with my other hand. She had the reflex to say something and tried to sit up quickly, but I signaled her to be quiet, we could not attract attention.

Waking up in an unfamiliar place in near darkness is unsettling, especially when your last memory is an unbearable pain that you still.

"Why are you helping me?" she asked me, puzzled.

"We'll talk when we're out of here. Get dressed, you can see everything."

A brief smile passed across her face like a flash of lightning, and instead of heeding me and getting dressed, she did just the opposite. She took off her underwear and threw it on the floor. I looked at her questioningly. On the bed, she hugged her legs, closing her eyes, as if she was too weak and sleepy. Now her body was only covered in darkness.

"They can also follow me through my clothes. It's a long shot, but it's possible. It's not that I'm trying to contradict you." She sounded tired.

"Cover yourself with the sheet then and we'll find something later. We're getting out of here."

But she was moving slower than a clumsy, uncoordinated turtle. I was being too fussy with her. I helped her cover herself with the sheet. She could barely stand. I picked her up and felt her fall asleep on my shoulder. I opted for the most unlikely and risky alternative. I walked with her down the hallway, as slowly as I could. I peeked out a bit and Jerry was awake, immersed in a book he was holding in his hands.

The guardians had given me incredible power, I could feel it. It was crazy, but I didn't have too many options left. It's hard to get used to the idea that you can become invisible at will. I walked slowly with Saya in my arms. Jerry, a police office, with a permanently kind expression, and whose hair was torn between its natural color and the silver that comes with age, looked up from his book as if he had perceived something beyond his senses.

For a moment, I put myself in his place, and it didn't seem right to walk out of there like that. He had helped us, and if I ran away like that it would call into question his professionalism. It wasn't fair. Across from him, one of the nurses who had been attending us slept snoring like a bear in an armchair much more comfortable than Jerry's precarious chair. I decided to reveal my camouflage gently.

I saw him blink several times and his book fell out of his hands. He stood up like a bolt of lightning and took a few steps back. The nurse snored even louder. Jerry was now behind me and only a few feet away from the front door. I could almost feel the disbelief and surprise of the police officer, standing there, so skeptical of what he was witnessing. He was shocked at witnessing the inexplicable.

"I am very grateful to you because you have helped us. Also to the man with the truck. I want you to know that neither this woman nor I killed that man."

I noticed Jerry moving a little closer to hear me better, still perplexed by the unusual sight of our blurred apparition.

"Those responsible are too far out of your reach and mine too. But believe me when I tell you that we are on the same side." A pause was made in the middle of that corridor bathed in dim light. "I'm sure that a crystalline feeling inside you knows I'm telling the truth."

"Who-who are you?" Jerry asked, his voice coarse from hours without articulating a word.

"My name is irrelevant, but I will answer your question. I am a connection between two worlds. A lover of good. A warrior for justice. A servant to the needy and a fierce enemy to the tyrant."

I kept silent for a few seconds so Jerry could understand the importance of my words. "I don't intend to get you in trouble with our escape, though I know your presence here is merely precautionary."

Jerry was attentive to every word that came from my lips. We had connected. I could tell he trusted me, despite the mysterious situation he was going through.

"Let's make a deal, Jerry. I turned and stared at him. He froze. Then I thought maybe it wouldn't be such a good idea. "Leave it, maybe you're not ready. Take care of yourself, buddy, and thanks again for helping us, I owe you."

Erasing my light trail, I walked toward the exit door with Saya asleep in my arms.

"Hey, you! Where do you think you're going?" I paused for a moment, chagrined by his frustration until I heard him say, "Tell me about that deal!"

He sounded determined and excited by the unknown. I thought about it for a moment, motionless before the exit, and answered him by uncovering myself to the light.

"Let's go out on the street. We will talk."

Chapter 39
The Art of Disguise

City of Raymond, Washington, 1996

By that time in the early hours of the morning, the air still held the cold dampness of the night, and Saya's body was moaning with a tremulous chattering of teeth. Even with everything, with the evil she did to me, and the evil I did to her, we were together. I felt an instinctive obligation to protect her, and she felt the need to be cared for, a strange irony of fate. So I pressed her against my warm, naked chest, and she settled down.

From her eyes flowed a transparent, saline liquid, well known to humanity, but which perhaps she was seeing for the first time. She looked up weakly, staring into mine, scrutinizing me with a stern, proud, icy sweetness. She was beginning to experience, for the first time, the subtle nuances of being truly alive. Her gaze became embarrassed, regretful. It was unnecessary to ask for explanations, and at that precise moment I made a promise to myself: from then on, I would keep that image of her and never again remember her in the awful hallway. I caressed her back tenderly and she withdrew her liquid gaze. I pressed my lips to her forehead and kissed her, and breathed in again the genuine smell of sticky sweat and tears.

"It's not that kind of kiss," I clarified to make her understand.

"I know. It is the kiss of compassion, of the innocent and solidary purity of those who are used to take care of others without expecting anything in return." Her words were losing their strength because of her weakness, she had to make a true effort to finish the sentence. "I am beginning to understand that you are more than just a feverish and tireless ambitious and selfish attitude. You are better than us. Now I have no doubts." And she began to shiver with cold.

"Keep your strength and rest, you will get through this."

The hospital door opened with the jolting creak that amplifies the silence of the night.

Jerry placed his cap on his head and checked the even curve of the visor with the touch of his hands, repeating a movement already automated by routine. The patrol car was parked a few steps away and Jerry waited with his hands resting on his belt buckle. The shared silence increased his excitement at rushing into the mystery of the unknown, although that parenthesis also made him hesitate.

"Let me tell you what the deal is, Jerry. You'll help us get out of town and I'll show you something they don't teach at the police academy. I think it'll be worth it."

The visor could not hide the air of suspicion on his face. Jerry was one of those non-conformists and daring people, those who do not frequent the comfort zone, he had a restless spirit and a thirst for knowledge, that was obvious.

"I accept on one condition, one question: can I trust you?"

"Before you got up from your chair, your question was answered. You should listen more to your inner voice; it knows more than you do."

Jerry shrugged slightly and opened the back door of the patrol car, confused by my cryptic response. I gently laid Saya's tired body lengthwise on the austere plastic seats, settling her in as best I could. I opened the passenger door and Jerry looked at himself in the reflection of his glass, wondering what kind of mess he was embarking on. He started the car and asked me,

"Where to?"

I stood for a few seconds thinking and told him,

"Today I'll be your partner for a few hours. Let's patrol and I'll show you what's hiding in plain sight."

The car, which looked so clean and decent on the outside, showed a very different interior. Seats eaten away by the rubbing of the gun on the backrest filled the whole cabin with yellow shavings. The grille separating us from the back seat could tell its own story of stoic endurance. It was dented from blows and with all kinds of biological remains that became mute witnesses of unmentionable human behavior.

The patrol car began to drive into the urban area. A thin line of fog waved through the streetlights accentuating the early morning hours. The occasional car could be seen on the plain crossing an intersection. We passed by a run-down colonial house.

"Stop for a minute. We need some clothes. Can I borrow a few bucks?"

Jerry looked at me snorting, uncomfortable. But he pulled the bills out of his wallet and handed them to me.

"Don't forget that I'm a policeman," he diplomatically reprimanded me.

I looked at the bills he had left in my hand and counted by hand more than eighty dollars.

"The indecent, the improper and the illegal always depend on the vision of the offended party. Stopping us here is no mere chance. If I had occasion to ask you for some clothes, you would give them to me without taking a dollar. Come out with me. I'll show you what I'm talking about."

Jerry looked around, fearful of being seen with me prowling the edges of that property. We reached the porch, where the laundry lay sheltered under the roof.

"Do you feel the energy of this house? The imprint of its inhabitants?" Jerry raised a skeptical eyebrow. "Don't worry; if you let me, I'll show you."

I approached him and placed my hand on his shoulder. A smile appeared on his face, and he closed his eyes to better perceive the sensation I was transmitting to him.

"You have noticed it, haven't you? We can all perceive these things, you just have to train your soul to do it, pay attention to those details that sometimes we feel, but go unnoticed. That's how you cops are; I'm sure with the bad guys you have your antennae well adjusted."

Indeed, the house was occupied by an elderly couple, and the energy permeating the entire household was one of excessive altruistic generosity and solidarity. Genuine brotherhood. I grabbed the oldest clothes hanging on the clothesline, a Navy veteran's T-shirt for me, some women's pants and a thick sweater for Saya. With the clothes pegs, I exchanged the bills for the clothes. Jerry stopped me and picked up the lying dollars.

"I'll talk to them tomorrow; I'll apologize for you. Keep the money, you'll need it more, and maybe you should also take those shoes for your friend."

I looked at them carefully: two pairs of shoes, one for men and one for women. I noticed that the neatness of these people was helping us more than expected. I took the money back from Jerry, nodded firmly and thanked him humbly, promising to return it, even though he insisted it was a gift.

I opened the patrol car door and woke Saya. She dressed almost in her sleep, as I turned my back to her in the doorway. I then tucked her in with the hospital sheet and let her rest again.

We got into the patrol car and before we started Jerry looked at me intently, unafraid, but with eyes sown with doubt. And so they would remain forever, because my existence and my reservations have never been exposed. He drove off without asking any questions.

"I guess you're not from here. Do you want me to take you to the bus station?"

"Later; first I need to contact your guardian angel." I told him this as if it were the most natural thing in the world.

"My what? I'm sorry, but I didn't understand you."

"You see, Jerry. I don't want to alarm you. The reason I'm with you right now and haven't left the hospital without you noticing is simple. You're in danger. Or so I think, I'm not entirely sure."

When I saw him reading in the hospital, before I even approached the hallway, I could see a small group of guardians around him, but they vanished all at once, there was no time to contact them, and I didn't know if they would appear again either. But I wanted to try.

Sometimes those who give their lives to protect and serve others also need to be protected; I am the living embodiment of that premise. Time passed in the patrol car and our relationship cooled as we drove aimlessly through the city. He didn't ask questions and I didn't explain either, although a cloud of impatience hung inside the car. Only the static of his radio station and the voice of a convoy of truckers on the highway distracted us from this voluntary silence.

Just at the same moment as I saw something out of the corner of my eye, Jerry got up the courage to say a few words to me.

"I've been worried about something for a while, but I'm not able to figure out what it is, maybe it's a kind of omen."

"Stop the vehicle, Jerry! It's here. It was worth the wait."

I got out of the car quickly. I ran to the corner where I had seen him; a particularly tall guard stood motionless in front of a store. His elongated arms and piercing darkness contrasted with the light above the prevailing haze. Jerry came to me walking slowly, as if something was weighing on him. Maybe he was wondering why this was such an unsettling journey. Or maybe he was questioning whether or not he wanted to know more. When he reached me, he looked at his hands on both sides and clenched his fists several times in an attempt to relax his muscles.

"That which you feel in your body is the strength given to you by the mere presence of your guardian angel. You will not get rid of that incredible energy until he is gone."

"What am I doing here?" He asked as if he could express his will in a dream.

"I don't have the answer to your question, but I do know that time is against us."

"I don't know anything about guardians. I don't understand anything!" A frustration emerged from him.

"It is your guardian angel, we all have one, and it is the one that protects us daily from so many dangers, if that's how you understand it better." I cut off the conversation to focus on the guardian. But the explanation produced more skeptical nervousness.

"But I'm not a believer," he replied, grumbling at the universe.

"Your beliefs will not change reality, only your ability to understand it."

The guardian took a few steps forward and his voice eclipsed my attention from any other sound.

"He's asking me to be quiet. To calm down. He says that later at home you can relax in your rocking chair, but now take out a pen and notebook from inside your jacket, and don't lose detail of what he is going to transmit to you, your life depends on it. He states that he has urged The Order to agree with me. That you should not be working today either."

"How do you know about it? What kind of witchcraft is this?"

He took a few frightened steps back. The guardian advanced towards him and placed his hand on his head. His whole body language suddenly changed. His hands loosened and his shoulders relaxed. The dark elongated silhouette retreated back to its original position with its arms parallel to its legs, again blocking the powerful light of the streetlamp anchored to the facade.

"Are you calmer, Jerry? Have you felt it?" I tried to make my voice as affectionate as possible.

"I have experienced this peace that I have just felt before. In my dreams, before I did this." And he looked at the shining metal star hanging on his chest. "What is going on?"

Suddenly, his eyes seemed to me deeper and his posture gripped by the tenacious fist of fear.

"There's no time for explanations. Get out the notebook, Jerry. I assure you it's important. You'll have time to think."

The guardian turned his gaze toward me and gave me a slight nod of affirmation that I interpreted as gratitude. Then he raised his left arm and pointed to the small white building, with its roof trimmed in red and its sign reading Raymond Federal Bank. And I began to repeat for Jerry every word conveyed by the dark shadow that appeared before me.

"It will happen here, on the 17th of this month, at thirteen hours and fifty minutes. It is your duty to save the life of one who could perish. The future is not written, it branches and is of unique direction. It cannot be corrected, but it can be redirected, and that is why anticipation is decisive."

"That day I work. I will be up to the task; I will not disappoint."

His enthusiasm was overdrawn, he radiated innate vocational motivation, determined and predisposed; it was obvious that his work was his passion.

"You'll have to take the day off," the guardian said sharply, and an indescribable grimace disfigured Jerry's eager face.

Immediately, he took a step towards me, with an air of protest. I turned my face to the ground, ordered him to stop with a wave of my hand, and focused solely on getting the message across.

"You will take the day off. And in advance, you will go to your cousin Colin's house. You'll ask him for the wheelchair he keeps in the basement. The one his late mother used. The Wilson family, who live on Thirteenth and Blake, needs it for their son. Your cousin will give it to you without objection and, when it's all over, you'll take it to the little boy."

Jerry's face underwent strange metamorphoses. His mouth hung open in surprise. The passage of age and such objective, unbiased employment had sapped the amount of magical thinking that every person stores from childhood.

"How do you know that?" he replied loudly, as if he were talking to a suspect.

"Don't interrupt, Jerry." I calmly brushed off his reprimand, and continued to relay the message, "Ten minutes before the announced time, you will pass the bank pushing the wheelchair and head for this corner. No one will notice you. You will need your sidearm, your taser, some ties, some shackles, a bib, a blanket, and your bullet proof vest."

Jerry was writing rapidly. He seemed to be concentrating, he was beginning to like what he was hearing, for an indelible, mischievous smile was paralyzing his lips and wrinkling the edge of his eyelids. A touch of tamed madness shone in him; he could smell the thrill. He had such eagerness to fight injustice. Now I was the bewildered one, it gave me food for thought. I had a lot to think about.

"Just a moment, please repeat it a little slower," I said to the guardian, whose accelerated, guttural words echoed in my mind with an almost disturbing echo. He fell silent for a moment and continued more slowly.

"Two males, Caucasian, medium height, strong complexion. One of them will wait outside with the vehicle started; the other armed with a bedpan that will rest on the passenger seat; the first will hide his face and he carries an automatic weapon, both will have military discipline and training. You must go alone, otherwise someone will die."

The guardian made a long pause and began to fade, letting the urban light pass through it.

"Good luck," he added.

"Don't go. Wait!" I shouted into the middle of that night set by fog and the whistling of the crickets. The shadow pulled itself together, thickening its darkness again.

"Show me. I want to see what will happen," I asked in thought, this time discreetly, so Jerry wouldn't know.

"I have told you just what you need to know, the rest you must improvise."

Another long pause made me aware of how my body groaned in the middle of that freezing night and how an uncontrollable shivering had taken over my jaw. A T-shirt was definitely not enough warmth.

"I will grant your request, but, as you know, you may not reveal any of it to him, otherwise fate will find its way to him."

"Nothing would upset me more."

Jerry was watching my silent conversation. He stared at me and then ducked his head to review the notes he had so hurriedly taken, used to unraveling his own handwriting every day after the usual *briefing*.

Standing there, trying to ignore my own shivering from the cold, I disconnected from the present. The guardian was sharing with me his capacity of perception. Everything was going fast and slow at the same time, crystal clear, as if suddenly my eyes had multiplied and I could see everything at a three-hundred-and-sixty-degree angle. The smells, the air swaying in the wind, the warm caress of the sun's rays, the sound of every bird, the typing of the computers, the faded voices inside the bank. Every single detail took center stage, and then the scene began to flow in front of me, sharp as a realistic dream in which you can't even think or imagine that you are asleep.

Jerry pushed the wheelchair. On the seat rested a blanket, and on it, a kitchen apron. I could feel his stress, the alarming anxiety that alerts us all to impending danger. He opened the door to the bank and for an eternal moment he stood on the threshold, holding it with his right foot and contemplating the whole interior, not undecided, but worried, as if he was doing something wrong and feared being discovered. The irony was that, as the guardian had told him, no one noticed his presence, neither to help him nor to observe him.

He was invisible to the attention of others. The door clanged as he let go, and Jerry stopped with a shrug of his neck. But all the customers were waiting their turn, or leaning on a shelf in front of the counter, filling out endless forms. The workers were sheltered behind thick glass, only connected to the customers by a small circular opening.

Older people and women, some with children, were the majority among the clientele. A man in a suit and tie was wandering around. He seemed too preoccupied to notice Jerry's eyes on him. It was easy to guess that he was the bank manager; he had that characteristic arrogant air of grandeur about him. But that didn't matter to Jerry; he just wondered that, if his mission was true, why no one else was able to see the disaster. Why a stranger predicted it, a week away, and without being involved.

Paralyzed in thought, doubt invaded his mind, and for a moment he looked into the glass and saw the hazy reflection of his own image clutching the wheelchair, and said to himself, "I am here to practice my profession. I will protect this place. I am a policeman. And he looked up at the huge surveillance camera that scrutinized the movements of those present, and a hot flush of ridicule tormented him for a split second. But then he pulled himself together, shook his head with a gesture more like a twitch than anything calculated, and moved to the corner the boy had indicated. Curiously, the same one where the camera rotated smoothly like a slowed pendulum. The only blind spot.

He put the brake on the wheelchair and looked at his watch; he didn't know the exact time it would happen and if it would be true; he looked at the blanket, the apron and then around. Nothing out of the ordinary. Then an older man with a mustache opened the bank door with force. Jerry's heart skipped a beat, expecting the worst, but the man didn't look up from his passbook and like an automaton he joined the end of a line of people.

The sunlight streamed through the windows bouncing off the whitish marble floor, revealing the shy existence of every speck of dust in suspension, while giving solidity and body to the whole display of luminosity. Jerry watched every movement and, although he was dressed in street clothes, his attitude was totally police-like, but no one had noticed that.

A man by a wheelchair was unremarkable. He had promised himself that he would stay until closing, even if he had to leave with the sting of the swindled. No one but him would know of his embarrassment, and that eased his fears. He recognized that he had nothing to lose except his time and a crazy promise.

Perhaps one day, between laughs and beers, he would tell how he had been tricked by a young illusionist. Irremediably, time continued to pass, and the workers looked even more frequently at the huge clock in front of them, the real boss and jailer that held their freedom.

In the image now, something snapped Jerry out of his recent observant routine. I think, well, I'm convinced he could sense a presence. I noticed it in his eyes. The guardians had arrived. Seven or eight, I didn't count them, but there were more than any ordinary person had concentrated before.

Jerry's survival machinery went into overdrive; however, he did not get upset. He did not lose his cool. The out-of-control passed him by unseen. He slowly peered out the window, no sudden movements. A dark Jeep parked in front of the bank's entrance and a muscular-looking man planted his military-booted foot on the asphalt. Jerry reached for his sidearm and cursed under his breath the veracity of the omens when he saw the man's face hidden by a black helmet, but above all by the rifle he held in his lap.

Instantly, he noticed that his sweater had some very familiar creases in it. He understood immediately that the man was wearing a bulletproof vest. Jerry changed his mind, put the gun in his hip holster and from behind his belt buckle pulled out the Taser. His guardian positioned himself behind him and spoke to him slowly. He would hear that powerful voice as an echo of his own ideas, but even if he had suspected it, it was not the time to question his inner voice.

He looked at the wheelchair, the blanket and the apron, and understood what he had to do. His eyes returned for a moment to the interior of the vehicle. The reflections of the sunny day prevented him from seeing the interior clearly, but at one point everything became crystal clear, and he could see the man behind the wheel. With a sharp jaw and a nervous demeanor, a baseball cap hid his eyes and his hands drummed on the steering wheel with a rhythmic drum beat that indicated his anxiety that it would all be over soon. The signs of fear, Jerry told himself.

When the robber entered the bank, the exact opposite happened to the moment Jerry did. For some strange reason, the customers and employees all sensed the danger, turning around practically in unison. And just in case their intuition had not been clear to them, the first thing he did was to demonstrate that he meant business with a burst of gunfire.

The thick glass was shattered, and the effect of the recoil also left a menacing line of dark holes in the ceiling. The most absolute silence took hold of the place. The robber fused the rifle butt, still smoking, to his right shoulder, and Jerry could see him switch the selector tab from burst to selective fire. Only his slow, short footsteps could be heard over the glass as he walked past each and every customer and employee.

"Everybody down on the ground, now!" They obeyed like a disciplined army. "Not you, fatty! I want you stuffing the dough into this bag, and you're going to do it faster than if you were in a pie-eating contest. Is that clear to you?" His voice sounded distorted from inside the helmet.

"Is anyone going to give me trouble?" he shouted madly, and repeated it, scrutinizing again the customers and workers, making sure that they had obeyed his orders; all except one, who had ignored the unspoken contract of life or death.

The robber's rifle stopped, pointing its barrel at the only person who had ignored the order. But soon he stopped paying attention to the man sitting in a wheelchair, covered with a brown blanket and an apron that prevented his drool from staining his clothes.

His open mouth oozed a mixture of saliva and air that transformed into parched whitish bubbles. His eyes were averted from the context, lost in infinity, and I believe a fleeting, deceptive thought of compassion scampered inside that black helmet. A brief inner reflection puzzled Jerry, who did not know what designs were in store for him next, and wondered to himself what kind of devious plan his guardian angel had laid out for him.

He was suddenly strengthened by an injection of courage as he realized that he was not alone, that it was all true. He could sense that someone or something from another world had deliberately helped him, had announced it to him and they were carrying it out together. And he felt protected by the uncorrupted and unshakable sense of good.

The robber maintained the discipline and order of military training. Jerry was looking for the right moment. It seemed that he would not arrive, that he would leave with the loot in the presence of a policeman. Like a flash, he imagined himself explaining why he pretended to be handicapped and did nothing to prevent the robbery. An unpleasant burning ran through his stomach for a second, and then he turned his gaze back to the situation at hand and concentrated again, pushing the thought away.

Paradoxically, the opportunity came in the most unexpected way. The robber walked among the customers without taking his eyes off the employees; he was watching to make sure that none of them would think of anything foolish and set off the bank's alarm. What the robber did not know was that the button could be reached with the foot from the counter and the same employee who was the object of his mockery, just out of thirst for righteous revenge and tired of putting up with such comments since she was a child, had pressed the silent alarm several times.

Had he not received such a humiliation, she would have waited for him to leave and would not have taken unnecessary risks, because after all, it was not her money. But neither Jerry nor the robber knew that detail.

Had Jerry been on duty, he would have flown like lightning to the bank, because his experience would have dictated that in all likelihood it would be a real alarm taking advantage of police relief and closing time for customers. But that day he had taken the day off, as he had been told, to be there like that, and instead another veteran police officer, about to retire, affectionately nicknamed the Commander, was cursing his luck at having to buckle his boots again and go to a false alarm.

Then, in one of those trips between bodies lying on the floor, the robber returned his defiant gaze on Jerry, he watched him for about three seconds, chewing gum. The barrel of his rifle was pointed at Jerry's chest, and then he thought it was time, because if an accidental shot occurred, only he would be affected. He lifted his chin from its theatrical crestfallen pose and uncovered himself from the blanket. Jerry was not stupid and knew that, if he fired his Taser first, the robber would fail to get his finger into the trigger guard and pull the trigger.

He shot at the legs, and the eyes behind the half-open visor stared at him, unblinking, flooded with disbelief, surprise and incomprehension. It took a few seconds for him to fall plummeting to the ground in unsettling spasms. Jerry hurried to identify himself as a policeman among all those present and to demand that none of them go out into the street because there was an accomplice, while he picked up the rifle and quickly frisked him.

He found a machete on his right ankle and threw it behind the wheelchair while insisting that no one leave the facility and that they remain calm. Jerry dragged the body to an ornate cylindrical column in the middle of the open space. The man was large and the panicked state of everyone present prevented them from offering assistance.

Jerry managed to drag him to the column, sit him down and place the handcuffs on his back, binding him to the fixture. He took a breath and looked out onto the street where the driver-accomplice was shaking his head impatiently, maybe he could that something was not quite right. Jerry had the impression that the wait was taking forever. He had to act quickly, or he ran the risk that the driver would finally enter the bank and the inevitable armed confrontation would ensue.

"Think, think, think, think," he said to himself, and cursed that they could have given him more information. He corrected the course of his thoughts and again focused on finding the solution. His wayward thoughts prevented him from listening to the voice of his guardian, which in his mind would spring up again as a brilliant, crazy idea.

But it could work.

Chapter 40
The Message

City of Raymond, Washington, 1996

He removed the robber's helmet. His gaze was lost, and from the corner of his right lip a transparent trickle of saliva was dripping down. The Taser had had the same effect on him as *electric shocks* in psychiatric movies. Jerry put on his helmet, picked up his rifle, and when he reached the counter, he asked the overweight clerk for the black money bag.

She handed it to him with a mixture of fear and resentment. Jerry took it diligently, but then he paused for a moment and turned to the clerk, raised his visor and fixed her with his gaze. In his line of work he had had to deal with hatred many times, and that was something he didn't handle well at all. The woman was confused by the galloping acidity of her rage.

"I'm here to protect you, I'm a cop. This is just a strategy. Don't forget that."

With one stroke he pulled down his visor. Jerry shouldered the bag and paused before heading out the door, checked the rifle, the remaining ammunition and set the selector to burst fire. Just in case, he left the clasp on the holster of his pistol unbuckled, caught his breath, constricted by the bulletproof vest, and walked to the car outside.

The sun's rays illuminated the day with a summer glow that created the false illusion that the street was longer. The driver was doing nothing but waving his hand for Jerry to increase the pace; he only focused his attention on the money bag, the rifle and the black helmet, and did not notice that the rest of his sidekick's clothing had changed, and that Jerry had been aiming at him without blinking since he had walked through the door.

The policeman's brain processed all the information like a well-oiled computer. Years and years of mental training and patrolling had turned the officer into a virtuoso analyst of danger. In an instant he jammed the butt of a gun in the knees of the agitated driver, who was insisting that he hurry with one hand on the steering wheel and the other waving it in the air, propelling his repetitive words.

Then the robber stopped his hand and stared at the strange, demeanor of the person in front of him as if he had had a sudden revelation. That kind of behavior was very familiar to me from past experiences. He had been tipped off and the guardian corroborated it with a statement I would have heard from two miles away, "He knows!"

That was it, the reddish ones had warned him of the ambush. But curiously I could not see them, because that vision was the precognition of the guardian. Jerry fired a long burst of shells into the front tire on the passenger side. The tire exploded, bringing that side of the car down more than an inch, but before the tire hit the ground the rifle was already aimed at the capped head inside the vehicle. Jerry paced in front of the Jeep while keeping his sights on his target, crossing his feet in such smooth side-steps that the barrel didn't move off target one iota.

"Raymond Police! Get out of the vehicle without opening the door!"

The window was fully rolled down, and the driver did not obey, but neither did he make any sudden movements, just staring into Jerry's eyes, which in the sun were perfectly distinguishable behind the darkened screen of the helmet.

"Get out of the window with your hands in front of you! I'm not going to tell you again!"

But the driver, whose long, unkempt hair stuck out over the brim of his cap, kept staring at him, pursing his lips half-covered by a thick carpet of beard, and would not obey. Jerry was running out of ideas. A hurricane of thoughts tormented his mind, which was torn between the duty to protect the life of every person and the conflict of safeguarding his own.

It was a clash of philosophies and, as a former military man, the robber had the advantage, because the military is trained to neutralize the enemy without hesitation, but the policeman must always calculate and select the lesser evil, even if it puts his own existence at serious risk.

The problem was, even though the car had a burst wheel it could still be driven so the driver, released the brake and the car began to move smoothly forward. The two held each other's gaze.

"Stop!"

It was the last command I heard him give before the guardian decided enough was enough, and the vision faded away as a dream fade into memory. Then the dark, anthropomorphic, haunting shadow that glowed blackness behind the glow of the streetlight waved goodbye, allowing the light of the streetlight to pass through, leaving with a final phrase floating into the night, something only I could hear, "There is nothing written.""

I had no time to protest or beg. He left as they usually do. They know what they are doing, or so I wanted to think.

"To what extent is life directed by destiny?" I asked myself. The truth is that I still don't have the answer. And another worrying concern was the guardian's demand that Jerry wear a bulletproof vest.

"What else did he say?" asked Jerry with innocent bad manners.

"You know everything you need to know. He's gone. That's all."

In the hustle and bustle of talking with the guardian, I had forgotten about Saya, but a movement glimpsed out of the corner of my eye reminded me. I walked to the back of the car and saw her snorting in annoyance, pulling her hair back in an awkward effort to spruce up her image. She was trying to beat the sleepiness. She was struggling to be strong, to be in control of herself. I opened the car door and we looked at each other in a wordless conversation that lasted several seconds.

"I'm fine. I know you don't want to ask me, but you want to know. I'm fine" She shifted uncomfortably in her seat. "They can come back at any time. I have to get away from here."

"I'll stay with you until you're far away." Her expression was beyond fear, she held all the tension in her shoulders and the fear of further betrayal was clear. "I will protect you until you are safe. I know you feel vulnerable and fragile. I know you are doubtful about the course you've taken. Personally, I think you have a chance now, and it's entirely up to you."

She brushed her unruly hair back from her face with the air of someone who has lost the thread of a conversation and is silent out of embarrassment.

"I know you don't want to ask me, but you want to know." And for the first time she gave a brief smile. "You have the opportunity to have a guardian. One of them has taken an interest in taking care of you; that means that if you help others and don't stray, you will quickly lose that fragile impression you have of yourself. You will become really strong and unshakable, and you will be afraid, of course, anything else would be foolhardy; but you will never be alone, even if you feel the darkest and most penetrating loneliness."

Jerry approached the driver's door, taking a quick glance at Saya.

"Is she like you?"-he asked me without thinking too much.

"Not exactly. She is very special. Her knowledge and intelligence can be overwhelming in this world. She is someone brave."

Jerry's face made it clear that he didn't understand and Saya's eyes moistened and a single a tear ran down the contour of her cheek.

"I'll drop you off at the bus station. It's open twenty-four hours a day and buses go everywhere. With what I've given you, you won't have much time, I admit."

His words seemed distracted by reviewing the hurried notes he had collected. He closed the notebook, slipped it into the inside pocket of his jacket and took care to zip it up.

"Thank you for everything, Jerry."

He was driving slowly, and the fog, far from dissipating, had become thicker. We must not have been far from the station, because we passed a huge bus with a sign that read Seattle. At the time, I was unaware that this fog would be responsible for an urgent call for Jerry.

"To all units. We have a 2-35, at the intersection of..."

Jerry turned on the rotating lights, and the whole street lit up red and blue. We were going at full speed, but the car didn't whine and the wheels didn't squeal. In fact, it seemed to me that before the call all the elements were crackling together, but now it was in its element, as if it had been created for precisely this moment.

In more than one curve I thought we would turn but Jerry was calm, more than used to driving at speed. With a smile to myself, I understood why that night of escape, so distant and so close in time, I could not detach myself from the Police.

"There has just been a traffic accident, and it seems that there are serious injuries." His voice sounded dry and shaky. It will serve as an excuse for having abandoned my post at the hospital.

Take the first bus, no one will ever look for you again. I'll help you with that.

His face was sorrowful but I could see that while his body was next to me, but his mind was already at the scene of the accident. I could feel his discomfort. His worry about arriving and his deep desire for it to be less than advertised.

A quick conclusion struck me. That cop and I were not so different, except for one thing. Jerry was very clear about his purpose, his raison d'être, his job was not his identity, nothing like that. It was a means to an end. However, I had been diving in quicksand for a long time and I was running out of air.

"Leave us right here, I can see the station. Go help those people. Remember, if it's serious they'll be there."

"There? Who?"

He stopped the vehicle and turned the steering wheel to make a quick U-turn.

"The guardians. They will guide you. You only have to silence your inner noise."

I quickly got out of the car and helped Saya too. Jerry rolled down his window as Saya leaned into me. I hugged her against me. Blue and red flashes filled the deserted streets. We began to walk slowly together.

I have always hated goodbyes. I can't stand them. I had nothing more to say to him and he had simply, I think, run out of words. Now we were even. My intuition told me something was up with Jerry, and context forced me to be fair to a good man, and in the end it turned out that his life was in serious danger.

The lights continued to swirl, adorning the dull, opaque fog. I didn't want to look back, but the purr of the patrol car's engine remained idling. Jerry had been blocked, watching me walk between lights and shadows. I stopped with Saya in the middle of the street, and an unexpected outburst of pain came from deep inside me,

"Do your duty!" I shouted at the top of my lungs as I stared at the distant bus station sign.

I don't know if I said it to him or if I was saying it to myself. Saya looked at me with a look of shock. She had begun to understand more, now, than she had in her entire life. That monster inside me slowly crept back into the recesses of my heart. I heard the rolling on the asphalt and the roar of the engine roaring away at full throttle.

Suddenly, the street seemed more inhospitable and depressing. A few lights illuminated the dark silhouettes of homes. I could see curtains twitch as people came in search of the voices that had disturbed their rest. They soon lost interest. They must have thought it was a drunken couple and soon they went back to their warm and comfortable beds.

Saya had more mental strength than physical strength, and it was that energy that drove her with every step she took. The station was completely empty, and in the air, there was that characteristic smell of gasoline and tires. The docks gave way to an asphalt buckled by the comings and goings of the coaches.

We took a brief rest in the green and rusty seats of the station. A chewing gum vending machine ironically reminded us of our state of need. Something sweet in our mouths would have calmed us down from all the anguish we had experienced.

The machine had been strategically placed in front to awaken the primitive desire for sugar. Saya tilted her head back and her long blonde hair shyly swept the floor with every move. We left a space between us. I remember the dull sounds of the night, it was something like an electric buzzing sound far and near at the same time, looking at the sky was starting to scare me.

A stray cat wandered oblivious to our presence, searching for who knows what, and time continued to pass slowly, and the cold was gripping the flesh of my arms. Saya was breathing noisily, her tongue clicking against the roof of her mouth. She was having a hard time. I was not happy about it, but surely the renewed imprint of humility and human empathy would remain in her memory.

A distant noise made me sit up alertly. We had been sitting there for more than thirty minutes and that noise seemed musical to me. Soon after, a huge silver coach was pulling into the station. It bore Greyhound lettering under a stiff greyhound in full race, and the colors of the American flag ran in endless lines all around the bus. The interior lights came on and a giant puffing sound signaled that the bus had stopped. On the front of the bus a sign read Portland, and as the doors opened, a gale of newly risen people sighed with joyful bells for having arrived at their destination.

I looked at Saya, terrified by the damp cold. She seemed to be waiting for my command. I stood up quickly and held out my hand to Saya, who looked at it for a moment in silent inner reflection on human kindness and solidarity. She took it with renewed strength, interlocking our thumbs as two old friends would.

As soon as I got in, behind Saya, I felt the pleasant warmth of the cabin. I pulled out the crumpled bills Jerry gave us and paid for our ride. I figured that we could still, hopefully, have a proper breakfast when we made a stop. Saya insisted that I sit by the window. I protectively refused, but she politely insisted. Finally, I gave in without further ado.

The coach approached the exit and as we started to drive, the lights went out, leaving over our heads a row of enveloping, dim green lights.

Before long, the bus was moving away from the city and into the darkness of the road. Hundreds of trees were passing me like a flock of sheep jumping a fence. Saya had curled into an acrobatic curl, her legs folded over the seat and her head resting on the armrest facing the aisle. The sound of the engine, the heating, the snoring of passengers, the trees and the immense accumulated fatigue weighed on me. I looked at the sky to prove to myself that nothing would ever scare me again, and a beautiful and hypnotic celestial vault fought to regain its prominence among the scattered mists.

In less than what seemed like an instant, I opened my eyes with difficulty. I didn't want to wake up, just to change my position, but then I was startled, as if in a split second I had recovered all my memory and until that previous moment I didn't even know who I was or where I was. The sun was shining brightly, and I cursed furiously for not having been alert, for falling asleep like a dormouse but the worst was not that.

I turned my head to look for Saya and instead an overweight woman was crocheting next to me. I had no choice but to put my hands to my head and pull my hair, already too long, back. I jumped up like a spring, sleepy and panicked, so fast that I hit the overhead luggage rack, rummaging through the crowd with blurred vision.

"Please, madam, let me pass." My desperate tone did not have the desired effect and the lady gathered all her paraphernalia far too slowly.

Finally, I made my way down the aisle hurriedly checking each and every seat. Saya was not there. I sat defeated in the last row, under the gaze of the other travelers.

I put my hands to my head again, unable to understand how I had fallen so deeply asleep. I took a deep breath to calm myself. It had definitely been a rude awakening. Another one of many. I rested my hands on my knees and a huge tattoo covered the entire inside of my right forearm. I couldn't get over my astonishment. I looked to both sides, in an already internalized ritual of paranoid security, and read the words written in pen on my skin: "Thank you for everything. I am indebted to you. Hide well or prepare for war. They will come for you. You are too valuable to them. Whatever you decide, I will wait for you under the Statue of Liberty, at the exact time of the winter solstice. You will need my help.

I laughed out loud, confirming the worst omens of even the most skittish travelers. The message was disturbing, but I basically cared little at the time. My entire being was focused on figuring out how it had been possible for it to write that on my arm and leave without my knowing anything. "They must have abducted me," occurred to me. And that absurd thought was what made me laugh. But soon the smile faded, and I regained my cool countenance.

Hide well or prepare for war.

Neither of these options were in my plans. Neither of them.

Chapter 41
Chambres

Portland, Oregon, November 1996

I could see that the bus was crossing a wide, fast-flowing river. We had been driving through the city for some time, but as we crossed the bridge, the travelers began to stir in their seats, regrouping their belongings, impatient to arrive. I, on the other hand, was in no hurry. No one was waiting for me there, and I had nowhere to go and no belongings to stow.

The bus station displayed a huge blue and gray sign with the same skinny dog stretched out. As in so many other cities, the station was flooded with people from all walks of life, from homeless and drug addicts fighting a silent turf war to elegant, faux-executive-looking men and women. A patrol of policemen probed with sharp hunting eyes at all the travelers, searching. I passed them and said good morning without stopping. I received from them an indescribable hoarse, improvised sound that sounded like a throat clearing.

I started to walk, breathing the unmistakable smell of the river in the air. As I walked, I took out all the money I had in my pocket, not even ten dollars, and then I told myself that no matter how little it was, it was much more than what Saya had. A little worry came over me for her, though I quickly dismissed my fears; she would manage just fine. Distracted in my thoughts, a gruff voice that seemed to speak to me brought me back to the reality I had put on the back burner.

"Hey, you want to earn a few bucks for your little collection?" shouted the driver of a light box truck, the kind that closes with a shutter.

"Are you talking to me?" I asked, surprised, although there was no one else there.

"Of course, who else?" he clarified in a singsong tone.

"What do you need?" -asked the survivor in me.

"Nine wooden boxes, about a hundred kilos. We have to put them in the basement of that art gallery. If you give me a hand, I'll give you fifty bucks."

I looked at him carefully for a few seconds, observing him.

"If you add a hamburger and a soft drink to your offer, we have a deal."

And I looked over to a fast-food establishment right there. In a couple of hours we finished the job. I helped him pick up the truck, and then he paid me, gave me sixty dollars, and told me that he was in a hurry, that that would be enough for the hamburger and soda.

I had a good meal. I was so hungry that I ordered two very big hamburgers, with fries and a giant drink. And then I sat there, watching the people. There was everything: families with naughty children, young people, some uniformed workers, a couple of people in suits, and then, in the reflection of the glass bulkhead, next to me, was me, an ordinary boy, expressionless and lonely, with strange, badly healed wounds, clean T-shirt and disheveled hair.

I walked through the streets aimlessly, and soon night began to fall. I didn't know the city, but a sign from another era caught my attention. It was blue with white letters, small and discreet, but well lit; it said Chambres. It was installed on a narrow dark red brick building.

I rang hard on the worn metal button attached to a black grille, and the door opened with a magnetic, intermittent sound. A smiling woman was sheltering behind a well-worn hardwood counter. She looked at me undisguised, though her friendliness did not diminish in the slightest.

After being presented with several options, I finally decided, as it could not be otherwise, I had to go for the cheapest: a private room with a small bed and shared bathroom. Twenty dollars was the price per night. When she gave me the key and I went into the room, everything seemed immaculate, exaggeratedly clean and spotless, unbecoming of an austere hostel. I took such a long, hot shower that I'm sure the twenty dollars was spent on that alone. My body was expelling all the accumulated dirt, and the fresh wounds stung when I rubbed them with soap.

I climbed into bed, which smelled of perfumed fabric softener, my stomach still full. I had forgotten the pleasurable sensation of being clean and clean, and during that time, before I fell asleep, I felt tremendously lucky.

"Thank you, thank you, thank you," I repeated, stammering, to who knows who.

I woke up as a new person. Suddenly, I felt lighter and stronger. Rested. In the morning, as I left the hostel, the same nice and friendly woman said good morning to me. I asked her for a good place to have breakfast and she pointed it out to me without stopping smiling for a moment. I could tell she enjoyed her work, even though to anyone's eye it could appear dull. I tried to smile back, but I think I got a strange, forced grimace.

Too much recent seriousness in my life had deactivated those muscles.

That pungent and exquisite smell of coffee awakened my senses; I ordered a strong latte and some pancakes with cream and syrup, the perfect mix of flavor. They brought me my change and those coins triggered a sudden thought. At the back of the window, a black pay phone bounded by two wooden dividers kept catching my attention.

Sitting there, without taking my eyes off the phone, I must have looked like a disturbed person. I kept thinking about it, I had to make that call. I needed to know how my parents were, Kingsley, my aunt and uncle, Father Damián; but I also felt the irrepressible need to call the boarding school and talk to Claudia and Paloma.

They took my plate away and I was still sitting there, thinking about what the right thing to do was. I pondered the pros and cons, and how that call might affect my own safety and that of my loved ones. I was scared, and although the letters painted on my forearm had already faded in the shower, Saya's phrase echoed in my head even louder. I had seen in the movies that if you didn't stay on the line for more than twenty seconds, no one could trace the call.

I plucked up my courage, took the coins and approached the phone. I dialed 34 for Spain and when it gave the signal, I dialed my home number. My mother picked it up. Her voice was muffled when she picked it up.

"Mom, it's me. How are you?" I asked naturally, still counting the seconds in my head.

Then a hurricane of words, disjointed and disjointed, mingled in the earpiece, all tinged with surprise, joy, disbelief and hysteria.

"Son, are you alright? What's happened to you? Is it really you? Thank God! I must tell your father."

"Mom, Mom. Mom, listen to me, please, I have to hang up in a few seconds." Silence fell behind the black plastic, only interrupted by the alternating crackle of the line crossing the ocean. "Don't worry about me, I'll be fine, I know it's not much, you'll have lots of questions, but I can't tell you anything else. A big kiss to all of you. I will call again. I love you all."

"Wait! Son, wait! Don't hang up!"

I pulled the receiver away from my ear with so much pain that I almost burst into tears between strangers and breakfasts. I could still hear my mother's voice, disconsolate, imploring me to extend the conversation a little longer, but I had to hang up. I had no choice. It was dangerous.

I headed back to my table. Those few meters were long. I struggled to walk, shuffling along, overwhelmed by my mother's discomfort. I plopped down on the black leather padded seat deflating gently behind my back.

"Another coffee, right?" asked the waitress with a certain obligatory glare.

I was stunned by the brief conversation and answered without even thinking about it.

"Yes, of course. Well loaded, like the one from before. Thank you very much."

She pulled out the glass coffee pot and refilled my cup. Then she poured a thin trickle of milk and went to another table. I stared at the strange arabesques the milk formed on the tinted coffee, more intent on focusing my thoughts on something else. I needed to avoid the swirl of emotions that was stirring inside me.

I hated to be the cause of any kind of pain. Still, there was nothing more I could do. If one day I were to wake up and tell a single fragment of my story, I have no doubt that someone would listen carefully, probably a psychiatrist, and seek my comfort by forcibly offering me a fully padded room and a straitjacket. In the meantime, I was unable to focus my attention too much, just staring at the curious figures formed by that mixture of milk over coffee.

I came to my senses and sort of patted myself on the back. I have never been one to worry; either you do it or you don't, and in either case the error may be present. Then I concluded that it is better to make a mistake by making decisions than to get it right, remotely, by purely random omission.

I took a long sip of coffee; it was just right, piping hot, but not burning. I savored its full flavor without taking my mind off my long-suffering, struggling, brave mother. I knew that when she calmed down, she would trust me. She would know that I must have good reasons for acting that way, however mysterious and paranoid they might sound.

I stood with my head against the glass, looking out of the giant window of the cafeteria at the incessant movement of people going to and from, all looking so busy. Urgency gripped them all and seemed to grant them no respite.

I looked at the ticket; the coffee cost eighty cents and, although saving had become imperative, I left a dollar twenty on the saucer. I took the last sip of that great coffee and as I put down the empty cup, I looked at the grounds stuck to the porcelain.

A sudden doubt came over me as I wondered whether, as I had heard so many times, their random arrangement would have any future significance. Of course, I was incapable of interpreting them, but the idea did not seem so ridiculous after all. I looked at them for a while, placed the cup gently on the table and stood up.

I walked the narrow aisle between the tables and the bar, dodging open newspapers and the fuss of effusive conversationalists who preferred not to take a seat, or were thirsty for the limelight. A rounded counter full of pastries invited customers to take something before leaving. Then behind me a very earthy sound chilled my blood. Ring! One, two, three. One, two, three. Ring!

Even when it was silenced, it seemed to keep bouncing back and forth between the glass and the walls.

My muscles tensed involuntarily; suddenly, the sleeve of my T-shirt was too tight on my arms and across my back. The waitress dropped the tray she had been carrying, demonstrating to me the unusualness of that call.

A waiter, who moments before seemed hyperactive, paused to look at his companion. The latter picked up the phone with a disjointed slowness. Only the three of us were intrigued by the call, the rest of the customers went about their business.

I read the lips of the waitress.

"Tell me?"

And I saw how her face took on a more ambiguous and indescribable countenance with each message, which in turn was accompanied by a sudden change in pallor. I made my way back through the crowd.

"How do I know it's not a joke? How do you know my name? Okay, yes. I think he's here. Just a moment."

The waitress looked for me in the crowd and when our gazes met, she stretched out her arm, tightening the firm and thick steel cord, pointing at me without blinking.

The waiter turned to look at me, intrigued, not having noticed my presence until that moment.

"I think it's for you and it seems serious."

Her hand was still outstretched offering me the handset while I watched with my mind collapsing with all kinds of hypotheses, discarding variables and closing off possibilities. It was black and white. If I had to fight again, I would fight tirelessly, but I cursed not being able to have a moment of rest.

I finally decided to pick it up after a few seconds, and in doing so I covered the microphone with my hand.

"Who is it?" I asked her harshly.

"I don't know. This is all very strange."

And she looked at the waiter with the eyes of a slaughtered lamb, in a kind of discreet distress alert.

"Male or female? Please answer. It is important."

The bartender was walking to the end of the bar quickly to get to us, and the waitress wasn't answering. Something very striking had been said to her on the other end of the line because she was puzzled. And inside I was growing fearful for my family's welfare, and I wondered if it had been worth calling my mother.

I couldn't risk turning my back on whoever was calling, it was purely a matter of security. What was certain was that somehow, they had intercepted the call. And if they knew where I was, then they could also know the whereabouts of my family. My teeth chattered as I completed the logical reasoning, while the waiter was already three steps away from me.

"Ask your colleague to calm down and take her away."

"Relax, I think the police are looking for you and they must be watching us, because they have read my ID badge."

The waiter, as conspicuously tall as he was scrawny, loomed over his companion with the Hollywood manner of a third-rate mobster, biting his lower lip and sticking out his tongue from time to time. Fortunately, he backed off, restrained by her. Wise decision.

I took the phone, while I concocted an escape plan from the cafeteria, which at that moment had been transformed into a mousetrap.

"Good. You have my undivided attention but watch your words before you incur a debt to me."

At that moment, I understood that I would be capable of anything if someone threatened my family.

"David, is that you?" The voice sounded feminine, old.

My body and mind had gone into fight mode, and it took me a few seconds to frame that voice.

"Paloma, is that you?" I asked, amazed and astonished at my luck.

"Of course, David. Don't worry, it's us. We finally found you."

"But how?" Stupid doubts assailed me, the result of the sudden stress release.

"The same way I found you in the Retiro Park. After calling your mother and, by the way, leaving her like a bundle of nerves, she contacted me and, in her phone, there was still some remnant, your peculiar imprint. I managed to visualize the place where you were. Don't think it was the first time, though." And a sincere laugh was heard with full tranquility, the one that people of a certain age know how to transmit. "It took calls to four coffee shops in Portland that matched the profile I had managed to see, and, of course, the hard and fast work of some efficient analysts whom I must congratulate. So our partnership is one big family, although that's the least of it now. Tell me, are you all right, did they hurt you?"

"Some wounds and bruises. Nothing major."

Although having tightened my whole body, the skin stretched and some of it had returned to ooze blood.

"This is the first time this has ever happened to us with a student and certainly never at such an early stage. We have a lot to talk about. Secrets to share. But first things first." Suddenly, her voice was a little far away from the microphone, confirming something with someone next to her I imagined. "Okay, David, the cavalry is heading that way. You'll see a lot of police cars coming in. Our contact in Portland knows what to do, but for all intents and purposes and in the view of the rest of the officers, from this moment on you are a protected witness to be guarded with top priority. He will arrange to have you taken to a secure location."

"I don't know if I want to. I... I wasn't looking for any of this!"

There was a heavy pause.

"No one can force you to do anything. Your life belongs to you, but at least let me see you, check that you are well and make sure that no tracker has been placed on, or in, you."

I was embarrassed to hear Paloma pleading. She had certainly never restricted my freedom, quite the contrary, and, above all, she had always been a true angel to all of us. I owed it to her.

"All right, we can see each other. But I warn you, I'm not going to talk to anyone." My tone sounded more authoritative than I would have liked, but that's the thing about emotions, they make everything real.

Then I noticed that there was not a single vehicle on the street, in either direction, and no one was walking on the sidewalks except for a man in a gray suit and blue tie who, with his long strides, was hurrying past the glass window, flanked by four police officers. Two of the officers stood in the doorway; the undercover policeman must have said something to them, because both drew their guns and held them discreetly, crossing their hands over their bellies. Others appeared on the sidewalk in front of them with long guns, pointing to the ground as they walked.

The man in the suit opened his jacket as if it were a curtain, hooking it behind his gun holster and revealing a golden badge hanging on his belt. Slim, moderately tall, with angular features and gray hair, he entered, put his hands in his pants pockets and studied the customers.

"I think your man just made his entrance. Elvis is in the building." And I snorted into the microphone, "What a media blitz."

"He will do everything in his power to ensure your safety. We have asked him to do so, even if it seems exaggerated to you. He thinks that all of us who have something different must keep up appearances. Life is often a theater, and we must behave as we are expected to behave."

"There he is! There! The boy you're looking for!" shouted the waiter.

"Go with him, do what he tells you and in a few hours we can meet." Paloma begged, worried that I would change his mind.

"What a show you've put on. I'm sorry, Paloma, but all this must change. These things are the real danger."

Everyone was staring. The uniformed policemen made an attempt to walk towards me but were gently stopped by the man in the blue suit and tie.

"It is possible, but our enemies never act in public. They do not risk being seen by crowds, let alone having their existence confirmed by a huge team of police officers whose testimony is so difficult to placate. This secret is only for a few."

"We'll discuss it. Ugly Harry is waiting for me, I have to go."

And unexpected laughter from Paloma and someone else rang through the tiny speaker phone.

I walked the distance to the exit. Less than three feet separated me from the agents and Harry, as I had nicknamed him. I stopped to look at the assortment in the warped glass display case.

"If you'd be so kind, let me have a tray of cakes; the rich kind, eh, not the kind that nobody eats," I blurted out.

The waiter looked at the agent for approval. He nodded his head a couple of times in agreement.

I kept watching the ones she picked up and made sure she didn't throw in any of those boring gritty or almond-covered cakes, aware of the prevailing silence and all eyes on me. She wrapped them and topped them off with a beautiful red bow, which contrasted visually with the white wrapper.

"How much is it, please"? I asked as I picked up the box from the counter.

"Nothing. It's on the house," she replied, anxious for me to get out of there, and with me the whole strange and surreal situation.

"I insist. I must pay. Otherwise it doesn't seem right to me."

I heard the air rush out of Harry's nose.

"Really, there's no need," he said with a terrifying, almost lunatic smile.

"I can't refuse a gift; it's a saying from my country, so cover me or we'll be here forever."

One of the uniformed agents clicked his tongue and snorted, impatiently.

"Well, that's thirty-two dollars, sir."

My eyes became like saucers, and as I gulped. I think my throat swelled up as if I had swallowed a boiled egg without chewing. My God, how could twelve cakes be so expensive? And, worst of all, I wasn't sure, but I don't think I was getting my money's worth. Well, send back a couple of cupcakes, I thought, but, of course, it was all wrapped up and people kept staring at me. The colors invaded my face.

Whispering, thinking out loud, I rummaged through my pockets for money, to the astonished gaze of Harry and his policemen.

"But how much does each cupcake cost? Holy cow!" I asked the nearest agent, who put his hand to his eyes, trying to remain serious. I think it had happened to him too.

It took me a while to get it together, but eventually the miracle happened. Thirty-two dollars and a few cents was all I had left of the money I had collected. I paid, took the cakes and walked over to Harry.

"We must hurry. We could be in danger." He said it quietly, but not so quietly that the policemen could not hear him.

"I've been like that all my life," I said, raising my eyebrows.

And with that the policeman, who had been holding back his laughter for a while, could hold it in no longer. He felt sorry to hear the truth that resounded in the background of my words.

"Well, boy, come on, let's get out of here," said Harry circumspectly.

"Whenever you want. But we must make a stop at my hotel, it's very close. That's all, I promise." Harry looked at the ceiling, searching for a lost virtue. "You see, I've learned to live with this. Don't think it's a whim. I'm not unaware of the threats, I'm well aware of them, but that's not going to stop me from fulfilling my desires, small or large." I breathed, staring at him. The fact that you and I are in this place talking is simply because I wish it.

Harry averted his gaze to my arms, observing with discreet brazenness the etched scars running across my skin, and the fresh blood from some poorly healed wound.

The uniformed officers came out and made a gesture. A retinue of vehicles positioned themselves in front of the cafeteria entrance. Motorcycles, a vehicle with police signs and another camouflaged with a red lollipop on the roof, and behind it, another identical formation of police vehicles.

"To the gray car," Harry said to me.

"The hostel I'm going to is the one over there, the one with the blue and white sign that says Chambres."

"Understood. Did you receive, comrade? Tell everyone. We are going to make a technical stop."

"Copy that, boss. At your orders," said the driver, who was dressed in civilian clothes, although he looked more like a policeman than the rest with his aviator glasses and that moustache that looked like a sticker.

The whole lot of them stopped in front of the hostel and Harry signaled me to wait.

"Now. You can go now," he said after receiving the *all clear* from one of the uniformed men who had entered as a group.

I got out of the car with the cakes and entered what the night before had been my palatial refuge. Small, shabby and austere, but comfortable, clean and well looked after. As I entered, there was the same charming and pleasant woman, looking worried about the police presence.

"Apologies for all the fuss. I bring you this gift. I must continue my journey and I did not want to say goodbye without thanking you for your kindness. I hope to see you soon."

And I left the wrapped cakes on the tiny oak counter, under the gaze of four armed agents.

The woman was puzzled by the strange situation. She was probably asking herself many questions, all of them unanswerable. But what would be clear to her is that one of her clients, like so many others I suppose, wanted to thank her with a detail for the "five star" service, recognizing that, although it may seem a modest job, kindness and enthusiasm in what one does changes everything.

I went out again, back into the bustle and incessant roar of human activity. Harry waited, standing by the car, and I stared at a huge building in front of me, playing with my imagination to take it apart, drawing in my mind its internal layout, its foundations and structure.

I looked again at Harry, who was restlessly making an arduous exercise of self-control so as not to rush me or offend me in any way, but at the same time wished to conclude the unforeseen and urgent mission that had been entrusted to him from New York.

We jumped in the car and sped off.

The sirens sounded shrill, in a continuous loop of alarm. Harry leaned a little to say something to me, but for a moment he thought better of it and returned to his seat position. But then he changed his mind again and leaned in next to me, loudly raising his voice to be audible over the noise.

"I know you're one of us and I don't want to ask questions. I guess, like everyone else, more or less, you'll have a talent. And yes, I know the threat that haunts you, though I've never seen them in person, or so I think. Can you tell me anything about them? Anything firsthand? You I am unable to penetrate."

I thought about it for a few seconds, trying to measure the words. Looking for the appropriate ones so as not to sound worrisome, always thinking to inform, but not to frighten. But what the hell, we were two grown men belonging to a secret society that used government means paid by the taxpayer to escape and fight our enemy.

"Unable to penetrate? What did you mean?" I asked him without paying too much attention to his questions.

"I am an interrogation specialist. Violent Crimes Unit of the Criminal Police. My talent is telepathy. Officially, I work with murderers, rapists, etc., and I'm very good at it. Unofficially, I interrogate "contactees", but those who survive are so deranged that I'm not able to extract much. You seem to be fine, and you are one of us, which simplifies things a lot, but even so, I am only able to perceive a single thought, something very strong. A woman occupies everything in you, am I wrong?!"

I looked at him, my jaw tight.

"Where did you come from?" He looked at me with such surprise and anguish that his gaze seemed, all of a sudden, deeply tired and aged. "I won't do that again. Sometimes I forget how delicate and intrusive my talent can be; I apologize."

And he leaned back on the seat, placing his fingers between his eyebrows, as if too exhausted by something he had sensed in me.

"They do not distinguish between good and evil. That doesn't exist for them. We're just a means to an end," I said, looking at the layout.

"They feed on our death. What does that mean?" he asked without hiding his intrigue.

"Look, my friend, I didn't even know of the existence of these beings; I was studying in a residence for promising young people, oblivious to all this sly battle. Confused and deceived, I have been persecuted and I have lost everything because of these "secrets", and when you have no one left to share anything with, you feel as if death has come to you in the middle of your life."

"You haven't answered my question and we're almost there." He wiggled his fingers and fiddled with his knees.

"You have already it, my friend. They feed on our death, because they have been dead for centuries."

He stroked his chin meditatively, his expression infinite and at the same time satisfied with what he had heard. I didn't lie to him, but I didn't tell him the whole truth either. It was obvious that at my side I had a good man, what shall I say, more than that, but I also felt the weight of his profession and the normative addition of our secret society. Of course, although in a different way, he and I were alike; we both prevented evil from multiplying and victimizing innocent people.

Too many enemies for lone warriors.

Within minutes, we had arrived on the tarmac at Portland Airport. A small, white, unmarked private plane awaited with the stairway unfolded and two flight attendants on either side of it.

"Good. This is where we part ways. Maybe one day we'll meet again, who knows. If not, good luck finding whatever it is you're looking for."

We shook hands and I boarded the plane, which exuded luxury and comfort. Two men in classic uniforms, with piped shoulder pads, welcomed me inside and introduced themselves as the people in charge.

"We will leave immediately. Some runways at the airport have been paralyzed because of our flight plan."

"Whatever you say. What do I do?"

They looked at each other.

"Follow the directions of the flight attendants, they will accommodate you."

Immediately, we shot skyward, making a banked turn at full speed. The lights of the police vehicles were seen as small, distant flashes, and the huge Columbia River became a thick, dark green line cutting across the land.

I looked out of the windows and saw two fighter jets escorting us on either side. I felt embarrassed; I myself had adopted an awkward posture on the enveloping cream leather seat. I refused the drinks offered to me by the stewardesses, who, no doubt, were also charming, but not like the hostess; their smiles were artificial and overdone.

They were papier-mâché smiles.

Chapter 42
Mockery

After a while, the stewardesses went to their cabin, and I was told to touch a button to if I needed them. A hatch closed and I was left there alone, surrounded by padded leather-covered seats, with buttons to listen to different radio stations, a newspaper and some magazines. I got bored of everything right away and missed having conversations of other travelers around me. Maybe I was too used to peasant life, but, without a doubt, and even with all its negative points, I liked the rampant greyhound bus better.

Sometimes, less is more.

The hours seemed like forever; I couldn't fall asleep, and the magazines were insipid. But finally the pilot announced that we were arriving in New York. We descended so fast that it seemed like something was wrong, but the stewardesses were quiet, talking between themselves and didn't seem concerned.

The plane taxied down the runway, turned to one side and continued. As daylight faded, we entered a huge hangar where several SUVs and a luxury sedan were waiting. A group of men were standing monitoring the entrance and there, looking entirely incongruous, was Paloma, an old woman in the middle of the tough guys.

Even from the plane window I could see both joy and grief on her face. The plane finally came to a stop and the stewardesses unfolded the ladder.

I stepped out of the plane and as I descended, Paloma approached cautiously. After our brief conversation it was clear to her that I no longer trusted them at all. They had withheld a lot of information from me, and that put me at a titanic disadvantage. Now I would be the one to keep my mouth shut. I wasn't going to say anything at all.

"Let me give you a kiss, David. Don't be angry with me, please, I beg you. We can explain everything to you."

"Your secrecy is a danger. But I don't think I could ever be angry with you."

I stepped forward and gave her two kisses.

"We all have secrets, David, and all will be revealed, but in due time. The only important thing right now is that you're safe. You've been released."

No one had released me, at least not voluntarily, but I kept my mouth shut.

"We will go to a safe place, and there we will answer all your questions and you will tell us what happened."

"Hold on a moment. If this is your idea of a deal, I'm not interested. I'd rather go on with my life and disappear from yours."

"Don't be defensive, we are all on the same side here. No one is going to force you into anything. We are one, and at the same time you are still free. Let's get in the car, today you will meet some people that will change the way you see things. Really, give yourself a chance, you have nothing to lose."

I was back to square one. The whole purpose of getting into this whole mess, of traveling to the USA, was to find Angie, and at that very moment I was not very happy with the results of my search.

We climbed into the sedan. The men retreated in military order, and some got into the SUVs, but others stood on the running boards, holding on to the roof rails.

We started our drive but immediately that feeling of just knowing something was wrong reared its head. I looked around me frantically. Paloma noticed my concern.

"Stop the car! Stop the car!" I shouted at the top of my lungs.

"Impossible. We must continue. We have orders," said the driver arrogantly.

Then I saw it. A long, powerful shadow appeared in the hangar. There was no doubt which one it was. It was Angie's guardian. There, totally dark next to one of the hangar walls.

"Stop the vehicle now!" But he still didn't listen, "Stop the car!"

I had no choice. Paloma tried to calm me down and at the same time to make the driver see reason, urging him to slow down, but it was all in vain; someone with more authority than her was calling the shots. I yanked the handbrake and kicked my foot through the window when I discovered my door was locked. A thousand tiny shards of glass scattered across the hangar floor, I jumped through, tearing my clothes in the process.

I looked at Paloma for a single moment, with an apology in my eyes, and began to run towards the long shadow that had altered my whole being. I could not let escape. I had to pursue it with all my strength, until my last breath.

Behind me I could hear the unmistakable metallic sound of men manipulating their weapons. I did not know what could happen, but I knew what I had to do. They were chasing behind me now. Someone fired his gun and the detonation sounded, bouncing off the walls again and again, until it finally disappeared.

"Don't move, son, nobody wants to hurt you!" said a condescending male voice.

A muscular man, wearing a black bulletproof vest and a blue T-shirt, was trying to convince me with a smoking gun aimed at me. And I thought about the light. I looked up at the cold light from the huge lamps hanging from the ceiling, which bathed the entire hangar in an annoying white, and then it became clear to me. The guardians had entrusted me with some virtues, and it was time to use them.

It was not even necessary to look at the bulbs; just by thinking it, all the lights dimmed, tinkling, until at last it was absolute blackness, though not for me. Like a nocturnal animal, I could see everything, in a bluish hue, but clear and precise as day. The bewilderment among them became apparent, and Paloma was shouting orders to them to let me go. I guess she thought I was too upset and was suffering from an episode of post-traumatic stress.

No one could imagine what was driving my steps, except that guardian and me. That one in particular.

I ran and ran after his elongated silhouette, between airplanes fastened with chocks, cables and hoses. Far away, lost in the darkness or stopped by Paloma, were the armed men. The shadow came to a halt in front of an emergency exit where it simply walked through the wall, oblivious to the laws of matter.

I pushed the green, horizontal bar of the door, tilting my face as I stepped out the other side, blinded by the orange sunset. The door closed automatically. If I could have, I would have turned off the sun at that moment.

It took me a few seconds to focus again, but I could see him, elongated and erect, with his arms held straight towards the ground, his characteristic color, or, rather, his absence of color, blurred from reality, dark as anything in the world, immobile and imperturbable. Its mere presence was almost unwelcome, and I could feel it was not there to protect me from any danger.

Its attitude was different. Mysterious and disconcerting. It could not escape me, no matter what.

I started running as fast as I could towards him. Something told me it was important. Perhaps this was the important thing, the ultimate clue. I almost fell on my face because of my anxious nervousness. I crossed the entire north wall in a few seconds, and when I had him in front of me, I was too out of breath to even say a word. I watched him fade away, being pierced sideways by the red and gloomy rays of the sun, fading away from reality.

"Hey! Wait, wait! Where are you going? Wait!" I shouted, discouraged but finally able to speak again.

He was leaving without saying anything to me. He had shown up for no apparent reason, for no reason at all. I looked in all directions looking for him. It was useless, I had learned his curious behavior. I knew for sure that he had left, but my resistance to frustration, my human condition, refused to accept it.

I had to brace myself against the rough wall. My hair was falling over my eyes. With my index finger and thumb I held my eyebrows, bouncing my breath on the palm of my hand. I felt dejected, indignant and bewildered all at once.

Then, something brought me out of my lethargy: a young, hesitant, feminine, raspy voice.

"Da-David, is that you?"

That familiar, soft, cracked voice came from some metal cages that housed huge used tires. Immediately, I was gripped by emotion. I was still out of place, and for a moment I didn't understand what she was doing here. I didn't have time to dwell on those thoughts because Claudia ran at full speed towards me. We almost fell when she jumped on top of me hugging me with all her strength, wrapping her legs and arms around me.

"I knew I would find you! -I knew I would find you!" she kept repeating, squeezing me.

Our bodies almost merged, so tight was our hug. I was captivated by her pleasant scent, feminine, subtle and indelible. Exactly the same characteristic sweetness as the day we flew to the USA together. Time stopped in that instant, as if it were a limited space in the world, just for the two of us. Slowly, and with a delicate softness, we stared at each other. Her eyes, bathed in the last rays of the sun, reflected a hypnotic and magical green. Her agitated breathing broke the silence. She was exactly the same.

My head started spinning. It wasn't possible, had I been so blind? But her demeanor, the way she looked at me, the way she touched me, the way she loved, everything was identical to my memory of Angie. She parted, with exquisite touch, the locks of hair partially covering her face and I stared at her for an eternal moment to catch her precious gaze in memory, joining our lips in an infinite kiss full of meaning.

How a simple act can say so much without words. Now I was sure, it was Angie. Claudia was Angie. My legs went weak as I came to grips with reality and how close I had been, and all the suffering I had endured to find her, obsessed in the search. How paradoxical, how ironic, how mocking. But I didn't care about all that. I had found her. It was not easy to grasp. It was as if an immense joy had hit me so hard, to such an extent that it had left me stunned. I needed to kiss her again, to caress her face.

"I couldn't bear to lose you again. I love you too much," she whispered, softly.

"Forgive me, Claudia. Forgive me for everything. I've been searching for a lifetime" I sighed trying to get rid of all the melancholy I was carrying inside. "But I have found you. I have found you."

Surely, she would not be able to recognize the scope of my ideas. By now the evening sky had turned a deep purple color, and in the distance, far, far away, an elongated, motionless silhouette, observant and darker than a shadow, faded into the horizon. "Thank you, thank you, thank you, thank you, thank you," I kept repeating to him. He raised his hand in greeting and disappeared.

"We must leave here as soon as possible. We must get away."

She looked at me in surprise, not quite understanding why, but she received the sense of urgency in my tone, although I could tell she was also dubious.

"Claudia, they are good people, I don't deny it, but they can't protect me. They would find me."

"I don't understand anything, nobody tells me anything." Frustration and incomprehension were evident in every inch of her body.

"I'll explain as much as I can, but now I must go. Are you coming with me?"

Every second counted. She, on top of me, her forehead pressed against mine, took a moment to reflect, her eyes piercing through me.

"I'm coming with you. Yes, I'm going with you," she nodded with conviction.

I took her by the hand, and we ran. I hesitated for a moment about which direction to take, but suddenly I understood. Claudia's guardian was not lost on that horizon by pure chance, nor was he just there as a distant spectator.

We escaped with the eagerness of two escaped convicts in search of freedom. I listened in the distance to the accelerations of the vehicles and the unruly voices of the armed men, restless, searching everywhere. I gritted my teeth and with my own hands I clenched the braids of the fence, opening a hole through which we could escape. My strength touched the limits of the reasonable, and Claudia looked at me both impressed and surprised.

We crossed in a hurry and got lost in a field full of wild bushes and unkempt grass; and when I was sure that no one was following us in the darkness, only then did we slow down.

The heat of the race moistened our faces. I grabbed her hand making her stop, approached her with the stealth of a feline and with delicate gentleness embraced her waist, pulling her close to me, containing my recent addiction to the taste of her lips.

"I love you too, Claudia. I love you."

I couldn't quite believe it. I had found her, after so much, or rather, she had found me. It didn't matter. I had her with me all that time and I was obsessed with looking for her elsewhere; but she, with no memory of another life, already knew it.

She knew from the beginning, and I did not.

I didn't.

Chapter 43
Uncertain Destiny

New York, November 1996

We held hands and wandered the unkempt terrain around the airport. We skirted the small peninsula, chasing the tireless bulbs of New York, returning to civilization and the anonymity of the big city.

Little by little, the ground under our feet was became more orderly, as nature gave way to civilization and bustle of vehicular traffic. A poorly lit bridge appeared in our path. Its narrow, slippery maintenance walkway led us between steel pillars. It was gloomy and dangerous, varnished by the greenish mildew of the prevailing fog.

Getting over the thundering bridge was no easy task, but we made it, and New York City shone before us.

At last we found a subway stop. Claudia was panting because of the pace I had been demanding, but she did not complain once. I stopped for a moment to contemplate the automatism of the commuters who, with routine habit, came out absorbed and with their gaze lost in infinity, calm and satisfied for having completed their daily cycle. I, on the other hand, at that moment, felt a little scared, overwhelmed by my responsibility.

I had Angie back. I couldn't believe it. Happiness was a word that was too small for me, because what I was feeling was so much greater. Claudia was by my side, and I would never let anyone hurt her again. It took us two long hours to get to our stop, in one of the most troubled areas of the Bronx. On the way, between transfers and rattles, we were catching up, talking about this and that. I was still clueless and confused by my new reality, meditating on my own morals.

I had to explain where we were going, and I also told her succinctly about Chloe. I could think of no safer place to go and no one more reliable to turn to.

As we left the station, I noticed Claudia clinging tighter to my arm. She was probably frightened by the decrepit buildings and the defiance on the faces of the groups we passed. But none of them bothered us.

I'm sure I took a few extra turns to get there, but I finally found the gate. I touched the intercom, and it didn't work. The gate was open, broken. As we entered, we received a blast of remixed smells. Beer cans, graffiti and torn mailboxes gave way to a wide staircase where a group of tweens cut watched us with suspicion.

"Move aside," I told them in a firm and authoritative tone, and we stepped between them.

As we climbed the stairs, we passed apartments with their front doors wide open. It was something of a relief to be reminded by those brief moments that normal life continued for others.

We stopped in front of the door. Claudia was staring at me; I think she was scared; I didn't ask her. I knocked softly. The door seemed fragile and hollow. Instantly, it opened a few inches, pulling a chain behind it and partially revealing Chloe's face.

"Dustin, is that you?"

The door closed only to open again quickly, this time fully, catching me in an unbridled embrace full of enthusiasm and joy. I couldn't help but be infected by her pleasure. I noticed myself smiling, relaxed and free, and also how blood seemed to flow more freely through my body here. It was pleasant but then I recalled why we were there.

"I'm very happy to see you, too. You look great."

Until that moment I did not realize that I had used my old name with her, and I made the appropriate introductions with Claudia.

"Chloe, let me introduce you to a very special friend: this is Angie."

Claudia instantly understood my intentions and played along without suspecting that those five letters joined together, some time ago, were her real name. I was talking to Chloe in a reserved manner. I asked her to give us shelter for two nights, but she got angry with me, offering me all the time we needed. I insisted on a firm promise to stay as little time as possible and then we would leave.

I needed time to let things settle down and reorganize my thoughts, digest everything that had happened and try to get a perspective on the bigger picture. Chloe started cooking something improvised in the frying pan, and unrestrainedly began to tell me about her new project. The day we met she had vowed to herself to change her life.

The whole apartment was different, it felt like an orderly, jumbled chaos. Hundreds of handwritten pages were scattered the sofa and piled up on the windowsill. An old turquoise-green banquette had acquired a renewed beauty through wear and tear, and next to it, like disciplined soldiers, two gleaming guitars awaited the moment to create magic in the right hands.

"I can't wait to see what you are capable of," I said to Chloe, happy to have been even partly responsible for this unexpected turnaround. In a way, and before I heard her sing, I was already moved.

"After dinner, I'll show you something I wrote, but promise me you'll tell me the truth; I don't want any false praise."

"I give you my word. I can't wait," I said enthusiastically.

Claudia was a bit shy at first, although that quickly changed thanks to Chloe's loving and generous treatment. It had been a long time since I had enjoyed a "family" dinner, and for a brief moment I felt a little dejected as I remembered all that I had sacrificed. But, when I noticed Claudia, playing with two French fries as fangs, sadness passed. I held her hand under the table and realized that everything I had fought for had been worth it, and that this moment and all those to come would be the best reward.

We cleared the table and helped tidy up. Then came the long-awaited revelation. The tiny living room was warm and cozy. It was lit by small candles and a nice little corner lamp, one of those with an opaque shade, and colorful glow. Chloe sat down on her turquoise stool. With subtle delicacy she rested the guitar on her legs and began to caress the strings.

The initial melody sounded familiar. I frowned, trying to recognize it, but since she said she had composed it, it didn't fit until she began to sing in a dreadfully mangled Spanish,

"La cucaracha, la cucaracha, ya no puede caminar, porque le falta, porque no tiene, las dos patitas de atrás..."

She stopped playing and stared at us seriously, waiting for the verdict. We couldn't stop laughing. It was unexpected and surreal, funny as hell. She laughed with us, happy with the effect of the joke. She was so funny.

Immediately, she began to play her real song, and we saw that she was a natural. The vibrant, harmonic percussion of the notes only lost intensity when she began to sing. It was as if her voice had been transformed, it was extremely sweet, but with a vintage tinge. Claudia squeezed my hand and my skin on my body tingled uncontrollably from the inside causing me an indescribable sensation.

Through music she managed to touch our souls. Claudia and I were enveloped in the gentle cyclone of her energy and we felt fortunate to be spectators of this prodigy: the art of drawing and coloring the air with feelings.

When the song ended, she opened his eyes and stared at us, waiting for some reaction. I clapped, surprised both by her talent and by my reaction, my ability to feel so strongly.

"How many people have you shown this to?" I asked in amazement.

"You are the first. I've been writing songs for days. I learned to play the guitar years ago, with my neighbor, and I put it aside when I met you, I knew I'd hit rock bottom and it was time for a change."

"You have to start sharing that gift. This hidden talent is more than a hobby: it's a sign," I repeated it, underlining it, "It's a sign."

"I completely agree with Dustin, you made me cry, it was beautiful."

"Thank you, guys, you're a great audience."

And we burst out laughing.

We talked all night, Chloe played many more songs for us and we dedicated much time to encouraging her to play in Central Park, of going to live music venues, of recording her own demo, of touring record labels. She needed to believe in herself.

Chloe insisted that we sleep in her bed, that she would spend the night on the couch. She knew that Claudia and I were much more than friends, but we both refused, not wanting to desecrate her intimate resting place.

Huddled on the couch in the dark, Claudia was deeply concerned about what we had done. Apparently, our tutor could not conceal her relief at my discovery. She had told Claudia that I had been found, but ordered her to stay in the residence because it was too dangerous for her to come to meet me.

They did not tell her anything else because the secrecy was absolute. Claudia thought about the request to stay behind for a moment and disregarded everything that had been asked of her. She took her savings and followed Paloma by cab. The driver had to stop at the private access control to the airport, but Claudia saw where the car stopped.

She continued on foot, trying to find a way in, avoiding the security guards. While looking for an entrance she noticed an elongated white feather dancing in front of her. It was strange, because it seemed to be rocked by a non-existent wind. She followed it until it landed on the fence, next to a gap without crisscrossing mesh, and she interpreted it as a magical chance.

She walked along the runways, passing mechanics, flight attendants, controllers, and she said good afternoon to all of them without stopping, with an astonishing naturalness. No one stopped her. Only herself, her uncertainty and the fear of being seen by the security of our people made her stop.

It was an armored hangar.

She was very worried about doing the wrong thing, about being absent from the residence and betraying Paloma's trust. She didn't deserve that, she told me. Suddenly, her concern and sense of guilt rubbed off on me, while making me reflect on my own selfishness, my confusion.

I came to my senses and understood that although Claudia had once been Angie and that essence was unalterable, no matter how much I wished it, Claudia was still Claudia, immersed in her context and uninformed about almost everything. I had to be as honest as possible, but I could not talk to her about the guardians; the rules of The Order did not allow it. Nothing, however, prevented me from talking to her about Saya or her fellows, but one thing went hand in hand with the other.

I started to feel overwhelmed by the complexity of it all, I could not find a simple solution and I perfectly understood all Claudia's doubts, all her worries. I made a spontaneous decision. I got up and knocked twice on Chloe's door,

"Chloe, are you awake?"

"What do you want?"

I listened to the movement of the bedclothes and the sound of her getting out of bed.

"Can I make a call? It'll just be a minute," I whispered again.

"You don't have to ask me, you're at home, you know."

I went to the kitchen with Claudia and closed the door. I picked up the phone and started dialing.

"Who are you calling?" Claudia asked me, impressed by my sudden outburst.

"Let's talk to Paloma. You're right, she doesn't deserve our indifference."

Claudia put her index finger to her mouth, nibbling as she always did when she was nervous. With care I caressed her face, finally landing on her hand.

"I have to talk to her."

As the phone rang, I wondered if it was too late to be calling.

"Hello?"

The voice on the other end didn't sound like the janitor's to me. It was someone more temperate and enigmatic.

"I will not speak to anyone else, and if it occurs to them to send any of our people here, I will take it as a hostile act."

"We have made mistakes, and we know it, but it has always been to protect you. We know this is not the time to talk about it. I will do what you ask."

The call was diverted to another extension.

"David?" It was Paloma, there was no doubt, but her voice sounded exhausted and discouraged.

"Hello, Paloma. I'm with Claudia. I found her at the airport, and I'm calling you so you won't be worried, neither for her nor for me. We are fine."

"We need to talk, David. You can't keep running away from yourself, and please don't involve Claudia. You must understand that you are my responsibility. I have made a commitment to take care of you."

I had to interrupt her, driven by a visceral energy.

"You almost killed me, you opened fire in the airport hangar! How should I take that, Paloma? Tell me!"

"I'm sorry, David, that - that was a mistake, a shot in the air to intimidate you into stopping, but, all in all, it was very revealing, we found out what you are, late. After they... But we found out."

"Paloma, please listen to me. I respect you very much and I am aware that you have always treated me better than well, but I need a few days to clarify my ideas, without anyone coming to look for us; I just ask for some peace, that's all. Do you think you can grant it to me? Remember, I'm choosing to call you now."

A muffled sound took up the entire communication.

"David... David, you have awakened very powerful enemies. I will try to give you a few days of calm, but you must understand that I am not alone in this and that there are dangers that you cannot gauge. There are dangers I don't even know about myself."

"Thank you, Paloma, thank you for everything," I said warmly.

"Promise me that you will take good care of Claudia and that you will call us at the slightest suspicion. Promise me."

"I promise you the first thing, I will take more care of her than of my own life. We'll call you in a couple of days."

"A couple of days, David. A couple of days. A big hug to both of you."

"Thank you, Paloma. Thanks, Paloma."

And I replaced the handset.

"Fixed."

I looked into her eyes and kissed her at length. I wondered again how I had been so blind. The disturbing phone conversation didn't distract me, it would be time to deal with that later. We needed to enjoy the present, we deserved it. The Order had shown me that we were meant to be.

I was trapped by Claudia, by Angie.

Things progressed and we had to make an effort to the sounds of our passion, of the noisy stumbles as we walked in each other's embrace. Glances charged with desire and soft caresses gave way to others of wilder and more passionate tints. Our bodies needed each other.

Clothes were becoming an annoying impediment and we shed them quickly. Naked, we gazed at each other. There was no hurry, I had been looking for her for a lifetime. I lay on top of her, engrossed in her eyes, caressing her rosy cheeks, savoring the soft touch of her full lips. She wrapped her fingers in my hair reactivating the passion.

Trying to be silent, we surrendered ourselves to one another right there on the couch. Our bodies became an instrument of connection. Little by little we stopped feeling with them, the increasing rhythm transferred us to a sensation far from the material. We were the perfect equation, the sum of our experiences, the subtraction of our longings. The product of our past concentrated in that instant.

We were indivisible.

We disconnected from the physical, from the earthly, from the carcasses, we were united. Our essences were free during an infinite and eternal breath of love in action. Moments of dizzying pulse, of invented breaths, of intertwined hearts; of surrender. We had become one. Then, now and always.

Without warning we returned to reality, between collapsed gasps and reunited looks. We did not know what had happened in that small room, we were far away from there, very far away. We laughed between uncontrolled whispers, covering each other's mouths. We kissed tenderly. Our lips burned, our eyes couldn't focus, and without saying anything we were back inside each other.

The connection was unbreakable. Claudia made me slide down the softness of her belly, our skin sliding on a thin, warm cushion of nonexistent air, and back again. We were drifting away from there, surrounded by the enveloping magic of our love. We smiled with spontaneous happiness.

Plain and simple happiness.

I woke up a few hours later, when the sky was lightening but the streetlights were still on. She was sleeping peacefully, wrapped in a vaporous quilt with a scent of lavender. Her tousled hair partially covered the innocence of her face with a warlike and sensual touch.

I decided to go out to get some fresh air and bring breakfast, but when I reached the street, I realized that I was too early. I started walking, watching the press and bakery vans working like discreet elves in a finely tuned machine. It got me thinking about my role, about what my part was in this unstoppable cog called the world.

Finally I found what I was looking for: a breakfast diner where I ordered breakfast to go for the three of us. I had taken the liberty of taking Claudia's purse; a little over a hundred dollars was hidden in its folds, a little and a lot at the same time.

I returned to the apartment surrounded by the aroma of coffee and freshly baked pastries. I opened the door and found a sleep

Claudia who soon perked up at seeing me arrive with breakfast. She ran to Chloe's bedroom to announce the news with the same joy as a lottery winner.

I don't think I've ever seen two women so happy about something so modest.

The sun was beginning to shine through the living room window. The two women were talking to each other as if they had known each other for years, and I was examining the architectural simplicity of the building across the street. Basically, it served the same principle as a bookshelf covered in exposed brick, but even with all the clothes hanging on the clotheslines, the plants in the windows and the cluttered arrangement of air conditioners, its beauty and resilience was undeniable. Lost as I was in my useless thoughts, I was startled by the insistent mention of my name,

"Dustin, Dustin, Dustin."

"What? -What's wrong?"

A chorus of laughter mocked me shamelessly.

"Are you plotting, or what? I can give you Chinese torture and you'll see how you'll stop laughing at me."

I grabbed Claudia and started tickling her.

Claudia and Chloe kept laughing, but I noticed a dark cloud thought hovering over my love.

"Are you all right, Claudia?" I asked, catching my breath.

"Yes, yes. It's just that I feel as if I've already lived this, I don't know."

And then I remembered that I used to play with her like that, when she was Angie, and the idea came to me.

The brilliant idea.

Chapter 44
Responses

New York, November 1996

Chloe gave us a copy of the keys and I promised her that we would help her change her *look* that very afternoon; *it* was something she was very worried about, due to the nature of her previous occupation. She needed a radical change, but without diminishing her beauty. At that moment, though, a powerful new thought dominated my priorities.

We headed into the street. It's funny how the eyes and the spirit adapt to the environment with astonishing speed. Before we knew it, everything had changed in Claudia and me. When you don't judge people under a false impression of danger, you integrate quickly. You coexist with the neighborhood, merging into the context as one more, no matter how different you think you are.

Our destination was Brooklyn. We took the subway and there were so many people that I immediately stopped thinking it was a good idea, but having already paid the ticket, we had no choice but to endure the crowd.

The coming and going of people was constant, and next to some of them the reddish beings wandered inseparable, like gum on a shoe, helping them in who knows what, but surely inciting their hosts towards the path of evil, towards their source of nourishment.

More than an hour later, after hundreds of faces seen and several transfers through the bowels of the city, we arrived at our stop. Only a few blocks separated us from our old, dilapidated factory, once our love bubble.

Claudia followed me, and I watched her carefully, trying to see if any scattered memories would emerge from her memory. They didn't seem to, judging by her constant questioning, until there were only two blocks away. She stopped abruptly.

"What is it, Claudia?" I asked deliberately.

"This is near the place where we came with the van, am I wrong?"

I snorted with some resignation. I had hoped for answers, not more questions.

"No. No, Claudia, you are not wrong."

"That night I had to go in, I remember that you were very angry with me, but it's that... I couldn't explain it, it was as if I had already been there. A very strange feeling. Crazy, isn't it?" She gave a half-laugh.

We stood in front of the dilapidated facade, observing it in broad daylight, infected by its abandonment. I noticed that Claudia was shuddering, but I didn't really know why, or, even if I sensed it, reason and disbelief were more powerful than intuition. Be that as it may, I could not give her clues, my guardian had clearly explained the rules. He trusted me to follow his instinct, even what seemed to me to be his most irrational instincts.

I removed the metal fence and concentrated on hiding us from view. The last thing I needed at that moment was to be interrupted. I was frustrated to have to keep secrets from her. I put those feelings aside and concentrated on visiting our old factory, and seeing if, with any luck, we could salvage something from the past. Nothing went as I expected.

"Why are you so interested in this place? It's in ruins. It's dangerous for us to wander around here. We should leave."

Her fears disconnected her from that sensitive faculty we all have.

"Let's go up to the second floor, I need to take a look," I insisted, in a last attempt to refloat a Titanic sunk in the deepest abyss.

"But what have you lost here?" Her voice sounded ruder than she intended.

"I wish I could explain it to you," I said to myself.

I went upstairs hoping that Claudia would follow me, but no. She stayed waiting for me by the bare and rickety stairs. What was my surprise when I got to the top: a pale reddish mound glowed dimly on the floor of what had once been our bedroom. I couldn't believe it; Daryl was there, again. But his energy, his imprint, was totally changed. Extinguished.

I stood and decided to project myself out of myself to communicate with him. I felt light as a nebula, but solid and firm at the same time.

Daryl was too faded, he looked devoid of vitality. I bent down to get a closer look. He sensed my presence and began to gesture at me. He wanted me to get away from him. To get out of there. But he was barely able to stitch the syllables together to form words. Weak and faded, exhausted and sickly-looking, he insisted, with the frailty of a worn-out old man, that I leave.

He was my best friend and despite all the betrayals, all the pain caused and the terrible consequences of his actions, something inside me refused to hold a grudge. Really, I knew I had to get out of there, let go of Daryl and return to my body and Claudia. I was completely unfamiliar with the world of the reddish, the way their existence was governed, but I felt very sorry to see my old friend Daryl like this.

He was paying for his mistakes, and the price seemed very high. I touched his head, with a friendly, concerned touch. He looked at me. His off-key, quartered look gave me a shiver that was hard to hide.

"I hope you can hear me, Daryl. How can I help you? You look bad, buddy."

But he kept insisting that I leave. His face reflected a deep sadness, an insurmountable grief. His voice grew fainter with every effort.

"Tell me what I can do for you, and I'll try to do it," I insisted.

But he shook his head, reaffirming his request to be alone.

"Relax, try to rest. I have to go, Daryl, but first I need to tell you something. It may not be important to you, but it's been a heavy burden for me all this time. I want you to know that I've forgiven you. That I understand, I wasn't very right about you either, and after all, we all make mistakes. In any case, the damage has been repaired. Take care of yourself, old friend."

I got up to leave, and then it happened. The sensation was much like a strong swirl of wind forming behind you. I had to turn around. It was the collision of energies that caused the immense contrast. His guardian had appeared before him. Was that possible? I stood transfixed, like a fortunate observer of a scene that was none of my business, or so I thought.

I was struck by the sight of the guardian bending down and resting his knee on the floor, tending to his protégé with uncharacteristic care. Daryl continued to sit, looking away, in a chosen and desperately muted solitude. I noticed that he was unaware of his guardian's presence until he laid his hands on him.

Daryl's dull reddish color began to fade and he slowly regained his lost appearance. His eyes were glowing again, and only then did he realize that something was happening. Something good. His legs were flailing on the floor and his hands were making the vain effort to push himself further against the wall, surprised by the unexpected and strange sensations he was experiencing.

Daryl was Daryl, I mean, there was no trace of reddish tinge left in him, or flaky, cracked skin. He was the spitting image of the day he passed away. Only then did he get a glimpse of his guardian. He was startled to have him so close.

"What is it, Dustin? What's happening?" he asked me, surprised at the dark and opaque presence of his guardian, as if I had something to do with it all.

"He is your guardian. He is something like your protector, your spiritual guide, I can't explain it easily; but don't doubt it, trust him."

Then the guttural and powerful voice of the guardian manifested itself, and Daryl, with a renewed appearance and vitality, witnessed the unusual presence with astonishment.

"You have succeeded in reconnecting with The Order. You have received sincere forgiveness for your deeds and you have submitted to an abstinence from evil. All this makes you worthy of transcendence. Now we will begin a new stage. A new opportunity."

The guardian stood up. His imposing stature brushed the top edge of the old factory. He held out his elongated hand to a still shocked Daryl. They both grasped each other tightly and Daryl sat up with a strong flash of enthusiasm in his eyes.

"What is that light?" asked Daryl, with the excitement of a child at Christmas.

"Goodbye, my friend. Good luck. I hope to see you again."

I could not see the light Daryl was talking about, but I knew it very well. The guardian was glowing with multicolored hues offering a more detailed view of his features. It was simply a fantasy image, like something out of a magical dream. Something incredibly beautiful.

"I hope so, Dustin. I hope so, buddy. You gotta see this! What a peaceful feeling!"

Their words sounded farther and farther away, as the two of them disappeared from my field of vision, gently fading into the center of the room, until they evaporated completely through that invisible portal.

I heard an unintelligible voice behind me. I had lost track of time, or maybe, in that parallel reality, things happened at a different pace; I don't know, the fact was that when I turned around, I found Claudia shaking my empty body that did not react to stimuli. I returned to my body and to the physical world.

My reaction was the same as when you are falling asleep and suddenly you feel as if you're about to fall. I reacted with an uncontrolled spasm.

"What is it, Claudia? Relax, I was just thinking, that's all."

I had a hard time blinking since my eyes had been open the whole time I'd been out of my body.

"You scared me! You've been gone a long time! You know, I thought you'd had a fit!"

She was both angry and relieved. I guess it must have been alarming. I tried to soothe her.

Our old room had ugly dampness on the walls, the same dampness that had peeled off the paint like dead skin. Certainly, there was nothing left there, only the broken scenery of an indelible and wonderful memory. I had made a big mistake bringing her here, hoping for more. It was time to live in the present and forget everything that had gone before. It was time to turn over a new page and really live my life. Claudia looked at the old factory with curious eyes.

"This place must have been very nice once upon a time. I can see that but what I don't understand is why you have come here twice."

I looked at her with an uncertain and resigned expression.

"Because I would have loved to live in such a place, especially with you by my side."

And I kissed her.

We walked out, careful not to step in any holes or trip over any debris, joking with each other. It was good to hear her laugh. But all that joy suddenly vanished as we left. To anyone's eyes, that sharp-faced gentleman was nothing more than a passerby who watched attentively as two young people laughed together. But he was not like that. He was something else.

I immediately grabbed Claudia and pulled her behind me. That man in the brown trench coat was by no means an ordinary passerby. Behind him, a small army of reddish men stared at me. He turned and walked with his back to us. He raised his hand, pointing to the sky and said, menacingly,

"Don't do it again, boy. Don't do it again."

And he put his hand back in his pocket as he walked sheltered by the red ones, turned the corner, and disappeared from view.

My heart was pumping a mile a minute. What had just happened? Who was that? He had managed to put me on my guard. What's more, I must admit, he had managed to scare me. Right then and there I realized that Claudia was my Achilles heel. I was afraid that something bad could happen to her. I needed to live a normal life, far from the reds, the guardians and creatures born under the heat of another star. The two lives were incompatible with each other. At least not with proper security. Could I choose? Was there a right choice? I removed the untamed hair from my face and breathed calmly to regain my composure.

"David, I didn't like that man at all. Let's get out of here. There's too much crazy around here."

"It's normal, we shouldn't have gone in there without permission. It is dangerous."

My explanation did not convince Claudia, but it made perfect sense. The secrets were back and I hated it with all my heart. I thought about it for a while. I needed to understand.

I deduced that the reddish beings behaved like an infectious disease, and the channel for reproduction was the selfish human need to see their darkest and most sinister desires fulfilled, whatever they might be. But for the first time I had confirmed, without intending to, that such a doom was reversible. The disease could be cured. The reddish ones could also transcend, it was complicated, it required a great effort, an unbreakable will, and I don't think there were simple instructions for it, but it could be achieved.

Daryl had succeeded, and I was happy for him. He had escaped the horrible need to feed on the evil of others, to participate in their success to feed it back, to see and cause pain, to condemn another living person to the terrifying fate he had suffered. He escaped that unsigned contract, that lucid nightmare.

Claudia's energetic vitality managed to extract me from my tangled hypotheses. I needed to enjoy the moment, to be with her. I needed her.

"There's so much to eat here!" she squealed excitedly.

We saw a horizon of gastronomic possibilities within our reach: Chinese, Italian, Mexican, Japanese, Turkish.

"You choose, Claudia. I am open to everything."

And out of the blue, she kissed me as if we were completely alone. People had to walk around us as we kissed on the street but I didn't care. I felt myself falling into a feeling of absolute sensual calm, a feeling of pure harmony.

When our lips disconnected, the energy still remained, and suddenly I was back to alertness, and I worried that I had let my guard down again, absorbed by that unhealthy and permanent paranoid psychosis. That paranoia blurred in the light, but no less true.

It was a pleasure to watch her eat. It was like having a Viking character in front of me, devouring everything as if there was no tomorrow. I was more interested in watching her than in eating. She was Angie, but it wasn't Angie. There was a clear essence, but obviously, it wasn't totally her. And it would never really be her.

For a moment, I briefly introspected and recognized that I wasn't Dustin either. I had changed too, I had learned from life's continuous mistakes and, though I was surely doomed to continue making them due to my imperfect nature, I unquestionably felt less naïve. More prepared. Evolved. Although I didn't know what for.

We walked along the walkway of the Brooklyn Bridge, filling the background of the tourists' photographs, improvised extras on a magical stage. The design of the bridge was simply masterful, and its construction a human feat. My architect's brain was throbbing inside me, but the situation was not ideal for it. I felt strangely driven by a different destiny, as if this life had other plans for me but I refused to accept them.

I was definitely no longer Dustin, and Claudia was definitely no longer Angie.

The sound of a motorcycle caught my attention. We had left behind the continuous throng of vehicles and pedestrians, and were on our way to catch the subway on the other side of the bridge. There was nothing special about that motorcycle, except for one thing: it had set off my sharp radar against evil.

The reddish ones always attracted my attention, but I could walk past them as long as their host was not in the exercise of his wickedness. In a manner of speaking, it was necessarily bearable; it would have taken a thousand lifetimes to deal with all the tyrants I came across, especially in such a crowded city. It was a different matter to indulge their harmful activity in my presence. That exceeded all my limits of tolerance.

When I saw the motorcyclist and the reddish being surrounding him staring at a large bag on the shoulder of an elegant woman, it was clear to me what was going to happen and what I needed to do.

I let go of Claudia's hand and in a reflex action, without even thinking for a moment, I ran towards the motorcycle. My hair covered my face, blocking my eyes. I didn't care, it was as if I was guided by a new sense. The motorcyclist was intent on snatching his target's bag and all I wanted was to get there before he could hurt her. I imagined her dragged along the ground, accidentally snagged by the strap of her purse. I needed to be faster, to get there before he did. Then I felt a powerful energy flowing through my body, and I reached her at a completely astonishing speed, defying logic.

That woman, in high heels and a frilly blouse, looked at me, motionless. She was scared of me and was unaware that the real threat was barely two meters away and getting closer. I felt a strange warmth in my hands, but I couldn't dwell on it, not at that moment. My body felt harder, stronger and more resilient than ever, almost as if it wasn't made of flesh and blood but was made of the most unbreakable steel.

Stunned to see me running towards her, she lost control of her arms and the bag fell to the ground. I passed close to her; I remember that my perception of the air behaved differently as I passed so close to her. Then the biker's gaze, driving with one hand and extending the other to the bag in an awkward posture, perceived my presence for the first time. It was too late for him. I jumped over the motorcycle crashing my right knee into his chest.

The motorcycle continued for a few meters without a driver, sanding the curb, to finally lose balance without major consequences. I landed with both feet on the ground, instinctively adopting a guarded position in front of that fiend.

"Get up! Come on, get up! Get your bag, you're on time! Come on! What's the matter, have you lost the urge?"

That impact on my knee must have hurt, however, I barely felt it. Something was different in me.

The helmet, which looked more like a military helmet than a motorcycle helmet, had saved him from hitting his head on the ground. His lips began to secrete a pinkish mixture of blood and saliva, and I immediately felt responsible for what had happened. I bent over him to inquire about his state of health. His reaction was to shield himself from me with a frightened fuss.

I think that the reddish ones had minimized the consequences of their "accident". A group of people were throwing a series of unfair phrases into the air. Instantly, I returned to the robbery that I had prevented, pursued by a huge shouting of hostile voices.

I sat up with self-assurance, slowly, seriously and calmly. Confident. Someone had called 911 from a coffee shop right there. The bag was still on the floor, at the feet of its owner.

Without removing my hair from my face, I picked up her purse and handed it to her. She took it obeying some deep reflex, but still confused by the strange experience. On this occasion, I believe that due to my own calmness the urban environment had been transformed into a silent open library. The curious looked at me expectantly, present and absent at the same time. The silence thickened the air, made it uncomfortable. The sound of several sirens was gaining intensity, and police cars appeared. It dawned on me that the police headquarters was just a few blocks away.

Claudia had not moved from the place where I let go of her hand, and the most disturbing thing was that she also harbored that kind of paralysis in her gaze.

I lifted the motorcycle off the ground by squeezing the clutch handle, its wheels spinning. Police cars were arriving and an ambulance was rounding the corner.

I could see that the starter pump was gone, and in its place was a mess of bare and poorly connected wires. I simply needed to get out of there. It was nothing premeditated. I got on the bike and gave it a pump to check that the engine was running well, and incidentally to get Claudia's attention, who remained frozen to the spot.

The police officers had already gotten out of the patrol cars. A couple was attending to the injured man, as if he were the victim of a simple accident, and others, who had just arrived, were asking what had happened. Claudia and I looked at each other, motionless, oblivious to the sounds of the ambulance and the growing crowd. A huge smile flooded her face. I returned it with a tilted nod of my head. Our complicity was complete. She dodged the chorus of indifferent gossips, moving right into the heart of the matter. With a swift movement, she climbed onto the bike behind me.

A sound stopped right next to me.

"Thank you for helping me. At first, I didn't understand what was happening, but then... Well, you were amazing. Thank you from the bottom of my heart."

Through the rearview mirror I could see a police officer approaching; I only had a few seconds.

"You're welcome. But I need to ask you something."

She looked at me quizzically, with that light of someone who is willing to listen. "Tell them what happened, if you want, but don't share our description. You've never seen me, okay?"

And I pulled back all the hair that fell over my face so that she could cross her gaze with me. Without taking my eyes off the woman's blue eyes, I pulled Claudia towards me and felt her hands tighten around my back. I clenched my right fist and released the clutch, driving away without looking back, at full speed.

I felt I was doing the right thing. I was finding my way.

My destiny.

Chapter 45
The Purpose

New York, November 1996

That motorcycle was really fast. It delivered its power so precisely, so intuitively, that you immediately felt it as an extension of your body. Riding without a helmet, the sensation of speed was multiplied. I didn't think about where we were going, I wanted to get away from there with Claudia; nothing else.

They say that we only use a small percentage of our brain capacity. That may not be entirely true. Without permission, a part of me had already decided on the route to take. I was shocked by that reality, chalking it up to an unconscious desire I knew nothing about.

I stopped for a few seconds at the first shelter I saw on the road. I needed to think about whether or not I would be able to continue. Sometimes it is not luck, nor the whims of fate, nor the challenges of life that test us. Sometimes it is oneself.

Something had guided me along that route and, although the terrifying pain of the experience seemed insurmountable, I decided to follow whatever that was. When I resumed drive, dazed by my thoughts and the deafening roar of the trucks, I thought it was necessary to return to the place. To close the circle. To defy fear.

Maybe I took a few extra detours to get there, maybe, but I found it easily. I unfolded the bike's stand and Claudia got off, staring unblinkingly at the gigantic half-opened entrance and the charred sign that still bore the slogan Simon & Sons Storage.

We left the motorcycle and walked in silence, as if we were one person. Claudia stared intently at the burnt walls that still carried the faint smell of ash. She turned from time to time to look at the gigantic space where once there had been a swinging gate. She needed to orient herself with references. I followed two steps behind her, watching for her reactions.

It was unbelievable, we were walking in the same direction as that fateful day. Her face expressed the effort of recovering something lost. She paused for a moment. She skin prickled as she fixed her eyes on a metal plate that was not flush with the pavement. Maybe that's where her foot was flayed.

We walked down the burned hallway, littered with fallen debris, until we reached the room. Faded police ribbons fluttered in the hallway at the mercy of the air, like broken dancers.

We broke through the tape. The room was covered by the brown rust and so much dust. She walked to one of the lockers, one among dozens, and stood in front of it, motionless, breathing hard. She stuck her finger into the place where there had once been a small lock and pulled out. It took a couple of tries, but finally the door gave way.

The condition of the locker was surprising. An expression of disbelief and sadness slowly covered her face as from the small top shelf she picked up a small box.

"Why do I feel this way? How could I have known this would be here?" Her back leaned against the lockers; she was weak with emotion. There's something you're not telling me.

I kept silent. It took me a while to react. I hadn't expected this. A part of me wanted to shout the whole truth, the whole secret. I would have spent less than a minute to sum it all up for her, but I couldn't. Instead, I kept quiet but felt a strange reflux in my belly.

Until I saw what I saw: a small spherical object. It was silver and similar to a tennis ball, but with something moving inside that was watching us without making a sound. It had crept out from behind a row of lockers. It lingered for a short time in front of us before shooting up and out of the window.

I didn't even have a chance to do anything. It was lightning fast, but I was sure that device belonged to the foreigners. Maybe they left it there as a system to gather information. Maybe they were trying to locate me. Maybe I was wrong. Too many unknowns. What was obvious was that the tranquility was gone and that feeling of exhausting urgency, which I had already conquered once, took hold of me again.

"What was that, David? When are you going to tell me what's going on?"

I hated to see her angry, and she had every reason in the world to feel that way. Put me in her shoes and I would have been less patient. My priority at that precise moment though was to protect her, and for that we needed to get out of there as soon as possible. I took her hands, holding the little blue box between us, and stared at her, trying to convey everything I felt for her. I joined my forehead to hers without blinking, immersed in the infinity of her eyes. I wanted to tell her everything without articulating words, because none of them came close to what I really felt for her. My heart tried to express itself with a soft and prolonged kiss full of affection, full of frustration, full of illusion, fear and love. Our eyelashes crossed at the same time, and I breathed in the rushing air leaving her lungs with the fleeting impression that our lives shared the same heartbeat.

"We have to get out of here. There is no time for explanations. We have to go." She clearly understood that the small flying object had broken our momentum and, by now she knew that my warnings were never unfounded. "Take care of what's inside that box."

She put it away without looking inside, and we hurriedly retraced our steps.

We got on the motorcycle, and left, fast. I cursed under my breath at those horrible creatures that were making our lives miserable. This was the final, decisive drop, the one that overflowed the glass and pushed me to make the final decision.

I could not continue this way. I had never had a messianic concept of myself, quite the contrary. I wasn't sure what I would do next either, but one thing was clear to me: all this persecution was not going to stop, neither for me nor for all the victims to come.

The courage I felt despite the absence of peace of mind unnerved my whole being. I was about to make the hardest decision of my entire existence. I was going to walk away from the love of my life voluntarily, consciously and decisively.

I had relapsed into paranoia. I looked up at the sky at every turn of the corner, looking for anything out of place. I stopped at the entrance to the freeway. I watched carefully, but nothing. Even so, I made use of the virtues granted by the guardians to put myself in invisible mode. I hoped that it would also serve to elude my presence from their technology, but I did not know what would happen.

I had to be more careful than ever, because when driving in those conditions no driver would be able to see us. The drive felt long and short at the same time. I didn't want to get there, I didn't want to face my own decision, I couldn't bear the thought.

I think, as we got closer, Claudia sensed my plans. She let go of my waist and detached herself from me. My soul was flooded with pain, and by now tears were falling freely. There was barely a block to the residence when Claudia started pounding her fists into my back.

I stopped the motorcycle, and I made every effort to stay calm and not break into a thousand pieces. That decision was proving to be the most painful thing I had ever experienced, and yet I had to feign a composure I didn't have.

"Listen to me! Listen to me! Listen to me, darling, please! Listen to me! I beg you, my love!" I said, chasing after her.

It was such a difficult thing. I don't think I'd really understood how hard it would be to walk away.

"No! I don't want to listen to you! I don't want to hear anything! -I need to be with you! I need you."

Claudia was trembling and her words were stumbling.

"Nothing in this world makes me happier than being with you. Nothing! But you must listen to me. I have powerful enemies, and I swear to you I have done everything to get rid of them. I've hidden, I've seen death, I've fought for my life, I've suffered, I've cried, I've run away, I've gone mad with loneliness, and I've longed for you so much that I've almost come to hate love," I blurted out. "But I've also won, I've found you, and I've wrapped you in my arms. And I finally understand. I must not take any more detours. I'm going to fulfill my destiny. I'm going to be the best version of myself. It's the only way. It's time to fight and I'm going to prepare for what's ahead. I need to do what I came here to do. Protect ..." Here I caught my breath. "Protect as many as I can."

"I will not leave you! I have loved you from the first moment I saw you! We belong together, don't you see? What can I say?" she shouted, while I dealt with the most awful internal battle imaginable.

"Claudia, I am not leaving you. This is not a goodbye, it's just a see you soon. Believe me, I have no other choice. If we really want to be together, this is the only way, believe me, I know," I said with conviction. "Find your own way, no strings attached. There is a hidden force guiding us, call it what you will, but it whispers the way. It has taken me a long time to understand it."

Claudia listened but I don't think she believed me.

"Don't depend on anyone, on anything, not even on me. With Paloma, with our people, it doesn't matter, if you listen to the dictation in the background of your heart, you will always see the path. I think that is the real mystery to be explored: the meaning of our presence in the world."

I held her face, calming her.

"No! I don't want to!" she lowered his voice, striving to regain her composure. "I'll help you with whatever you have to do. We've done it before and it worked out fine."

"This is different. You must trust me. I'm asking you, please. Trust and everything will be fine. We will be together, and we will live our lives with the greatest gift you can give us. With love and peace of mind."

We held each other's gazes like two negotiators unable to reach an agreement.

"You don't even deign to tell me anything! How shameful and sad! It's true, I don't want a life full of secrets."

Anger coursed through her, and she began to move away from me, towards the residence. I followed a few steps behind her so she picked up the pace, running away from me, obfuscated in her outburst of anger.

She reached the doorbell and without looking back, rang it. I walked the last few steps slowly, and as she noticed me approaching, she gave no respite to the button, she kept it pressed constantly, staring at the security camera, until the metal door creaked open.

At the last moment, I grabbed her hand with just the right amount of force, in a way that she could let go if she wanted to. She froze. Never had I felt so afraid of myself, and never had I needed someone's support so badly. She turned crestfallen, hiding her pain.

"I love you; do you hear me? I love you, and nothing that happens can change that because our love is eternal. You and I are infinite. I simply ask you for a pause, a moment of our existence. I need to put myself at the service of others. I need to answer the call. Fix the mess. Respect myself."

"David, don't talk to me about eternity. I've already lost you once," she said. "Those scary nights, crying for you, thinking you might be dead. That-that was endless."

I'd never seen her so angry. I feel like a fool, a complete imbecile.

I removed her hair from her face, infected by her anguish, by the feeling of guilt.

"Nothing that could happen to me should make you feel stupid, okay?"

"You don't understand. You don't understand anything"

And there was an abrupt, tense and disconcerting silence between the two of us.

"I was stupid for not finding the time to tell you how much I loved you right away, for not talking to you about what was happening to me with you and for not asking you if it was happening to you too. I didn't know if I was losing my mind, and I didn't ask any of those questions because I suspected that your heart was distracted. You were looking for something else, and I was afraid to declare myself, to lose what I already had. And now that you are back, that something has changed in you, now that I have everything, that I am happy, you tell me that you are leaving. That you must stay away from me."

I was stunned. Then words flowed from within me as if drawn from a higher intelligence, or perhaps as a reflection of experience and presented at that moment in the form of wisdom, I'm not sure.

"I've spent a lifetime looking for you, I've never given up, and finally I've found you, it's you. You are my happiness. But I cannot forget the reality with which I am in line, and that is that the same gift that drove us away is the one that has brought me back to you; that is to say, we are connected, we live to be together."

She seemed half convinced.

"But if I continue to shirk my purpose, my destiny, my dedication to others, our happiness will be interrupted and I will have failed myself. I will have failed my duty, the purpose of my existence. It has taken me lifetimes to understand this."

When you know you have found the truth, the universe conspires to make the unthinkable happen. The right words appear, with the perfect tone, the right touch and the right look. Love has curious expressions, and the sacrifice we were agreeing to was further proof of its unwavering endurance.

Paloma walked slowly along the path that divided the greenery from the mowed grass and connected the access to the residence. I had great respect for Paloma and, ultimately, for the secret society to which she belonged, but my intuition told me that I should not be what they wanted me to be, I could not become their instrument. I had to be myself and I was convinced that the obstacles, the details, would resolve themselves. It was not about trying to do things alone. On the contrary. I would never be alone if I followed the path of my purpose.

"Promise me that you will come to see me from time to time. Promise me and I'll be satisfied."

The crackling of the gravel under Paloma's feet could be heard, and suddenly the idea of Claudia flooded my imagination like an overwhelming light.

"I promise that we will see each other as much as possible. Wherever you are, I'll be with you, so don't worry about that. But you must promise me that it will be our secret and that you will be careful not to think about me in public; there are very sensitive people who might discover us, and that would not be good for us."

A huge smile of joy spread across her face, followed by a lunging embrace, sealing our pact with a series of kisses, finally leading to a softer, sweeter and calmer one".

I let go of Claudia's hand. I took off Kingsley's pendant and held it in my hand for a few seconds; it meant a lot to me. I slipped it over her head and made sure it was centered on her chest.

"Listen to me. Never take it off."

And with that I left. I drove slowly by her, wishing to cross our complicit gazes for that last moment. Instead, I was puzzled by the fragility of my memory as I watched her gazing at the inscription on the ring she had taken out of the little blue box: Dustin & Angie-1977. She lifted her face to meet my eyes, and I saw so many questions in her silence.

Her awakened intelligence was beginning to connect the invisible and impossible signals, and a cloud of skepticism was settling on her face. I think she began to understand that the pseudonym under which I introduced her to Chloe was more than just a measure of self-protection. None of it made sense because she was the one who sensed the hidden presence of the little blue box, and now in her mind a million questions were pushing each other, trying to clarify the unexpected mystery that had been presented to her.

"I love you!"

I moved my lips silently for her to read as I passed. I gave a salute to Paloma, who was already behind her, and gazed once more at the love of my life before leaving, winking at her, to reaffirm our complicity.

Claudia's expression remained meditative as I drove away. She seemed absorbed in thought, but, at the same time, looking at me with deep suspicion and glowing skepticism.

I accelerated hard, picking up speed, on my way to fulfill my destiny. I was going to do what I was born to do and I knew, no, I had the clear certainty that the hidden plan had been revealed to me.

"Wait! I remember! Wait!" I stopped the bike at the sound of her screams. Claudia came running, I rushed to meet her, and she jumped on top of me, embracing me.

"I remember you. The train, you pulled me off the train. I remember. Tell me I'm not crazy, please tell me," she begged, whispering in my ear.

"You're not crazy, Angie. No, you're not crazy." I was shocked. "I couldn't tell you, I was forbidden. I'm sorry, my love." Our foreheads touched. "No one else can know, ever."

I set her down on the floor and we stared at each other, breathing in with emotion, recognizing each other beyond the patterns of time.

"We have an appointment in Paris." She gave me back the ring. I squeezed it tightly and we kissed, stretching every second, breathing together, synchronizing the rhythm of our hearts.

"Leave now," she said.

She let go of my hand, caressing my fingertips, and walked towards Paloma, looking back at me as she walked. I stood there, feeling the giddiness of emotion, chewing over what had just happened. I got on the bike and gave the steel beast gas, pulling away with a smile.

I smiled because I felt that I had stopped being selfish, hedonistic and indecisive. I felt that I was tuning my existence to the designs of The Order and that intelligent force of the universe was showing me, showing me the way. I was right.

I felt it in my chest.

Chapter 46
Love Is Salvation

That motorcycle was, quite simply, spectacular. It was the best I had ever ridden. But there was a problem: it was stolen and had an owner. I drove slowly to Chloe's apartment. I needed to say goodbye to her, give her a hug and wish her all the luck in the world in her new life I could really relate to her.

It was late and the night began to steal the clarity of the day. I could breathe that cold and humid air of the plants mixed with the remaining strength of the increasingly absent sun. I could not leave the bike alone, so I rang the doorbell forgetting that it was not working.

A group of youngsters looked at me, somewhat undecided what they thought of me. Two reddish ones were feeding on one of the young men. The other four saw him as their leader and would soon have reddish ones of their own.

I took the initiative and approached them. I stood in front of them. We were all about the same age. The boys began to move restlessly, crossing their gazes with each other, just because of my silent presence in the place. They turned to their leader, looking to him for a solution to what could be a provocation. He stood up and walked down the four steps until we were facing each other, he noticeably unfriendly, as if I shouldn't even be looking at him. I took a couple of steps back; I needed peace.

"I need to ask you a small favor, I don't know if you'd be willing to do it."

He burst out laughing as if he were in front of a madman.

"Get out of my sight before they take you out in your coffin!"

One of the boys approached the bike and quickly realized that the bike was stolen.

"Hey, buddy, did you blow this bike yourself? That's pretty tough, man!"

"Well, we already have a motorcycle," he said to the big guy.

"You ain't got shit. And you stay away from it right now, if you don't want to end up crying at home with your mother."

"Yes, the bike had a different owner and I have to give it back to him. I've come to say goodbye to a friend, and I need you to keep an eye on it while I go upstairs, that's all. If you do me this huge favor, I will be grateful."

The big guy burst out laughing again and the rest of them looked at each other in bewilderment, badly pulling out false smiles that revealed an underlying insecurity. The boy, surrounded by reddish people, clenched his fists and gave me an ultimatum.

"You aren't taking this bike with you! This is our neighborhood and we're in charge, we're the Pumas, do you understand?"

And then I couldn't help it. I laughed like I've rarely laughed in my life. Actually, it wasn't that funny, but when they told me that their gang was named after a big cat I just started laughing. I was laughing so hard that even the big guy caught it and started laughing too, confessing,

"Damn it, man, Pumas was that dumb ass' idea." And he pointed to a dark-haired, scrawny boy who was still sitting on the stairs.

"The puma is the *ninja* of the jungle, and he's also fierce, like us. I think it's cool," the skinny guy defended himself as best he could, while we all laughed.

568

"I like you, white boy. That's why I won't beat you up, but you're not taking the bike."

"Dude, come on," I said, shaking my head.

The laughter suddenly stopped, and a tense atmosphere took over. It had been so long since I had laughed like that that I was incapable of getting angry with them. He tried to throw a punch at me, but he didn't even manage to raise his fist above his waist because I had already grabbed his head. I felt a lot of compassion for that young man, and I needed to resolve this in the best possible way. I pulled his soul out, just a couple of centimeters, not enough to disconnect it from his body. And I directed his eyes towards his reddish companions. His face reflected the most terrifying horror and I talked to him, in that other parallel universe so close to ours.

"Do you see them? Tell me if you see them! Answer me."

He was unable to speak, only a rasping scream could be heard emerging from his being and continued to do so even when I returned him to his body. He sat on the floor, truly affected by what I showed him. His friends looked at me fearfully, full of surprise and uneasiness, not quite knowing what had just happened. There was no need to ask him again.

That's how I understood it.

I walked upstairs. Hallways with open doors, old people, children and mothers went about their lives with no regard for their privacy while I ran along the landings. I knocked on the door. Chloe appeared, looking unfriendly. Fortunately, it was only temporary.

"Dustin, that's enough! You always knock on the door like the police do!"

It was something I didn't know, because they had never knocked on my door, but I had no choice but to believe her in view of his genuine reaction.

"I'm sorry"

And I ran my hand behind my head, rubbing it in embarrassment. I stepped inside and could see that I had interrupted some rehearsal, by the notebook and pen hastily thrown on the couch.

"I have come to say goodbye to you. Claudia has returned to her place, and I am going to devote myself to what I must do. I have listened to that inner voice, the one I'd been ignoring but that has always been my guide and my destiny."

The quickened breathing after climbing the stairs reflected the excitement of sharing my decision, especially with her. We had so much in common. Immediately, my joy became hers, and although she didn't know the details, we were both enveloped in that aura of kindness and beauty that you can share with like-minded people.

We gave each other a big hug. We wished each other all the luck in the world and promised to see each other again, because some relationships, no matter how much time passes, become unchangeable. I walked down the stairs slowly, I was enjoying that building that to most would be pitiful, but that, for me, had become one of the most beautiful places in this world because inside you could breathe humility, eagerness to improve and creativity.

Arriving at the gate, I was pleased to find the motorcycle in the same place where I had left it. Next to it, standing there, the big man was waiting. His expression had changed. It no longer reflected the haughty cockiness of the beginning; instead, a kinder countenance had settled on his face. I didn't want to say anything; I thought there was no need to explain, and I got on the motorcycle.

"Wait, dude, who are you? What did you show me?"

His questions tumbled out, his voice already that of a man. I crossed my hands over the tank and made myself comfortable, balancing the bike on its wheels. I purposely paused. I needed to convey to him the strength of emptiness, the energy of calm.

"I am the one who has shown you the truth, so now you must keep it with you. And what you have seen is your future. You are young, healthy, strong, and I venture to think that you are even quite intelligent. No one needs to commit evil acts, this life provides you with everything in abundance, but you must behave with generosity. We are all born pure. It is up to you to return to the right path; it is your chance, do not waste it. Take care of yourself and take care of as many as you can. Thanks for keeping an eye on my bike."

I looked in the rearview mirror and started quickly.

It was the first time I had done something like this, and I did it with the intuition that it would work. The guardians had entrusted me with more powers than I had had time to explore, but, at the time, I had more important matters to think about.

After several crossroads and a couple of kilometers, a brick building with blue gates and a huge antenna on it caught my attention. On its roof waved, loudly and in discreet night solitude, the American flag, and in front of it, vans and police cars were coming dangerously close to each other taking advantage of the space. I had no choice but to interpret it as a signal. I stopped in front of the police station.

The officers were going in and out; paradoxically, they were too busy at work to notice that, on the sidewalk in front of them, a young man was watching them on a stolen motorcycle. I removed the cable splice and the engine stopped slowly, as if it didn't really want to. I put it in neutral gear and pushed it across the road to a gap next to the access. A voice startled me.

"You can't leave the bike there." His voice sounded harsh and sharp.

"You'll see, officer. Good evening. I believe this motorcycle is stolen; I have brought it here to be delivered to its owner."

"And where did you find it, boy?" the policeman asked me, surprised.

"Not far away," I answered ambiguously to avoid making something up.

Because, although for me I was doing the right thing, and there was no doubt about that, I did not know the ins and outs of the law. The policeman looked at the motorcycle and then looked at me again, and I think he came to the conclusion that it was impossible that I was responsible for its theft. Then the energy in his voice, his attitude and his kindness towards me changed dramatically.

"I don't know you at all, but I'm proud of you." And he put his arm around me, pulling me into the police station. "Come on in."

The sign on that door said: "Police only". He sat down in front of a yellowish computer, which betrayed the number of cigarettes that must have been smoked in that room.

As he worked on the computer, I kept thinking that I should get out of there, and even began to wonder how I would spend that night, and what I would have for dinner, because again I was out there, alone again and with nothing.

"Well, officer, if you don't need anything from me, I'll be on my way."

Finally, the rotating hourglass disappeared, and in its place a red message took all the attention on the screen.

"Bingo! Here he is. His owner is going to be very happy," exclaimed the policeman.

"I'm very glad, officer. If I may, I'd like to keep my name out of it. You know, I don't want any trouble."

"You won't believe it. Have you seen? Good deeds always bring good things. The owner is offering a $1,000 reward to anyone who finds the bike. And don't worry about that, we don't need to get your information or anything. Now, yes or yes, you have to stay," he said, raising his eyebrows.

I thought it was strange to see a police officer smile so much. I got a laugh out of it, and so did he. Lately, I noticed myself smiling more. Something was changing inside me.

I could see a room full of people. It was the place where the complainants were waiting. The energy in the air was one of frustration, negativity and I could even sense a desire for revenge, which is not the same as justice. Agent Romansky took me to another room; it was a dining room with a coffee machine, a soft drink machine and a television, which he affectionately called the immortal.

I was embarrassed, I didn't want to abuse his hospitality, but I didn't want him to be offended either, so I took a strong cup of coffee. I didn't know what the night would have in store for me, and I hadn't watched TV for so long that I was hooked immediately.

They had the news channel on; everything was bad: violent protests, wars, catastrophes, and to top it off they were announcing rain in New York. Some agents sat near me. They greeted me naturally and continued their conversation. It was not the first time someone like me was among them. I got up and changed the channel, because none of them were watching. I found the A-Team, and immediately lost myself in the story. I lost track of time and space.

Agent Romansky appeared with a woman, just as one episode ended. She can't have been more than thirty-five years old and surely was too elegant to ride a motorcycle. The policeman introduced us, and she took a small wad of bills straight from her purse.

"Please, this isn't necessary. It was nothing, I am satisfied with your joy. Don't be angry, but I don't want to accept your money."

She looked me up and down, and from the way I looked, she drew her own conclusions and was even more surprised.

"You can't imagine what that motorcycle means to me. It's not just rubber and metal, for me it's the present materialization of a memory."

A memory. Her words were so accurate that it seemed almost impossible to me that it was an eventuality. Was I going crazy? I was hearing such personal messages from other people's mouths. I pushed the idea out of my mind, as if it were nonsense. Later I would realize that these coincidences were not such nonsense as I had assumed.

Romansky, with that freedom that only an authority can take advantage of, took the lady's money and forced it into my pocket, and, of course, it was not appropriate to stop him.

"You can't be ungrateful, boy. You deserve that and much more."

Romansky's voice eclipsed the sound of the A-Team's adventures, the chimes of typewriters, the chatter of the crowd and the sirens of cars leaving the police station in their eternal rush.

I left the room with a dubious excitement. For some reason, I felt ashamed that I had accepted that money, but, on the other hand, it seemed to me that it was undeniable that The Order had arranged that I should lack nothing from now on.

Finally, I stayed with that thought, and I knew that by having accepted the purpose of my existence I had also adjusted with the universe. With the energy. With the whole. And, in that way, I found the inexhaustible source of abundance that I had avoided until then: dedicating myself to others.

Dedicating myself to The Order.

New York, December 21, 1996

The weeks passed by quickly. At the same time, I had the impression that the last encounter with Saya had been buried in my distant memory, and, to tell the truth, a part of me didn't want to see her again. I guess we all have to struggle with those internal barriers; and forgiving from the heart is one thing, but such a sharp pain always leaves a mark.

Anyway, I was working on fixing myself. I had become an expert nurse of myself. During that period I had no rest, because there were so many people in need, so many lives to protect and so much injustice that sometimes night and day came together.

I was never in the same place, rotating through the city, through the suburbs, identifying and solving the most difficult cases. I focused on those that could cause serious harm to people. The only time of the day that I dedicated to myself, and I am not so clear about it, was my training. I fought in so many disciplines that, sometimes, and with the forgiveness of those opponents, I forgot some rules of combat; but in real life there is no such honor so inculcated in the martial arts and no such sportsmanship.

In real life working against evil is a life and death struggle, without rules, without scruples, without conscience or remorse. That's how it works. I felt the need to live as the opposite: full of respect, empathy and mercy. So my task became doubly difficult. My body was becoming a museum of scars, but also a material instrument of The Order, stronger, tougher, faster, stealthier and with a more awakened mind. With a purpose.

But that day was different. I was going to meet again with Saya, and something very bright and deep in my being told me that it was essential, that it had to be so, that something greater than me, than her, than the guardians had arranged it. And I felt pushed, encouraged and excited to serve, in absolute silence, humanity, or at least a small part of it.

The fact is that I arrived very early. The snow had fallen for days and had formed a powerful compact layer on the ground. A few stray flakes floated in the air, as if moved by the sound of the sea horns and the mournful flapping of seagulls.

I kept staring at the imposing statue never losing sight of its meaning. In fact, it was the same reason why I was there waiting for Saya, on alert, aware of all the powers that the guardians had given me in case I was ambushed, and at the same time without the certainty that she would come.

A female silhouette blended in with the dozens of Victorian lampposts raised on concrete pedestals. It must have been her. As I approached, her image gave me the appearance of a beautiful and elegant woman from Eastern Europe, dressed in a tight black coat whose color brought out the golden tone of her hair. My footsteps on the snow crunched like bubble wrap as her coat fluttered in the wind.

"Good. I see you're doing well, better than the last time I saw you," I broke the awkward silence between the two of us.

"We both know why we're here," she said. We know they're coming back. They're going to come back more and they're going to get to you, and they're going to do whatever it takes to make that happen."

She paused, waiting for me to say something.

"I don't know what to say to that."

I needed to connect the latest developments. To hear what she had to say.

"You are in danger. All of humanity is in danger; in fact, they are going to focus much of their resources on coming here to seek the solution to transcendence, they are desperate to know what lies beyond and you are a key that opens that door."

She took another short break, waiting for me to say something. I merely shrugged my shoulders.

"Almost all governments have had contact with our civilization. It is practically an open secret. Our plan is to create chaos, war, violence and disaster, and to achieve this we have given you increasingly cruel and powerful technology, tools and weapons, and even if you don't want to ask me, I will tell you why. It's very simple: only when times are hard do protectors and people like you surface. I assure you this is true across the universe. You, my friend, are the first one we have ever seen who has been so deeply connected to the other side. I know they will do whatever is required to possess you and use you as a portal."

My face remained unchanged as I took this in. It was a lot to hear. Saya took a few steps towards me, our faces were a span apart, and these last words rang in my ears with a slight, soft threatening tinge, even though Saya had distanced herself from them.

"They will go after you, they will go after me, they will go after your family, your friends, your acquaintances, they will even go after your pet if necessary to get what they want, and they will not stop until they get it."

It was paradoxical that such sharp words emanated from such a beautiful person. I finally made up my mind to ask.

"And how long do we have until they come back?" I asked, feeling surprisingly calmly, although inside I kept thinking about Claudia, my parents, Kingsley and everyone else.

"Maybe six months, eight at the most, depending on your calendar." I managed a half-smile that did not go unnoticed by her. "What makes you so happy?" she asked me.

"This short time may not seem like much to you compared to the eternity you have been alive, but to me it is a huge breath of fresh air. We have plenty of time to prepare ourselves, to improve, to protect ourselves, to love, even."

She clearly didn't understand why I added love to that list.

"Saya, there are many kinds of love, and all of them, without exception, are connected to the universe you are talking about. Love is what makes us strong, what connects us to that other side, and you, believe it or not, have already begun to strengthen yourself."

"You talk as if you think we're going to survive. That we'll be able to hide."

And for the first time I saw a note of fear in his eyes.

"Do not be afraid. Do not suffer, do not anticipate a pain that does not exist. I am making a plan. I am going to tell you a secret, one that I want to share with you. Your thoughts are a free product of your creative essence, that which you imagine is created in your mind, and reality responds and corresponds by adapting itself until it fulfills your desire. That is why I guarantee you, not only that we will survive but that we will win, and I know that the process has already begun." I smiled calmly and assured firmly. "We are not alone."

And I discovered that, in this body, this beautiful and strong body lived a frightened, fragile and helpless being from another world, and I embraced her with all my love so that she could feel for the first time that incomparable energy. The energy of creation. The energy of life.

—Reality is ours. We can shape it. We are allies of The Order. Trust.

Acknowledgments

To my indefatigable guardian, Loli, tireless and cheerful fighter. To my beloved uncle, wherever he may be. To my dear brother Tope, to Belón, to Antonio, to Raúl, to Javier, to Juanillo; and, especially, to Victoria Andrés Parada, my dear squire, sorceress and teacher. I love you all.

To my editorial advisor, Lucía F., spearhead of EBL publishing house's extraordinary team who has carefully paid attention to every detail of my book.

Above all, this thanks goes to you, who, however this story has come into your hands, have given it light, movement, sound and color, doing something prodigious: transforming words into experiences of your own. That's how amazing imagination is. When you pay attention to it, with some repose, and allow that treasure to guide you, you end up perceiving the powerful presence of The Order and its guardians. It is simple, it connects with the rational limit. It is something that begins by observing the signs, by questioning synchronicity. The apparent chance that surrounds us, in this life and in the next.

Thank you from the bottom of my heart.

See you soon.

www.ingramcontent.com/pod-product-compliance
Lightning Source LLC
Chambersburg PA
CBHW022358110726
47903CB00004B/1047